A Stalemated War:

At Home and At Sea, 1805

by

John G. Cragg

A Stalemated War: At Home and At Sea, 1805
Copyright © 2018 by John G. Cragg
BeachFrontPress@gmail.com

Dedicated to

My sons

Mike and Phil

and to

My most encouraging and
helpful critic

**Olga Browzin
Cragg**

Preface

This is a work of fiction. It follows on from the first three volumes in this series, *A New War: at Home and at Sea, 1803, A Continuing War: at Home and at Sea, 1803-4* and A War by Diplomacy, 1804. They are available at Amazon.com and other Amazon sites by searching for my name or the title. The present tale takes place in 1805. A great many things have changed in the more than two centuries that have elapsed since that date, including items and phrases that may be unfamiliar to many readers. To help those who are curious, a glossary is provided at the end of the book. Items which appear in the glossary <u>are flagged</u> on their first appearance in the text by an * as in, for example, taffrail*.

Chapter I

Captain Richard Giles maneuvered his ship, *Glaucus*, alongside the French frigate that was engaged with the vessel of his friend, Captain Tobias Bush. In fact, Bush's frigate, *Perseus*, was engaged with French frigates on each side, but so far was giving as good as he got. The vessel that Giles was approaching had undoubtedly suffered much damage and many casualties so that Giles should be able to turn the tide of battle easily. He would come alongside his opponent, unleash a single, but no doubt overwhelming, broadside and then grapple and board the enemy. His boarding party should be able to sweep aside the French defenders on the first ship and join with Bush's men to defeat the second vessel.

"Grapple when we are alongside! Boarders, prepare! Starboard guns, fire as you bear!" Giles roared. *Glaucus* crept alongside her opponent, but then nothing went as planned. The muskets which were firing into the crew of their adversary from the quarterdeck* and the fighting tops* seemed to be hitting no one. In fact, the marines were cursing that their muskets wouldn't fire. Giles could see the gunner on the leading cannon pull his lanyard, but instead of its roaring out as it sent its ball hurtling into the enemy, all that happened was a weak bang with the cannonball rolling out of the gun's mouth to drop harmlessly in the water. The charge must have been defective. Then the same thing happened with the next gun, even as the enemy returned its own, all too effective cannon fire, sending apparently, though unbelievably, thirty-six-pound balls into *Glaucus*.

A shout from the bow made Giles glance to larboard*. Emerging from the fog bank was another vessel, a French line-of-battle ship, with its guns run out just waiting to fire on his frigate. That broadside would destroy *Glaucus*. Giles had no choice; he must surrender. His ship was helpless, and there was no point throwing away any more lives.

"I surrender! Surrender!" he bellowed, hoping that all would hear. The signal midshipman was nowhere to be seen. The ship was suddenly rocking as he struggled to get to the flag halyard to lower their colors. Even as the scene faded from his sight, he discovered that the halyard was jammed.

"Richard, wake up," a voice intreated. "You are having a nightmare. It's all right. It is just a dream. I am here. You're safe."

Giles knew that voice. It was the one that filled many of his dreams, his wife Daphne's. What was she doing here? She shouldn't be on board *Glaucus*!

The battle faded. He was being held around the shoulders by Daphne. It had been a dream. He was at his home, Dipton Hall. He was with Daphne. He still felt shaken by the nightmare, but its terror was rapidly evaporating. But he shouldn't have such dreams, and he certainly shouldn't let Daphne know that he had them. That wasn't right. It wasn't manly. He had never heard of other captains having nightmares about battles; none had ever mentioned them to him. In the wardroom* when he was a lieutenant, some men had mumbled or cried out in their sleep, but no one ever talked about it or asked each other about such events. At that time, he hadn't been bothered by dreams, not of this sort, anyway.

"I'm sorry," he mumbled. "I shouldn't trouble you."

"No trouble," Daphne lied ignoring the anxiety his dreams were causing her. "I'm here. It's all right. Go back to sleep."

Giles laid his head on the pillow again. Soon his breathing evened, and he was clearly asleep. He slept without further dreams until well after dawn.

The winter sun snuck feebly over the trees that hid the church from Dipton Hall. It shone weakly into Daphne's bedroom where Giles was still lying in bed, his head propped up with a couple of pillows. The nightmare was now just a hazy recollection that his sleep had been disturbed. He was enjoying one of the perks of being an invalid: not getting up when his wife was roused before dawn by her maid, Betsy. He really should get up, but he would sneak a few more minutes in bed, just because he could. He reflected on how lucky he was, not only to be alive, but to have such a marvelous wife, a healthy infant son, and more money than he would ever need. Daphne unquestionably headed the list of his good fortunes. Vibrant, unconventional, spontaneous, imaginative Daphne.

He fondly recalled how they had first met on the road between Dipton Manor, her father's estate, and the village of Dipton. She had started by greeting him warmly, quite forgetting that young ladies were not supposed to greet men to whom they had not been properly introduced. They had discussed drainage, not a subject he would expect to interest any young lady, and she knew a great deal about the ins and outs of the matter. Furthermore, he had realized that she had not spent any time trying to evaluate how good a marriage catch he might be, as so many young ladies had done in the past when he was first introduced to them.

He had fallen in love with Daphne Moorhouse immediately. Soon he had realized that he must marry her. Luckily, she was as taken with him as he was with her, even though she had always claimed that she wanted nothing to do with marriage. Marrying her had turned out to be the best decision he had ever made. He was amazed that she had agreed to be his wife, and he was still finding out more and more about her. Everything he learned about her confirmed how lucky he had been to win her. Now she had been supporting him through his nightmares, nightmares that he should not even have and that he most surely should not be inflicting on his wife.

His reverie was broken by Daphne entering the bedroom. "Still in bed, Richard? And on a fine day like this?" she asked.

"I should get up," he responded and tried to push up from the pillows as a first step in getting out of bed. A jolt of pain shot through his damaged shoulder and was clearly expressed on his face.

"Easy does it," commanded Daphne.

She helped Giles out of bed, supporting most of his weight on the wounded side to lever him into a position where he could get up. Betsy, uncannily, showed up just at the right moment to summon the footman, who was acting as a valet, to help Giles.

Giles's getting ready for the day at the time when he did was fortuitous. Within minutes, Mr. Jackson, the doctor and surgeon turned apothecary, appeared.

"Good. You are up, Captain Giles. Let me see how your exercise is going."

"Do I have to?" Giles asked petulantly.

"Only if you don't want to lose the use of that shoulder and find that you cannot lift your arm. The exercises will hurt, unfortunately. Without them, you won't recover fully."

Mr. Jackson aided Giles to sink down so that he lay flat on his back on a particular place of the floor where earlier the apothecary had chalked some lines. He then helped his patient to position himself in just the right way.

"Raise your injured arm, as I showed you until it hurts too much."

Giles swept his arm along the surface of the floor, keeping it straight at the elbow. He started grimacing in pain as it neared the level of his waist. He had to cease when his hand was only a bit above it. Mr. Jackson marked the place where Giles's elbow stopped with a piece of chalk.

"Now the other arm," the surgeon ordered.

This time the hand was parallel to the shoulder.

"That's a bit better. But you should be able to raise your arms until they are straight up over your head. Now try bringing each arm up straight in front of you."

Giles again demonstrated his lack of flexibility.

"You will have to keep working on it, Captain Giles, if you don't want to be handicapped for life. Your stiffness is not just the result of your wound. It also comes from not using your arms regularly. I would guess that, since you are the captain of your boat, you never climb the rigging, if that is the right term, or otherwise use your shoulders very much."

"I'm afraid that's true," agreed Giles in a surly voice. He was about to correct Jackson by pointing out that he had been referring to a 'ship,' not a 'boat,' but he desisted when he suspected that his friend was only misusing the term to get him to act pompously. The doctor was one of the few people that Giles encountered who was totally uninterested in exactly what was his own status or that of the person to whom he was talking.

"Now, I expect you to do fifteen of each of the exercises twice a day," Mr. Jackson stated. "Daphne, I count on you to make sure that he does do them."

Further discussion of Giles's shoulders was prevented by the butler, Steves, appearing to announce, "Mr. Summers and Major Stoner are here to see Captain Giles."

"Oh, as officers of the Ameschester Hunt, they will be wanting to talk to you about the kennels, I expect," Daphne said. "I told you how Major Stoner blurted out their need to find a someone to provide a place to keep the hounds while he was getting up the courage to talk about marrying Lady Marianne. Incidentally, you should congratulate Major Stoner on his being engaged to your half-sister."

"I know, though I think commiserations might be more in order."

Mr. Summers had indeed come about whether Giles could be persuaded to provide a place at Dipton Hall to keep the hounds of the Ameschester Hunt. The Hunt had been forced to find a new location for its kennels. Major Stoner's warning had given Giles and Daphne a chance to consider their answer, though they were not immediately going to indicate that they had already made up their minds. Major Stoner had not wanted the President of the Hunt to know that he had told Daphne about their needs. He was afraid that Mr. Summers would feel that the Major was intruding into his command of the institution, even though that was precisely what he had been doing.

Mr. Summers began by hoping that Captain Giles's wound was healing properly and went on to effusive expressions of gratitude for the role that Captain Giles had played in keeping the nation safe. He seemed to be quite stalled on this subject, repeating how proud the neighborhood was in having one of their members defeating French ships. Of course, Daphne was aware of how much Giles's exploits, which had been widely publicized, helped to reassure a nervous nation that the Royal Navy could contain the French threat, but this was getting to be ridiculous. She had always been aware that Mr. Summers was uncomfortable discussing matters of business with a lady present. The implication that she could even be consulted on how to resolve important problems was anathema to him, even though he knew that in dealing with Dipton Hall, Daphne was the one deciding on all issues when Giles was away. She had only partly assuaged his discomfort by pretending that all decisions would be entirely Giles's own. Now she realized that the poor man was overawed by dealing with a man of much greater wealth and land-holdings who was also a national hero.

Just as Daphne was wondering how to intervene to get Mr. Summers to come to the point, Giles took the task from her.

"Mr. Summers, I appreciate what you are saying, but surely you did not come here just to praise my service in the Navy, which is, after all, no more than my duty."

"Oh, no, Viscount Ashton, but I could hardly ignore your illustrious deeds. Why the Naval Gazette…"

"Forgive me for interrupting, Mr. Summers, but I prefer to be addressed simply as Captain Giles. It is much more convenient in the Navy, and indeed, that is also the case when dealing with civilian matters. After all, being called 'Viscount' as a courtesy is of no significance."

"I apologize, my l…, ugh… Captain Giles. I meant no offense."

"None taken, Mr. Summers. Now, what did you want to see us about?"

Giles had put a slight emphasis on 'us' which pleased Daphne no end. It told her that Giles was fully aware that carrying out anything they decided to do would undoubtedly fall on her shoulders to accomplish and so he would do nothing without her consent.

"Well…ugh…I hate to ask when Lady Ashton? Lady Giles?…"

"Either will do, Mr. Summers, but I prefer Lady Giles while my husband is known as Captain Giles," Daphne stepped in before Mr. Summers could get lost in the maze of what might be a correct title.

"When Lady Giles and you have been so generous to the Hunt. However, we do have a dilemma. It's about the hounds. We were hoping that you could help out directly or, at least, aid us in finding a solution."

"About the hounds?"

"Yes, Captain Giles, You see it is like this." Mr. Summers then started to elaborate on the problem.

The difficulties were easily summarized, Daphne realized, but that was not how it seemed to come out of Mr. Summers's mouth. The old colonel, who had been providing a place for the hounds of the Ameschester Hunt, would no longer do so. Hosting the dogs had included providing a house for the professional master of the hounds as well as the kennels in which the animals were kept. The Master's job did not just involve looking after the hounds and making sure they were up to snuff when it came to finding and tracking a fox. Also, and equally importantly, he had to train puppies from an early age so that they could take their place in the pack when the time came. No one else among the members of the Hunt seemed to be in a position to provide a home for the hounds and the Master of the Hunt. Mr. Summers started to catalog all the various excuses that had been presented. Giles saw no point in hearing them, so again he intervened to move the discussion forward.

"So you want us to take on the hounds, do you?" Giles asked.

"Well, yes."

"And the financial aspect?"

Giles's direct approach rather startled Mr. Summers, and there was a lot of humming and hawing before it became evident that Colonel Redfern, the landowner who had been hosting the pack, had been putting a lot of his own money into the job. Completely ignoring Major Stoner's presence, Mr. Summers explained that he thought that Colonel Redfern had been willing to do it as a way to try to get into local society. His colonelcy was in an Indian regiment, and he had become very wealthy as an Indian nabob. Nevertheless, he had not been welcomed automatically into Ameschester society's higher reaches. Mr. Stoner indicated quite clearly that Colonel Redfern had been trying to buy his admission by supporting the hounds. When that had not worked, the Colonel had lost interest. Mr. Summers did suggest that the Hunt might contribute more to whoever would take on the task, but the Hunt's funds were very meager, very meager indeed.

Major Stoner was looking both furious and shame-faced at this telling, though he said nothing. Daphne felt for him: his position was much the same as Colonel Redfern's though on a lower scale. She would have to think of something to assuage the hurt that Mr. Summers was inflicting so mindlessly.

Mr. Summers went on to explain that Colonel Redfern had developed gout which would prevent his taking part in the hunt or doing much else and so he was not willing to host the hounds anymore. He went on at some length about how inconvenient and unfeeling was the Colonel's decision. How could he expect to be welcomed in the neighborhood if he was not willing to pull his communal weight?

Daphne could see that Giles was getting more and more annoyed at these comments and stepped in before he lost his temper.

"Are you suggesting, Mr. Summers," she interrupted the harangue, "that you would like Dipton Hall to provide a home for the kennels?"

"Well…ugh…ugh…yes, my lady. It would be a tremendous help if you and Captain Giles could see your way clear to taking on the hounds."

"We'll have to see consider it very carefully before making up our mind. Being responsible for the hounds is a serious matter, and there would be a considerable expense in taking them on, as I am sure you are aware, Mr. Summers. Captain Giles will have to examine the matter closely before we can give you an answer. There is the question, in particular, of how we might be able to accommodate the kennels without the dogs' barking causing too much disturbance. We can't have evensong in the church interrupted by the baying of the hounds."

"Relative to that, Lady Giles," said Major Stoner, "did you hear that Mr. Wark is selling his estate?"

"No, I hadn't."

"Yes. It has to do with the effect of the raid by the revenue officers and also his arrest for trying to have your tenant, Jacob Nestor, wrongfully hanged for poaching. Mr. Wark needs money both to pay his lawyers and to have some cash when he gets to Botany Bay. You heard that he and Sir Thomas Dimster are to be transported, have you not?"

"Yes, I knew about Sir Thomas. His son is our steward, but I hadn't heard about Mr. Wark. I'll be glad to see him out of the neighborhood."

Sir Thomas's attempts to thwart Giles's rights had been stopped by Daphne's agency which had led to his trying to get his revenge on her by harassing one of her tenants. That action had also failed miserably, with the result that Sir Thomas and his henchman, Julius Wark, had been arraigned on capital charges. They had apparently avoided the noose but had been exiled to Australia.

"Thank you for bringing to our attention the need for someone to take on the hounds, Mr. Summers," Giles said in a voice indicating that the discussion was at an end. "Major, might I have a word with you separately? About Lady Marianne."

After Steves had shown Mr. Summers out, Giles turned to Major Stoner. "I have not had a chance before to tell you how happy I was to get the news that you are engaged to my half-sister, Lady Marianne. I haven't been here enough to get to know you properly, Major. However, from everything that Lady Giles has told me, Lady Marianne is fortunate that you will be her husband. I hope that we can get to know each other better soon."

"That is very gracious of Lady Giles, I must say. Very gracious! Especially as I am afraid that I rather got off on the wrong foot with her originally. I think that I may have insulted her by expressing what I now know were completely unfounded beliefs about ladies participating in the hunt."

"Oh, Major, that is all forgotten. I have learned that you are quite able to change your mind, and that is what truly matters," Daphne intervened.

"I am sorry about the remarks that Mr. Summers expressed about Indian officers," Giles resumed. "I can assure you that I do not share them. If it is any consolation, my father-in-law suffered from a very similar prejudice when he first came to Dipton, a prejudice that, no doubt, Mr. Summers shares since he strikes me as only being two generations from the foundry floor and such men are often the greatest snobs."

"I agree completely with Captain Giles, Major Stoner," Daphne interposed at this point, "but there is one little matter about which I would like to consult with my husband before you go. Richard, if you could just come with me into this corner."

Giles was somewhat nonplussed by this request but agreed.

"Richard," Daphne said in a low voice, "I think we should provide Lady Marianne with a dowry."

"Do you? That is a bit of a change in tune, isn't it?"

"It is. But I have been observing them. It is not a marriage of calculation as I thought at first, but one of genuine affection."

"For a hard-hearted manager of broad estates, you really do have a romantic side, don't you, my love," Giles teased. "All right, I shall tell him about it now. £15,000?"

"That's generous, but it does sound a reasonable contribution for you to make."

"Major Stoner," Giles said after going back to the Major. "My wife was reminding me of my status as head of the family. My father has rather abdicated his responsibilities, as I imagine that Lady Marianne has explained to you. I am not only welcoming you myself but also as the *de facto* head of the family. In that connection, while Daphne could not very well mention a marriage portion* for Lady Marianne when you talked to her, I am happy to say that Lady Marianne does have one of £15,000, presently invested in consols*. I know that, in the past, my half-sister has felt rather abandoned by her family. I hope that this will make clear how we regard her as a valued relative and also that we are glad that she has chosen you to be her husband."

"That is extremely good of you, Captain Giles. Extremely good! And completely unexpected. Completely! I know that Lady Marianne will be very encouraged to hear of it. Very! Especially as it is, of course, completely unexpected."

"I think I had better tell my half-sister about it now, don't you agree, Daphne? Major, I hope you can join us for luncheon."

Chapter II

"Richard," Daphne asked after luncheon was finished, "do you feel that you are able to ride?"

Giles was startled by the question. It indicated that Daphne no longer regarded him as an invalid.

"I believe so. What do you have in mind?"

"I would like to ride up to where our wood joins Mr. Wark's. I haven't been there for ages."

"You wouldn't be thinking about his land in connection with the kennels, would you?"

Daphne blushed at her intentions being perceived so easily. "Yes. The best place for the kennels would be up near the wood, where the foxes are and where the hounds would be out of the way, but the best spot is very close to Mr. Wark's land, and it would be difficult if the pups ran off in that direction."

"Let's go look. But I certainly am not promising to buy Mr. Wark's estate, not without a lot of investigation."

"Daphne blushed. She sometimes forgot how easily Giles could see through her strategies to get him to agree to one of her projects.

"Of course not. I was only thinking that a ride would do us good, and having a place to go always makes a ride more enjoyable."

Giles looked at Daphne in a way that suggested that he doubted this story, but he ordered Steves to have the horses prepared before following Daphne upstairs to change for their outing. Daphne and Giles's ride quickly took them to the cart track that separated Dipton Hall Wood from Mr. Wark's. While Dipton Hall Wood had had much of the underbrush cleared away to allow easy passage through the trees, it appeared that the wood on the opposite side of the track had not been touched for years.

Daphne halted at one point. "There is some fine timber in there," she said. "I wonder why Mr. Wark has never harvested it."

Giles stared at his wife in surprise. He knew that she was an expert when it came to agricultural matters, but that she could quickly evaluate the value of timber from a distance amazed him.

"Are you sure it is valuable?" he asked.

"Not sure. I'd have to examine it more closely, but, yes, I'm pretty confident that there are opportunities there."

They rode on a little farther.

"There is supposed to be a track, or a right of way, somewhere along here that leads to the road that serves Mr. Wark's estate," Daphne said. "But I don't see it, and I think we are close to our boundary."

"Would that be it?" Giles asked. He was pointing to a mass of tangled, dead tree branches that seemed to cover a small section of the edge of the wood on Mr. Wark's side of the track. Daphne looked at it more carefully.

"I think you are right. I wonder why Mr. Wark blocked it in such a complicated way."

"Probably because it is a public right of way, unlike the stretch we have been on which belongs to us, and he does not want people to use it to get through his wood. He certainly doesn't want people to explore his property. I wonder why."

"It would be interesting to find out, but not now. It is getting late."

Somewhat reluctantly, they turned their horses towards home. The light was already failing, and as they neared Dipton Hall, the glowing windows looked warm and welcoming. The air had a nice touch of wood smoke in the air for Dipton Hall still burned wood rather than coal. There was a heaviness in the air that promised snow before dawn.

Daphne and Giles dismounted under the portico, handed their reins to a footman who would pass them to a groom and entered their home. Steves held out a silver server on which rested a single envelope.

"This arrived by courier from the Admiralty, sir, while you and Lady Ashton were out." Steves refused to call Daphne 'Lady Giles' because it was of lower precedence. He was very unhappy when Giles insisted on being called 'Captain Giles' rather than 'Viscount Ashton'. Even 'Sir Richard Giles' would be better in Steves' opinion, but his master was adamant. "Captain Bush arrived a few minutes ago," Steves continued. He wishes to see you. Major Stoner is still here. They are in the large parlor with Lady Marianne and Miss Crocker."

"Very good, Steves. Lady Giles and I will change before joining them."

Giles was opening the missive from the Admiralty as they mounted the stairs to get changed.

"What is it, Richard," asked Daphne. "Word of your next assignment with *Glaucus*?"

"Not really, though it may turn out that that is what it is about. I have been summoned to meet with the First Lord on Thursday of next week. At the Admiralty. No hint of what it is about."

"I wish they wouldn't call on you so soon, especially after your illness, but I suppose that there is nothing you can do about it."

"Not really. Not with Boney hankering to invade England. I wonder if Captain Bush also got a message from the Admiralty and that is why he is here."

"The only way to find out is to get changed so that you can ask him."

Daphne and Giles found a blazing fire in the parlor where the company was just as Steves had told them it would be.

"Captain Bush," Daphne greeted him after curtseying to his bow. "It is good of you to visit. You must stay to dinner."

"And you, Major Stoner, I hope you can join us," Daphne added after Captain Bush had indicated his acquiescence.

"Captain Giles has just received word that he must go to London, to the Admiralty, next Thursday," Daphne started the conversation. "I imagine it is about his next task for them. Have they contacted you as well, Captain Bush?"

"Yes, my lady. However, I have received rather different news. My ship, *Perseus*, has been condemned as not being worth repairing, so I am now without a command. I shall be looking forward to spending time here in Dipton."

"Yes, we've missed you. My father in particular, since you are the only one who shares his passion for the battles of antiquity."

"I do hope that Captain Bolton will return soon," broke in Catherine Crocker. "It seems unfair that our marriage depends on the whims of Bonaparte and the Admiralty."

"That's the price we have to pay when we fall in love with a sailor in time of war," Daphne told her, indicating quite firmly that this was not a suitable subject for conversation.

Conversation then became general. It was mainly about local matters until dinner was announced and continued so through the meal. Only when the ladies had been led away to the drawing room by Daphne and the cloth* had been drawn did Giles raise a subject that had been bothering him all day.

"Major Stoner, you mentioned earlier that Mr. Wark is selling his property."

"Yes, or so I heard from a couple of reliable men in Ameschester yesterday. Mr. Wark's land is always of interest to the Hunt since he won't let us cross his land. We lost a very nice fox there earlier this season when it took refuge in Mr. Wark's wood. Very annoying! Very! Of course, landowners have the right to refuse to let the Hunt cross their land, but not many are as adamant about it as Mr. Wark, and he has hardly any fields whose hedges and fences might be damaged. The usual reason people give for not allowing the Hunt on their land is the damage that might come to the hedges and fences or that fields might be trampled in a way that would make plowing more difficult.

Nonsense of course! Totally! But there you have it. Most of them don't mind the dogs chasing the fox across their land, but Mr. Wark won't even allow that. I suppose that it has something to do with the smuggling. He'll be no loss to the county, no loss at all! That is certain."

"I might ride over there and have a look at the property," Giles said.

"I wouldn't if I were you. One of the men in the Hunt, Mr. Cornwell, you probably know him, told me he was curious and went to see the property. He was chased away by men with clubs. They said that they could only allow people who came with Mr. Wark's permission, which they would have to get from his solicitor in Ameschester. Never heard such nonsense! Outrageous! Can't imagine why they would stop gentlemen from examining the property. Can't expect anyone to buy it if they can't just see it whenever they want. The grounds anyway." exclaimed the Major.

"It might have something to do with where the smugglers hid their wares," remarked Captain Bush, thoughtfully. "I was puzzled to learn how little the revenue officers found when they descended on the place with the dragoons. Admittedly, the raid must have come as no surprise after Wark's involvement in smuggling was blurted out in open court, but I am surprised that what they found was almost in plain sight. You would have thought the smugglers would have removed everything before they came."

"Maybe they had removed most of it already," suggested Giles.

"I think it is more likely that it was hidden too well, or the smugglers bribed the revenue officers," retorted Major Stoner. "I know there has been no sudden shortage of smuggled goods in the area. None at all!"

"I am surprised that there is so much smuggling this far from the coast," Captain Bush resumed his musings. "How do they get it so far inland without being caught?"

"Simple," replied the Major. "They bring it by water. Couldn't do it by land, not in quantity. Not possible especially with heavy items. Not possible at all!"

"Heavy items?" Giles asked.

"Yes. Many smuggled goods are quite heavy or bulky, like salt or tea or tubs* of gin. Many of the goods like that which are sold here have been smuggled."

"Are they indeed. I would never have guessed it."

"Just ask your butler. He will know."

"I still do not quite see how the smuggled goods get here. Could you elaborate Major Stoner?"

"Well, I can't say I am an expert on it," replied the Major. "The River Amesnott which, of course, flows through Ameschester is part of the canal network. The goods arrive by barges. Usually, I have heard, coal barges. Then there is a backwater quite close to Mr. Wark's estate, where the barges can be pulled in and unloaded without anyone knowing. It seems to be such general knowledge that I suspect that the revenue officers must be deliberately turning a Nelson eye to them. It must then be a very short distance to Mr. Wark's estate."

"I cannot say that I like this large amount of smuggling," remarked Giles. "Its principal purpose is to not pay the taxes which are put on many imported goods. Those taxes must be helping to pay for the defense of the kingdom, including, of course, money for the navy. Smuggling must be making the amount of money available to defend our shores smaller. I don't see why so many people connive with the smugglers."

"The people I know don't see it that way," responded Major Somers. "They feel that with the income tax now raising funds for war, the other duties are too high. And a lot of them are skeptical about where the money goes. They have all heard of suppliers who are making a fortune out of the war, not to mention the unpopularity of the extravagance of the Prince of Wales."

"I am still puzzled about how Mr. Wark kept all his smuggled goods so that no one knew where they were. I also wonder how he got them from the canal to his place," said Captain Bush. "If he was as big a part of the smuggling trade in these parts as he is said to have been, I don't understand why the revenue men found so little material when they raided right after that remark was blurted out in court. It made it very clear that he was storing smuggled material."

"Probably someone was bribed to look the other way – revenue officers and the magistrates are not above being persuaded to ignore the noses on their faces, and the dragoons would have only done what they were told to," said the Major cynically.

"Well, I am now very intrigued about Mr. Wark's property," said Giles. "I am going to see my lawyer in Ameschester tomorrow. Maybe he can tell me how to get to see Mr. Wark's property if he is selling it."

The conversation then moved on to other topics, and Giles forgot about it until he was in bed, about to blow out the candle.

"Daphne, my love, I have to go to Ameschester tomorrow to see Mr. Snodgrass. I would like to have you come with me if you wish. Will you come, please?"

"I'd love to, but I thought your legal work was just about some tiresome deeds to the properties, and I am surprised you didn't ask Mr. Snodgrass to send them here."

"That is what my dealings with the lawyer were supposed to be about, but the arrival of the letter from the Admiralty reminded me that I should make sure that all is in order concerning you and Berns before I leave. I want you to be there so that everything is clear to you in case the worst comes to the worst. Furthermore, I want to ask about Mr. Wark's property and how we can get to see it fully. I know you will be interested in that. And for both topics, I would like to have any suggestions you might offer."

"Richard, we can't just show up out of the blue and expect Mr. Snodgrass to see us right away."

"Don't you think that he would be sure to see us if we arrived at 11:30 unexpectedly? I imagine that we are already his richest clients, and we can only get richer. Surely he knows on which side his bread is buttered."

"Richard! That is despicable, even if what you say is true. I don't want to flaunt how rich we are, even though we are, or to presume special favors even though people will give them to us just because of our titles."

"I agree with you, my dear. It is never a good idea for the well-off to rub people's noses in how much more fortunate they are than others. That is why I asked Steves to send Geoffrey first thing tomorrow to make an appointment. Mr. Snodgrass's clerk can tell him whether it is feasible and Geoffrey can be back here before we leave. I indicated that he should take Dark Paul. It would be a good idea to give that horse some exercise before the Hunt meets on Saturday. I don't want my mount to be spending the day trying to unseat me again."

"I should have known you were teasing about the appointment. I just hope that your shoulder will allow you to ride in the hunt. Is it wise to use Dark Paul?"

"We'll see."

Chapter III

Giles and Daphne arrived in Ameschester just before 11:30 a.m. Geoffreys, the groom whom Steves had sent to arrange an appointment with the lawyer, had returned to say that 11:30 would be convenient for the lawyer. He neglected to mention that, as he was leaving the lawyer's rooms, he had heard Mr. Snodgrass tell his clerk to inform Mr. Hawkins that his 11:30 appointment had to be canceled.

Mr. Snodgrass's chambers were in an old building on the market square. They were on the first floor and provided a cheery view of the snow-sprinkled square through leaded windows. Mr. Snodgrass himself was the epitome of everyone's impression of a country solicitor: slightly plump with a stereotypical belly, red cheeks framed in white mutton-chop whiskers, and a pair of spectacles that had slipped down his nose. The only thing that belied the impression of a pleasant, dedicated and not very bright lawyer was the shrewd sparkle of his eyes. They indicated an underlying shrewdness that the pleasantness tended to hide. Seeing that Daphne was being ushered into his room ahead of Giles did not surprise him at all.

"Mr. Snodgrass," Giles opened the conversation, "it is good of you to see us at such short notice. I hope it didn't inconvenience you."

"Not at all, not at all, Viscount Ashton," the solicitor declared, not mentioning that it was another client who had been inconvenienced. "I am delighted that I could accommodate you and Lady Ashton."

"One thing, before we start, Mr. Snodgrass. I much prefer to use my naval rank rather than my civilian title in ordinary discourse."

"As you wish, Captain Giles. As you wish. Does Viscountess Ashton have the same preference?"

"Yes indeed, Mr. Snodgrass. 'Lady Giles' is quite grand enough for me," Daphne replied pleasantly.

"I hope you didn't come here just about those papers that need signing. There is nothing complicated about them, and they could easily have been dealt with by my sending them to you, or I would have been happy to visit Dipton Hall."

"That is not really why we are here," Giles replied. "I am likely to be called to continue my duties in the navy very shortly. I wish to have my affairs all in order before I go."

"Very wise, especially as there have been many changes in your life recently such as the birth of a son and the deaths of your half-brothers. What was simple before may be a good deal more complicated now."

"Indeed. I wish to make sure that Lady Giles has as much authority as possible if I die."

"That will largely be possible. Widows have much more independence than any other women. There may be some problems with the various restrictions on your inheritances that must devolve to your son. Unfortunately, we should also cover the possibility of Lady Giles passing away while you are absent and make provision for any other children you may have in the future. It would be best if you nominate guardians for your children in the event that Lady Giles dies, or the requirements of the entails* on some of the properties happen to require guardians for your son so that those parts of his inheritance could not be handled by her."

"Can you get the terms of the entails from my family's London solicitors?"

"Oh, yes. There is nothing secret about those provisions. I suggest that you name several guardians, in order rather than jointly. The reason is that if you only name one, and he dies, his heir or executor will become the guardian, which may not be what you want at all. If they are all listed, they will all have to be involved when any decisions are made, which can be very awkward."

"I hadn't realized that the subject of guardians might come up. Let me see -- I will name Mr. Moorhouse, Lady Giles's father, my brother, Lord David, though that is not his proper title as you probably know, and finally my friend Captain Bush. Of course, I would like a provision that they are to follow Lady Giles's wishes as closely as possible."

"Anything else about the documents you want me to prepare?"

"No, but there is another matter I would like to discuss with you."

"Yes?"

"I hear that Mr. Julius Wark's estate is for sale. Do you know who is handling it?"

"I believe it is Mr. Shuster, the lawyer with an office on the opposite side of the square. If you are interested in the property, you would have to see him so that you can obtain permission to view it. I am told that Mr. Wark's servants are very unwelcoming to people who want to examine the property casually. Even those with permission are prevented from examining anything but the house by men with cudgels. It is a bad situation. I am told that it is not Mr. Wark that is behind these difficulties, but Mr. Twist."

"Mr. Twist?"

"You may not know him. Mr. Twist has a large residence in the best part of Ameschester and does not participate in the Hunt. Rumor has it that he is heavily involved in smuggling in this area, possibly even the leading figure. Some people think that he is trying to frustrate buyers of Mr. Wark's property so that he can pick it up cheaply for himself and continue its use as a center smuggling. This information is all second-hand, you understand. You really should talk to Mr. Shuster if you are interested in the property."

"It sounds quite intriguing. When we are finished here, I think we will call on Mr. Shuster."

Giles and Daphne crossed the market square to the less elegant side of the place. Mr. Shuster's rooms seemed to be in terrible disarray. Both Mr. Shuster and his clerk appeared to be searching through piles of papers for some lost document. The arrivals could tell which of the two was the lawyer and which the clerk only by the fashion in which they were dressed; they were both engaged in the same task.

Mr. Shuster looked up from a paper he was examining. "What can I do for you? As you can see we are very busy right now."

"I have come to get authorization to inspect Julius Wark's property. I gather that you are the one who grants it."

"Yes. Are you seriously interested in buying it?" the lawyer asked rather abruptly.

"I might be," Giles replied. "It depends on what condition it is in and whether the price is fair."

"All right. Jenkins," Mr. Shuster addressed his clerk. "give this man one of the authorizations. It is around here somewhere. Now Mr. ..."

"Giles."

"Giles, I should warn you that Geoffrey Twist has stationed several ruffians at Hillcrest Grange – that is the name of Mr. Wark's estate – to discourage anyone from examining the property or making an offer on it. I can give you permission, but you may find that Twist's men will stop you from examining everything."

"How is that possible? Surely it is illegal for him to try to interfere with Mr. Wark's affairs in that way."

"It is. However, with Wark in prison waiting to be transported to Australia, and with the magistrates and constables afraid of Mr. Twist's bully boys, there is nothing I can do about it. I can only warn you. After that, it is on your own head. Do you still want the authorization, Mr. Giles?"

"It is Captain Sir Richard Giles, Viscount Ashton, to you, Mr. Shuster," Daphne intervened sounding very annoyed. "Of course, we want the authorization. We are not about to be intimidated by some dishonest bully, I can assure you. If we like the estate, we will make a reasonable offer that you will be bound to present to Mr. Wark."

Giles had to struggle to suppress the wide grin Daphne's outburst caused him. He had guessed that his wife had a temper and could be extremely forthright when the circumstances warranted it, but he had never seen this side of her before. Mr. Shuster and his clerk were completely taken aback. Ladies simply did not talk that way, except to their servants.

Jenkins scurried to produce the needed paper, and Mr. Shuster signed it promptly.

As soon as they were seated for luncheon at the Fox and Hounds, Giles could hold back his amusement no longer. "You certainly put that lawyer in his place," he praised Daphne.

"Oh, dear, I was so annoyed with Mr. Shuster and how he was treating you that my tongue just ran away from me. I really shouldn't have expressed myself so forcefully, should I?"

"I don't see why not. I never thought you were a shrinking violet. I was quite proud of you."

"I shouldn't have talked about 'we' rather just about 'you,' should I, Richard?"

"I don't agree. You know it will be our property *de facto* even if it is my property *de jure*." Giles expression indicated that he was rather pleased with himself for using legal Latin. " I don't care who knows it. It should be more convenient for you if people realize from the start that you are actually in charge."

"I wish we had talked about the guardians before seeing Mr. Snodgrass," Daphne changed the subject.

"I should have consulted you. I hadn't thought of the need before this. I just thought you would take care of everything if I perished."

"As Mr. Snodgrass pointed out, there are other contingencies and, anyway, even a widow cannot handle everything."

"If you don't like the names I specified, we can just change them."

"No. I cannot think of three better men to be Berns's guardians if he needs them. I just would like to have been asked, even though I know it is your decision."

"I understand."

"I don't imagine that you have already asked them."

"No. As I said, I hadn't thought about the subject before this."

"Then I think we should have them to dinner so that you can ask each one. It would also give us a chance to see if they have any suggestions for dealing with the Mr. Twist. I hate the thought of his getting away with his actions, especially as the property is right next to ours."

"I agree with you. I am sure that we will find a way to put him in his place."

"Just be careful that your plan is foolproof. You are in enough danger at sea without running risks at home."

The minute they arrived at their home, Daphne sent out invitations to the three men designated as guardians. Only as she was preparing the notes did she realize that the men had one thing in common: they were all without wives. In her father's case, the situation wouldn't change unless Giles's father, the Earl of Camshire, died and he could persuade Lady Camshire to marry him. That would be ideal in terms of his being the guardian for Bernard. The Earl most definitely would not be a suitable guardian. Daphne's brother-in-law, Lord David, was likely to marry someone who would advance his hopes of becoming a bishop. There was little she could do to ensure that, if Lord David were named the guardian, the woman taking her place would be a loving substitute should Bernard be left without parents. Captain Bush was another matter altogether. A bit of careful matchmaking was in order there. Her mission of getting all her female in-laws married – and off her hands – had met with complete success, though not always in the way that she had planned. She would now turn her match-making talent to other uses.

Giles and Daphne returned from Ameschester to find that Major Stoner had invented some excuse to visit, though it was quite clear that he had come to see Lady Marianne, whatever the supposed reason might be for his visit. He had to be asked to stay for dinner. His dining at Dipton Hall wasn't an uncommon occurrence. The Major very frequently found some pressing matter or other that brought him to Dipton in the afternoon. Daphne wasn't quite sure how much this was due to the attractions of Lady Marianne and how much to the superior cooking of Mrs. Darling, the cook at Dipton Hall. However, she had no objection to his being present. To do something about balancing the numbers, she might as well invite Captain Bush's mother and sisters as well as the man himself, though that choice would not advance her match-making at all.

Having decided about the guest list, Daphne gave Steves the invitations to be delivered and told him to tell Mrs. Darling how many might be expected for dinner. It did somewhat amaze her how imaginative meals could be served when she sometimes gave the cook the numbers of guests to expect only at very short notice. Surprisingly, Daphne would never have suspected that the reverse of the coin was that when the number of guests was small, the servants ate unusually well the next day.

Giles was able to take the three men he had designated earlier in the day aside before dinner to ask them to be guardians. Each was enthusiastic, though Captain Bush did say that the prospect made him wish even more strongly to find a suitable wife. That settled, the party went into dinner in a convivial mood discussing local matters and local gossip without mention of the war or politics or the dastardly doings that had led to Mr. Wark being in such dire straits.

Giles waited until the ladies had withdrawn before raising the subject of Mr. Wark's property and the warning he had received from Mr. Shuster. A lively discussion followed.

"It seems strange that this man, Twist, would be taking an interest in the property," Captain Bush remarked. "Isn't he a town dweller with a fine house in Ameschester?"

"Yes, he is," responded Mr. Moorhouse, "but I have heard that he is deeply involved in the smuggling trade – not the actual smuggling, of course, but with selling the contraband that arrives in this area."

"I've also heard rumors that that is what he is doing," added Major Stoner. "In addition, I am told that he is keeping people out of Wark's property because he is storing smuggled goods there."

"I understood that when the revenue people looked into it, they found very little material and hardly anywhere to store it," remarked Giles. "Why would this Twist person want to preserve the place for the smuggling trade?"

Major Stoner laughed. "Not much was found because the magistrates who conducted the raid had been bribed to stop their search after finding a small amount of the stuff. They got enough material to make sure that Mr. Wark would be convicted, but no more. I am told that there are lots of hiding places in the woods if you look for them. The magistrates did not find them because they did not look for them."

Giles was beginning to wonder about Major Stoner. The man seemed to know far more about the smugglers than one would expect. But, surely, he could not be allied with them since, if he were, he would not talk about the subject so freely. Even so, Giles was beginning to wonder if Major Stoner was a suitable addition to his family.

"You seem to know a great deal about the smugglers, Major," he remarked.

"Í suppose I do, Captain Giles. My information has come quite inadvertently. You see, I have a favorite pub near my estate. The Soldiers' Rest, it's called. I go there quite often, especially as sometimes it gets lonely rattling around in my big house. There is a splendid group of men who visit that establishment regularly. First-rate people, first rate! Excellent conversation, excellent! They are quite willing to let me join them. Anyway, there is a corner of the snug that cannot be seen from the lounge, but everything said at one table of the bar can be heard if you are in that corner. I use it when my friends aren't there.

"Several times lately I have been in the corner when a group of rowdies enters, and they sit at that table. I couldn't help overhearing their conversation, not that I didn't want to.

Knowing about other people's doings makes life much more interesting, don't you think? I learned that they were involved in smuggling and got to hear quite a bit about how it is conducted around here. Very interesting, I can tell you. Very interesting!

"The last time I heard them, they were laughing about how Mr. Twist had put one over on Mr. Wark. He had bribed the magistrates who were conducting the investigation necessitated by that outburst in court that mentioned that Mr. Warp was keeping smuggled goods on his property. The magistrates found only enough material to ensure that Mr. Wark would be convicted of smuggling and then they looked no further."

"I am horrified to hear about the magistrates," said Lord David, "though I did get some sly remarks when I was named to the bench about how bribing our magistrates was not unknown."

"I didn't know that you are a magistrate, Lord David," said Captain Bush.

"Yes. It seems to be automatic when one is a Member of Parliament, though, of course, I can only serve when I am not in London."

"Something really should be done about this disgraceful situation," said Mr. Moorhouse, "but I don't know what."

"Well, I still want to see the property and so does Daphne," said Giles. "Obviously, I can't take her to Hillcrest Grange when there is this sort of a problem. I guess that the rest of us should ride over there with a group of men that can sweep the ruffians aside so that we can examine the place."

"Excellent idea," said Captain Bush. "We could bring along my coxswain, Tramorgan, and yours, Giles. Also that groom you have, Griffiths, who was in the cavalry. And anyone else who might be useful with a cudgel."

"I'm not sure that I like that idea," Lord David intervened. "It is making more trouble without actually getting to the root of the problem."

"I agree," chimed in Major Stoner. "It really would be a good idea to involve the dragoons, so that we can find out how much stuff is there."

"You are right," Giles conceded. "It would be better if we could put an end to it once and for all, at least as far as this gang is concerned. I would particularly like to get this man Twist."

"Well," said Major Stoner, "I think you are right, quite right, but how are we to do it? Can't go off half-cocked. Wouldn't do at all! Not at all! But here are some ideas about how we might round up all these smugglers and give you a free hand towards using the property of Mr. Wark as needed for the Hunt."

The Major laid out his ideas and a plan was formed with contributions by all those present. The port was passed around several times as they tried to make their scheme foolproof and to ensure that they could handle all contingencies. The scheme could not be implemented the next day, but the following one would serve nicely. The gentlemen broke off their discussion only when everything was understood, agreeing not to mention a word of it when they joined the ladies.

Giles did tell Daphne about their intentions when they had retired to bed, just before blowing out the candle.

"I'm coming with you," she announced when the full plan had been laid out.

"You are not. This is not lady's business," Giles retorted.

A heated discussion broke out, with Daphne pointing out that the first part of the undertaking might be more convincing if she were present with Giles. They argued for several minutes until Daphne won her point. However, she did have to agree that she would withdraw before the time arrived to implement the later and even more important parts of the plan.

Chapter IV

Giles and Daphne led a small cavalcade along the right of way through Mr. Wark's property, Hillcrest Grange, an hour after dawn. The previous day they had arranged for the brush that hid the entrance to the track to be cleared away. The group who had planned the trap that was being set for Mr. Twist and his henchmen was accompanied by the two coxswains and the former cavalryman, Geoffreys, along with some of the outdoor servants of the three principals. In addition, they were accompanied by a company of dragoons that Major Stoner and Lord David had arranged to support them.

The cavalcade proceeded to where the track joined the road that ran past Mr. Wark's drive. There they found another mound of brush closing off the passage. They moved enough of the branches aside so that Giles and Daphne could walk their horses through the gap. The rest of the party remained on the track. Their presence was hidden from the road most conveniently by the remaining pile of brushwood.

Giles and Daphne turned right on leaving the barrier and trotted their horses to the drive that led up to Hillcrest Grange. The residence was some distance from the road. It was an austere, grey-stone building with no remarkable architectural features. The couple had gone hardly one hundred yards up the drive before they were met by four burly men armed with cudgels and a couple of ancient muskets.

"You can't come in here. It's private property. Turn around and get back on the road if you know what's good for you," snarled the man who appeared to be the leader of the group.

"I have authorization granted by Mr. Shuster to examine the property," Giles replied. "Here is the document he gave me."

Giles handed over the piece of paper. The leader took it and appeared to study it carefully. He was, no doubt, having trouble deciphering the words, Daphne noted: he was holding the document upside down.

"You can examine the house, but not the grounds," the ruffian stated, returning the paper to Giles.

"The permission includes the grounds, all the grounds," retorted Giles. "Stand aside."

"You cannot go into the woods. Those are my orders. If you are not content with seeing just the house, then get out of here," commanded the leader of the guardians.

They had reached the first critical part of the plot. Giles raised his riding crop as if to strike the man when Daphne intervened.

"Captain Giles, don't attack them. You might get hurt and then what would happen to me?"

"You are right, Lady Ashton. There are better ways to deal with this. I will get the new magistrate and a company of dragoons, and then we'll see if they can prevent us from seeing every inch of the place."

"We'll be back tomorrow morning, with support, to examine the property completely, my good man," Giles told the ruffian condescendingly. "You can count yourselves lucky that Lady Ashton accompanied me today. Otherwise, I would have given you a much-deserved thrashing, but that would not have been suitable for her eyes."

Giles and Daphne turned their horses and rode at a slow walk down the drive and turned left. They were well out of sight of the men guarding Hillcrest Grange before Giles broke into a loud guffaw.

"You were marvelous, Daphne. So alarmed at the idea of my getting into a brawl."

"I just hope they took us seriously."

"Only time will tell."

They turned left when they came to the track by which they had come and pushed past the branches that blocked the way. The rest of the party was keen to learn what they had discovered.

"That should put the cat among the pigeons," Lord David remarked after Giles had told the tale.

"The next few minutes should tell us whether it worked," Giles replied.

The words were hardly out of his mouth when they heard the sound of a horse galloping towards them from the direction of Hillcrest Grange. Through the brush-wood screen, they could see one of the ruffians who had stopped Daphne and Giles riding post-haste along the road that led to Ameschester.

"Looks as if they have taken the bait," said Giles. "With any luck, Mr. Twist will come with his smuggling workers, and we will catch them all red-handed. Of course, he may only send underlings, but I would dearly like to catch him too."

"Even if he does not show up," said Lord David, "we may be able to catch him implicitly. I told my groom to watch Mr. Twist's house to report any messengers who came urgently this morning. He may be able to provide enough evidence to convict Twist, even if that villain doesn't come himself."

"Very clever of you, my lord…ugh…Lord David," sputtered Major Stoner, who still had a great deal of difficulty reminding himself that Lord David wasn't a lord at all. It was a family joke since all the acknowledgment of his noble parentage would consist of his being called the Honorable Reverend Giles. "Very clever!"

"I imagine that it will be quite a long while before anything happens here," said Mr. Moorhouse. "I think I shall take a break and return after lunch."

"Very sensible, Father," remarked Daphne. "I shall return to Dipton Hall and make sure that the arrangements for the cold luncheon, which we are providing, are going as planned."

Giles could hardly remind her that her role in the adventure was supposed to end at this point. Her mentioning lunch brought to his attention that the schemers had made no provision for the men who would be awaiting the developments that would warrant the capture of the miscreants. He would never treat the crew of *Glaucus* that way, and there was no excuse in this case for his not making sure that the needs of this group of supporters would be filled. Daphne was proving herself to be too integral to this adventure for him to send her away at this point.

The rest of the company settled down to wait for the next developments. The military men were used to waiting for something to happen and to keeping alert as the time dragged on tediously. Lord David had no such experience, but he had brought a writing block with him and was composing his next sermon.

Only a short time seemed to have passed before Daphne returned with a group of servants bearing the makings of a fine repast. They consisted of bread and cold meats and pies, enough for all the soldiers and the other men who had come to take down the smugglers. There was a cask of ale for refreshment as well as several bottles of wine for the gentry. Everyone pitched into this picnic heartily while the sergeants made sure that none of the dragoons had too much ale. Giles made sure that those who had been delegated to watch for developments along the road were relieved in time to get their share of the meal.

With lunch completed, and the picnic cleared away and taken back to Dipton Hall, Daphne lingered with the group awaiting further developments. The soldiers, their officers and the other members of the party seemed to be treating her as a mascot and good-luck charm. Giles did not have the heart to order her to return to Dipton Hall, especially as he was not sure that she would not find some entirely reasonable reason not to obey him. He chose to overlook his previous stern orders only telling her that she must hang back if there was any danger.

The men had just settled in for another lengthy wait when they heard the sound of horse beats from the direction of Ameschester. Before long, a small cavalcade, led by a man dressed as a gentleman and followed by some rather scruffy retainers, cantered past the mouth of the watchers' track. A few minutes further wait saw the arrival of several carts. Giles let the carts disappear down the road before going onto the road to see where they were going. Not surprisingly, the carts turned into the drive leading to Hillcrest Grange. Earlier, the spies Giles had set to watch the entrance to the drive had reported that the destination of the first group of riders had been the same. Everything was falling into place nicely.

Giles signaled to the men in his group to mount up. Following their plan, before they reached the point at which they could be seen from Hillcrest Grange, they paused to let some of Giles's gamekeepers and other servants sneak up the side of the cleared space along the drive to take up positions to discourage anyone from leaving the scene by going into the woods. A second group snuck along the road, keeping low in the hope that they would not be spotted by any of the miscreants who were closer to the house. When he guessed that the two parties were in place and there had been no cry to suggest that they had been spotted, Giles signaled for the raid to begin.

A bugle sounded from the cavalry who then started forward at a walk, moving next to a trot, and then to a canter. They thundered down the drive quite terrifying the group of men who were near the carriage house. Their leader, the man who had led the mounted party which Giles and his confederates had seen earlier, indicated that they all were surrendering and would offer no resistance. Several laborers who were in the stable block ran out and headed towards the woods, obviously hoping to escape. They found their flight blocked by the men whom Giles had sent around the perimeter of the cleared space. Confronted by armed men who looked very eager to try their aim, the would-be escapers yielded and were herded back to the main group.

"Let's see what we have here," Giles said to his brother. Examining what was in the carts revealed several tubs* that were marked as containing cognac. They were of French origin and had no revenue stamp.

"These are obviously smuggled goods, and smuggling is unquestionably a crime," declared Lord David solemnly. "As a magistrate, it is my duty to arrest all these men and seize the goods, which I hereby do. Everyone we have found here can be presumed to be involved, at least until such time as we hear their cases in open court."

Lord David turned to the one man who was dressed as a gentleman. "Now sir, may I have your name, please?"

"I am Daniel Twist, esquire," replied the man in question, rather to Giles's surprise, for he had never heard someone include the term that indicated that he really was a gentleman when introducing himself. "Of Ameschester."

"I see," remarked Lord David. "Well, as the only gentleman here, I must presume that you are in charge, Mr. Twist. Clearly, it is a major operation and has defrauded His Majesty of much-needed revenue. That is a very serious crime. I don't think that we magistrates have the power to deal with such major crimes, so I order that you be held in Ameschester gaol until the next assizes. Pity. Especially as the next time the judges are here is several months away."

"Constable," Lord David addressed the Dipton parish constable whom he had had the foresight to include in the little anti-smuggling venture. "Please take Mr. Twist to Ameschester gaol and tell the gaoler that, on my orders, he is to be held for the next assizes. You can tell him that I will be along shortly to complete the formalities needed to confine him. Take him by the back route to Ameschester through Dipton which we used to get here.

"Now, you others. You are also in very serious trouble. It is likely to have very serious consequences, especially as some of you were armed. I can't speak for the other magistrates, but they may feel that hanging or transportation is the appropriate punishment so that you will be held for the assizes."

"That's not fair," shouted one of the men who had been caught. "The magistrates have been involved in this here smuggling as much as any of us."

"Damnit, Jimmy. Don't you have no brains? We could have counted on the other magistrates to let us off if you hadn't let the cat* out of the bag. Now we're for it," said a large, swarthy man.

"So you may be," Lord David confirmed. "Of course, if you help us to break up this smuggling ring, we might be more lenient towards you, perhaps much more lenient. I am afraid, Jimmy, that you don't have much choice since I suspect the others won't trust you after your remarks. You will just have to help us. All of you remember that things will go much easier on you if you tell us all that you know about these activities, and the more you tell us, the harder it will be on the ones who don't. That fellow Twist seemed to me to be the sort to get as much as he can by ratting on everyone else, don't you agree, Captain Giles?"

"It seems most probable to me," said Giles. "That's certainly the way it works in the Navy. Anyone who steps forward now will undoubtedly get off more lightly than the others. Who will volunteer to join Jimmy here?"

Several men looked enquiringly at their companions wondering which choice would have the worst consequences for themselves.

Finally, one man said, "I reckon that we are in enough trouble right now without making it any worse. Anyway, it looks to me that this smuggling lark is finished. I am not going to suffer by keeping quiet only to help those who have been gaining the most. I'm going with Jimmy."

That broke the ice, and three others joined the first two in spite of the black looks and muttered threats from the remaining men.

"Major Singer," Giles addressed the officer in charge of the dragoons. "Please delegate a few men to take this lot to Ameschester gaol. By the back route, of course. We'll keep the three who have volunteered to help here."

As the officer told off the guards, Giles continued, "We should push those carts out of sight in case other members of the smuggling band are about to arrive.

"Mr. Baker," Lord David addressed the senior revenue officer, "you and your colleague might start by cataloging how much contraband is in the coach house and stables."

"Now everyone," Giles ordered, "hide so that you cannot be seen from the road. There may be some more of these rogues who will come to remove their goods. Hendricks, take your under-keepers into the woods and see if you can find out why Mr. Wark was so reluctant to have anyone go into them."

The remaining men again retreated to the edge of the woods where they could not be observed from the road and settled down to wait. The minutes seemed to drag terribly slowly for those who were not used to the need for patience before action could be taken. Giles and Captain Bush, together with their coxswains were well used to inactivity as were the cavalry officers and men, but time seemed to have stopped for Lord David and Mr. Moorhouse and most of the others. They were about to conclude that this was a waste of time when they heard the sound of a horse on the road. After several agonizingly long minutes, a single horseman turned up the drive. He was followed by a dozen or so workmen on foot who preceded several carts.

As he neared the house, the horseman began to look about anxiously. "What has become of that idiot Twist? His message said he would be here because we had to remove that last shipment as soon as possible. He is supposed to be here. What's going on?"

"Perhaps he has already come and taken the first part of the cargo away, Mr. Richards. It took me a while to find you today, and we had farther to come," said one of the other men.

44

"You may be right. We had better get on with it. Open the doors, and we can start loading."

Giles and his group remained in hiding as the carriage house doors were opened and the workmen started loading the carts. Then, led by Lord David, they emerged to confront the second group of smugglers.

"I am the Honorable David Giles, Justice of the Peace and Member of Parliament for Dipton. May I inquire who you are and what you are doing?" he asked of the leader who was directing the loading of the carts.

The man addressed looked a bit dismayed by this request, but he decided to try to brazen the situation out.

"I am Henry Richards, sir. Mr. Wark was kindly storing some of my goods in his coach house and, since he has decided to sell his estate, I have come to remove my belongings."

"I see. So these goods belong to you and not to Mr. Wark?"

"Yes, indeed."

"Is that also true of the remaining goods in the coach house?"

"It most certainly is."

"Very interesting. Mr. Baker," Lord David instructed Mr. Baker, "please be so good as to examine the things that have been loaded into the cart."

The revenue agent began to look over the goods that were in the cart. "There are several tubs of brandy here, my lord. It looks like some wine also. None of them has our stamp."

"So they are all smuggled?" Lord David asked.

"So it appears, my lord."

"'Mr. Giles' will do. The title is only a bit of a joke."

"Very good, sir. Yes, it would appear that no excise has been paid on any of the goods. Of course, we haven't had a chance yet to examine much of what is in these buildings."

"It does look like that will be a large undertaking, a very large one. What will happen to the material after you have finished cataloging it?"

"Well, sir, it is still the property of its owner. Once he has paid any fines imposed for the smuggling, then he can claim his goods by paying the duties owed, together with compensation for our services, of course. I imagine the owner must be presumed to be Mr. Wark, since this is his land, even though he was in prison at the time it was put in the stable house. Though, Mr. Richards claimed they belonged to him, so he might be considered to be the owner. If Mr. Wark or Mr. Richards doesn't claim the goods and pay both the taxes and the fine, then the finder is given the opportunity to pay the excise – and, as I said, our fees – in order to acquire the goods."

"It's getting late," Giles interrupted when it appeared that Lord David wished to prolong this discussion, "and it will be dark soon. I suggest that a company of the dragoons be left to round up any more smugglers who appear and that we retire to Dipton Hall. You are more than welcome to join us, Major Stringer, and you, Mr. Baker.

The group that had been formed to deal with the smugglers broke up then, with the leaders making their way to Dipton Hall. They arrived just as the winter evening was closing in and the temperature was dropping below freezing. Daphne had anticipated their return and had blazing fires and mulled wine ready to warm them. The men sat long over their port and Madeira that night as they recalled little details of the day's adventure and talked about the prevalence of smuggling. Mr. Baker was most informative of the difficulties he faced since there was little sympathy for his efforts to collect taxes when both necessities like salt, tea, and gin and even beer were taxed along with more luxurious items such as fine brandy or French lace. None of those who were listening confessed to filling their cellars with smuggled casks or otherwise supporting the smuggling trade, though Giles was sure that all of them enjoyed smuggled items. He was rather glad that Steves's practice was to decant all the wine before bringing it to the dining room so that there was no need to try to keep from Mr. Baker the fact that none of it had ever been in the presence of revenue officials.

Daphne and Giles were about to snuff out the candles after they had gone to bed when Daphne remarked, "Richard, do you realize that in all the fun you were having today with the smugglers, you never did examine the house or find out what the woods at Hillcrest Grange are like?"

"You're right; we didn't."

"Well, there isn't much time before you have to go to London. I would much rather you see the situation before you go rather than leave it to me to make such a major decision by myself, or go through all the barriers to a woman buying property on her own."

"On the last point, I am sure that Mr. Edwards can smooth the way for you. He should. He has made enough off me as my prize agent that you can be sure he will give you the very best service since he undoubtedly hopes for more business from us. However, you are right. I trust your judgment completely, you know, but I would like to see what we may be acquiring. We do have a couple of days before I will have to leave. Would you like to investigate Hillcrest Grange again tomorrow?"

"Yes, that is exactly what I hoped you would suggest."

Daphne and Giles returned to Mr. Wark's property the next day. They brought with them Timothy Fellows, the chief Dipton-Hall gamekeeper. While they assessed the residence, Mr. Fellows could start evaluating the woods. They had seemed to be an impenetrable jungle when they had been at the house, but they were the principal lands included in the estate, which seemed to have no fields, but did have some paddocks for horses. Mr. Wark must have been buying hay, oats and other agricultural supplies. Giles and Daphne would have to check the land title to make sure that there were no fields scattered elsewhere that went with Hillcrest Grange about which they knew nothing.

The house itself was dusty and showed evidence of a lack of being cared for properly. Mr. Wark had clearly not been concerned as his furnishings became shabby and his curtains lost all hint of freshness. It struck Daphne as a bit of a mystery. Even if Mr. Wark had been one of those many landowners who had not been able to maintain their incomes in difficult times, his reputation as a major smuggler seemed at variance with the poverty displayed in his dwelling. However, it was none of her business. The house's condition could be used to justify offering a lower price. With a bit of money devoted to it, the house could be made into a very attractive place for a gentleman and his family.

Giles's reaction to the house was total dismay. It seemed to him a gloomy place where it would be disheartening to live. Unlike Daphne, he could not envision how it could be a pleasant residence. He only started to see it as Daphne commented on the improvements that were possible and how they would transform the building into a lovely place to live. She even suggested that it might well be a place where Giles's niece, Catherine Crocker, might like to reside with her fiancée, Captain Bolter, after they had married.

Daphne's enthusiasm converted Giles to the advantages of acquiring the property. There remained the question of what the grounds were worth. As they stood near the front door, idly observing that Mr. Baxter and his assistant were busily noting all the contraband that had been discovered the previous day while they wondered about the nature of the estate, they were joined by Mr. Fellows.

"What do you make of it, Mr. Fellows?" Giles asked. Daphne was still not used to Giles habit of addressing the senior managers of the estate with the title 'Mr.' rather than just by their last names, a habit that he must have developed in the Navy. She noted that Fellows was also surprised and flattered by it. Maybe Giles's habit was a shrewd move to keep the loyalty of senior servants.

"It's a damned strange place, sir. At the edge of the wood, it appears to be impenetrable underbrush, but that isn't actually the case. There are spots where you can push back the underbrush, and then you find tracks leading into the woods. Quite well-used tracks in my opinion. They lead to copses of holly and yew and other plants that aren't quite natural. When I examined one carefully, I found a disguised opening, and when I had pushed the brush aside and maneuvered around a holly bush, I found that there was a way into the area. Inside there was a shed, quite a substantial one."

"What was in the shed?"

"I don't know, sir. It was locked."

"You should have broken the lock. Go and do it now."

"Captain Giles," Daphne intervened. "I don't think that is a very good idea."

"Why not?"

"First, because Hillcrest Grange belongs to Mr. Wark and we do not have permission to break into a locked shed. Second, if we did break in, we can be pretty sure about what we would find since the shed is hidden away in this manner. Then we would have to inform Mr. Baxter. He would have to catalog the contraband. Next, he would have to have the fine assessed as well as the duty. Finally, he would have to give Mr. Wark another chance to set things right.

"Mr. Baxter doesn't work exactly quickly. As a result of discovering what is in that shed, everything about the property would be tied up for much longer. That would be particularly the case if his involvement led to him examining the wood and finding more storage places. I think we should let sleeping dogs lie, at least until we have made up our minds about taking on the kennels and buying Hillcrest Grange."

"You are quite right, Lady Ashton. Let's go back to Dipton Hall and consider the question carefully."

When they had changed from their riding clothes, Giles and Daphne huddled together in her workroom assessing the case for acquiring Hillcrest Grange. Giles was eager to purchase the house so that they could rent it to his friend or someone else who would make interesting neighbors. He was not particularly interested in adding to his land holdings, which was not surprising since they were considering woodland and not arable land whose proper management was his hobby. Daphne looked at their possible addition to the estate primarily as a matter of business. She did believe that the harvestable trees would complement the present timber activities of Dipton Hall and looked at the transaction first as a matter of the value of the logs they could expect to sell as well as the rent for the residence. Both found that they were keen to have the kennels, partly to solidify their position as the premier family in the area and also to encourage a sport which they both enjoyed. They agreed that they should buy Hillcrest Grange.

"Oh, Richard," Daphne lamented. "I wish that you didn't have to leave tomorrow. I would so like to have you here, especially to handle this."

"I know that you are perfectly capable of taking care of it."

"Not without involving a lot of other people. I am a woman, remember. A married woman. I can't just buy someone's property."

"I suppose. But what can we do about it? Do you think that Mr. Snodgrass could set it up so that you can make all the important steps?"

"I don't know. But I don't want to have our last day taken up with your going to Ameschester. I do so like to be with you!"

"I do too. But if we skip luncheon and take the carriage, we will still be able to be together. I don't think it will take Mr. Snodgrass very long to find a way that we can get what we want despite the fact that you are a woman."

"But, Richard, we can't just barge in without an appointment and expect him to do some work immediately."

"Oh, Daphne," laughed Giles, "how I love it that you still think of yourself as being simple Daphne Moorhouse, who, of course, Mr. Snodgrass would not consider a particularly valuable client. In fact, you are now Viscountess Ashton, soon to be the Countess of Camshire, married to one of the wealthiest landowners in the county. A landowner who is known for his peculiarity of letting his wife make all the important decisions about the management of the estate. I am quite sure that Mr.

Snodgrass will find no more important business than to be of service to us immediately."

With that worry settled, they had the carriage brought to the portico and went to Amesbury. On the way, they talked excitedly about all the projects and changes they had in mind and whether young Bernard should be entered for Eton, Harrow, or Rugby, a decision in which, Daphne knew, most mothers would not be involved.

Giles's appreciation of Mr. Snodgrass's priorities was correct. The lawyer grumbled about the outrageousness of the suggestion that, in effect, Daphne could take her husband's place, but when he put his mind to, found a way that would accomplish their intentions. He also agreed to enter into negotiations with Mr. Shuster to purchase Mr. Wark's property, a task he took on with ill-concealed glee since he would undoubtedly be taking from the clutches of his rival any legal matters that might arise in future in connection with the property.

Daphne and Giles resumed their excited chatter when they were once again in their carriage. Only as they neared Dipton did the weight of their impending separation engulf them. They were turning up the driveway to Dipton Hall before Daphne made up her mind that she should share her latest suspicions with her husband.

"Richard," she began, "I think I may be with child."

"What?" he asked rather neutrally since he had been lost in thoughts of what lay ahead. Then what Daphne had said registered with him. "With child, Daphne? Oh, how wonderful! What a marvelous parting gift. Are you sure?"

"Not completely. I haven't seen Mr. Jackson yet, as you know. Don't get your hopes up too much, though. I may not be pregnant. And even if I am, Mr. Jackson has warned me that a lot of pregnancies end themselves, for no clear reason, quite early on."

"Oh, I hope that doesn't happen. I am completely delighted with the thought of another child. I only wish I could be here to help you through the delivery. Of, course, with luck that may happen. I don't know what the Admiralty has in mind for me."

Chapter V

Giles walked from Norad's Hotel, where he had spent the night, to the Admiralty. He had somewhat misjudged the time it would take, with the result that he arrived a little too early. Unlike his recent visits to the Admiralty, when he had been summoned to receive new orders, he was not immediately taken to the First Lord's office. Instead, he was ushered into the large waiting room. It was notorious as a place where officers could wait for hours, even for days, to see the official with whom they had business, even ones who had ordered their presence on that day at a time specified.

Giles had never before been in the room, but it seemed to meet the rumors exactly. A host of men glanced up at him as he entered. Some were lieutenants, many quite elderly lieutenants, and others were post-captains. He nodded to two or three whom he knew and was about to settle onto a chair when he noticed that his old friend, Captain Henty Bolton, was seated in one of the corners. The two of them had served at the same time in the Caribbean and had more recently renewed their friendship with the result that Bolton was now engaged to Giles's niece, Catherine Crocker.

"Captain Giles, what brings you here?"

They were on a first-name basis, but its use in public would not have been appropriate for a captain to use in addressing another one above him on the naval list.

"I don't know, Henry. My last commission was on Admiralty orders, but it is finished. I had expected to receive a new 'requested and required' letter attaching *Glaucus* to some admiral or other, not an order to show up here for some unexplained reason. And you?"

"As you may remember, I was comfortably ensconced in my position as captain of *Hermosa*, attached to the Channel Fleet. Unfortunately, I lack both seniority and influence, and I was only filling in for a Captain Durrell who was nominally in command of her. I received a letter stating that Captain Durrell was about to assume his command and ordering that I bring *Hermosa* to the Nore* before handing her over to this Durrell chap. When I asked around about him, I discovered that the scuttlebutt was that he was made post almost immediately after he had passed his lieutenant's examination*. Since then, he has not been to sea, the pleasures of St. James* being more attractive to him than those of the command of a ship. However, it seems that he is now in need of his full pay, so I have been relieved of my command."

"That sort of thing is a disgrace," Giles protested, loudly enough to cause many raised eyebrows among the other waiting officers. It was considered not only bad form but also highly dangerous, to call attention to the weaknesses of the naval appointment system in the very lair of the flunkeys who were instrumental in indulging the strange requests that their superiors made in the implementation of the system of influence.

"I agree, Richard, not that that does much good. So I am here to beg for another command, hopefully before my present one expires at the end of the month."

Before Giles could commiserate further with his friend, he was summoned to the First Lord's presence.

"Good of you to come," the man in overall command of the Royal Navy greeted Giles as if the Captain were doing the Admiralty a favor by appearing. "You acquitted yourself very well in a difficult situation in Russia. Now, I have another possibly tricky task for you."

"Yes, my lord? Incidentally, congratulations on your elevation to the peerage." Sir David McDougall had recently been created Baron Gordonston, the lowest rank of the peerage, for services to the Crown. Malicious rumor had it that he was furious that he not been made at least an earl.

"Thank you."

The First Lord wandered over to a map showing the English Channel on which he pointed to a location in France. "As everyone in Britain must know, Napoleon is planning to invade us. He has been assembling a huge fleet of small craft, centered on Boulogne, here."

The first Lord pointed to the chart before continuing. "He has also assembled a very large army on the heights above Boulogne – here. We are not at all sure where he intends to land, a surprising gap in our knowledge given the number of spies whose reports we are receiving and the amount of planning that the French must be doing. Of course, Bonaparte has always been good at disguising his strategic and tactical intentions, but our not having any real knowledge of his plans is worrying.

"It is not a very seaworthy armada he has gathered in Boulogne. Well, you know about that. You saw it not so long ago and burnt some of it. Best show we've had against that build up!

Boney will need some pretty calm days and favorable winds to get his army across the Channel, and that flotilla could not defend themselves successfully against even a weak naval force while they were making the crossing. In other words, he has to have complete command of the eastern part of the Channel for a considerable amount of time when the weather is favorable for him to have any hope of success. Still, there is no doubt that the bulk of his forces is encamped outside Boulogne, and that the invasion fleet of small boats is ready to go. All he needs is command of the Channel for a few suitable days.

"To defend the Channel, we have the North Sea Fleet which is usually cruising off the Goodwin Sands, here." Lord Gordonston was again pointing to the map. "Its base is at the Nore. With the wind from the east or north-east, they could be among the invasion craft before Napoleon could establish a strong enough beachhead for his invasion to succeed. There is, at present, no major enemy naval force to the east of the North Sea Fleet. The Dutch fleet has not been rebuilt since Camperdown*, though we cannot be absolutely certain that they are not hiding some newly built ships where we cannot see them. The Danes are neutral, at least for now, and do not have a fleet that could seriously challenge our North Sea one.

"At the western end of the Channel, the situation is more complicated. The Channel Fleet is usually patrolling off Ushant, but there is always a good number of ships at Spithead, here. It would take them some time to intercept the fleet of small boats intending to invade us, but they could easily get there before many of the craft had made the crossing, indeed before all of Boney's boats could even have left Boulogne.

"The main French fleet is bottled up here in Brest," the First Lord pointed to the location of the great French naval base. "It is being blockaded closely by the Channel Fleet. Even if the French all got out of the port without being seen – a difficult task given the narrowness of the entrance so that their exit will take quite a long time – they are bound to be discovered before they can get around Ushant and into the Channel. As long as this is the situation, they won't be able to pry open the Channel on their own. They will need help from elsewhere to defeat the Channel Fleet. Even if our ships are blown off station by gales, the French will need time to get out of Brest after the wind has eased enough to allow them to sail, so we can expect to catch them. In the worst weather, the Channel Fleet takes cover in Tor Bay, here." The First Lord thumped his knuckle on the map to indicate the default location of the fleet in foul weather. "As you can see, it is still in a position to intercept any French fleet that uses the opportunity of a storm to sail up the Channel.

"To have much chance of success, the Brest Fleet would have to combine with other French or Spanish fleets to overwhelm the Channel Fleet and still be able to defend the invasion craft against the North Sea Fleet. Of course, the Brest Fleet might be successful if it could combine with other ships we do not know about so that they could gain entrance to the Channel with enough force left to protect the invasion crossing. That's what I worry about, even though the admirals all tell me that they could not have such ships.

"The other significant French fleet is at Toulon*. Nelson is blockading it. I'm not sure that he is the man for the job – the French once gave him the slip there – but he had to be given a major command, and that seemed the best one. If the Toulon Fleet should get loose in the Atlantic, it could do a great deal of damage. The Spanish fleet could also sail, and the two fleets might arrange to join the Brest fleet, in which case we will be in real trouble.

"Your frigate, or any number of frigates, can't affect fleet battles directly although all our smaller ships are invaluable in shadowing the enemy fleets and conveying their locations to our larger ships. However, I have a special task for you that would be much more useful than just attaching you to one of the fleets."

"Yes, my lord?" Giles was glad that the lecture on the current situation was ending. He had been learning nothing new.

"I have my doubts with respect to our information about the strength of the French Navy, especially about its strength in the Channel and on the west coast of France. Everyone seems to believe that their ships are mostly in Brest with a small force at the Garonne. Our reports about the sizes of those fleets are supposed to be pretty accurate, and that is where our spying efforts have been directed. But there are a lot of other harbors along the coast. While they may not be suitable as an anchorage for a whole fleet, they could each hold a few ships of the line, enough to seriously change the picture. Some of those ports certainly have adequate facilities, such as Lorient where large ships have been built. Napoleon has been building more ships. That we do know. They are not just the cockle-shells to get his army across the Channel. In a lot of these places, it would not be too difficult to hide one or two large ships from observation from the sea, and that would particularly be the case if their top-masts were sent down along with the main-sail yards and canvas.

"I fear that the enemy may have a significant number of ships hidden away and could coordinate their movements to join together with the known fleets to present us with a far more powerful force than we are presuming will confront us. Hardly anyone believes that my fears have any basis in fact. I do not have a sea-going background, so it is easy for others to state that my fears are unfounded. Asking our blockading ships to look into the matter runs the risk that people will see what they expect to see – or rather not see what they already know is not there. This is where you come in."

The First Lord paused a moment, possibly to take a last reflection on whether his orders would be wise.

"Yes, my Lord?" Giles nudged him along.

"I am commissioning you to look into the minor French ports and to do everything you can to determine what naval ships, if any, they may be harboring. I also want you to intercept any vessels leaving such ports to find out what they have seen there. Those ships will probably be smugglers so you will have the authority to seize them and their cargoes if they are indeed smuggling. You cannot, in reality, seize their ships, but you can order them to report to the customs houses on arrival, with the seizure of their property and having their crews impressed into the navy if they fail to do so. Of course, you can turn a blind eye to their doings if they agree to supply information to you.

"I am assigning you two other ships to aid the information gathering. One is the small frigate *Flicker*, twenty-eight. She is pretty well the smallest frigate in the navy and the smallest command for a post captain. She is Dutch-built, and of very shallow draft, so she can get in closer to land than almost any of our ships of any strength. Better certainly than our brigs*. Her captain, unfortunately, died of some stomach trouble on her last voyage. We are about to appoint James Flemming into her. He is very young and has just been made post. Son – second son – of the Earl of Hashborough. Not supposed to be very bright, but his father is very influential."

"Has he had any relevant experience, my lord?"

"Not really. He spent his time as a lieutenant on *Herculaneum* – seventy-four – Captain Trumper. Did nothing notable, but his father controls a couple of seats in Parliament and has some connections with important army contractors. And his older brother has always been in poor health, and I hear that he may die soon of his ailments."

"Might I suggest, my lord, that Captain Flemming's appointment is truly inappropriate? From your description of the mission, it will require someone with experience in handling a ship in difficult situations, appreciate what he is seeing when having only imperfect views of harbors, and be able to deal effectively with difficult characters. The wardroom of a seventy-four is a poor training- school for such matters. I am sure that Captain Flemming would be better off in a frigate assigned to one of the fleets where he can learn from being part of a group before being expected to perform well in a rather loosely defined mission where independent judgment may well be required with little time for reflection." Giles realized that he might well be exaggerating what would be required of his subordinate, but he had no desire to rely on someone whose only claim to a command arose from his father's importance.

"I take your point, Captain Giles, but I don't know where we could find at short notice the paragon you describe."

"I hate to presume, my lord, to make a recommendation. However, just the right man is downstairs, waiting to discuss his next command with someone in the Admiralty."

"Who might that be?"

"Captain Henry Bolton, sir. He is very experienced. I served with him in the Caribbean, and we have more recently renewed our ties. He is very much the sort of man whom I want."

"Newsome what do you know about Captain Bolton?" the First Lord asked the Second Secretary, who had been discretely following the conversation.

"Not very much, sir. He has yet to hold a command of his own as a post-captain, but he did distinguish himself as a commander in charge of *Dragonfly*. That led to his being made post. He is totally without influence, sir, which is why he is lucky to have landed a job filling in for Captain Durrell."

"It is also why he may make a good candidate to command *Flicker*. Look up the information we have on him, please. I will see him right after Captain Giles."

"I must remind you, my lord, that Captain Flemming's father is very influential. In addition, Captain Flemming might well become the next Earl of Hashborough."

"I am aware of it. I am also aware that Captain Giles is one our best frigate captains and is now quite rich enough that he could easily leave the service if we don't pay attention to his naval preferences. In addition, he also has control of two seats, and he is certain to become the Earl of Camshire. I don't think he intended to use his influence and he based his argument on Captain Bolton's merit, but to say that Captain Bolton is without influence is not quite right. Now, do as I say."

A somewhat intimidated Second Secretary scurried away, presumably to get the necessary docket. Giles was stunned to have it so clearly stated that he really did have serious influence with the government and that, when he made a suggestion, it would be interpreted as an exercise of that power.

"Well, that's settled, unless there is something seriously untoward in Captain Bolton's record," the First Lord got back to his instructions. "Now, the other ship is a sloop, *Firefly,* schooner rigged. She is commanded by Commander Franklin Archer. Just been promoted. Served in the sixty-four *Thunderer* before being given this command. *Firefly* has just had her copper renewed. She is one of our fastest ships and points* very high. She unfortunately also has a deep draft. However, between her and *Flicker* you should be well equipped to catch the smugglers from whom you hope to get information and co-operation.

"Now, any other questions?" It was clear that the First Lord did not expect any.

"Where is *Firefly* now, my lord?"

"Newsome, where is she?" The Second Secretary was present again, though Giles had not noted his return.

"At the Nore, my lord, as is *Flicker*. Sir, have you mentioned reporting?"

"Not yet. Captain Giles, you will be sailing under Admiralty orders, of course, but in waters under the command of some very senior admirals and more junior ones who are under them. They will not be pleased to see three ships of the type they always claim are in very short supply which they will be unable to commandeer. In addition, most of the reports about which I am suspicious come from them or members of their command. They won't be happy about your orders, so you are to insist that your reports be forwarded to the Admiralty unopened. I'll give you written orders to that effect which you can show to them if needed.

"One last thing, but very important. I don't know if you have heard, but Lieutenant Correll has asked to be temporarily relieved of his duties. His father recently died, after inheriting his brother's estate. A substantial one, I understand. Correll wants time to make the proper arrangements before he returns to sea. I suppose I should say, 'if he returns to sea.' I hear that he is now a very rich young man. Anyway, you will need a new lieutenant. I understand that none of your midshipmen has passed his exam."

"No, sir. They are still too young to take the examination*."

"Then, I have just the man for you. His name is Etienne Marceau. He is from a noble French family. They only just got out of France before having their heads chopped off. He has been a midshipman in *Quixote*, thirty-six, and has recently passed the examination. He speaks French very fluently, and he can speak as if he is a Norman workman as well as in a more elevated tone. I was thinking that it might be helpful for you to have someone who is fully fluent in French and can sound like a member of the lower classes. I should mention that his family are friends of mine and so you would be doing me a favor to take him on."

"That was quick," thought Giles, "give a favor, get a favor." However, the First Lord's argument made sense, and he had no candidate to suggest himself.

"He sounds eminently suitable, my lord. I shall look forward to making his acquaintance as soon as possible."

"He shouldn't delay your sailing. He is currently in Kent. Newsome, send the orders for him to join *Glaucus* as soon as possible. Do you have Captain Giles's orders? Good. Well, Captain, I wish you luck in this new undertaking. I will anticipate your reports eagerly."

With that, the First Lord turned to his desk, obviously seeking his next task. Giles found himself escorted from the room by a lackey with no waste of time. He did stop by the waiting room to wish Captain Bolton success, only to find that another servant was summoning his friend to a meeting with the First Lord.

"Richard, this summons from the First Lord has happened unexpectedly quickly. I have my barge at the Admiralty steps and will be returning to the Nore when I am through here. Would you like me to give you a ride?"

"Indeed, yes. I will get my things from my hotel and meet you at the steps."

Giles was amazed that the Admiralty had acted so swiftly on his suggestion. He would be very pleased to have Bolton under his command, even though he did have some misgivings about how the influence-system worked. For all the First Lord knew, Captain Bolton might be a dud who should never have been given a command, just like Captain Flemming. Flemming would undoubtedly be given some command, possibly one in which he could do a great deal of damage.

It did not take long for Giles to return to Norad's hotel and collect his luggage and Carstairs, his coxswain. He did take the time to write a note to Daphne explaining that he was going to sea. He added that Captain Bolton would be joining him as captain of a frigate. They arrived at the Admiralty steps before Captain Bolton had returned to his barge. While he waited, Giles was amused to notice how Carstairs had latched onto Captain Bolton's coxswain. The man would undoubtedly be going with his captain to his new command. Giles had inadvertently let Carstairs know about Bolton's changed status, and Carstairs had lost no time forging the links in the chain that held coxswains together when their captains were on similar missions. It was not just the captains of the navy who formed an invisible connection joining the ships together. Their coxswains did likewise.

Captain Bolton's arrival at the landing steps was marked by the very wide grin on his face. His step was feather-light as he strode happily along.

"I am sure that I have you to thank for my good fortune, Captain Giles. Indeed, Lord Gordonston indicated that you had put in a very good word for me. Thank you so much."

"No thanks needed, Henry. You fully deserve it, and I am delighted to have secured you to back me up. I don't know yet what sort of a ship *Flicker* is, but I am sure you will have her up to snuff quickly."

"You can count on me, sir. Oh, this has secured my future. You now need have no worries about how well I can provide for Miss Crocker."

"I never doubted it. I just hope that this commission will allow us to get enough time ashore that you can get married. I know that Catherine would like nothing better."

With that, both men stepped into the barge. The tide was on the ebb, and Captain Bolton's crew was well trained. In minutes they were shooting under the arches of London Bridge. Then the sights of the river, St. Paul's Cathedral, the Tower of London, the crowded pool and docks sped by. They arrived at the Nore in no time at all.

Captain Bolton brought Giles to *Glaucus* before rowing to *Hermosa* to collect his belongings after which he would go aboard *Flicker*. If all was in readiness in that ship, as it was supposed to be, he could weigh anchor in the morning. Giles invited Bolton for a late dinner on *Glaucus* after he had read himself into *Flicker* and he would ask Commander Archer of *Firefly* to join them. If all was in order, they should be able to sail on the morrow's tide.

As Giles had intended, Commander Archer arrived before Captain Bolton. Giles wanted to get to know his new subordinate. Archer was a reedy young man, one without a commanding air. He was also very young. Giles wondered how the man had got his command so early. He hadn't read anything in the *Naval Gazette* that would have produced an early promotion based on merit.

"Tell me about yourself, Captain Archer."

"Yes, sir. I joined *Tremendous*, seventy-four, when I was sixteen, though my father had had me entered* in her books at age twelve. I started, of course as a midshipman. That was five years ago. I served in her in that rank until I passed my examination and was lieutenant in her for another two years. Then I was promoted to my present rank."

"That is a very rapid rise in rank, Captain Archer, isn't it?"

"I suppose it is. My uncle, Oliver, Lord Bordalls, you know, and my aunt, Lady Bordalls, have been very generous in pressing my case."

Giles's heart sank. Here was an extreme case of promotion by influence rather than merit. Of course, Captain Archer might be an excellent seaman, despite his rapid advancement, but Giles doubted it. Service solely in a seventy-four was hardly likely to produce an officer skilled enough to handle a schooner in battle. Well, there was nothing much he could do about it immediately. With any luck, the Admiralty might have assigned Archer an experienced and capable lieutenant who would know what he was doing.

"I notice that *Firefly* is anchored very close to the shore, Captain Archer," Giles remarked to change the subject.

"Yes, sir. When I brought her out of Chatham, we were anchored almost on the other side of the fleet, but my lieutenant didn't know what he was doing so our anchor dragged, and we ended up where we now are. The port Captain ordered that I should stay there until I was ordered to move."

Before Giles could inquire more into the accomplishments of his new subordinate, Captain Bolton was announced. His friend burst in full of enthusiasm about his new command, though it was evident that he thought that there was much work needed to bring her up to the standard he wanted. Giles suspected that there was more to what Bolton had discovered, but with Commander Archer present, he was not about to tell what it was.

Giles had invited *Glaucus*'s principal officers to the late dinner as well as the two ship's captains. He was a believer that all should be aware of what was required of them and the purpose of their endeavors; he had little use for commanding officers who took joy in the petty power of limiting subordinates' information to enhance their own importance. The main part of the discussion was ensuring that every ship would be ready to depart at the turn of the tide the next day. The party did not linger long over their port after the King's health had been drunk. Most had responsibilities to make sure that everything would be ready at the appointed hour. Captain Bolton was the first to leave, not surprisingly since he was the only one who would be trying to take to sea in a crowded anchorage a ship and crew with which he was completely unfamiliar. Giles would have to wait to find out what were his friend's misgivings about his new command.

The following morning brought a series of squalls ripping through the anchorage. They were unpleasant and annoying but not serious enough to prevent sailing at the appointed time. At seven bells of the forenoon watch*, Giles told *Glaucus*'s signal midshipman, Mr. Fisher, to hoist the signals for *Flicker* and *Firefly* to sail. He hardly needed to supervise *Glaucus*'s getting underway once he had given that order, since Mr. Hendricks, his first lieutenant, was thoroughly experienced in handling the frigate. Instead, he turned his telescope on *Flicker* and *Firefly*. His sympathies went out to Captain Bolton with the job of taking his ship to sea in difficult conditions. His friend had not had any chance to be involved in his crew's training, but if anything went wrong, Captain Bolton would be held responsible by all the other officers in the anchorage if not by a court-martial. *Flicker*'s anchor was being recovered smoothly, but the unloosing her sails when the time came seemed to be a bit ragged, with men not being entirely sure of their stations.

Giles shifted his attention to *Firefly*. She seemed to be having problems raising her anchor and smoothly sailing away. First, she raised her sails too soon, including her jibs, which must have significantly increased the difficulty of recovering her anchor with the ship yawing somewhat from side to side. Then when the anchor was off the bottom, she slipped sternwards unsteadily, her rudder not catching the water to spin her onto the larboard tack*. Finally, Commander Archer did get her under control, and she gathered way close-hauled on the larboard tack, sailing among the anchored ships rather than turning downwind as soon as possible. Her present course would only just clear the stern of a huge, cumbersome seventy-four ship-of-the-line. Giles could just make out her name: *Tremendous*. All should have been well, though *Firefly*'s course left little room for error.

A sudden, strong gust struck the schooner. She should have loosed her sheets* to parry the gust and have turned to starboard to avoid the swinging battleship. Instead, she turned to larboard. A severe collision seemed to be inevitable. However, luck returned to *Firefly* at the last moment. Her bowsprit had just started to poke through the stern windows of her victim when the gust suddenly intensified. It caught *Firefly*'s jib and wrenched her bow to starboard while the massive second-rate*'s stern swung to larboard. However, much of the stern casement was ripped from the gigantic ship that towered over the sloop. *Firefly*, coming clear of the lee of her victim, was about to be flattened by the wind when her main sheet parted. The pressure that was threatening to capsize her was relieved. Somehow she recovered, and with her mainsail flapping uselessly in the wind, she sailed free of the peril that had almost destroyed her.

Glaucus and *Flicker* had to reduce sail and wait for *Firefly* to get her mainsail under control again before she could join them. Giles supposed that there was no real point in questioning Commander Archer on what had gone wrong. Nevertheless, he summoned the young officer to report to *Glaucus*. He waited impatiently for his order to be fulfilled, wondering what, in the name of all that was holy, had happened.

It didn't take long after Captain Archer arrived on *Glaucus*'s quarterdeck to discover the source of the collision with *Tremendous*. In answer to Giles's query, Archer replied, "Sir, it was the fault of my quartermaster who turned the ship in the wrong direction."

"How did that happen?"

"I don't know, sir. We had lots of room until *Tremendous* took it into her mind to swing towards us. Totally unexpected, of course, but I did notice it at the last moment."

"You had the con, Captain Archer?"

"Yes, sir."

"And then?"

"I ordered the quartermaster to turn to the right – starboard, sir. Instead, he turned to larboard, so we scraped *Tremendous*. Luckily Mr. Latimer, here, told them to turn the other way before it became more serious."

"Mr. Latimer?"

"Yes, sir, my master's mate."

"Is he experienced?"

"Not very. I didn't like the old man who was *Firefly*'s master, so I had him replaced with Mr. Latimer whom I had known on *Tremendous*."

"I see. What exactly was your order when you became aware that you were about to crash into *Tremendous*, Captain Archer?"

"I yelled, 'Starboard your helm,' of course, sir?"

"'Starboard your helm?', are you sure."

"Yes sir, of course, I wanted to turn to starboard."

"Good God, man, don't you know that that is the order to turn the ship to larboard."

"Is it? Surely not. That doesn't make sense."

"There are many things that may not make sense in the Navy, Captain Archer, but you are supposed to have learned them as a midshipman or lieutenant. Didn't you ever stand watch* while *Tremendous* was under sail when you served in her?"

"Of course I did."

"And didn't you give helm orders?"

"No, sir. I always just told the master's mate of the watch what I wanted, and he instructed the helmsman."

"I see. Don't you think that you should have signaled your apologies to the captain of *Tremendous*?"

"Oh, no. Captain Morrow was on deck and saw that all was well. I doffed my hat to him and bowed. I am afraid he just shrugged and looked away. He knows me well, of course, since I sailed with him, as you know."

"Now, your grounding when you were getting under weigh?"

"Yes, sir. No harm done. Just one of those things that can happen."

"Tell me about it."

"Well, sir, since I had never taken a schooner off a lee shore, I ordered my lieutenant, Mr. Blemkinsop, to take charge. I am afraid that he made a mess of it."

"Mr. Blenkinsop is an experienced mariner, is he?"

"Not really, sir. He served with me in *Tremendous* as a midshipman. Only just passed his exam before I received my promotion. The lieutenant who was in *Firefly* before I took command did not seem to like me. Anyway, he resigned right after I had first met him, and I had to find a new lieutenant. Randy Blenkinsop was just the right fellow. Son of Lord Rye, you know. Terribly good at riding to hounds is Randy. Capital fellow to have on board."

"Did he have experience handling a smaller ship with fore-and-aft sails?"

"No, sir. That is why I ordered him to take *Firefly* to sea so that he could get the experience. I am afraid he did make a bit of a cock-up doing it."

"I see." Giles realized he had been uttering that expression quite a bit even when he meant, "I don't believe it."

"I suggest, Captain Archer, that in future you take command yourself and rely on your master's mate for ship handling. Possibly you should go over with him just what the helm orders mean."

"I couldn't do that, sir. Mr. Latimer is a very good fellow, but he isn't a gentleman. It wouldn't do to take his advice, would it, sir?"

"That wasn't a suggestion to be questioned, Captain Archer. It was an order to be obeyed."

"Aye, aye, sir."

How in the world could Britain win the war, with the 'interest' system producing this sort of an officer? Giles ruminated after he saw the commander over the side. No doubt Archer would be made post very soon in exchange for some obscure favor done to a politician. If his incompetence didn't get him court-martialed first, he would no doubt rise to be an admiral with a whole fleet to mismanage.

Chapter VI

Daphne watched Giles's carriage drive away. She stood under the portico of Dipton Hall, waving until the coach was out of sight. She knew, of course, that she had married a sailor on active duty and that his profession would take him away for long periods of time. However, that was no real consolation when he had to leave once again. Even the thought that he had remained at Dipton for an unusually long period of time after he returned to Dipton badly injured from his previous voyage did not cheer her up. She just hoped that he would come back safely this time, completely uninjured, and soon. What she did know is that she would far rather have Giles, even if only for short periods, than anyone else in the world.

Daphne realized that the best cure for what she was feeling because of Giles's departure would be to keep active. There was any number of things she could do, and that needed to be done. She had to see to the accounts and make sure also that all was ready for spring. She had to visit her father's tenants and check that everything was well with them. She had a steward, who looked after such matters for Dipton Hall, but she had yet to find a suitable one for Dipton Manor. Then there was Ashton Place. Giles had inherited it a few month ago. The house was rented, but she wasn't sure that the farms were being managed to their full potential. She had yet to visit the property to see just what had been added to their family fortune. She would have to arrange a trip there in the near future. But first would come the kennels for the foxhounds of the Ameschester Hunt. However, before she could tackle that challenge, she would have to purchase Hillcrest Grange and deal with the material that was hidden in its woods. She had no time to sit around moping just because Giles had had to follow his vocation.

Daphne was about to set off to see her father's tenants when a bout of nausea hit her. Yes, she was probably with child, but she had better make sure that that was what her problem was. She called for her maid only to be told by Steves that Betsy had gone out. When she asked why and where her servant had gone, Steves replied that she had mentioned something about having to see Mr. Jackson.

Daphne was surprised. She could not believe that Betsy would be ill without first telling her. What could be the matter? The mystery was soon solved when Betsy returned with Mr. Jackson.

"What in the world is going on?" Daphne demanded.

"Hopefully, nothing serious." Mr. Jackson replied. He had known Daphne since she was a small child and he had always dealt with any health issues she had, from a cold to a sprained ankle, not to mention the gamut of childhood illnesses and her first pregnancy. "But Betsy told me that she was worried about your health. You have been sick to your stomach quite frequently, and you have been very irritable recently. You don't seem to be yourself, she said. You were hiding whatever was bothering you from your husband, she thought, but you couldn't fool her."

"That's nonsense."

"Maybe it is. Have you been nauseous recently?"

"Yes, just a few times. Nothing serious."

"Any headaches?"

"A few. But not very bad ones."

"Are your breasts a bit tender?"

"Now that you ask, I suppose they are more so than usual." She thought for a minute and blushed. Modesty required silence on this subject, but not telling Mr. Jackson everything would be foolish. "Of course, my husband has been paying some attention to them," she spoke in a whisper.

"Any unusual food wants?" Mr. Jackson paid no attention to this bout of modesty on the part of his patient.

"No."

"But my lady," burst out Betsy. "Mrs. Darling told me that you have gone to the kitchen a couple of times to order some pickles."

"I don't see why that has anything to do with anything. It is much easier to go to the cook directly, when I crave something, than to have to bother all the servants. If I were to ask you, you would ask one of the maids, and she would have to go to the kitchen to ask the cook, and then, likely, Mr. Steves would get involved, and one of the footmen would be delegated to bring it to you, and finally I would get it, by which time the desire for a pickle might have passed. Much quicker, and easier all around, for me to ask cook myself."

"Daphne, that's all true," Mr. Jackson broke in before Daphne could fully establish the case of how reasonable she had been, "but you are also exhibiting all the symptoms of being with child, even down to the glow in your cheeks which is not really seasonable for the middle of winter."

"Well, what then? Do you want to examine me?"

"Not this early in the pregnancy, no. I know that you are perfectly healthy and should have no trouble bearing another child. An examination wouldn't tell me anything. I now know that you and Captain Giles are to be congratulated on the prospect of another offspring."

"Oh, I already guessed *that*. I told Captain Giles just before he had to leave. I presume that I can now go about my usual affairs."

"Of course. I imagine you have my instructions from last time. You won't have to curtail any activities for quite a while. Just don't ride that horse of Captain Giles and, if you insist on doing so, don't fall off him. Breaking your neck would not be good for the baby." Mr. Jackson did not seem to be able to restrain himself from teasing Daphne about one of her more inglorious adventures in the past, even though she had not been with child at the time.

"That's all you want to do? Don't you need to examine me? You did last time."

"You were farther along then, and I would have been checking how easy it would be for you to have babies. I know all that now."

Daphne was a bit disappointed. She realized that she had wanted Mr. Jackson to make a fuss over her new condition. She should have known that she wouldn't get that sort of sympathy from him. As far as he was concerned, she would simply have to resume her usual activities until her pregnancy was much more advanced. He didn't believe in coddling ladies when they were expecting, or even confining them when their time became close. She had better start seeing her father's tenants as she had intended. She also knew in her heart that it was the best way to avoid moping over Giles's absence.

Two days later, as Daphne was going over some accounts in her workroom, Steves announced that Mr. Snodgrass would like to see her. The lawyer entered to give the news that Mr. Wark had accepted the offer that she and Giles had made for his property and that the sale would be completed in record time.

"I think that this man, Wark, really needs the money as soon as possible so that he can safely arrange to have it available in New South Wales. I think I may have encouraged you to offer too high a price since I didn't know how pressing was his need for cash. I did think at the time that there would be a good deal of hard bargaining before we could agree on the amount, Lady Ashton," the lawyer reported. "I apologize if I let you pay too much."

"Oh, you couldn't have known either. We offered a sum that is much less than the value of the place to us, so I am satisfied. Indeed, I am thrilled with our success. When can we take possession?"

"It will take a couple of days to complete the transfer. I am sure that it will be yours by Monday – and if it isn't, I will let you know."

"Thank you, Mr. Snodgrass. One other thing before I let you go."

"Yes?"

"Ashton Place. Captain Giles has inherited it from his brother, as you may know. Can you look into the legal details? I think that I need to know all about them before I decide what to do with the place. What restrictions there may be, and so on. Captain Giles's London solicitors have all the details, I know, but I don't want to make a trip to London to see them, and it would be much more convenient if you could get all the information so that you can answer my questions when I think of them."

"Of course, my lady. I will commence the process of finding out immediately."

With the news of the new purchase, Daphne resumed her tasks with increased enthusiasm. She wanted to inspect Hillcrest Grange as soon as she could. She warned her gamekeeper and her chief forester to be ready to accompany her on Monday. She also contacted the man who had been in charge of the changes that she had had made to Dipton Hall to be ready to survey the new house that she would be renovating.

Three days after Giles had disappeared down the driveway, Daphne and her niece were breakfasting when Steves brought in the mail. Daphne checked hers and found a letter from Giles. She had reached the place where Giles mentioned that Captain Bolter would be joining him when Catherine let out a most unladylike shout of joy.

"What is it?" Daphne asked, not wishing to be distracted from reading the last few lines of Giles's note that were telling her that he wished he was able to take her with him on his new assignment.

"Captain Bolter writes that he has been given a ship all his own. It's great news."

"Yes, it is," Daphne responded in a distracted way. Catherine kept reading.

"It's a frigate. Called *Flicker*. Isn't that a wonderful name for a frigate! Only a small one, apparently, but Captain Bolter writes that it is all his."

Daphne did not bother to comment as Catherine gave the highlights of her letter.

"Oh, goodness! He says that he only got it because Captain Giles demanded that he be given it. Oh, isn't Uncle Richard marvelous, Aunt Daphne?"

"I think so," Daphne replied with a smile. Her niece's enthusiasm was infectious.

"Oh, can you believe it? He will be sailing under Uncle Richard's orders. Nothing could be better. Oh, now we are bound to be rich. Uncle Richard is always at the forefront of adventures, isn't he?"

"He has indeed been fortunate, but don't count on it, Catherine. At least, I don't think he is overly foolish, which is much more important. However, full pay is very much better than half pay, you know, and Captain Bolton has secured that status whatever his luck with prizes may be."

Daphne felt pleased with her response to Catherine's enthusiasm. Richard had mentioned Captain Bolter's appointment to her in his letter although he had given no indication of his role in his friend's receiving it. She thought she had done a good job of pretending to be startled by the news, rather than disparaging it by hinting that it was old news to her.

She looked up to see that Catherine was rereading her letter with the same delight as she had experienced on first learning its news. That did remind her of something that she now should tell her niece.

Daphne had not told Catherine about how she and Richard wanted to buy Hillcrest Grange, even though, if they did get it, they intended to offer it as a residence to Catherine and her new husband. It had been all too possible that Mr. Wark would hold out for too much money or that someone else, possibly one of the king-pins of the local smuggling trade, would offer more than the amount that she and Giles had agreed on. It would have been cruel to build the girl's hopes up only to have them dashed if the purchase had fallen through. Then in the excitement of getting the property, its relevance to Catherine had slipped her mind. She should let her niece know immediately.

"Catherine," she began. "Captain Giles mentions in his letter that they will be assigned to home waters. With any luck, they will be able to get ashore in England again for short periods and quite soon. It is possible that you and Captain Bolter will be able to get married soon."

"I hope so. Lord David has read the banns, after all, and Captain Bolter arranged for them to be read in Norfolk. We intend to get married as soon as he can get here."

"I am aware of that." Catherine had, indeed told her these plans several times, and never seemed to realize that her aunt might be fully aware of what the engaged pair hoped to do.

"When you are married, you will have to have somewhere to live – and more importantly, where the two of you will want to live," Daphne continued.

"Oh, we've talked about that. Captain Bolter hopes to find a house somewhere near here, though he hasn't been able to look for one yet. I thought that you would let me stay in Dipton Hall until he could find the right place. I suppose I should have asked you."

"Of course, you are welcome to stay here while Captain Bolter is away. And the two of you are more than welcome to remain here until you find a suitable place. You know I enjoy your company. But you will also want a home of your own as soon as possible, no matter how nice you may think your uncle and I are. You have heard us talk about Hillcrest Grange, I am sure."

"Yes, no one could live here without hearing about it."

"Well, what you don't know is that Captain Giles is going to buy it."

Catherine thought it might be judicious not to say that she had heard all about it from her maid who had heard it from Betsy. Instead, she replied, "Are you, truly? I did know that you were thinking about it, but not that you had purchased it. "

"Yes, we have. The house itself needs quite a bit of work, but after the repairs and improvements have been made, we thought it might be just the right place for you and Captain Bolter."

"Do you think that we could afford the rent?"

"Yes, I was sure you could even if Captain Bolter were only on half pay. But if you are interested, I think it would be a very good idea if you are involved in planning the changes that are needed, especially as you have much better taste than I do."

Catherine jumped up and threw her arms around her startled aunt. "Oh, Aunt Daphne, you are the best aunt ever. And Uncle Richard as well, of course."

This reaction to her words was far more than Daphne had expected. Had she ever been so spontaneously enthusiastic?

"I'll be going over there to look into some things on Monday. I hope that you will be able to come with me."

"Of course I will! You are so wonderful!"

Daphne left the table to get on with her tasks with renewed enthusiasm of her own. All she would need was

Richard's presence to make everything perfect. "Oh, that this stupid war would end soon!" she wished, even though her wishes on the matter were of no consequence.

Chapter VII

Dawn the following morning saw Daphne set off with Catherine Crocker and a group of men, some to evaluate the possibilities of the house and lands of Hillcrest Grange, others to start working on straightening out her acquisition. It had rained overnight, but the skies were clear, and it was quite warm.

When they arrived at the first set of brush that had been used to block the track that joined Dipton Hall to the road leading to Hillcrest Grange, Daphne detached a couple of men to start a fire to get rid of the barrier once and for all. The fallen branches at the other end of the track received the same treatment. Daphne had brought a man knowledgeable in what was required to turn a little dirt track into a decent road. He was left with a helper to survey the work needed to make a proper connection joining Dipton Hall to Hillcrest Grange.

As Daphne and her followers neared the residence of Hillcrest Grange, a motley collection of servants, some who by their dress were indoor workers and others who worked outdoors, met them. These people were probably hoping to be taken on by the new owner. Daphne did not have time to deal with them at that point. However, one of the people she had brought with her was her steward, Thomas Dimster. He was delegated to take the names and particulars of the servants so that she could decide on whether to keep any of them. The only exception Daphne made was for a woman who claimed to be the housekeeper. Someone who held that position should know the peculiarities of the house; maybe she could help Catherine look it over. If she proved to be satisfactory, Daphne would retain her in her position, at least until it became more evident what the altered house would require.

Daphne went inside the residence with Catherine for a quick look around. She then suggested that Catherine should examine the features of the house more carefully while Daphne saw to getting the work on the grounds started. She was bursting with curiosity as to just what the

hidden sheds might contain.

Catherine was delighted to be able to take her time evaluating the house. She was glad not to have her aunt on hand when she was only trying to sort out possible ways of improving the rooms. With Daphne away, Catherine could form her thoughts without having to explain them to someone else while they were still jelling. She had brought her sketchbook with her, and started drawing, on the left half of the paper how the entryway looked now, and on the other half, how it would look with her improvements. The right side of the pad got a lot more erasures than the left one. As she penetrated farther into the house, the housekeeper was kept busy opening and closing drapes and moving bits of furniture around.

Daphne went outside to find that the revenue officer, Mr. Baker, and his assistants had arrived. He had brought Major Strange and his company of dragoons with him, suspecting that it might be necessary to guard the treasures he would be finding. Daphne ordered the brush that was hiding the entrances to the woods to be moved into piles and set alight. She then led the way to the shack which she had examined with Giles. Once again she instructed that all the brush hiding the building be cleared away and burnt.

It was the work of a moment to break open the door of the shed. Daphne had expected to find barrels of brandy and bottles of wine. Instead, they found that the storehouse was full of bales of tobacco and chests of tea.

"Why in the world would Mr. Wark be hiding tea and tobacco?" Daphne asked Mr. Barker.

"Because they are smuggled, of course," replied the revenue officer. "Look how none of them has any revenue stamps. They have all been smuggled into the country."

"I never realized that smuggling involved such bulky items. I thought it was just wine and spirits and luxury goods like French lace that were brought in illegally."

"Oh, yes, my lady. Almost every item that is subject to duties or excise taxes attracts the smugglers. All it takes is for the taxes to be high enough to reward people for avoiding them. High duties seem always to attract the efforts of smugglers no matter what the material may be.

"I'll have to get these goods assessed, Lady Ashton," the revenue officer continued. "As I told you, we will calculate the excise taxes to be assessed on them. Then you can pay what is owed to the crown and take possession of the goods. Otherwise, we will have to take them on behalf of the crown and sell them for whatever they will fetch."

"Oh, Mr. Baker, which would be more advantageous for us? Captain Giles would know what to do, I am sure, but I don't understand any of it."

"Well, my Lady, it is straightforward. If you can sell the goods for more than the tax with a bit of profit to reward you for your trouble, you should acquire the goods. If not, then we will have to sell them for less than the tax. It doesn't matter to me. I get paid the same either way."

"What would you advise, Mr. Barker? I have no idea what they might be worth."

"Well, my lady, I can't say. It is not my decision, and I might be held responsible for steering you in the wrong direction."

"Oh, I won't tell anyone, Mr. Barker. I just don't know what to do."

"Well, I can tell you that on the coast, the smugglers are selling these sorts of goods for less than what the excises would be if they were paid, so it wouldn't be worth anyone 's while to pay the duty on them in order to then sell them to others. Farther away from the coast, in a place like this, you might well get more than you would have to pay in taxes. However, it is very expensive to bring all these goods inland, especially when one has to keep them hidden from prying eyes or to pay substantial bribes to get people to look the other way as they make their way from the coast. Of course, it is also costly to bring in legally imported goods to Dipton since transportation costs are very high when they are carried by land, and you would have to worry about the goods being stolen before you got them here. There is very little legal trade in these parts as far as we can discover, so I imagine that you could sell whatever the smugglers have stored here for a very nice profit even after you have paid our fees."

"I see, Mr. Baker. That is very helpful. I'll leave you to your work."

"Thank you, my lady. There is one other thing, my lady."

"Yes. Mr. Baker."

"Well, I heard someone mention that there were other sheds scattered throughout these woods, equally well hidden."

"Yes, I think so."

"I would suggest that I seal them with one of our special tags. That way, we will know if someone tries to break into them before I can do their inventory. It would remove suspicion and also make it easier, if any of your groundskeepers happen to catch some strangers, to establish whether they have broken into any of the sheds. If the other sheds are anything like this one, they are filled with valuable property that will belong to you if you pay the duties."

"That's a good idea. Mr. Baker. I will see to it."

"One other matter, Lady Giles. May I ask that a couple of companies of the dragoons be   allowed to venture onto your new property tonight?"

"My new property?"

"Yes, this one, Hillcrest Grange."

"I suppose so. But why do you want to?"

"You may not know it, but there is a stream that runs past the boundary of Hillcrest Grange, quite close to the road. It flows into the River Amesnott which is, of course, part of the canal system. For the first several hundred yards, or so, the stream – it's called Scalders Creek – can accommodate a canal barge. There is no towpath but one can pole a barge up the stream, or so I have been told."

"What does this have to do with me, Mr. Baker?"

"Mr. Wark built a landing stage on the creek, and that's where the contraband in which he was dealing was unloaded. At night, of course. Then he arranged for carts to carry the goods to his woods here, to keep on filling these storehouses. The landing is on what is now your property."

"How did you find out about this?"

"The information came from some of the people we caught who decided that it was worth telling us as much as they could to escape punishment for being involved in the smuggling ring."

"So what does that have to do with tonight?"

"A new shipment is expected. Coming in what is ostensibly a coal barge; at least that is what the boat pretends to be. My informants expect it to enter Scalders Creek around six o'clock – it will be full dark by then. It is said that a gang will be ready to unload it – the contraband, that is, not the coal which is used as a disguise. The coal is supposed to go on to Ameschester tomorrow."

"And you want to be on hand to apprehend the shippers?"

"Yes, my lady."

"What will you do with the coal?"

"Provided that the bargeman cooperates with us, I shall let him go on to Ameschester and unload his cargo in the usual way. With luck, we will be putting an even bigger dent in smuggling around here."

"That would be a good thing, I suppose."

"Oh, yes, my lady. But it won't be popular with your neighbors."

"What will you do with the contraband?"

"The best thing would be to let the smugglers unload it before arresting them."

"Why? That seems a bit odd to me."

"My lady, it's the standard problem that we face in apprehending a contraband shipment. If we seize the barge as soon as it docks, we will end up being in possession of the barge and its cargo. We would have to find some way to dispose of them. We are not really in that business. And there is no benefit to us since anything we got paid would have to go straight into His Majesty's coffers. If the illicit cargo is on your land when we seize it, and you want to pay the duty, it would just be more of the sort of material you now own and will be arranging to distribute. Since the carts the smugglers use are likely to be abandoned, you can claim those too. Of course, we have to collect a service fee first before the goods can be released."

"Of course," Daphne sounded a bit ironic. "All right. Your proposal won't add to my problems, so it sounds like good business. Good luck, Mr. Barker. Just remember that I haven't yet decided whether I will want to buy any contraband which is mysteriously found on my property."

Daphne was intrigued by what Mr. Barker had told her about the landing stage at the creek. She realized that she knew little about the countryside around her new property. It was odd the way in which the two parishes had little interaction, even

88

though they shared a boundary. She had never explored the area around Hillcrest Grange; indeed, the first time she had even seen the house was when she had visited it with Giles. Her ignorance must have something to do with d the track that joined Dipton Hall to Hillcrest Grange being blocked even though she now knew it to be a right-of-way. She vaguely knew that the road running past Hillcrest Grange only met the one from Dipton at Ameschester and that there was no other straight-forward connection between the two since they passed on opposite sides of a small hill. She wasn't even sure about how many other properties were in the vicinity of Hillcrest Grange. She would have to do some exploring when she had time and meet her new neighbors. Right now, while Catherine was busy planning and everyone else had been assigned their jobs, she might as well find out more about what Giles and she had bought.

There was a large meadow area on the other side of the road where the driveway to Hillcrest Grange turned off. It had probably been used for grazing horses or possibly cattle, in the days when Hillcrest Grange had been a more usual type of estate engaged in agricultural activity. What had happened to Mr. Wark's horses? He must have had some, but there was no evidence of them at present, except for a few broken pieces of harness in the stables. Certainly, no horses had been included in the sale of Hillcrest Grange. Possibly he had sold them all when first he got into trouble over his smuggling activities.

Daphne rode her mare, Moonbeam, past the entrance to the track to Dipton Hall and entered an area that was new for her. On one side of the road, the woods of Hillcrest Grange continued; the other side consisted of land that might have been marsh meadows at one time, or even arable fields, though they had been neglected for years. Further along, she could see a line of willows. That must mark the stream that Mr. Butler had mentioned.

Daphne stopped to examine the land more carefully. There were real possibilities of bringing modern techniques to enrich it and make it productive. How Giles would match her excitement! He had been a bit disappointed, she knew, that their acquisition didn't seem to present many agricultural challenges. She would have to get it surveyed. Maybe she could even persuade Catherine to make a sketch of it which she could to send to Giles.

She set Moonbeam in motion again, keenly looking about as different aspects of the land presented themselves to her. She almost missed a turnoff to a muddy track leading towards the stream. The laneway had ruts and hoofprints from having carts dragged over it. Mr. Wark's distinctive way of trying to disguise possibly intriguing aspects of his property was evident in piles of brushwood, though they had been somewhat pushed aside, perhaps to allow horses to pass single file.

Daphne turned Moonbeam into the track and soon came to the stream. At one point the bank had been improved by having small logs pounded into the stream bottom with earth being shoveled behind them to make a landing platform. Crude though it was, it would allow a barge of modest draft to be docked right against the land for unloading.

Daphne's excitement at what she was learning about the new property increased. This landing might well be exploited to provide a much better way to get the crops of Dipton Hall to market than the tedious haul along the road to Ameschester which was now the only way to get them there. It seemed that the possibilities opened up as a result of buying Hillcrest Grange were much more extensive than either she or Giles had realized when they decided to acquire the property.

Time had slipped away as Daphne had been making her discoveries and ruminating on their implications. It was time to collect Catherine and make their way back to Dipton Hall before the early winter dark closed in on them.

Catherine was reluctant to leave her sketching even though the light was failing. Once extracted from the house, she chattered on about what exciting possibilities there were for improving the house. Daphne paid only minimal attention. She was thinking about the lands of Hillcrest Grange, not the residence.

Only while Daphne was changing for dinner did the enormity of the situation occur to her. She already had more tasks than she could handle easily in looking after Dipton Hall and her father's estate. There were also all the other undertakings requiring her attention that she had enumerated before going to Hillcrest Grange. Now there were still more matters that would require her attention because of the opportunities opening up as a result of her exploration of the newly acquired property. The problems arising from the smuggling and what to do with the haul that the revenue men were uncovering were now added to the others. How in the world would she cope, especially as she was now pregnant? Well, moping about it would only make things worse. Daphne squared her shoulders as Betsy finished doing up her buttons and set off to see Berns before dinner. He was her pride and joy. He gave her more pleasure than any of her endeavors on her properties.

Chapter VIII

Daphne came down for breakfast well before dawn. She was surprised to find Catherine already at the table. As soon as a footman had poured her tea and set a plate with her usual breakfast of one poached egg, one rasher of bacon and a small portion of devilled kidneys in front of her, Catherine burst out with a request.

"Aunt Daphne, can I go to Hillcrest Grange again today, please? I want to keep on considering how it should be decorated and other improvements might be made. Even what would be the best use of some of the rooms."

"Use?"

"Yes, Mrs. Laver – that's the housekeeper's name – pointed out that the drawing room and the dining room are the same size, but the drawing room is more easily reached from the kitchen than is the dining room. And the morning room is on the north side of the house, while it would be much better on the south side. Things like that. And upstairs which room would be best as a nursery."

"It sounds as if Mrs. Laver is being very useful."

"Yes, she is. She tries to sound respectful of Mr. Wark, but it sometimes seems to be a great struggle for her," Catherine giggled thinking about it.

"I am not surprised. Servants have to be respectful of their masters, no matter how awful they may be. Positions are not easy to find, especially the more senior ones, and disrespect for the masters, no matter how justified, can ruin their hopes of further employment."

"Why is that?"

"Think about it. Suppose that you were thinking of hiring Mrs. Laver. If she said bad things about Mr. Wark, you might presume that she would gossip unfavorably about you. We all do things that can annoy servants, and they can't retaliate by telling other people whom we know about it. Even if they do tell other servants about their complaints, they run the danger that the criticisms will be passed on by those servants to their masters or mistresses and so do the same sort of damage if ever they need to find employment elsewhere."

"I'd never thought of that."

"Anyway, to get back to the subject, you can certainly go to Hillcrest Grange today. Of course, you will take Enid with you." Enid was Catherine's lady's maid. Daphne was afraid that Catherine, in her excitement, might forget that no lady, especially an unmarried one, would go anywhere without at least her maid.

"Yes, Aunt Daphne." Catherine clearly felt that there was no reason for the reminder. "There is one thing I wanted to ask you."

"Yes?"

"Can we make any alterations to the actual building?"

"What did you have in mind?"

"The windows are tiny. Hardly any light gets in, especially, of course, in winter. It is not just how gloomy the furnishings and paint and so on are that makes the house so unattractive. It's also the weak illumination."

"I suppose you are right. It certainly is a rather ugly building from the outside. Larger windows might help that too, I guess."

"They would, I believe."

"Let's talk to Mr. Harris, our builder, about it. He may have some ideas, before we go overboard with plans. He is coming here later in the morning, partly to talk about the stable block and largely about the kennels we might build. If you can wait until he is here, you can explain to him what you think might be needed, just as a rough idea, you understand. There is no point putting a lot of work into planning it if carrying out the plans will be prohibitively expensive."

Catherine seemed torn between her wish to dash off to Hillcrest Grange and her desire to see the builder who might be able to help put some of her grander ideas into action. She chose the second alternative.

She did not have to wait long. Daphne had hardly retreated to her workroom before Steves announced that Mr. Harris had arrived. He was a burly, red-nosed man who made no pretensions of gentility, but who did exude a quiet air of confidence. Daphne had first employed him to build the stable block, where she had not thought there was any need for an architect. Luckily, Mr. Harris was both an architect and a builder, having taken up the first profession when finding that he was supposed to work, as a builder, from architects' plans that were impractical. He had at first been very doubtful about taking directions from a lady, especially as his first task in working at Dipton had been to get her to think in specific terms about what she wanted. To his surprise, when he pointed this out to her, Daphne had been quite willing to sit down with him to work out what was needed and even to consult the stable-master about what would be best. Soon he had become confident about dealing with her and found their talks helpful. Indeed, he now much preferred his visits to Dipton Hall to any of his other employers who were more demanding even when they did not know what they wanted or, if they did, why some things would be much more expensive than others.

"My lady, I hope you are pleased with the stable block."

"Indeed, I am, and I will be looking forward to your adding the finishing touches when the weather is more favorable. However, I wanted to talk to you about a couple of other matters."

"Yes, my lady?"

"First, it's about the kennels. I think I may have mentioned them to you earlier. We have decided to take the hounds of the Ameschester Hunt and have chosen the general area where we want to build them. Let me tell you what we are thinking."

A protracted discussion about the needs of the kennels ensued, in which it became evident that Mr. Harris, although he was active in the Ameschester Hunt, knew little about kennels, while Daphne had only a vague idea of what they required. Mr. Harris suggested that perhaps he should first see what sort of facilities Colonel Redfern had for the dogs and talk to the man who was in charge of them, Charlie Maddox. Daphne agreed and was about to announce that she would go with him when she remembered her resolve to do less, not more. Mr. Harris, no doubt, could make the initial inquiry. She need go only if he ran into a reluctance on the part of the colonel or the master of the hounds to talk frankly about what was needed and how Dipton Hall's facility could benefit from not repeating the weaknesses of the current establishment.

"There is one other matter, Mr. Harris," Daphne announced when she had finished writing a note to Colonel Redfern asking for his cooperation.

"Yes, my lady?"

"You may have heard that Captain Giles recently purchased Hillcrest Grange."

"Yes, I have."

"Do you know the house?"

'Not really, my lady. I have only seen it at a distance from the road. It did not leave much of an impression on me."

"Captain Giles is going to rent it to my niece and her husband. It needs considerable internal work, and it might make sense to make some other changes to the structure at the same time. Bigger windows and things like that. Anyway, my niece – Captain Giles's half-niece, Miss Crocker – has some ideas about it. I'll call her in, and we can discuss it."

"Oh, no," thought Mr. Harris, "not another female with their typical lack of sense about building." However, what he said was, "I am sure that will be very helpful, my lady."

Catherine was summoned, and she came with her sketch pad and with bubbling enthusiasm about how the house could be improved in a way that somehow made Mr. Harris even more apprehensive about having an easy collaboration with her. To his surprise, he found that she was expecting fewer changes than those which might be practical. She also had the skill to sketch out what she had in mind which made everything much clearer, even though they could hardly be called working drawings. Before long, the builder became enthusiastic about the possibility of substantially improving the house for a reasonable expenditure. He noticed that Daphne was listening with benign approval to Catherine's suggestions. He had been afraid that Daphne would want the minimal number of changes possible. Lady Ashton was an excellent patron for whom to work, but she was always conscious of the costs of what she was ordering. He had been worried about getting into the middle of uncomfortable disputes between the two women, with one wanting the elaborately expensive and the other not wishing to spend money.

Their discussion ended with agreement that Mr. Harris should accompany Catherine to Hillcrest Grange (with Enid, Daphne specified firmly) and that he could then make his way to where the kennels would be located so that he would have a feeling for the lay of the land. Daphne made it clear that she did not want any more reshaping of the site than was necessary

Daphne was about to call Betsy to help her change so that she could visit some of her father's tenants when Steves called her attention to the even more pressing duties that had arisen from her role as the wife of a prominent landowner. The butler entered the workroom bearing a calling card on his silver platter. Lady Blenkensop had come visiting. It was usual for ladies to engage in morning visits with each other, partly to exchange news and gossip, partly to relieve in small measure the encompassing boredom of their lives. Daphne had been spared this while she had been nursing Captain Giles because she had let it be known that she was far too busy during her husband's rare presence at Dipton Hall to encourage casual visits. Earlier she had established that she was at home only on Tuesday and Friday mornings. This accommodation of local mores had done something to reduce her reputation for eccentricity among the gentry of the area. Today was Tuesday. Giles was away. There could be no valid reason to not be at home to Lady Blenkensop.

Her visitor was a strikingly tall woman whose generous figure was only somewhat disguised by the flowing type of gown that was now in style. She was a lady of firm opinions, though they always seemed to agree with those of her husband, Sir Havard Blenkensop. There was, indeed, when other ladies got together in her absence, some speculation about whose opinions they were. Her husband was a rather stupid and lazy man who seemed to be able to spend hours in his library without ever turning the pages of the book he was reading. Did Lady Blenkensop agree with him, or he with her?

The necessary beginnings of conversation concerning health and children had only just finished when Steves entered to say that another lady, Mrs. Griffiths, had arrived. She was the wife of an army major who had leased a nearby property.

When the further round of inquiries about health had been completed, Mrs. Griffiths started the more serious conversation by remarking, "Can you believe it, my dressmaker informed me yesterday that her supplies of French lace are much diminished, and she had nothing suitable for my gown for Baron de Roy's Ball. I cannot understand it, especially as she said that she had little hope of getting more soon."

"How awful!" said Lady Blenkinsop. "I wonder if the problem affects any others of us who are preparing for the ball. I know Baron de Roy's Ball is not nearly as important an event as yours, Lady Aston, but still one would not like to appear in ancient rags."

"That is hardly likely to happen in your case, Lady Blenkinsop. I would have thought that your existing wardrobe would furnish materials enough for your dressmaker to make a splendid new gown," retorted Mrs. Griffiths. "There is an even stranger shortage than my dressmaker's problem with her lace, Lady Ashton. Major Griffiths has complained that Andrews, our butler, has informed him that he has not been able to restock the cellar with his favorite claret, or really any acceptable claret at all. You can imagine how annoyed this made Mr. Griffiths. Why, he even accused Andrews of drinking too much of the wine. He does too, Andrews that is, though I am afraid that Mr. Griffiths does often end the evening in his cups."

"What in the world can be the problem that there appear to be shortages of such important supplies?" Daphne wondered.

"Sir Havard says it has something to do with the arrest of Mr. Wark and Sir Thomas Dimster and more recently Mr. Twister, but even he doesn't understand what the problem could be."

"It's a sudden dearth of smuggled goods," Mrs. Griffiths stated decisively. "That's what Andrews says."

"Smuggled goods, Mrs. Griffiths?" responded Lady Blenkinsop. "Surely not! Maybe in your case, but not in mine!"

"Fiddlesticks! Everyone uses smuggled goods. They just don't ask where they come from. Ask your dressmaker, dear Lady Blenkinsop, and your butler. Why I wouldn't be surprised if even Lady Ashton has smuggled drink in the cellar or untaxed salt and tea in the larder, or smuggled finery in the wardrobe. We all know that dear Captain Giles has been so fortunate that you can afford anything, Lady Ashton, but you simply cannot buy honestly-obtained materials around here. Have you encountered any shortages, Lady Ashton?"

"I haven't. But with Captain Giles away and not doing much entertaining recently, we might not have had a chance to run out of important supplies or to order new gowns. I'll have to ask Steves. I don't know for a fact that we have any smuggled goods."

"You are just like everyone else, Lady Ashton. What we don't know, we can't feel guilty about. So we don't ask, just pay the bills."

"You and Sir Havard are going to the ball, are you, Lady Blenkinsop?" Daphne changed the topic. She knew all too well that she was, or would be when Mr. Baker was finished, sitting on a large hoard of all sorts of smuggled goods which she didn't know how to sell, even though they would then be legal. It had not occurred to her that storing this material would have ramifications for her neighbors. And for everyone else as well.

She could hardly wait for the proper time for the ladies' visit to end, as dictated by unwritten rules so that she could explore further how she and others were affected by smuggling and especially by the suspension of the illegal activities. She was particularly concerned since she had played a significant role in hindering the easy trade in illegal goods. It had certainly not been her intention or Captain Giles's to inconvenience the local gentry.

When the allotted time was up, and Daphne could bid goodbye to her guests with a good conscience, she sent for Steves. He turned out to know quite a bit about how smuggled goods got distributed. It seemed that, to a large extent, the smugglers had taken over most of the trade in all the materials that were taxed heavily. Most of the wines and brandies available were illegal, though the smugglers did supply a small quantity of legal liquors for the retailers to show to the revenue people when they came around, which was not often. He laughed and said that the tea chests that were bought for Dipton Hall, "at a very good price, my lady," were all stamped by the revenue service. The containers were picked up by the supplier when they were empty "as a service, you understand," and he noted that the same chests came back often in the next order or two. He readily admitted that the cellar at Dipton Hall was full of smuggled wines and brandy.

"It is quite different here than in London, my lady," Steves explained. "In London, I could get legal goods or smuggled ones. The smuggled ones were cheaper by a bit, but the delivery was more haphazard as the smugglers had to avoid the authorities in order to deliver the material. They usually did have better merchandise, but not always, and there was always a risk of serious inconvenience and fines for dealing in the stuff. Of course, the Earl of Camshire always ordered me to find the cheaper goods, and not to mind the law. I don't think Captain Giles would take the same tack if he were aware of how much was smuggled here, but he wouldn't have any choice, other than to do without. Quite a few people around here probably would prefer legal goods, if the prices were close, but, right now, no one is bringing the legal items, or so I am told. It would be just too expensive."

"How do you know all this, Steves?" Daphne asked.

"Some from my own experience in getting all the things we need, my lady, and more from other butlers. We butlers get together regularly on our days off or at other times when we are not on duty. The others know more than I do because they have been here longer."

"I wonder why the revenue officers don't stop the trade."

"Why, my lady? They are as much part of the trade as anyone. Mr. Baxter, who was here for dinner the other evening, is hand-in-glove with the smugglers. They let him intercept specific shipments, often of the poorer quality material. He looks good, and the penalties for the few people they were able to catch were always quite mild. Sir Thomas Dimster made sure of that, at least he did before you had him thrown off the magistrates' bench. A few hours in the pillory for ordinary people, no more, and the smugglers made sure that no one got hurt while serving their sentence. All a bit of a game, you see. And of course, Mr. Baxter and the other revenue officers were paid by the smugglers, or so I am told."

"I understand that the supplies have dried up recently."

"So it would seem, my lady. All I know is that the man who used to come around to take our orders – and tell us about anything particularly good that was available or things that just now were not available – has not been here for a while. Lying low, I suppose, until things blow over and someone else takes over. Arresting Sir Thomas, Mr. Wark and Mr. Twister seems to have put a crimp into the operation. If I may say so, my lady, you and Captain Giles have put quite an obstacle in front of the smugglers conducting their business."

"Were those men behind the smuggling?"

"So I understand, though others must have helped with the finance and got part of the profits. I don't know who they were – their butlers are too loyal, I believe, to tell if they happen to be local gentlemen. There was a fourth man in charge, I understand, who was responsible for arranging for the distribution of the material, but I don't know who he was. I never thought to ask when placing my orders."

"He was in control of delivery."

"Yes, my lady, or so I understand. Indeed I think that he was in overall charge of the operation. Sir Thomas was the man keeping the law at bay, and Mr. Wark was responsible for storing the material either on his property or elsewhere. Mr. Twister was the gentleman who arranged to get the material to the Ameschester area and turn it over to Mr. Wark. As I say, I don't know who this fourth person is. I will ask if I see the man who took our orders, but that fellow is not from around here. The person who might know is Mrs. Carstairs, down at the Dipton Arms. She must have been placing the orders for the inn, what with Carstairs being away most of the time with Captain Giles."

"Thank you, Steves, you have been very helpful," Daphne concluded the interview. It certainly left her with more questions than answers. Who was the mystery figure behind the smugglers? Shouldn't he be put out of business and punished like the others? If he weren't, wasn't he likely to find others to fill the roles held by the people whose crimes had been revealed? How was she to get rid of the smuggled goods that were now in her possession? Especially if she couldn't trust Mr. Baxter?

Daphne knew that Giles did not approve of smuggling; indeed, he would probably be distressed to learn where their wines and other materials came from, even if there were no other practical way to get them. One way to avoid using smuggled goods would be to keep such items from coming to Dipton so easily. Then, possibly, an honest route could start. The legal goods would cost more, of course, but the money that was paid in excise taxes helped to maintain the navy to which Giles was so committed. If there were more money for the navy, the war might not last so long, and then the chances of his being home might be better.

Daphne's first step in a so-far nebulous plan would be to find out about the mysterious fourth leader of the smugglers who had been supplying the wants of Ameschester and vicinity. Maybe, as Steves had hinted, Elsie might have an idea of who the man was. She owed her a visit anyway. Elsie, as a former servant and now an inn-keeper, couldn't visit her, at least not if propriety was to be observed, but Daphne had the excuse of taking tea in the parlor of the Dipton Inn to visit Elsie. It was usual for ladies who were not traveling to visit an inn, but it was not really improper. Daphne knew that she already had so many tongues wagging about her unconventional behavior that one more dubious action would change nothing. Not that she cared about what others thought, but since the birth of Bernard she had realized that it might be better for him not to have a mother who was the subject of so much disapproving gossip. Uncharacteristically, Daphne realized that she should wait a little while before visiting Elsie, not because of propriety, but also because of the many other pressing matters on her plate.

Chapter IX

Glaucus and her two accompanying ships had quickly examined the coast to the east of Calais. As Giles was well aware from earlier service, Admiral Gardner kept scouring that part of the coast to hinder French shipping. He knew that there was no harbor where the French could hide line-of-battle ships, or even frigates, without their presence being quickly known. The ports around Boulogne were so jammed with landing craft that he was sure that they attracted the attention of many British spies. Any large ships hidden in those ports would soon be reported to the Admiralty. If the French had as yet unknown vessels tucked away somewhere along the coast, he expected them to be found farther west in Normandy, Brittany and even farther away in the many safe havens of the Bay of Biscay. He wasn't really surprised that Dieppe had proved clear of French warships: it was still too close to Boulogne. Now, as he sailed west, the chances seemed to be better.

Giles's ships were to the west of Dieppe, about four miles offshore, close-hauled* on the starboard tack. Ahead and to larboard, white chalk cliffs rose straight from the sea. However, Giles knew, at their base shingle beaches extended for some distance from the cliffs. Five or six miles ahead, a battery had been established on the top of the cliff to add protection for coastal traffic even though the cliffs gave protection against any invasion force. The battery had been placed well back from the edge of the cliffs, possibly because of instability of the ground closer to the brink.

"Deck there, sail ahead, twelve miles," hailed the lookout at the head of the fore topmast. Giles grabbed a telescope and started up the starboard ratlines. Usually, he would have sent a midshipman to supplement the lookout, but he was aware that he was in need of exercise. He reached the foremast top* and decided that, despite the extra effort required, he would not take the easy way through the lubber's* hole. Instead, he followed the path up the shrouds* that skilled topmen always used, on the outside of the top with nothing to catch him if he slipped. He arrived badly winded at the top of the fore topgallant mast and took a moment before leveling his telescope. He was panting in great gulps of air. He would have to climb the masts more often. He expected his crew to be fit. He should be so himself. He had not driven himself hard enough after his convalescence. Now he was paying the price.

Having caught his breath, Giles turned his telescope on the distant sails. Having had years of practice, he automatically adjusted for the fact that the image was upside down and reversed. What he saw was four sets of sails, not two as initially sighted by the lookout. The first two appeared to be brigs; the latter two were only luggers. Even as he watched, he could see the brigs altering their courses to starboard, probably seeking the protection of the battery on the top of the cliff. They must be French.

Giles studied the situation for a few minutes. He knew that the chart had shown shallow water a bit off the beach below the cliff, but with deeper water nearer the shore. He couldn't help wondering if the chart was accurate, or if a mistake had been made at some time as the original had been copied and recopied by various masters. It could be important. The battery was so high and back from the cliff's edge that the guns could not be depressed enough to shoot at targets close to the shore, which was where the approaching ships appeared to be headed. If there were a shoal, they would be trapped. The basis of a plan formed in his mind.

Giles decided not to try to keep up his bravado by sliding down the backstay as he would have as a midshipman.

The result would probably be bleeding hands that hurt abominably, not something which would impress his crew. When he reached the deck by the less spectacular method of climbing down, he ordered the Master to heave* to and the midshipman of the watch signal the other captains to come aboard. He noted with distress that his calves and thighs were burning from the unusual exercise. His convalescence had been too easy-going to prepare him adequately for returning to duty.

When they arrived on board, Captain Bolton was treated to the full honors due to a post-captain while Commander Archer had to be content with being welcomed by Giles alone as he came through the entry port. The three retired to Giles's cabin where they were joined by Mr. Brooks, the Master, who was clutching his chart. Giles quickly explained what he had in mind. *Glaucus* would double back to where he could get close to shore before turning to capture the enemy vessels who were seeking the protection of the fort. Captain Bolton would continue on their previous course until it was safe to get close to the shore and then come back in between the coast and the shoal. The enemy vessels would be trapped and easy to capture. When Commander Archer wondered why *Glaucus* and *Flicker* wouldn't be blown out of the water by the guns of the fort, Giles explained that the fort's guns couldn't be depressed enough to bear on the two British frigates.

"The only way for the fort to hurt us would be for them to so diminish the charge that the balls would travel no distance at all before falling on top of us. I doubt that they have been making the appropriate charges or even tried to determine how much power would be needed to accompany their objective," Giles explained. "We'll be quite safe."

"What is my role?" demanded Commander Archer. "You can't just leave me out."

"*Firefly* will remain near the point where *Glaucus* and *Flicker* part ways, well out of range of that fort."

"So I *am* being left out, while you get all the prize money."

"No," Giles replied testily. "I want you here because the two luggers might be able to escape across the shallows and I want to capture them as well as the brigs. Just remember that you draw more than either of us, so be careful not to pursue the luggers too close to shore."

"But you will get all the prize money."

Before Giles could reply, Captain Bolton muttered, loudly enough that the others could hear him, "Don't be more of a fool than God made you, Archer. You will still be getting a largely undeserved one eighth of all the prize or head money that we earn."

The meeting broke up following that remark. *Flicker* resumed the course that the group had been sailing before the meeting. *Glaucus* turned back on a broad reach. *Firefly*'s rig did not allow her to back one of her sails to maintain her position, but she slowly sailed across the wind with only one sail set and that one not drawing properly.

The four French ships kept on their course. The trap was sprung. The enemy would not be able to escape when they realized that the protection of the shore battery was illusory

Glaucus and *Flicker* arrived at almost the same time to the points where they should turn according to the charts. Giles noted that the French brigs were anchoring in front of the fort. The cliffs make the wind fluky so *Glaucus*, now having to sail close hauled, was considerably slower than *Flicker* as they closed* on the enemy ships. *Flicker* did nothing to slow up her progress; she would reach the French first. The cliff-top battery remained silent. It was clear that the French could not swivel their cannon enough to have them bear on either of the frigates nor could they depress them sufficiently to guard the brigs.

Giles was nervous. The French ships seemed to have taken a long time to furl their sails. Even as he realized that something might be wrong, the French brigs undid their anchor lines and threw them overboard. The lines were buoyed for later pickup, and the two vessels were under sail again. They made for *Flicker*. The naval brig already had her gun ports open and her cannon run out. The merchant brig started to open disguised gun ports on the side that Giles could see, behind which lurked guns, not very large ones, but nevertheless they posed a menace to a small frigate which the enemy took by surprise. Worse still, men were pouring onto her main deck from below. This brig must be a privateer with an extra large crew available to man any captured vessels. The extra sailors were aboard so that they could take prizes into port while allowing the brig to continue hunting for more ships. In this case, with the extra men still aboard, they posed a major problem for Flicker. If the two French ships could come alongside *Flicker*, the large crew might well be able to capture her before Giles could enter the battle. They might then even use *Flicker* against *Glaucus*.

Glaucus was still a long way from the other ships. At that distance, Giles could not count on his broadside to be effective. Furthermore, turning his ship to bring his broadside to bear on the enemy would involve a significant delay before he could come up with the other ships. In addition, *Flicker* was so close to the two brigs that an errant shot might damage the British frigate rather than one of the enemy ships.

Giles did have one surprise for the French. *Glaucus*'s most powerful guns were the two long twenty-four pounders he used as bow chasers. In moments, the brigs would be in range. The French would have no reason to expect to be attacked by such powerful guns for no other British ship had adopted the change to using large cannon as bow chasers in the way that characterized Giles's frigates. The surprise factor might help his cause quite apart from any physical damage that his guns might do.

He shouted out orders to Mr. Marceau, the lieutenant in charge of the bow chasers, to be ready to fire them as soon as they bore on the enemy. He ordered the helmsman to pinch up into the wind. The two cannon roared out. *Glaucus* resumed her course with very little time lost in her race to get to the other ships. At such long range, Giles had no reason to expect the cannonballs to have a decisive effect, and this was the case of the starboard ball. It only caught the corner of the taffrail* of the privateer and did little damage though some murderous splinters might have injured some of the crew.

The larboard shot was a different story altogether. It passed over the taffrail and struck the wheel, killing the helmsman and scattering splinters everywhere. The cannonball continued on to bounce off the mizzen mast before being stopped by hitting one of the broadside guns. The slaughter caused by the splinters from the mast cutting a swath through the massed attackers waiting for a chance to board *Flicker* must be appalling. The loss of the wheel made the brig turn, and the extra strain thus produced caused the injured mast to split and start to fall to larboard. The ship, which had been about to come alongside *Flicker*, veered to larboard so that it became an easy target for that frigate's broadside. The devastation among the packed, would-be boarders on the privateer's deck must have been horrendous.

Captain Bolton resisted the temptation to board the privateer. The French brig-of-war was converging on *Flicker*, and he needed to deal with her first. She was coming up on his starboard side, probably intending to board immediately since in a broadside-to-broadside battle *Flicker* had the more substantial weight of metal. It did not surprise Giles that Captain Bolton did not let this second threat have her way.

"Starboard your helm," Bolton must have instructed the helmsmen. His orders, "Fire as you bear. Then load with grapeshot*," could be heard on *Glaucus*.

The broadside roared out, surprising the French brig and striking her before she could respond. Her broadside, when it came, was ragged for *Flicker*'s shot must have put some of his rival's guns out of action.

Bolton must have ordered his helmsman to larboard his helm since Giles could see the wheel spin so that *Flicker*'s guns would continue to bear. The second broadside roared out, sweeping the brig's deck and thereby causing any hope she might have had of boarding *Flicker* successfully to die. *Flicker* continued her turn and was now positioning herself off the stern of the brig. Bolton's next broadside would destroy his target.

"She's struck,*" bellowed one of *Flicker*'s midshipmen. Giles could also hear Captain Bolton's response, "Cease fire!" Immediately following the order, the French ship's mizzenmast started to lean over, and, with increasing speed, it went by the board.

Glaucus was bearing down on the privateer. After the mauling she had been given by *Flicker*, she had no hope of resisting the larger frigate. Before Giles could order his broadside to fire, the target hauled down her colors.

Giles looked back to where the two luggers had been moored. They had made no move to try to assist in the battle, but now they were hauling up their anchors, apparently hoping to slip away while the larger ships were clearing up after the fight. A shot from one of Glaucus's stern chasers put that idea out of their minds. Giles ordered his first lieutenant to board the privateer in order to receive her surrender. Mr. Hendircks was to take enough marines with him to control her large crew. He instructed Midshipman Stewart to take possession of the two luggers.

A cannon boomed out from the top of the cliff. Startled, Giles looked to sea wondering what the gunners could be aiming at. He glanced to seaward and was horrified to see *Firefly* aground only a half-dozen cables away. His orders for *Firefly* to stay in deep water had been explicit, and they had not been obeyed.

"What the bloody Hell is that damned *Firefly* doing on the shoal," Giles bellowed, just to let off steam, not expecting an answer.

"Sir, she set sail to come towards us when the men appeared on the deck of the second French brig, and it looked like she might take *Flicker*. I called the deck, but no one could hear me. I didn't think it was important enough for me to leave my post," the masthead lookout called down.

"I'll have that nincompoop flogged for disobeying orders," Giles muttered to himself.

Having vented his anger, Giles started to think about what to do. The tide was still falling, and even though *Firefly* must have found an unmarked passage to get so close to shore, there was not much hope of getting her off the sandbank quickly. Another cannon fired above them, and Giles watched as the ball missed *Firefly* and hit the sea several hundred feet beyond her. Looking back at the cliff-top, He could see a cloud of smoke that told him which gun had fired. Through his telescope, he could see when it was next run out that it was at minimum elevation. The French were unable to hit the schooner without changing what they were doing. That handicap wouldn't last long. Only a small reduction in the charge, or doubleshotting the guns would make it possible to hit their target, and the gunners had lots of time to find the range before the ship could be refloated. It was quite a different problem from the earlier one of trying to drop a cannonball on a moving target.

He had little choice as to what to do. He turned to the signal midshipman. "Order *Firefly* to abandon ship and to join us," he commanded in a normal voice before turning to examine the cliff more closely.

A gully cut through the face of the cliff to the right of where the battery was located. Giles's telescope revealed a steep path winding up towards the top. It was only a presumption that the track would lead somewhere near the battery at the top, but Giles was quite ready to take the chance that it did.

"Mr. Macauley," he called for *Glaucus's* lieutenant of marines.

"Sir?" the response came immediately since the officer had been standing right behind him.

"Take a look at that ravine in the cliff side." Giles handed over his telescope.

"Aye, aye, sir...I've got it."

"Do you see the path?"

"Yes, sir."

"Do you think that your marines could get up that path and take the battery?"

"We could certainly try, sir. Success would depend on what we find. But it seems that we could easily retreat if we meet too much of a force when we get up there."

Macauley struggled to contain the smile that threatened to break out on his face. He knew that the captain had already reached all these conclusions. This type of consultation was just Giles's way. Involve those who were to undertake a mission in its planning rather than just giving orders without accepting any comment. After he recognized what it was, he had found that the technique worked well with his marines.

"Then take your men and some of the seamen to help you and get it done. Take Mr. Marceau and young Mr. Fisher with you."

"Aye, aye, sir."

Lieutenant Macauley could hardly restrain his delight at being given an important assignment. He strode away issuing a string of orders to look after all the details needed for his foray ashore to succeed. It seemed no time at all before he was reporting that his mixed force of marines and sailors was ready to leave. As the lieutenant had expected, Giles sent him on his way with a wave of his hand and no further comment.

Giles was now concentrating on *Firefly*. Archer had still not abandoned ship. Through his glass, he could see that, instead, the commander was loading – indeed overloading --all the ship's boats with what looked like cabin supplies and special furniture. What had got into the man? To emphasize the stupidity of what was happening, the next cannonball clipped the top of the sloop's mainmast. Whether the French were adjusting the charge deliberately or it was a random variation was not yet clear, but they could destroy the boats lying alongside their target at any moment.

"Resend the signal to *Firefly*, Mr. Dunsmuir, if you please." Giles realized that he couldn't care less if Archer should be killed, but a lot of good men were being put at risk by the commander's foolish behavior.

Giles refocussed his attention on the land party. They were already all ashore, and the redcoats were scrambling up the steep path. Soon they disappeared around a bend. They must be nearing the top. Giles wondered if the track curved back towards the battery or if it continued inland. The chart was no help. It didn't even have a sketch of the cliffs.

The crack of a single pistol shot came from the battery. It was followed by a small fusillade of muskets, only four or five. Then silence. What had happened? Surely, there should have been more noise, even if *Glaucus*'s party had been ambushed or encountered an impassable barrier at the top of the path. If Lieutenant Macauley had been successful, there should have been far more noise.

Another ball whistled overhead. Giles turned to see where it would land. The French must have found the range, using a double-shotted gun for there were two splashes close to the larboard side of the sloop. Those shots did have one good effect. *Firefly*'s boats pulled away smartly from the ship and headed towards the shore. Even then, Commander Archer did not seem to be able to get it right. Instead of veering off from the line linking the ship to the battery, where the next balls were likely to fall, he went straight along the most dangerous route.

The next pair of cannonballs struck their target. One hit *Firefly*'s mainmast while the other one struck one of her guns, causing it to burst through the side. There appeared to be some other damage whose exact nature could not be determined from a distance. Still, the sloop looked as if the damage could be repaired, at least well enough to enable her to limp back to harbor. It was undoubtedly fortunate that he had insisted that Commander Archer abandon ship. If the crew had remained on *Firefly*, the butcher's bill would have been substantial, and all to no purpose.

Giles once more looked at the battery to see how many cannon would now shoot at *Firefly*. To his surprise, all he could see was one empty embrasure where the gun that had been firing had rolled back from the parapet after its last discharge. He could make out no activity there either. Then he spotted a red coat in the embrasure. Through his glass, he could make out Lieutenant Macauley waving his hat. The battery must have fallen, and only just in time. Another five minutes and *Firefly* would have been reduced to matchwood. Giles heaved a sigh of relief. *Firefly*'s vulnerable position had not been anticipated when he first decided to capture the French brigs.

Chapter X

Giles was tempted to throw Commander Archer into irons to await a court-martial for disobeying his clear order to remain away from the shore. But such an action would do little good. If he did so, *Glaucus* was likely to be tied up for a long time waiting for the trial to go ahead. With Archer's influence, he might still escape from a court-martial with only a mild reprimand. The sloop needed work to be serviceable again. Archer and his lieutenant were the only officers he could spare to oversee the repairs to *Firefly* since the French brigs also had to be repaired, manned and provided with officers to see them to Portsmouth, the nearest major English naval base.

Commander Archer's launch had almost been swamped by a cannonball that had plunged into the sea within yards of the boat before she could leave the sloop. It was a soaked and bedraggled group that appeared on *Glaucus*'s quarterdeck. Given his opinion of Commander Archer, Giles took quiet glee in ordering them to return at once to start making repairs to their ship so that she would be ready to sail as soon as possible. Only as he saw them returning to their boats did he feel a pang of guilt. He really should not have taken his disdain for Archer out on the rest of *Firefly*'s crew.

Giles's next chore was to deal with the two luggers. Midshipman Stewart had them rafted up to *Glaucus*'s side and was waiting patiently for his captain's attention.

"What did you find out, Mr. Stewart?" he asked.

"They are both smugglers, sir. One English and one French."

"How do you know that they are smugglers?"

"In both cases, sir, their cargoes are drink, wine in one case and brandy in the other. The liquids are in tubs, not barrels."

"Tubs?"

"Yes, sir. They are tiny casks, long and narrow, that can easily be carried on a man's back. Legal drink is carried in much larger barrels, not very suitable for landing on a beach or some such clandestine place."

"How do you know so much about smuggling, Mr. Stewart? I would have thought that you were sufficiently isolated at Butler's Hard not to have much of it going on."

"There wasn't, sir, and all the way down the river the banks are not suitable for landing cargo, but once around the corner at the mouth of the river, the shore soon turns into a beach which is ideal for landing cargo surreptitiously. When I was a boy, lots of people used to go down from Butler's Hard when a cargo was expected, and they would talk about it later."

"You'll have to tell me more about the smuggling some other time, Mr. Stewart. Now we have to deal with these luggers."

"Yes, sir."

"Did you find any documents or logs?"

"No, sir, nothing.

"The French lugger is a prize, and her crew are prisoners, which is a nuisance since we already have many prisoners. Giles stated. "We'll keep the ship, of course, but you can take the crew ashore when Mr. Macauley is finished there. The lugger can join the other prizes when they go to England. I will have to wait to see what *Flicker* needs, and the other prizes, before I decide who to send in them. I guess the French lugger is worth something. Otherwise, I'd scuttle her, though the cargo must also be worth a good lot of money."

"Aye, aye, sir."

"The English ship is more of a problem. We know what she is, but I am not sure that the evidence of smuggling would stand up in court. Anyway, I don't want to waste time taking them in and getting them tried. I will see the captain in my cabin in a few minutes. Let him stew a bit. He may not know how limited are my powers, even though we have been given a place in the revenue enforcers."

"Aye, aye, sir."

Giles's next task was to see what the state of affairs was with Captain Bolton and the two brigs. Instead of ordering the junior captain to join him on *Glaucus*, he had the jolly boat, the only one of *Glaucus*'s boats not engaged in other activity, row him to *Flicker*. Bolton greeted him cheerfully even though his ship had lost several crew members due to the French *brig's* broadside. He did have two problems. The one broadside the brig had got off had done a lot of damage. One of the cannonballs had clipped the foremast about eight feet above the deck. It had gouged out a significant part of it, greatly weakening it. The hit had scattered splinters all over the place. They had accounted for most of the injuries to members of the crew. Even though *Flicker*'s carpenter was in the process of fishing the mast by attaching stout timbers about it, it might not stand up in a blow or if pressure was put on it by sudden turns of the frigate.

Flicker's second bit of damage was probably the more serious one. Somehow a vagrant shot had holed the frigate below the waterline. That in itself was not serious. Carpenters in the navy were highly skilled at plugging holes in such a way that a vessel could continue for a very long time before a more permanent repair could be effected. The problem was that the cannonball hole had revealed that one of the affected planks was rotten. It should be dealt with as soon as possible so that the rot would not spread farther. One had to worry particularly about rot getting into the ribs of the ship, compromising her seaworthiness much more seriously.

Properly repairing this damage was a dockyard job. Heaven only knew when the Portsmouth dockyard would get to it. Giles was not at all sure that his influence would do much to shorten the wait and Captain Bolton had no leverage at all that would help to get the small job done quickly. Should he risk Bolton's ship by keeping it with *Glaucus*, or should he send *Flicker* to England immediately with the strong possibility that he would not see the small frigate again on this cruise?

He was turning this dilemma over in his mind when a solution came to him. He was on excellent terms with Mr. Joshua Stewart of the shipyard at Butler's Hard. Midshipman Stewart was his son; he had built *Glaucus* as well as Giles's previous ship, *Patroclus*; and Giles's visit to his house with Daphne had cemented a strong friendship. Giles was sure that Mr. Stewart could fit repairs to *Flicker* into his dockyard's schedule much more quickly than would the royal dockyard. Giles would send Midshipman Stewart to England in the French lugger together with the damaged frigate, and his presence would make his father even more willing to help.

An additional benefit to the plan was that Captain Bolton would have an opportunity to marry Giles's niece, Catherine Crocker. If his friend had to spend all his time hectoring the Portsmouth dockyard to fit his frigate into their schedule, he would have to stay in Portsmouth hoping to sneak his job into a pause in the 'more important' tasks that they were performing for those with influence. If *Flicker* went to Butler's Hard for the repairs, Bolton could get married and find a few days for a marriage trip. Giles would not have to wait very long to have a frigate with him again whose captain he could trust implicitly. He could see no downside to his idea.

Captain Bolton was reluctant to return to England to repair his ship until Giles mentioned the benefit of Bolton's being able to marry Giles's niece while he was there. Bolton's only objection was a regret that Giles would not be able to attend the wedding. Giles countered that hesitation by pointing out that it might be a very, very long time before they both were in England at the same time so Giles could be at Bolton's wedding. He knew that his niece wanted to marry Captain Bolton as soon as possible.

Both French brigs needed some repair before they could proceed. The one whose wheel had been destroyed would take a bit longer to fix than the other one. However, both ships, as well as *Flicker,* would be ready to sail in a few hours. Giles wasn't sure that *Firefly* would be afloat and repaired by then. He would send more men to help Commander Archer. He wasn't even sure if Archer would be able to get his ship to Portsmouth safely. Ship handling did not seem to be among the Commander's virtues. He would write to Lord Gordonston about Archer's deficiencies.

"There is one thing, Richard," Bolton said.

"Yes?"

"I only have a very inexperienced – and not very able -- third lieutenant. If my first and second lieutenants are commanding the brigs, I am not sure how well we could handle

Flicker if we got into a fight or even a serious blow. I know we don't have to sail very far to get to Portsmouth, but you know the Channel – it's completely unpredictable."

"What are you suggesting?"

"I know – everyone knows – that Mr. Stewart will make a first-rate lieutenant when he is old enough to pass the exam and has enough time at sea. I think it would be better if you let him captain one of the brigs, instead of my second lieutenant."

"All right. It will be good for the youngster. But won't it harm your second's prospects?"

" No, it won't. He is a long way from ever being ready for his own command, and this won't set him back at all."

Giles returned to *Glaucus* to find that Lieutenant Macauley had not yet returned. What could be keeping him? Lingering on shore ran the danger of the French having some armed force near enough to try to interrupt his retreat from the fort. However, Macauley was an experienced officer. He would not linger on shore without a good reason. In the meantime, Giles would deal with the English smuggler.

He called for Mr. Stewart. He began by explaining to the midshipman that he would be commanding one of the brigs when it sailed to Portsmouth with *Flicker*. Then he told him how he hoped that the older Mr. Stewart would fix the frigate as quickly as possible. It would give his junior officer a chance to see his family.

"I am honored that you chose me for the task, sir," the lad responded to the news. "But you don't need me to persuade my father to work on *Flicker*. Just knowing that Captain Bolton is sailing with you would be enough to make him give the repairs to *Flicker* priority. Even without that, he would do the repairs much more quickly than any navy dockyard, and at half the price. However, I shall be pleased to see my family. I should be able to take the packet that will be bringing you letters and news so that I can return before *Flicker* is ready. No matter how quickly my father can get to work on her, cutting out rot can take some time and I am sure you can use me here."

"Thank you, Mr. Stewart, I certainly can," Giles responded. "Now fetch the captain of the English lugger."

The man whom the midshipman introduced to Giles was a sturdy-looking fellow, with a brick-red, weather-beaten face, partly covered by a bushy white beard. He must have been over forty. His name was Fred Creasey.

"Thank you, Captain, for rescuing my crew and me. The Frenchies had us by the short hairs, you know. I thank you for intervening. Having said that, I'll be on my way."

"No, you won't, Captain Creasey. No bill of lading. No log, only a note saying how many casks you took on board. Tubs, in fact, not barrels. You are nothing but a smuggler, and I will turn you over to the authorities. Your lugger will be sailed to Portsmouth, and you will be held a prisoner on *Flicker* until Captain Bolton can turn you over to the proper authorities. I imagine they will hang you."

"That isn't fair, your honor. I'm just a poor sailor trying to make an honest shilling supplying England's urgent needs. Portuguese wine, sir, Portuguese wine. Got blown off course and taken by those damn Frogs."

"Nonsense. Even if I believed your tale, I am quite sure that the French wouldn't have left you sailing your ship unsupervised if you were their prize. And honest traders don't use tubs. You are nothing but a smuggler. You are trading with the enemy, and you are trying to defraud His Majesty of the funds needed to defend our country. We'll leave it to the magistrates in your home port as to whether they believe your story or not."

"I guess you have caught me, fair and square, Captain. I hope you realize that you are condemning me to the noose with that decision. The beaks* at Harksmouth have it in for me, even though their cellars are full of wine that I have brought in. I don't suppose that there is anything you can do so that me and my crew can avoid swinging."

"There might be, there just might be."

Giles went on to describe what he wanted: news of naval craft in the small French harbors that Captain Creasey would visit in the course of obtaining his cargoes. The smuggler had recently been in Aber Ildut in Brittany, but it was too shallow and to hold any warships. Indeed, Captin Creasey had found it a disappointing port at which to obtain his goods. Supplies and suppliers were very limited, though he was quite pleased with the cargo he had picked up there. But he wouldn't count on being as lucky if he went there again. He would be happy to go elsewhere next time. He would also inform Giles about any discoveries he made.

"I'm as patriotic as the next man, your honor. Just have to make a living, you understand, and if I don't do it, someone else will. Free trading pays better than fishing. I'll meet you when I'm next here. Did you know that the people who supply our goods have a network of fishermen and others who let us know where government ships are, especially the revenue cutters, but also the smaller Navy ships, even frigates since you sometimes hunt us? I won't have any trouble finding you."

"Very good. Any of the ships of my squadron will do. And if I am not around, you must tell the Admiral of the Channel Fleet. If I find out that you haven't, I'll stand witness that you are a smuggler."

"No need for that, Captain. I'm glad to do my bit to beat the Frogs. This war is not good for my business either. I'm as patriotic as the next man, but a man does what he has to survive."

"All right, Captain Creasey. You may go. Try to steer clear of others of His Majesty's ships. They are not likely to be as lenient as I am. Mr. Stewart, escort Captain Creasey back to his lugger and let him sail."

"Aye, aye, sir."

The boy was back soon. "Why are you letting that ship go, Captain? Surely he is a criminal whom we should apprehend."

"It's a long story, Mr. Stewart. He is more valuable as a source of information than as an extra cargo seized by the revenue service. Furthermore, I am following my orders even though I find them distasteful.

"Yes, Mr. Stewart, my orders are from the Admiralty. They are the people who think the information is worth more than the elimination of any particular smuggler. Maybe they are right. Now, you should go over to Captain Bolton and find out what he wants of you."

Giles turned away. What was his next task? Of course, what had happened at the battery? Had Lieutenant Macauley returned? When he put that question to the officer of the watch, he was told that Mr. Macauley had just embarked in the smallest of his boats. The marine lieutenant appeared to have a strange officer with him. 'What was that going to be all about?' Giles wondered. He knew that he would have to wait until the boat came to *Glaucus*. One might want to be a dashing frigate captain, but the truth of the matter was that, like it or not, most of the time one had to be a patient, not a dashing, frigate captain.

What a day it was turning out to be, Giles reflected. Quick planning to capture French ships. Then a burst of action as his little force carried out the plans, with some unforeseen difficulties. Now here was Lieutenant Macauley coming undoubtedly with more news that would require him to make more decisions. Where would the latest information lead him before he could take to his bed?

Chapter XI

Giles was surprised that Lieutenant Macauley was not the first man out of the boat. Instead, a tall, unknown man was first to board *Glaucus*. The newcomer was wearing what appeared to be the remnants of a Captain's uniform. He looked to be older than Giles, for his tousled locks and several days' beard were showing a good deal of gray amid his dark brown hair. Whoever he was, the stranger saluted the quarter-deck before turning to Giles, indicating that he was familiar with navy ways.

Lieutenant Macauley immediately followed the stranger on deck, so close behind him that, while the newcomer was facing the quarterdeck, he scurried forward and announced, "Captain Giles, may I introduce Captain Chockley to you, of the His Majesty's Frigate, *Vigorous*."

"Welcome aboard, Captain Chockley. I am horribly busy now. My servant may be able to find you more suitable attire.

"Mr. Miller," Giles addressed the officer of the watch, "pass the word for Furguson. He is to find suitable clothing for Captain Chockley.

"I apologize, Captain Chockley, I am in the aftermath of a battle, and all sorts of things are demanding my attention. I hope to have time to welcome you properly before long."

"I quite understand, my lord, needs must…"

"Thank you. Oh, Furguson, here you are. This is Captain Chockley. See what you can find him in the way of clothes. His have been rather hard used, as you can see. Captain Chockley, I'll welcome you properly later.

"Now, Lieutenant," Giles addressed Lieutenant Macauley, "what is this all about and where are my men?"

"Sir. I followed your orders to take the men up the ravine over there. We were fortunate. At the top, there is a spur to the path that curves back toward the top of the cliff, and we came out very close to the battery. All the French soldiers were engaged in looking at how their firing at *Firefly* was going. Before they knew it, we had them surrounded, and they surrendered without a fight. There was one laggard who had been out of sight behind one of the guns which was not in use. We found out later that he had been drinking a whole bottle of brandy. Anyway, he must have seen what we were doing and suddenly appeared with a musket which he was trying to aim at us. I fired my pistol at him, and he threw down his weapon before passing out."

"You shot him?"

"No, sir. I missed. I expect it was the effect of the brandy, not my bullet, that put him on the ground."

"Very well done, anyway, Mr. Macauley, but then what happened?"

"We rounded up the gunners and their helpers. We were about to come back to our boats when I noticed some movement in a window on a building a bit back from the cliff. I only got a glimpse, but I thought whoever it might be was wearing a military uniform. The building, I learned later, was formerly a small monastery whose monks were forced out at the Revolution.

"I pulled out my other pistol and pointed it at the officer who had been in charge of the battery. 'What is that building?' I demanded. 'I will shoot this officer if someone doesn't tell me. Then I will just keep shooting each of you until someone does tell me.'

"I don't speak any French, as you know, sir, but I got Lieutenant Marceau to translate. The officer was only too happy to tell us what the building was. Then he added that it was occupied by a small detail of soldiers together with a few English prisoners of war. The soldiers were preparing the way for a much larger group of prisoners who were being moved to a prison near Boulogne.

"This information, of course, snared my interest. I took several marines with me and went towards the building. When we got there, the soldiers had left by the back door. I didn't think it was worth pursuing them, though now I believe that I should have.

"We broke open the door and found two men in shackles, Captain Chockley and his second lieutenant. Captain Chockley told me that his ship had been wrecked on a lee shore and the survivors had been captured. They had been kept in a prison near Quimper, in Brittany, but then orders came to transfer them to Boulogne. A small group of the French soldiers had been sent ahead to find a place for the night, while the prisoners and the rest of their guards would follow shortly. Captain Chockley and his lieutenant were made to accompany the first group so that the crew would be leaderless, or so the French sergeant in charge of the advance party had told Captain Chockley.

"When I heard that a platoon of French soldiers was on the way with the captured crew of an English frigate, I suspected that you would want to ambush them. So I brought Captain Chockley with me to tell you about this development. I left the rest of my men and the other prisoners at the battery, under Lieutenant Marceau."

"I see. So you are saying that we have the chance of rescuing the crew of an English frigate that the French have captured?"

"Aye, sir. At least those who survived the shipwreck, sir, and some others seamen who were in the same goal. Captain Chockley did not know how many Frenchmen there were among the guards, but the number is substantial."

"Have you staked out a good place for an ambush?"

"Yes, sir. The path from the beach crosses a road at the top of the cliff, a little back from the edge, and with a dip because the gully that we climbed up hasn't fully finished the break that it makes in the cliff. There are bushes on each side of the gulley through which the road runs. I figure that we can ambush them there. Captain Chockley indicated that the French usually moved the prisoners with one group of guards at the front of the column and with another one bringing up the rear."

"Sounds like a good plan. Let's get to it. I'll come with you, and we can bring Captain Chockley as well if he is willing."

Fortuitously, Captain Chockley returned on deck at that point. He was wearing Giles's second-best coat and trousers. They were a bit too large for him, but they were much better than the clothes in which he had arrived.

"Captain Chockley," Giles greeted him. "I must apologize for not welcoming you aboard with the proper ceremony."

"I was hardly surprised, my lord. The end of a battle is not the time to stand on formality."

"That is good of you to say, sir. Incidentally, in the Navy, I do not use my title. Makes things much simpler all around. Now Mr. Macauley tells me that the rest of your crew can be expected to arrive at the battery over there before very long."

"Yes, Captain Giles. At least those who survived our shipwreck."

"I intend to rescue them. I hope you will join me so that your men know immediately that any orders given to them should be obeyed at once."

"Of course, I will be happy to. They have been treated much more harshly that have my officers and me."

Giles was much more out of breath when they reached the top of the ravine than was Lieutenant Macauley, but he was glad to see that Captain Chockley was even more winded. The marine pretended not to notice and found something to ask his subordinates while waiting for his commander to recover.

"How do you propose to mount the ambush, Lieutenant Macauley?"

"I think we have to divide our forces, sir, since the enemy will also be divided. I suggest that I take half of the sailors to attack the afterguard. You and Captain Chockley can stay on this side of the dip with the marines and the rest of the sailors and attack when the French soldiers are abreast of your position. I would suggest, sir, that just before you attack you have Captain Chockley loudly order his crew members to lie down and then you should immediately fire on the guards. I'll attack the rear guard when I hear that you are attacking the leading group."

"That's a good plan. Make sure to warn us if anything comes up that would require us to change it or to call off the ambush. One of the ship's boys should be able to carry messages quickly. Your marines here can fire their muskets and reload as usual. You might tell them before you go. I am sure they would obey me, but you should let them know what I intend so there will be no surprise. The sailors might as well attack with their cutlasses, yelling like banshees. The French are unlikely to be marching with loaded and primed muskets, and surprise will be worth much as an ill-aimed volley of musket balls. I suggest that you also attack with cutlasses immediately after firing."

"Aye, aye, sir."

The sun was already setting so it was likely that the ambush would take place after sunset. Giles wasn't particularly worried about that. His sailors were well practiced in carrying out orders in the dark. The almost-full moon would rise just after sunset and would provide enough light, even in the bushes, to allow the attack to proceed effectively.

The last glow in the west had almost faded away when Midshipman Fisher sprinted along the road to where Giles's men were hiding by the side of the road. He was out of breath and had to get his wind back before blurting out his message. Giles put a finger to his mouth to indicate that the lad should whisper.

"Sir," the boy squeaked, "Lieutenant Macauley sent me to tell you that there is a troop of six dragoons leading the soldiers and prisoners. The cavalry is a little bit ahead of the marching soldiers, sir."

"Thank you, Mr. Fisher. You had better stay with my group. Be ready to attack the leading guards after the horses have passed us. And pass the word to the rest of our men that they still are not to attack until I give the word.

"Mr. Marceau, pick six of the sailors to come with me and the marines. We are going to go down the road a short way. Tell them to come here at once, but quietly.

"Now, Corporal Jones," Giles directed the man in charge of the marines in his force, " there are six dragoons coming along the road ahead of the soldiers and their prisoners. I want your marines to shoot the riders. Are your muskets loaded?

"Aye, sir," responded the marine corporal, biting back the temptation to add "of course."

"Good. Divide the targets among yourselves; I don't want you all to aim at the same trooper. After you have fired, reload and fire at any who are still in the saddle, without waiting for an order to fire the next volley. If there are no more targets, fix your bayonets and attack."

"Now, you lot," Giles whispered to the sailors whom Lieutenant Marceau had designated to help him. "We have to deal with these riders. When the marines fire their volley, charge the dragoons with your cutlasses. I hate to do it but slash the back legs of the horses even before you take on the riders. You can take prisoners as long as there is no threat to you. Otherwise, kill the frogs, even if they are surrendering.

"Captain Chockley, as we agreed, yell to your crew the second you hear the muskets fire and then charge the leading group of the prisoners' guards. Now, come along with me, you men who have been selected for my group, quietly. Good luck, all."

Giles led his contingent fifty yards farther down the road. They hunkered down behind a screen of bushes waiting for the French dragoons to arrive. By luck, the moon was shining down the roadway so Giles's men could see what was coming while they were in the shadows of the bushes.

They didn't have long to wait. The jingle of the horse harnesses announced the approach of the cavalrymen. Giles could see the troop approaching at an easy walk, two by two. They weren't paying much attention to where they were going and were chatting animatedly with each other. Giles let them come past the place where most of his men were hidden waiting to attack the marching soldiers. That group had just come into sight. By luck, he had chosen exactly the right distance to proceed down the road with his special force. The horses would reach his position just as the French soldiers guarding the prisoners drew parallel with his waiting sailors.

Giles bellowed, "Fire!"

The muskets roared out just after he heard Captain Chockley call, "*Vigorous*, lie down!"

Giles had no time to evaluate the situation. With his sword drawn, he charged out of the bushes. The volley had shot two of the dragoons from their saddles. One of the other horses bolted, but even as Giles took a second to stare at it, its rider collapsed on one side of the horse and was being dragged along by his stirrup. One of his sailors slashed the back leg of another of the horses. At the same time, his mate took a nasty gash on his shoulder before slicing his cutlass across the Frenchman's belly. Another horse reared, and before its rider could get it under control, two of Glaucus's sailors were pulling him from his saddle.

That left only one cavalryman still mounted and unwounded. With his saber raised high, the dragoon swung his horse toward Giles. Just as the horseman was upon him, the horse reared, possibly because that was what he had been trained to do when riding down a man on foot. Giles was able to sidestep. As the horse came down, he parried the saber-slash from its rider and followed through by slashing his opponent's thigh to the bone. Blood gushed from the wound indicating that Giles had severed an artery. The horse charged on for several yards and then slowed and stopped. His rider toppled from the saddle and fell to the ground. The man was finished.

Giles could not rest on his laurels. "Follow me," he bellowed and raced off along the road. The ambush of the leading group of guards had been entirely successful. The soldiers who were supposed to be guarding the captured seamen had surrendered at once when they were attacked so unexpectedly. The men from *Glaucus* had suffered no injuries. So far, the only casualty to Giles's men was the sailor who had been slashed while the dragoons were being defeated. That wound was already bandaged, and the man's arm had been put in a sling.

Lieutenant Macauley appeared at that point. He was accompanied by several men who did not quite look like ordinary sailors or French soldiers. It was hard to tell who they were since the moon had gone behind a cloud.

"I'm happy to report, sir, that we captured the afterguard without a fight," declared the marine lieutenant.

"Excellent. Do you know if the prisoners are all right?"

"I haven't had a chance to examine them with any care, sir. I thought it was more important to report to you. There are far more of them than we expected."

"Oh?"

"Yes, sir. Among them, I discovered some officers. I brought them with me, sir."

The men that Giles had noticed coming with Lieutenant Macauley stepped forward.

The oldest of them took the lead. "Captain Hugh Fortingale, at your service, Captain." Thank you for rescuing us. I was in command of *Indomitable*, thirty-six."

"Glad I had the chance, sir," replied Giles. "I am Captain Richard Giles of His Majesty's Frigate *Glaucus*."

Another man spoke up, "I am Captain Percival Hornsworth, of His Majesty's Frigate *Incomparable*. It is about time the Navy saw about rescuing me."

"And these others?" asked Giles.

"My three lieutenants, useless creatures as they turned out to be. But for them and the wretched behavior of my crew, I would not be here," declared Captain Hornsworth.

"And the others?" Giles asked, for there were several other individuals in the group of men.

"My officers, my lord," replied Captain Fortingale. "May I introduce Mr. Fletcher, my first lieutenant, Mr. Farnsworth, my third, and Mr. Black, one of my midshipmen. I am afraid that the rest of my officers were killed when my ship was taken."

"I'm sorry to hear about them, Captain. Incidentally, I don't use my title in the Navy. Let me introduce Captain Chockley, captain of H.M.Frigate. *Vigorous*.

"Now, there seem to be many more prisoners that can be accounted for by the crew of *Vigorous*. Do you gentlemen know anything about them?"

"Yes, Captain Giles," replied Captain Fortingale. "Some are from my ship, the members of my crew who were able to walk, and some are from Captain Hornsworth's. There are also men from other ships, which ones I do not know."

"Any idea how many there are?"

"Well I haven't had a chance to count them, especially the ones from *Vigorous,* but I would guess that there are upwards of two hundred and fifty men, maybe three hundred."

"Good lord, and we already have a lot of prisoners. How are we going to get them all to England, I wonder."

"Simply shoot the prisoners, Captain Giles. No other choice," said Captain Hornsworth. "And leave most of the seamen behind, if you must. But I tell you, we must get away before any more frogs arrive to recapture us."

"Well, I am not going to shoot any prisoners. That is certain, Captain Hornsworth. Somehow I will get them all to England as well as our men."

"I am senior to you, sir. I order you to shoot the Frenchmen and to leave any of our sailors behind who are crippled, or wounded or otherwise superfluous."

"Do you, Captain Hornsworth? What is the date on which you were posted?"

"Seventh of August, 1801."

"Is it! Then you are junior to me, sir, for I was made post on the eighteenth of September, 1799. You will now obey my orders. Captain Fortingale, may I ask whether you are senior to me."

"I am not, Captain Giles. I became a post-captain on the ninth of July, 1800."

"Captain Fortingale, are any of your petty officers among the prisoners?"

"Yes, sir. The bosun and the master of arms and a couple of master's mates. Unfortunately, my master and my lieutenant of marines perished when we were taken.

"Captain Giles, I do have some bad news for you."

"Yes?"

"At our last stop, where we joined the other group of prisoners, we learned that we were to be followed by a large number of French troops headed for Boulogne. In fact, we were ordered to leave so that they could occupy the inn to get some refreshment before they followed us along the road. I don't know what their plans were exactly, but it did sound as if they had to make a night march because of all the time they had wasted along the road so far. They may not be very far behind us."

"Mr. Macauley, please have Captain Fortingale point out his warrant officers and other reliable men to you. They can help in making sure that the prisoners and the seamen can get into our boats in an orderly fashion. Arm as many of his crew and of *Vigorous*'s as you can with the weapons of the French soldiers. Have them guard the prisoners we have just taken. I want you to form a rear guard with your marines and our people.

"Mr. Marceau, would you lead the French prisoners, and their guards, followed by the other seamen to the shore, please. Mr. Fisher, get down to the beach as fast as you can and use the jolly boat to go to *Flicker*. Ask Captain Bolton to send as many boats as he can to help take everyone off the beach. Tell him that there will be roughly two hundred and fifty men to add to his troubles and have him sort them out among *Flicker* and the two brigs."

With a chorus of "Aye, aye, sir," the designated officers dispersed.

"What about me? What am I supposed to do? I must be taken off immediately," demanded Captain Hornsworth.

"Then you had better accompany Mr. Marceau and help him to see to an orderly loading of the boats. When that is completed, you may go to *Glaucus*."

"And what about you? We don't know when the French are going to arrive. Are you just going to go off to your frigate immediately and abandon us?"

"No, sir. I will be with the rear guard or sorting out any problems that arise with the evacuation that require my attention. I expect that I will be one of the last to leave the beach."

Giles began the climb up to the road where his rear guard was stationed. Lord, he was already tired, and there was still a lot to do and hazards to run before he was back on *Glaucus*. By rights, he should be settling in his cabin to write to Daphne about their capturing the French brigs. Now heaven only knew when he would be able to tell her all about this unending day.

Chapter XII

The various groups sorted themselves out, and the crowd on the road started to diminish as more and more men disappeared down the gully. When all that remained was the substantial rear guard, which included the marines, Giles decided to accompany the last of the sailors to the beach. Some distance before they reached the shore all movement stopped. Giles pushed the crowd for the rest of the way to the beach to see what the problem might be. It was simple. The men had to wait for the boats which had taken the first batch of rescued seamen to the ships to return so that they could take the next load away. Captain Chockley had had the men line up rather than spread out over the beach. The evacuation would take quite a long time since so many more people had to be taken off the beach than had come ashore from *Glaucus*, and it would be more difficult to load a disorganized rabble than an orderly line of men.

Giles went back to the afterguard. He explained that they were to wait until the gully was almost clear before making their descent. They should be ready to try to hold back the French force until all the men presently waiting for boats had been taken off. Then he turned around to go to the beach again, having to ask people to make way as he neared the bottom since they were jammed up as they waited for their turns at the boats. The evacuation would take some time. There were not very many boats, and there was a large number of men to embark.

At the beach, Giles found both Captains Chockley and Fortingale. There was no sign of Captain Hornsworth, even though he was not the senior captain and Giles had ordered him to oversee the loading of the boats. The other two captains had taken on this task without being told.

"How goes it, gentlemen?" Giles asked.

"Very well, sir," replied Captain Chockley. "We sent the wounded in the first boats and then the prisoners with some seamen as guards. Now we have to await the boats' return so that we can load the next group. We have sorted the order of embarkation and reckoned how many trips will be needed. Getting everyone here off will take three more loads at least, sir, and, with the rearguard, we will probably require four. Luckily it is not a rough night."

"What happened to Captain Hornsworth? I asked him to supervise the loading."

Captain Fortingale replied sourly. "His idea of supervising the loading was to take the first boat out to your ships. Your coxswain ... Carstairs? ... insisted that he go to your frigate, *Glaucus*, rather than the other one, even though he had jumped into the first boat that was ready to go and it was going to *Flicker*. Very persuasive fellow your coxswain! Quite scared Hornsworth, I believe. I don't know why he so wanted Hornsworth on your frigate. I would just as soon not be shipmates with that lout."

Giles laughed. "I imagine that Carstairs took one look at Captain Hornsworth and recognized a problem when he saw it. Captain Bolton, who commands *Flicker*, is very near the bottom of the list. He also has an unwarranted respect for rank. If either of you is on *Flicker*, please try not to overwhelm him. He is an excellent officer, but a bit deferential."

Giles took the trip back up the path at a much more leisurely pace than he had previously in scaling the heights. On the way, he ruminated on the situation. He now had a huge number of men to transport to England. Far more than he could safely accommodate on *Flicker* and the two captured brigs. He would have to take a large party of them to England on *Glaucus* and suspend using his ship to keep on exploring the coast. He could, at least, renew his supplies in England, even though they were not very low. Knowing the problems of getting action from the authorities ashore in Portsmouth, he could count on at least a week before *Glaucus*'s needs were filled. That would give him a few days at Dipton. He could see Daphne. And it would allow him to attend Captain Bolton's wedding. Maybe rescuing all these prisoners and capturing many French soldiers wasn't such a disaster after all.

"Any signs of the Frenchmen?" he asked Lieutenant Macauley when he reached the top.

"Not yet, sir."

"There will still be quite a wait until the beach is clear, I am afraid. I suggest we establish an ambush up here with some of the men and another a lot down the path to the beach. We'll want to startle the French and make them regroup as they come after us, while our people mounting the ambush can leave immediately and get down to the next spot. We can leap-frog down the path setting ambush after ambush. That should slow them enough so that we can all get away."

"Aye, aye, sir."

"That wasn't an order, Lieutenant. I was making a suggestion. You know more about fighting on land than I do."

"It strikes me as an excellent plan, sir."

"Then you go and find the next ambush place while I hide my group at the entrance to the path. Of course, the French may not show up at all."

"Aye, aye, sir."

Macauley selected a group of sailors to form the first party. Giles noted that he left his captain with all the marines. He directed his men into the bushes where the path branched from the road and settled down to wait. With any luck, the full force would be back on board the frigates before the French soldiers appeared. Giles was well aware that wine and efficient military actions did not go well together. The enemy might well be delayed by overindulging in the tavern where they had paused. Unfortunately, he could not count on their dawdling to that extent. Better to assume that they were coming and be pleasantly surprised when they did not arrive rather than to presume there was no danger and find out that he had been wrong.

The group waiting at the junction of the road and the path had to wait quite a long time. Giles was starting to wonder if they would get away without a fight when he became aware that his group might not be able to sneak away without a confrontation with the enemy after all. The noise of the French coming preceded them. They were singing loudly, and when the file of soldiers came into sight, it was evident that they were marching very sloppily. Giles decided that he should just let them pass his position in the hope that they would proceed through the dip where the road crossed the gully and miss the path to the beach.

The French indeed did almost miss noticing the path. Only when the last of the soldiers had passed Giles's position did the French sergeant who was bringing up the rear look to one side and call out, pointing towards the path. He yelled something in French and screamed the same words again before running forward, past the last of the soldiers. The file of infantrymen stopped, probably waiting for their officers to give instructions.

Several minutes passed before the enemy sergeant returned. With him were a couple of officers. The three men stood examining the path for several moments. In the dark, it may not have been easy to see that a large body of men had recently left the road to take the path that led steeply downwards. The French officers had a lengthy discussion, probably about what they were observing, while all the while the English watchers were on tenterhooks about what might happen.

Finally, the French conclave concluded. It appeared that they were going to explore the path using quite a substantial number of their soldiers. Giles whispered to his men to be ready. He let the enemy party group together at the entrance to the path before he cried "Fire."

The muskets barked in unison. Giles's orders were that his men were to take off down the path without waiting to see the result of their volley or to reload or to receive further orders. Giles himself did pause to see what effect the ambush had had.

The Brown Bess musket, with which his men were armed, was notoriously inaccurate, so Giles was surprised to see how effective the surprise attack had been. Most of the shots must have hit someone among the packed French mob. Many of the wounded lay on the ground where they had been standing. The other soldiers took cover in the bushes on the uphill side of the road, many of them helping their wounded comrades to safety. Nevertheless, the intersection of the road and the path was still littered with bodies.

Giles could hear the clamor of many voices explode as the French tried to evaluate their position. The enemy would hopefully be engaged in a lengthy discussion as to what to do next. Giles set off down the track to catch up with his men.

A couple of hundred feet down the path Giles was met by Lieutenant Macauley. The marine seemed to be alone. "Lieutenant, where are your sailors?" he asked.

The marine laughed. "Well hidden, sir, just through there. Their muskets are all loaded and primed and their bayonets in place."

Even knowing that they were there, Giles could see nothing that hinted at the presence of the men.

"Well done, Mr. Macauley. Now take the group of men who were with me on the road to form your next ambush. I'll stay here to spring the trap."

"Aye, aye, sir. The latest report from the beach is that the boats are returning to the ships and that the next trip should be the last one. I asked the captains who are overseeing the loading to make sure that the last boat, which is the one that will take our party, will be large enough to hold us all. Captain Chockley thought that there would be no difficulty in ensuring that."

Lieutenant Macauley led his group of men down the path while Giles melted into the bushes where the lieutenant had indicated that his sailors were hidden. There they were, all ready for the enemy to appear. The sailors clutched their muskets in a way which showed that they were determined to make every shot count. Giles was glad that he had drilled his crew in how to handle muskets as well as cutlasses. Most captains did not, since they saw little prospect of their being used. The marines, by contrast, treated handling a musket as a not very interesting or challenging task; countless hours of drill had made this the case.

It took some time for the French to appear. They came creeping down the gully very cautiously, the leading soldiers seeming to want the backing of more men before taking another step that might put them in danger. Very good, thought Giles. The same sergeant whom he had seen earlier kept trying to push other men ahead of him, but that only slowed matters down more. The officers who were in command of the soldiers had yet to appear.

Giles waited for the group to get close enough to make sure that at least some of the musket balls would strike their targets. The prospect was helped by the enemy being bunched together. A more adept officer would have spread his men out to reduce the damage that concentrated fire could do. As it was, it was likely that even a misaimed shot would hit someone, as long as it was not aimed too high or too low.

Giles had only his pistol as a firearm and knew that he needed to be very close to an enemy to have any hope of hitting him. The hostile party crept closer to where the British waited. The sergeant, who was in the lead, was nearer to Giles's side of the track than to the other one. The path at this point was narrow. Giles waited for the sergeant to draw parallel to him. Then he pulled the trigger as he roared, "Fire!"

Giles's had been aiming at the man's chest since it was the largest area of the soldier that presented itself and so was the one he was most likely to hit. It was a fortunate choice. The ball took the sergeant in the head, killing him instantly, Giles guessed. The rest of the British force fired immediately, well before the enemy had any chance of retaliating. Those Frenchmen who were not hit turned around and stampeded back up the path. None of them fired a shot from his musket at the British, but one of them stumbled and shot the soldier in front of him in the back. Giles saw that shot out of the corner of his eye as he moved back, just before he turned to run down the path behind his men.

The next place of ambush came up quickly, and once more the group running down the path continued past it to the spot that Lieutenant Macauley had chosen for the next confrontation. Giles was left again to command the ambush with the men who had already taken up their hidden positions.

It seemed to be ages before Giles heard the noise of the French cautiously descending the path. He had no idea of how much time had passed. Was it getting close to the time when they could run down to board the boats, or would there be more ambushes to set? If so, how many? These thoughts were interrupted by the French again making their presence known. This time, Lieutenant Macauley had chosen a place where there was a small clearing through which the path ran steeply. Giles would take advantage of the situation by opening fire when most of the Frenchmen were milling about in the open wondering what lay ahead. Lieutenant Macauley had stationed the men in a group on one side of the path where it again entered the woods. Giles had changed this to spread them out along the edge of the clearing with the path in the center of his line, ready to fire as the enemy appeared. He would not be surprised if his men would have time to reload again before the French got themselves straightened out sufficiently to resume their advance. He should get two chances at them.

Once again, the French were heard before they were seen. They paused as they entered the clearing, possibly afraid to cross what might be an open killing ground. The clearing was well lit by the moon, and the light made it difficult for the French to see into the surrounding forest. A French officer appeared, probably a captain, Giles guessed, though he had no knowledge of the uniforms of the French army. The man spent some time organizing his men for an advance.

Giles waited until the French were half-way across the clearing before he ordered his contingent to fire. Several men at the front of the enemy formation were hit. The rest ran back to the comparative safety of the woods. Giles had his men wait and reload while the French decided on their next move.

It took a while, but the panic caused by his unexpected volley didn't last as long as Giles had hoped. This time, the French were organized into a column before they emerged into the clearing. Led by the same officer, they marched toward the English four abreast. All that was needed was the drumming that was said to be the key to the French Army's implacable march to victory.

Giles let the column come towards him. The very density of the formation meant that his muskets should deal a hammer-blow to the French advance during which the English party could retreat to the next ambush point. On came the French, seeming to get bigger by the moment. Giles knew that he must let them come very close for him to have the best chance of causing havoc. He was sure that the marines would wait for the command. He just hoped his crew members would follow suit. They were not trained, as infantry were, to stand in the face of an approaching menace, but he believed that he could trust them to rely on him to time their volley to be effective without putting them in too much danger.

The French kept advancing. For the first time, Giles realized respect for infantry who had to stand firm while a danger bore down on them. At least he and his men were not waiting out in the open. He resisted the desire to fire at once and flee. What was the expression? Wait until you can see the whites of their eyes? But in the moonlight he wouldn't be able to see them, would he?

On came the French. At last Giles could wait no longer. "Fire," he roared. As he had ordered while they were awaiting the second appearance of the French, his men kept to the bushes as they left with no rushing until they could reach the path in a place which was out of sight of the clearing. Giles hoped that the French would not be sure whether or not he had retreated, and would fear being caught in the open again by the English if they tried once more to get to the place where the path reentered the woods. That hesitancy should slow them down.

Giles's men went down the path in small unorganized groups. That was what he would expect from his sailors who were used to being presumed to know what they needed to do without being told. Even the marines forewent the parade-ground formation which was their norm.

The English sailors and marines came to the next ambush location to find that Lieutenant Macauley just waved them along without pausing. Giles was the last of the group to reach that place where Lieutenant Macauley was waiting for him.

"Is this our next place of ambush, Mr. Macauley?" Giles asked.

"It was going to be, sir, but we can proceed directly to the boats now. Before we get there, all the other men will have been loaded, and we will be the final ones."

The two officers followed behind their men, moving steadily down the poorly lit path. They reached the beach to find that their group was already scrambling into the two launches that were waiting for them. Captain Chockley was still overseeing the operation. He had the honor of being the last man to board before the crew of the final launch to leave the beach ran the boat into deeper water so that they could return to *Glaucus*.

The boat was just pulling up to Giles's frigate when a glace toward the moonlit beach revealed a group of French soldiers venturing cautiously out of the woods. They were far too late to do anything but watch their enemy sitting safely at anchor, out of range of any guns they had with them.

However, one piece of bad news awaited Giles's arrival. *Firefly* had not just run onto a sandbar when it attempted to join *Glaucus* and *Flicker* earlier in the day. Instead, Commander Archer had succeeded in running her onto some rocks, not the usual shingle or sand that Giles would have expected to make up the shoal. In doing so, he had torn the bottom out of her. This fact only became evident to him and his people when the tide came in, and *Firefly* showed no inclination to float. 'Had it really been only that same day,' Giles mused, 'that his little squadron had first seen the French brigs' topsails?' So much had happened since that it seemed much farther back in time. How his lot had changed. Instead of continuing his inspection of the small ports of France, he now had to take his ships and their prizes into Portsmouth, crammed with French prisoners and rescued British seamen, to whom were now added the sorry crew of *Firefly*.

Giles's only consolation in contemplating the voyage ahead of him was that he did not have very far to go. Even in good weather, everyone would be uncomfortable with each ship crammed with far more people than she had been designed to carry. Heaven help them if the unpredictable Channel decided to unleash one of its notorious storms. On *Glaucus*, it would be rendered even more awkward by having on board three post-captains and a commander, all of whom would be facing courts-martial when they arrived home. In the case of the captains, furthermore, they would have to be crammed into Giles's day cabin, in a way unbefitting of their rank. How glad he would be to see the last of them! How happy he would be to see Daphne, Bernard, and Dipton even if only for a few days.

Chapter XIII

Daphne always enjoyed her forays to the Dipton Arms. She had known Elsie for years, in fact since she was a young girl. With no one else for Daphne to confide in, the two had become much more than mistress and maid.

Daphne wasn't the only one who was with child. As a matter of course, Carstairs had been at home when Giles was at Dipton and with the same result. Elsie was a couple of weeks ahead of Daphne, but, otherwise, they were both awaiting the arrival of a child whose father was likely to be at sea when the babies arrived. Elsie had more difficult pregnancies than Daphne, but it was still early days, and the real discomforts were months away.

Daphne insisted on seeing Elsie's child before they could have tea in Elsie's private parlor. The child, who with Carstairs's full approval had been named Daphne, was a charming little girl. Like Daphne's son, Bernard, she was almost on the edge of exerting her independence. Then the two friends got down to discussing all the latest doings in the neighborhood. It was a one-sided exchange of news. Elsie's contacts among the lady's maids and other servants gave her as much gossip about Daphne's strata of society as Daphne had, though Daphne could hold up her end of the conversation with information about the broader world outside the immediate neighborhood. Also, Daphne could explain better what their two husbands were doing since Carstairs's understanding of the overall situation of *Glaucus* was more limited than what Giles felt free to communicate to his wife. Not that Daphne had much recent news. The men had not been gone very long.

Where Elsie had the advantage over Daphne came in the doings of the ordinary people of the neighborhood. Such folk drank, and therefore talked, at the Dipton Arms, and Elsie picked up much of what was being said. Indeed, she knew more about what the revenue officers were doing at Hillcrest Grange than did Daphne, even though Mr. Baxter was allegedly keeping Daphne, as the owner of the property, informed.

Elsie did confirm what Daphne had heard about the shortages of goods that were usually smuggled into the area. The innkeeper was getting worried about the situation, for her cellars were starting to look very empty. The man who had come regularly to take her order had not been by since the hidden cargo of the most recent smuggling-barge had been seized, and the three principal figures behind the smuggling trade had been arrested. Elsie did know that there was a fourth leader, but she had never heard who he was, nor had she ever had reason to ask. She would try to find out, but she wasn't hopeful because she suspected that he lived on the other side of Ameschester and no one who frequented the Dipton Arms might know who was the mystery kingpin.

Daphne wondered how to discover the identity of the man who might know about the network for distributing the smuggled goods. Mr. Snodgrass, her lawyer, might know. She resolved to visit him in Ameschester the following day.

Daphne's visit to the town advanced her search not one iota. Mr. Snodgrass said he had no idea who the individual might be. A stop at the bank, where she was a most valued customer, met with what she was sure was genuine ignorance, though the managing partner did promise to make inquiries about who might be the mystery man. She had to return to Dipton Hall frustrated at her lack of progress, especially as she had to set to work on her other tasks. She would have preferred to pursue the mystery if she could think of any way to proceed usefully.

Friday brought more visitors to Dipton Hall and more discussion of the growing shortages of goods that the ladies always expected to be readily available. To Daphne's surprise, it became evident that most of them did not realize that the materials that they thought were so necessary to their enjoyment of life, and even more to their husbands', were smuggled into the country and had avoided the duties that were owed on them. It seemed very strange that they knew so little about the extent to which they consumed goods on which the taxes had been avoided. Only the prevalence of smuggled wine and brandy seemed to be widely known, and their shortages were ascribed to the breaking up of the smuggling ring. The other materials caught up in the same circumstances were believed to be unavailable for utterly mysterious reasons.

Daphne had learned from Steves and Elsie what were the prices that they were paying for the goods on which duties had not been paid. They were a good deal higher than the charges that Mr. Baxter had told her she would have to pay for the windfall that had accompanied the purchase of Hillcrest Grange. Daphne could undoubtedly sell them for less than the going rate and still turn a handsome profit. How could she distribute them if she did pay the taxes? She could hardly set up as the purveyor of quality foreign goods, could she? She giggled as she thought of the handbills that she might have printed saying, 'Lady Daphne Giles, Viscountess Ashton, offers for sale exclusive French lace and brandies on Friday next at ten o'clock at Dipton Hall.' Doing so, she realized, would at least deal with one of her annoyances. None of the ladies in the area would call again at Dipton Hall. They would not want to associate with someone who was so brazenly engaged in trade.

Such thoughts did nothing to hide Daphne's dismay at having such a direct means to turn a profit but not having the knowledge to be able to exploit it. Giles, she was sure, would know how to handle the situation satisfactorily, especially as he had little prejudice against people who were in trade. But, of course, he was not here, and he did rely on her for the efficient handling of his interests. That was precisely what was at issue here.

The key to solving Daphne's dilemma came from a source that she should have known would be useful, but had forgotten. Major Stoner was at Dipton Hall when she returned from Ameschester. His being there was no surprise. The Major was lured by the presence of Lady Marianne. When Daphne mentioned her problem to him, the Major knew the answer.

"It sounds like it might be Sir Lester Brownlee. He has an estate quite close to mine. You probably don't know him,

Lady Ashton. His residence, Gaymound House, is, after all, quite a distance from Dipton, and Sir Lester is not a member of the Ameschester Hunt. His title – he is a baronet – is of long standing, though I don't know if any of the Brownlees ever made much of a mark for themselves. He is rumored to have various commercial interests – as an investor, not as a man of business, you understand. I suspect he may be the man involved in the smuggling trade. Not sure, of course, but I have heard jokes about his involvement when I was visiting the inn where I go regularly. I know him, of course, though not well. If you like, I can introduce you. Gossip has it that he is a bit hard-up for money. The stories about his not very proper activities, which he needed to keep himself in funds, seem to have become more prevalent after you so successfully broke up the smuggling ring."

"I did nothing of the sort! Do you think I could talk to him? What would he and others think if I had you introduce me to him?"

"I'm the last person to ask about others' opinions, Lady Ashton, but I would say your reputation for being unconventional and having nothing detrimental stick to you would see you through any awkwardness."

"Is that truly my reputation?"

"I suppose I shouldn't have said so, but, yes, it is. Only the insufferably proper resent you, you know. Most of the others just wish they could be more like you."

"I can always count on you to tell me the unvarnished truth, can't I, Major? It is rather refreshing. Well, I would like to meet this mystery man."

"Then I'd be happy to accompany you so that I can introduce you. Indeed, you and Lady Marianne could visit my residence, Sydbeck House, for luncheon. Then we could go on to ask your questions of Sir Lester. That would be a splendid idea, I do declare. Do you know, Lady Marianne has never visited my estate, and she would undoubtedly like to see it before we are married. Looked at that way, it is you who will be doing me a favor."

It had started to snow and seemed to be promising to dump a lot of the white stuff before morning. Lady Marianne wouldn't let Major Stoner set out in the dark in such conditions. Indeed, it required several more days before the Major could return home and make sure that his cook had the proper ingredients for a special luncheon. So Daphne and her half sister-in-law had to contain their eagerness to visit Sydbeck House for several long winter days before they could set out in Daphne's carriage to see Major Stoner.

Neither Daphne nor Lady Marianne had ever seen Major Stoner's estate. Lady Marianne luckily had the side of the coach with the best view of the residence as they approached. It would be her future home, but she knew almost nothing about it. Description of anything nonmilitary was not among Major Stoner's abilities. The house was a well-proportioned block of yellow stone featuring large and symmetrically positioned windows and capped with a beautiful cornice. It's only weakness was the doorway, which was hardly more than a double door with a small covering over it. Sydback House was not a large building unless it extended far to the back, but it was very prettily situated. Lady Marianne's spirits rose. It was much more handsome than she had expected. Maybe she would be able to persuade the Major to improve the portico.

Major Stoner must have been anticipating their arrival for he came out to welcome them even before his butler could announce their arrival. The Major hovered nervously as they were helped out of their warm cloaks and it was he, instead of the footman, who ushered them into the drawing room.

Major Stoner was not a great conversationalist and having the two ladies in his drawing room threatened to leave him speechless. Daphne dealt with the situation by commenting on how the snow had delayed their ability to visit. Had he been much affected by it at Sydback House? Lady Marianne contributed very little to this conversation, and it was petering out rather quickly when Daphne thought to express delight at one of the Indian artifacts that graced the room. That remark got the Major going. He turned out to know a great deal about Indian art and Indian ways. Once started, it took only a few comments, indicating that his listeners were interested in what he was telling them, to keep him going. Daphne had never before heard the Major talk of his experiences in India, except in passing and almost in an embarrassed way, as if his service there was of dubious value, except as a way to make money. Now he showed that he had made himself knowledgeable of all aspects of Indian culture and appreciated them in a manner that took

Daphne by surprise. She had expected him to be one of those people who automatically thought everything to do with a foreign country must be inferior, especially one that was miles and miles away.

The Major's exposition continued through lunch, and it was only interrupted when Daphne broke in to suggest that they should visit Sir Lester Brownlee's residence. Lady Marianne wanted to know if she could stay behind and have Mrs. Lavers, Major Stoner's housekeeper, show her the house in more detail. Luckily, Daphne had brought Betsy, her maid, with them in anticipation of such a request, so she and Major Stoner set off in her carriage together with Betsy.

Gaymound House, the home of Sir Lester Brownlee, was a ramshackle building, showing the signs of various additions, made at different times and in whatever style might then have been in vogue at the time. It also gave an indefinable air of not being looked after properly. Daphne thought that, if it were hers, she would tear the house down and start again. Possibly Sir Lester didn't care about the place or couldn't afford to maintain or improve it.

There was already a carriage at the unprepossessing entrance to the house. No one came out of the house to help Daphne and Major Stoner alight and greet them. Indeed no one even opened the front door for them. They had to knock loudly before a surly footman opened it and asked, rather rudely, what they wanted. Before Major Stoner could reply, Daphne saw Mr. Snodgrass, her solicitor, standing in the entrance hall.

"Lady Ashton, how nice to see you. What are you doing here?" the lawyer asked, rather abruptly Daphne thought.

"We are here to see Sir Lester, Mr. Snodgrass. May I ask you the same question?"

"Haven't you heard? I thought everyone would know about Sir Lester. I suppose it must have been the snow that prevented you from hearing the news. Just before the snow storm, Sir Lester left the area, with his wife and children and a considerable amount of baggage. They said nothing to the staff here about where they were going. They did stop in Ameschester for luncheon at the Fox and Hounds, and several patrons heard Lady Brownlee haranguing her husband. They could not help hearing that Sir Lester was taking them to Bristol to get a ship to carry them to America. I believe a place called Baltimore was mentioned. Anyway, Lady Brownlee did not want to go to America and couldn't understand why they were leaving. Sir Lester lost his temper in the end, and it came out that he had to leave to avoid creditors and possible conviction for his role in smuggling."

"Needless to say, the news spread all over town very quickly, and many merchants and others found that Sir Lester had been borrowing not only from them but also from the bank and other people. He would run up bills and then pay part of what was owed, and could then get more credit. Many of the men of business thought that the money came from his involvement in financing the smugglers and so had no worry about being paid back. What they didn't realize was how much

Sir Lester was borrowing from others and how much he was losing gambling.

"To make a long story short, they engaged me to try to sort out the debts and assets, and see how much the loss would be. That's why I am here, to see what possessions Sir Lester left behind and to have a quick look at the property. It is just as well they did retain me. I only barely prevented the butler from absconding with the silver, and there is any number of other items that could easily disappear. Clothes and furnishings and glassware and I don't know what else. It will all have to be cataloged and auctioned off.

"I dismissed all the servants on the spot. They won't get paid, I am afraid, but I can't run the danger that they will take off with whatever of value they can carry. Most of them thought that the family was just off visiting Lady Brownlee's relatives in Staffordshire, though the butler knew the truth. I will have to get some trustworthy people to look after the place until I can have the auction held.

"But I am forgetting my manners and proper priorities. May I inquire why you want to see Sir Brownlee?"

Daphne explained about her suspicion that the baronet would know about how the smuggled goods came to be distributed throughout the area.

"I may be able to help you. Very perceptive of you, Major Stoner, to realize what Sir Lester was up to. Everybody in Ameschester thought that he was a passive financier of the smuggling, but I have found some papers that show that he was very heavily involved in conducting the business. I suppose that no one suspected since Sir Lester and, even more so, Lady Brownlee expressed such contempt for people who made their money through trade or the professions, or anything like that. The yield on his estate is negligible now. I imagine that he has been quietly selling off parts of it. Sir Lester did keep records of various aspects of the smuggling. I suspect he may have been the chief organizer. I also discovered some notebooks about its operations. You are welcome to them, Lady Ashton, they are of no value for winding up his affairs. I must apologize for not realizing that Sir Lester must be the man about whom you were wondering when you visited my rooms.

"Simons," the lawyer ordered one of his underlings who was at hand, "fetch those documents we found in Sir Lester's library and give them to Lady Ashton, please.

"Lady Ashton, I hope they are useful. If I can help in any other way, be sure to let me know."

Daphne and Major Stoner found themselves once more outside. Daphne was just as glad. She had not been interested in Sir Lester except as a source of information, and she had been afraid that the Major would want to gossip with Mr. Snodgrass about his neighbor. Daphne also made her excuses to the Major for not staying long at Sydback House, pleading that it would soon be getting dark and there might still be snow in the hollows. She did have to endure, on the trip to Dipton, Lady Marianne's recounting all the marvelous things about the Major's house, but how Daphne's sister-in-law could make a lot of improvements if the Major approved. It was quite clear that her fiancé's home had more than met Lady Marianne's expectations.

It took a whole day for Daphne to go through the papers that Mr. Snodgrass had given her. Sir Lester had indeed been the king-pin of the smuggling ring, taking the lion's share of the proceeds and, it appeared, guiding the work of the other ring-leaders. Daphne also learned the names of other gentlemen in the neighborhood who were silent investors in the smuggling endeavor. She realized that she would never again be able to go to the start of the Ameschester Hunt without seeing various gentlemen of impeccable reputation who had invested in the shady enterprise.

Daphne did discover all the details of how the smuggled good had been distributed, who had bought what, and which intermediaries had been in contact with the customers to take their orders and inform them about deliveries. All she would need to do was to contact the intermediaries, and then she could, no doubt, dispose of all her windfall. A little calculation told her that the profits would be huge, especially as she would not have to pay the various intermediaries a premium to handle illegal goods.

She realized that she had the knowledge to dispose of the materials in the hidden storehouses. But did she want to? Sir Lester had used as a buffer between himself and the distribution of the goods, Mr. Shuster, the shady lawyer. That must have been how he avoided being known as the man who distributed smuggled goods. That was an occupation utterly inappropriate for a gentleman. Daphne realized that people would think that her taking the lead in disposing of the smuggled goods would be regarded as being absolutely inappropriate for a lady in her position. Certainly, she could not be seen to be directly involved. Of course, it wouldn't bother her if she got that reputation, would it? But how would Giles react to her getting involved in trade? He gave her a lot of freedom, but going into business was hardly what a nobleman would expect of his wife, especially when they were the leading figures of the area and had all the money they needed.

Of even more importance in considering what to do, Daphne realized that she didn't want to have much involvement in dealing with the smuggled goods. She had much better uses of her time. In particular, she wanted to have more time to enjoy being Bernard's mother, to read, and to play music. However, she wasn't about to let Mr. Baxter get away with making the profit by just giving him her goods. She wouldn't use Mr. Shuster, the shady lawyer who had handled Mr. Wark's affairs: she couldn't trust him. Approaching Mr. Snodgrass to arrange the selling of the goods would probably only lower her in his opinion without getting him to agree to act. However, couldn't she use someone else? She was dubious about involving her steward, whose father had been so close to the smuggling trade; he had an occupation that was just suitable for a gentleman without means, but getting him involved in *trade*? No! And what would her niece Lydia, Mr. Dimpster's wife, think of his undertaking such a task?

She was torn. She did want to find a way to dispose of the goods. It offended her practical sense not to be able to find a way to sell the material to the benefit of herself and her neighbors. But she didn't want to spend any time doing so. She was overburdened as it was. Furthermore, did she really want to risk Giles's possibly unfavorable reaction if she went ahead to make a profit out of them? They certainly did not need the money. These thoughts preoccupied her attention as she finished going through the records of Sir Lester Brownlee's nefarious undertakings.

Chapter XIV

Daphne's problem of how to find someone to distribute the now legal contraband that was scattered about Hillcrest Grange was solved the next day, completely unexpectedly. She had scarcely settled down in her workroom when Steves announced Major Stoner.

"Major, it is good to see you. Lady Marianne and I enjoyed our visit to Sydback House. Lady Marianne talked of nothing else as we returned to Dipton. She is in the morning room, I believe. I am surprised that Steves did not tell you"

"It's you I have come to talk to, Lady Ashton, if you'll let me. You are the only person who knows anything about my finances and can help me in suggesting what I should do."

"Whatever is it, Major?"

"You know that I returned from India with a very tidy sum of money that I had earned trading on my own account. You have no idea how easy it is to make money out there if you have a small amount of capital to begin with. I did it by starting with my major's pay which, of course, I couldn't spend during the voyage to India. Not very much money, it is true, but it was enough to get me started."

"Yes, I recall, Major. You must have had a real flair for business to turn such a small sum into such a handsome fortune."

"Well, not really, Lady Ashton. If I had stayed a year to two longer, I might have been a true nabob, but the climate did not agree with me, and I had to come home. I had accumulated enough to buy Sydback House, which, as you know, provides only a very small return in rents. I invested the rest in consols which yield a comfortable, but not large, income. Instead of being content with my lot, however, I thought that, if I had a greater income, I would be more respected in the neighborhood. It was foolish, I know, but that's what I thought. I sold some of my consols and put the money in a bank in Leister that promised far better returns. 'Promised' is the proper word. Within a month of my placing my money with them, the bank went bankrupt."

"How awful!" Daphne exclaimed. "are you sure that the money is gone?"

"So I am told. Things still weren't that bad, but I now was convinced I needed more income. My agent suggested that I invest in a very promising canal company. They had already started digging and had even opened part of the canal. They needed additional capital, but they were already paying dividends to the early investors who had financed the first steps. Those investors were getting a very handsome return, much more than consols pay. So I sold some more consols and invested in the canal. The better returns would go some way towards making up for what I had lost in Leister."

"So things are looking up for you again, Major?"

"Unfortunately, no, Lady Ashton. I learned yesterday that the canal company has gone out of business. Most of the reports of the progress being made and the money being earned had been fabricated. The company seems to have used the proceeds from new investors to give dividends to old investors. I don't entirely understand how it was done, but my investment in the canal company is now worthless."

"Oh, how dreadful, Major. Bad luck, twice in a row. It seems terribly unfair! But why have you come to me?"

"I thought I would talk to you before breaking the news to Lady Marianne. Obviously, I cannot keep her to her commitment to marry, since I have lost my money. I just don't know how to break the news to her."

"I wouldn't be so quick about deciding that, Major. You could sell your estate and move into more modest quarters, for example."

"Oh, I couldn't do that after getting Lady Marianne's expectations up so high, especially as she has seen Sydback House, and loved it."

"Well, let's see. Lady Marianne will be disappointed, no doubt, but her position when she was married to Captain Choker was even worse, so she may be able to accommodate your reduced circumstances. However, before pursuing that line, I may be able to help out a little."

"Oh, Lady Ashton, I couldn't accept money from you and Captain Giles. Your gift to Lady Marianne is already very generous."

"That wasn't what I had in mind. I need someone to oversee the distribution of all this contraband that has come into Captain Giles's hands as a result of purchasing Hillcrest Grange. There is some urgency to get it sold since all our neighbors are running short of things that the smugglers bring in. Can you believe it? Some of the ladies are worried that their dressmakers will not have the materials to make stunning gowns for Baron de Roy's ball.

"The papers that Mr. Snodgrass gave me makes the smuggling operation all very clear. They list who were the agents that Sir Lester was using, and how they had people under them who collected the orders and arranged for the deliveries. You could take that on for me, and it would be of great assistance. It might be a bit of a come-down for you, for it hints at being in trade and you have worked so hard to prove that you are indeed a gentleman."

"That doesn't worry me, Lady Ashton. I do have to earn some money, and pretending to be above such matters hasn't got me very far socially, has it? I'm still not a gentleman born, and, of course, I never will be. Except for your family, everyone treats me as a bit less than them. I would not be ashamed to work for my money, and any effect on my social status wouldn't matter much. I could still be a contributing and participating member of the Hunt – it is not reserved only for gentlemen. In some ways, I would rather it is out front how I make my money rather than it be a secret that leads to people muttering unfavorable speculations behind my back."

"Good, so will you think about taking on this task for me, Major?"

"Yes, indeed, my lady, but it only solves my problem temporarily, of course. Once your hoard of smuggled goods has gone, I'll be back in the same pickle."

"I am not so sure about that, Major," Daphne replied. "The amounts involved are quite amazing. In addition, the papers give a great deal of information about the smuggling ring all the way from the coast up to Dipton, which seems to be the end of their operation. I have done some calculations. The goods could be brought in, duties paid, and the materials distributed up the waterway in the open. The savings from not having to hide what is going on and bribing officials would pay the customs charges so that the enterprise could be as profitable as the smuggling has been, probably more so. I know that in India you had quite a lot of experience in organizing and dealing with rough customers, so you might be the ideal person to deal with setting up this enterprise and taking the business away from the smugglers."

"That prospect sounds both challenging and exciting," replied the Major. "I must confess that I am a bit bored with the life of a landed gentleman, especially since I know nothing of farming. It would, of course, require capital to get it going. You can't expect the seamen who are bringing in the goods to be paid by credit."

"I'm not sure about that. However, you are right. I, or rather Captain Giles, can finance that side of the endeavor. He hates smuggling because it's robbing the government of much-needed money to pay for the war. This enterprise might be a way to cut down on how much illicit activity goes on at the expense of the Crown. That is a clear benefit for him in addition to its turning a nice profit. As you know, providing money to finance an enterprise is not regarded as soiling one's hand with trade – why it isn't, I cannot imagine."

"If your scheme works out, it would be the solution to my problems, Lady Ashton. It would also provide me with challenges of the sort which I would welcome. The life of a country gentleman with limited activities turns out not to appeal very much to me."

"Then I suggest you look at the papers that Mr. Snodgrass gave me and see if we have enough information to proceed. Now, I am sure that Lady Marianne is resenting my monopolizing you. You should see her before getting into the documents."

Before turning to other tasks, Daphne reflected on how much her opinion of the Major had changed. At first, she had thought him an opinionated buffoon. Then, as she saw more of him, she thought of him only as a way of getting Lady Marianne out of Dipton Hall. Now she found him a worthwhile business partner and a most acceptable in-law. Well, such musings didn't get her tasks done, but the most pressing of them had been dealt with this morning.

The next person to want Daphne's attention was Mr. Harris, the builder. He had a set of rough plans of the kennels for

Daphne's inspection. He had designed a utilitarian building that incorporated all the requirements stated by Charlie Maddox. Furthermore, Catherine Crocker had proposed some improvements to make it a more attractive structure but at a somewhat higher cost. Catherine had provided sketches of how the building would appear if it were built as Mr. Harris had designed it, and how it would look with her suggestions.

Daphne called Steves to find Catherine, and she showed up so quickly that Daphne suspected that she had been waiting close at hand to hear about her aunt's reaction to her suggestions. There was no doubt that Catherine had talent. Her improvements would make the building merge with the landscape much more harmoniously. Mr. Harris's ideas were good, but Catherine's additions improved them substantially. The increased cost was significant, but not outrageous. Daphne promptly authorized building the kennels according to Mr. Harris's concept, but with Catherine's features. That decided, they moved on to discussing Hillcrest Grange.

Mr. Harris and Catherine had collaborated in designing changes that would make Hillcrest Grange a much more attractive structure. Larger windows and a more impressive entrance improved the outside appearance while providing practical advantages by making the rooms lighter and the welcoming of guests more congenial. Changes to the interior made the space more useful and easier for the servants to perform their duties. Catherine had indicated changes in the use of some of the rooms, that would not requiring rebuilding, but she also suggested some interior alterations that would make the space allocated to the bedrooms and dressing rooms more appropriate. The proposed improvements had all been illustrated by before-and-after sketches by Catherine. Daphne was surprised how much better the rooms would look with the color changes that Catherine was introducing.

"These are ambitious plans, Catherine," Daphne remarked. "The only thing that strikes me is that the house remains jammed up against the woods at the back. You can't get a good perspective of the back of the house, and the rooms there have no attractive views from their windows. I wonder if anything can be done about that."

"I'd wondered about that concern myself, Lady Ashton, but it would make a much more extensive project," said Mr. Harris. "I have been hesitant to suggest it, especially with the need to build the kennels soon."

"Yes, I can appreciate your point," said Daphne, "but I do think that it might be better to at least have overall plans as to where we should be going rather than to do the planning piecemeal. What are your ideas, Mr. Harris?"

"The woods at the back would need to cut back quite a lot to make a useful space for landscaping and to allow some additions that I think would improve the building. If they were removed, the property would be significantly enhanced in my opinion.

"You may want to cut the woods back anyway. In the past, it looks as if they were used for providing timber, but not recently. There are many fine old oaks and some serviceable elms and maples in the bit of woodland near the house. If you had them cut, the timber would probably pay for the landscaping and many of the costs of improving the house."

Daphne had never even thought of using the land which she and Giles had acquired with Hillcrest Grange for timber operations, partly because she knew nothing about forest management. What Mr. Harris said seemed to make sense, but did she want to get involved in such a project? How difficult would it be to find a reliable man to manage the forests, for it would require skills that her gamekeepers did not possess?

Maybe Mr. Edwards could find someone who could undertake the task. She had to remember her resolve to make time for herself, not to start more projects for her to manage.

"I'll think about it, Mr. Harris. In fact, no, we will proceed at once if someone to oversee the selection and felling of the timber can be found promptly. With the war on, I know from Captain Giles that the shipyards badly need good oak wood. We could use the canal landing to ship the wood to the coast."

"These plans look splendid. Can I have copies to send to Captain Giles, whose approval will be needed for such an extensive project? I am sure that he will be happy with the plans for the kennels so that you can start on those straight away, Mr. Harris. We have already decided where they would go, and Captain Giles, I know, simply wanted buildings that would merge well into the landscape. He had no definite ideas about how they would look. However, he needs to be consulted about the changes to Hillcrest Grange. I'll tell him about them in my next letter if you can get the drawings ready, Catherine."

Daphne was able to escape from her workroom as the others withdrew. She spent the time before lunch with her son. Afterward, she took her mare, Moonbeam, to visit her father's tenants. They were her friends, much more so than the ladies with whom she exchanged visits. She had known them since she was a girl and visited them more to find out how they were getting on and to exchange parochial gossip than to make sure that her father's lands were being well tended. Those visits were one of the activities that were being limited as she became busier. She knew that she preferred them to many of the other tasks in which she had become engaged, challenging and important though they might be.

It was several days before Major Stoner returned to Dipton Hall. He came well before lunch, asking for Daphne rather than Lady Marianne. He had been busy.

"I have been able to sort out pretty well how the operation worked," the Major began. "Sir Lester was indeed the spider in the center of the web, and quite a web it is. I did wonder how he kept his reputation as a gentleman if he was the man running the distribution of the illegal goods. His secret was to use several subordinates who did the actual business with the customers. They had people to gather the orders and others to see to the delivery of the material. He even had them pay the bribes to Mr. Baxter and the other revenue officers to turn a blind eye to what he was doing and to make sure the officials were zealous when anyone tried to do any smuggling on their own.

"I certainly have enough information so that I can get all your goods sold with a very tidy profit after expenses. We don't need to use the intermediaries; there is enough information in the documents that I can easily manage that side of the business. And since the goods will all be legal, distributing them will be simpler and cheaper. Of course, we may get some complaints about not having work for nearly as many men, but that will just have to be endured. So I would suggest that it would be very profitable for you to pay the duty and let me arrange the sale and distribution of all the material stored presently at Hillcrest Grange."

"That sounds very attractive. I presume that you have allowed for some money for yourself."

"Yes, my lady. Of course, I have. I was thinking that thirty percent of the net profits would be a fair payment."

"How much would that be?"

"Well, we can't be sure, of course, but I would expect it to be in the neighborhood of £2,500."

"That much! I am surprised. Yes, I think you should go ahead if you are content with that amount."

"Oh, I am, Lady Ashton. The sum goes some way to recouping my losses. That does bring me to the second area about which I found out a bit of information that I suspect could be used to get more profit."

"This is concerning how to bring goods on which the duty has been paid into the area?"

"Yes, my lady, though I am not entirely clear how we could change the business from a smuggling one to a legitimate one."

"Why is that?"

"What I can make out from the papers, and you can probably learn more from that than I can. I was never very good with numbers. Luckily serving in the Indian Army didn't require much ability in that line, what? I had just enough to ensure that my ventures made a pretty penny."

"Quite, Major," Daphne interrupted for there was a distinct possibility that they might get completely lost in the sidetrack that the Major was exploring. "What did Sir Lester's papers indicate?"

"Well, I think – but, as I said, I may be wrong – the smuggling operation begins in Harksmouth. I sense that the Custom House officers there must be well paid to ignore illegal activity, for the contraband seems to be unloaded onto a public dock of some sort and then transferred to the canal boats. Not picked up off a beach or a quiet cove or somewhere out of the way as I had expected. It's then loaded onto a canal boat and brought up here. Some entries suggest that sometimes the barges carry the goods to other destinations instead, but I can't quite figure out what is going on. To make your ideas work, you would have to find out what is happening in Harksmouth, and how to get the deliveries from abroad out of the hands of smugglers."

"There must be some way, Major. Let me have the papers, and I'll see if I can glean any ideas from them. I am having several people for dinner today who might turn out to have some ideas about the subject. I have invited Captain Bush, as well as his mother and sisters, and Mr. Harworth and his two sons. He is the vicar of St. Mary Minor. It is the parish church for Hillcrest Grange, and I have discovered that the living* is in the gift of Hillcrest Grange, so Captain Giles bears some responsibility for it. I have invited my father, and he sent me a note to say that he would be bringing Mr. Justice Amery, who is staying with him during the Ameschester assizes. Something to do with deficiencies in the Judges' Rooms in Ameschester With those men, particularly Justice Amery and Captain Bush, you may be able to get some useful suggestions.

It was a large party that gathered for dinner at Dipton Hall that afternoon. For once, the numbers of men and women were almost in balance, and a lively evening it turned out to be. Mr. Harworth was a widower and had been for some time. He was an Oxford man, whose time there had overlapped Daphne's father's though they had not known each other. His two sons were up at Oxford, in his old college, and were destined for the church. Mr. Harworth turned out to be a good conversationalist, with a dry sense of humor, which made him a worthwhile addition to any party, especially as he lacked the sanctimoniousness that plagued so many of his calling.

The Bush sisters both enjoyed reading. They had borrowed many books from Mr. Moorhouse's collection and were well able to hold up their ends of the conversation with those next to whom they were seated. Those gentlemen consisted of the Harworth sons as well as Major Stoner. While Daphne had invited Mr. Harworth from a sense of her duty to the holder of the living in the gift of Hillcrest Grange, she had also had in mind that a widowed clergyman might be just the match for the widow of another one. Mrs. Bush fitted that description. The fact that there seemed to be an immediate attraction among their offspring was a bonus. Daphne was never above a bit of matchmaking whenever she had people whom she thought were in need of spouses. It quite pleased her that, when the ladies withdrew, she was immediately quizzed about what she knew about the inhabitants of the vicarage of St. Mary Minor. The fact that she knew little did not prevent a lively conversation continuing, based purely on speculation and rehashing of the little amount of information that had been gleaned already about the three Harworth men.

Discussion in the dining room concerned subjects that the ladies would undoubtedly have considered more frivolous than those taken up in the drawing room. Justice Amery was particularly interested in the discoveries about smuggling in the neighborhood and grilled Major Stoner about what he had found out about Harksmouth.

"I knew that corruption in the customs-house service was endemic, but this is a clear indication of the scale to which it must exist in Harksmouth," pronounced the judge. "To be able to transship from the vessels bringing in the material on to canal boats indicates that the customs officials are being paid to look the other way. And with suppliers of various goods being involved, so that they cannot all be brought in on the same ship, there must be warehouses of some sort where they can 'hide' the goods. Everyone in the vicinity is bound to know what is going on."

"I hadn't thought of it," said the Major, "but I can see where you must be right."

"You mentioned, Major, that you suspected that the local revenue officers here might not be completely honest."

"Yes, I suppose I did. I don't see how Mr. Baxter and his assistants could be so unaware of what was going on, while also he seems to have a very good idea of what prices the smuggled goods command in this area."

"You also indicated that he suggested the terms that he would expect from Lady Ashton if she were to pay the duty."

"Yes, I don't remember all the details, but I do recollect him saying that the duty on brandy is one pound, one shilling, nine pence, three farthings. He would expect a ten percent commission so he would be charging Lady Ashton one pound, four shillings. It stuck in my mind since I thought the commission rather high, though I confess that I pay quite a bit more than that for my spirits."

"You are quite right. Mr. Baxter seems to have added five shillings to the duty which is, in fact, sixteen shillings, ninepence, three farthings. I remember it because it is such an odd figure. Mr. Baxter also is not supposed to take an extra commission. Trying to extort extra money is illegal in these circumstances. I wonder how we can trap him so that he can be brought to trial."

The conversation then turned to how to discover what was the situation in Harksmouth. They needed to learn how the goods were brought into the port. Furthermore, Mr. Justice Amery pointed out that they should try to find out how the customs-house officials in Harksmouth were involved. He thought he could arrange help there, and stressed that his interest was two-fold. First to punish the offenders and second to ensure that smuggling did not re-emerge with a new set of officials.

"We'll have to make sure that those behind the present activities in addition to the customs officials are arrested and punished. It should not be as hard to curtail the business as it is in places where the customs officials are not so corrupt. Usually, there is an army of men involved in getting the containers carried from the beaches or other landing places to wherever they can be hidden or sent on their way. Those people have been known to take violent exception to having their livelihoods compromised by zealous law enforcement."

When the gentlemen rejoined the ladies in the drawing room, separate groups formed. The younger members seemed to find much to discuss when they were away from their elders. Mrs. Bush and Mr. Harworth had a great many anecdotes to exchange of experiences arising from living in a parsonage. As always, Lady Marianne and Major Stoner found new subjects requiring comment that had arisen since their last meeting. Mr. Moorhouse, Captain Bush, and Justice Amery formed a separate group with Daphne and Catherine, but before they had even found a topic of conversation, Justice Amery indicated that he had some matters to discuss with Daphne separately.

"Lady Ashton," the judge began, "I hope that you can help me with Mr. Baxter and the other customs officials."

"In what way can I be of assistance, my lord? I have realized that the smuggling here could only have been so extensive if the officials deliberately looked the other way."

"Yes, I am sure of it, but it will be very difficult to prove. Fortunately, I think the discussion while the gentlemen were enjoying our port suggested a way in which they might be brought to justice. I will, however, need your help to implement it."

"Yes? I will be quite willing to do what I can. Indeed, you may know that Captain Giles is backing Major Stoner in a venture to establish a legal trade in the items that in the past have only been available here from smugglers. It would help if we could count on the revenue officials to deal properly with smuggling attempts."

"Major Stoner mentioned that Mr. Baxter would be charging you with duties on the goods found at Hillcrest Grange before he can release them so that you can sell them. He would also be charging a commission of ten percent, the Major said."

"Yes, that is indeed what Mr. Baxter suggested could occur when he has completed his inventory of the goods in question."

"Furthermore, he mentioned that the duty on brandy would be over twenty-one shillings a gallon."

"I think so. I don't remember the exact figure, but I do remember that it was over a pound and also involved farthings. Exactly how many has slipped my mind. How is that number relevant to unmasking Mr. Baxter as a criminal?"

"There are two aspects to it. First, as an officer of the Crown, Mr. Baxter is not allowed to charge a commission, though it is known that a commission of two percent or less would not lead to trouble. Much more importantly, the duty on brandy is only a small amount over sixteen pounds. Mr. Baxter might have made a mistake, but I imagine that he did not and will report that the goods were transferred to you at lower rates of duty than he is going to charge you. That is a serious crime, especially for such a large sum, for it is defrauding the Crown, not just yourself."

"Good heavens! I would never have thought to check that the rates that Mr. Baxter was quoting were not the correct ones."

"What I am suggesting is that you get a signed bill of sale from Mr. Baxter stating the basis of his calculations. It should also clearly state the ten-percent commission."

"Yes, I would do that in any case. I can insist if Mr. Baxter is reluctant on the grounds that I have to report any such transactions to Captain Giles, even though he has authorized me to complete such matters without his explicit consent."

"I know, even though it is so very unusual. Generally, men in Captain Giles's position arrange that their affairs will be managed in detail by a male agent rather than by their wives. Of course, I realize that you are not the typical wife."

"More to the point, Captain Giles is not the typical husband. But how would having the bill of sale help to trap Mr. Baxter?"

"I would like you to make a copy for your records or to send to Captain Giles, or whatever you would do with the document, and let me have the signed copy. Mr. Baxter will have to submit a record when he turns in the money he will claim to have collected as duty. The figures will not agree with those in his bill of sale, and he will be caught trying to defraud the government. Incidentally, the government will reimburse you for the overcharge, whether or not the excess sums taken by Mr. Baxter are recovered or not."

"That is reassuring. But it is not crucial. I have decided to buy the materials at the price quoted by Mr. Baxter, so, from my point of view, it is just a windfall. I will be happy to go along with your scheme and hope that you succeed."

When Daphne and Justice Amery returned to the more general group, she suggested that it would be pleasant if they had some music. All the ladies played or sang, with varying levels of accomplishment, and Daphne thought that with three unattached men such an activity could only help with her vague match-making endeavors. She also enjoyed playing for company and was happy to provide herself with an opportunity. How Captain Giles would tease her about her match-making. He had already observed how she, who had claimed that she wanted never to marry, was quite eager to help others to do so. She had to admit that the married state certainly suited her, as did the maternal one. Daphne was tired out by the evening. However, on her way to bed, she found time to peek into Bernard's nursery to see that he was sleeping soundly. She wished that Giles was there to see his son with her.

Chapter XV

The schemes that Daphne and Mr. Justice Amery had devised worked smoothly. Mr. Baxter did indeed present a long list of the items that he had cataloged, with duties that had to be paid on each of them together with the basis of the assessment. He even included in the document a summary of what was owed as the commission which he required to release the goods. The evidence of the guilt of the revenue agent was clear.

The parish constable had already been alerted that he would be needed, and Mr. Justice Amery and Major Stoner had arranged for some dragoons to be behind the stables at Dipton Hall at the critical time. One of the recently appointed magistrates was enjoying the hospitality of Dipton Hall in the drawing room. He was joined by the revenue officer for Ameschester, a Mr. Worthington, whose appointment had not been revealed to Mr. Baxter as yet. They were enjoying the hospitality of Dipton Hall in the drawing room just at the time when Daphne was completing her transaction with Mr. Baxter.

When the signed paper had been exchanged for a bill of exchange drawn on the Ameschester Bank, Daphne rang the bell for Steves. However, the summons was not answered by the butler. Instead, the magistrate and the new revenue agent came, accompanied by the parish constable who had been waiting in the servants' hall. Mr. Baxter was arrested and taken to Ameschester jail. The new revenue agent returned to Daphne the bill of exchange she had given Mr. Baxter, and she was happy to issue him a bank draft for the correct amount. Mr. Worthington, of course, got no commission since that would be illegal, but Daphne did indicate that she would like to consult with him about how best to make sure that any further shipments had had their taxes paid properly and how to keep smuggling at bay. However, Mr. Worthington would be given an honorarium for such service since it was beyond his duties speaking strictly.

Major Stoner set out immediately to make sure that the various warehouses of Hillcrest Grange were emptied. He started with the dressmaking and millenary supplies which were so desperately needed to assure that the ladies of the region could be ready for The Baron de Roy's ball which was rapidly approaching. Daphne took advantage of the visits of several ladies to spread the word that Major Stoner had only undertaken the task of having the goods sold in order to make sure that the inconveniences caused by the end of the smuggling ring would not impact more than was absolutely necessary on the preparations for the special event. This way of looking at the Major's role in distributing the goods completely changed people's appreciation of the Major's endeavors. It turned what would normally be considered a very demeaning undertaking into an act of public benevolence.

The Baron de Roy was the only nobleman in the vicinity of Dipton Hall, other than Giles himself. His title was of ancient origin, and his residence, Besterdale House was on an artificial island with a moat around it, though the medieval battlements had been torn down a long time ago. The house was said to be quite comfortable though in an old-fashioned way.

All this information had come to Daphne from the gossip of others. Baron de Roy's estate was quite a long distance from Dipton Hall as measured by roads that carriages could use, though it was much closer by paths suitable only for horses or on foot. He had been widowed almost two years previously and had been a recluse since then. Daphne had seen him at recent meetings of the Ameschester Hunt, but otherwise scarcely knew him. It was only following her marriage to Giles that she could be considered to be in the same social strata as he was, and no reason for their meeting had as yet occurred.

The occasion for the ball was Baron de Roy's youngest daughter's coming out. He had habitually avoided his duties in the House of Lords and had little general influence in the county, while over time the holdings of his estate had diminished. As a result, he did not mark the coming out of his daughter by taking part in the London season. Instead, he was celebrating the occasion with a ball at his estate. The news that he was ending the period of mourning for his wife had set tongues wagging in the parlors and drawing rooms of the region. Not only did it indicate that his daughter was officially taking her place as a marriageable young lady, though it was rumored that her dowry would not be significant, but also because the Baron was now on the list of highly eligible gentlemen.

The ladies of Dipton Manor were all determined to attend the ball, so Major Stoner was pressed into service to accompany them since they could hardly go without a male escort. He had been dreading the event, for he was sensitive to being snubbed by those who felt he was beneath their notice, a fear that was enhanced by his recent endeavors in disposing of Daphne's smuggling loot. He was overjoyed to find that he was being lionized as the gentleman who had stepped into the breach opened when the supplies so necessary for a successful ball had been seized by the Revenue Service. Instead of being regarded as a stepped-up shopkeeper, as he had feared, he was considered to be someone who had taken a successful and vital leadership role, most certainly exactly what might be expected of a prominent gentleman. Although he knew that the credit should go to Daphne, he had no objection to taking it himself, especially as he knew that Daphne would prefer that her role in the events be minimized. For the first time, Lady Marianne began to think that possibly, in accepting the Major's proposal, she had not reduced her own status significantly. Indeed, the Major was being shown more respect than her late husband had ever earned for himself.

As always at balls, there was a distinct shortage of men who wanted to dance with the ladies, particularly the ones who were already married or committed to matrimony. More gentlemen than ladies were drawn to the card rooms or to talking in groups entirely ignoring the dancing that was happening. As a result, Daphne spoke with a more extensive circle of women than just those with whom she exchanged visits. However, she also received more than her share of invitations to dance, which surprised her as she was aware of her reputation as an independent woman with definite ideas of her own, not one who would want to spend a dance just admiring the views of her partner. One of the daring ones was Baron de Roy, who must have regarded her as a safe choice in the sea of single women for whom he would be a great catch.

Daphne's other frequent partner was Captain Bush, who despite having only one leg and one arm enjoyed dancing and, to the undoubted frustration of the many ladies who thought that they were the ideal mate for the war hero, asked either Daphne or Catherine Crocker to dance. Daphne spent some of the time while dancing with him lecturing him about how it was his duty to dance with other ladies, but to no avail. He ignored her suggestions until Baron de Roy brought his daughter, in whose honor the ball was being held, to meet Daphne. That occurred just as Captain Bush was approaching her for another dance.

"Lady Ashton," said Baron de Roy, "may I introduce my daughter Penelope?"

"Delighted, Miss de Roy. Your father is providing a splendid way to present you to society. Miss de Roy and My Lord, may I introduce Captain Tobias Bush? He has long been an associate of my husband. Captain Bush, this is The Baron de Roy and his daughter Miss de Roy."

"Oh, Captain Bush, you must be the hero about whom there were such glowing reports in the papers," Penelope squealed. "How brave you were, and how brave to have surmounted your wounds so well!"

"Yes, indeed, Captain Bush," added the Baron. "We are very proud to have such a famous sailor in our neighborhood, one who has given so much for his country. I was amazed to see you dancing just now. Your overcoming so staunchly the personal costs of your service is an inspiration to us all."

"Thank you, my Lord. Miss de Roy, do you have any places on your dance card?"

"Yes, I do, Captain Bush."

The two stepped aside to discuss any empty spots among the dances to which she was already committed.

"I am afraid, Lady Ashton, that the ball has not been quite the success that I anticipated," Baron de Roy took up the conversation with Daphne.

"Why not, my Lord? Everyone has been having a good time."

"Quite right, but I am afraid that I did not think of the implications of having it at this time. My wife, my late wife, would have known better. So many of the young men are away in London or elsewhere that there are not as many as I am sure my daughter had hoped there would be, and many of those who are here seem to be a bit intimidated by her being a peer's daughter. I probably should have arranged to participate in the London season, but I do hate life in the capital, and I detest the House of Lords. I am afraid I have been very remiss in taking my seat in the House, so my London acquaintances are not extensive. I am so glad that Captain Bush has asked her to dance. I must say, he is remarkably agile for a man with his handicaps."

"Yes, he doesn't let them stand in his way more than is necessary. I thought he would leave the sea when I first met him, soon after he sustained his wounds, but my husband had little problem persuading him to take command of a frigate when he had recovered. He is now waiting for his next ship, I believe, and then I would not be surprised if he were off again. He is very shy, though one would not expect it in a hero, and he has yet to make a large number of true friends here. Of course, he is unmarried. I had hoped that his finding a wife might make him less keen to do more than his duty. His recent service in the North Sea has made him a rich man, I know."

Daphne's conversation with Baron de Roy then turned to other matters, but before he took his leave to attend to other guests, he suggested that they should see more of each other as leading landowners in the area.

To Daphne's surprise, Captain Bush seemed to have captured Penelope's imagination. Not only did he dance with her twice, but when supper came, he was the one whom she chose to take her into the supper room. Daphne had been wondering about finding a suitable mate for Captain Bush. Connection with a peer, even a minor one, could not hurt his career and the fact that Miss Penelope was not used to London society might well increase the chances of keeping Captain Bush near Dipton, as Daphne wished.

Daphne noticed that the romantic connection between the Harworth and the Bush families seemed to be progressing smoothly. Mr. Harworth and Mrs. Bush had spent quite a bit of time chatting with each other while each of the young Harworth men had danced several dances with Captain Bush's sisters. In each case, the gentlemen had taken the ladies into supper. It was really quite satisfactory how things were working out. By the time that the party from Dipton had to leave, Daphne was well satisfied both with her own enjoyment of the ball and with the advances that seemed to have occurred in her match-making endeavors.

On the day following the ball, Major Stoner left to go to Harksmouth to gather information about the smuggling. It spoke highly of his interest in establishing an alternative source for the luxuries and even necessities which were now not available in Ameschester that he would miss the next meeting of the Ameschester Hunt. Of course, the stockpile at Hillcrest Grange would not last very long, and Daphne and the Major had agreed that it would be easier to run their venture if an alternative group of smugglers did not emerge to start providing contraband material before Daphne's duty-paid items cornered the market.

Daphne's first task after the ball was to interview some estate managers whom Mr. Edwards had recommended. She was lucky. The second candidate turned out to be ideal for her father's estate which Daphne had been managing since before her marriage. The new manager would take over the day-to-day running of the estate that had become a burden to her, though she would continue to visit the tenants, whom she still regarded as being her friends despite her rapid rise in the social pecking order. The candidate was a Mr. James Harvey, the third son of a prosperous landowner in the next county, who had become interested in estate management rather than one of the more usual professions such as the bar or the church. Daphne liked him from the minute she met him and found that he was well acquainted with the problems, possibilities, and pitfalls of adopting modern ideas of how to use the land.

The real find of the morning, however, was a Mr. Henry Drew. His name had been included in the men recommended by Mr. Edwards because he knew about forest management and Giles's prize agent thought he might be useful at Hillcrest Grange. Mr. Drew was not the son of a gentleman. Instead, he was the offspring of a tenant farmer. He had had considerable experience in the New Forest in managing a large area of woodland, but his services there were no longer needed since the owner had decided to cut down all the oaks, mature, nearly mature or too young, willy-nilly, because of the fierce demand for timber for shipbuilding. When that had been done, the owner had no more need for anyone other than a gamekeeper for his woods.

Daphne was impressed because Mr. Drew had already had a look at Hillcrest Grange before he came to see Daphne and had definite views about what needed to be done both regarding harvesting timber which had been allowed to grow too old and in terms of maintaining a healthy forest. Mr. Drew was more than ready to do what was required to manage both the felling and the transport of timber. Daphne engaged him as soon as she realized that he would be removing most of the management of Hillcrest Grange from her shoulders and at the same time turning it into a productive addition to Giles's holdings.

When Mr. Drew had left, Daphne leaned back in her chair, contemplating how much less time would be required to manage the estates as a result of her morning's work. That satisfaction was emphasized by Nanny Weaver's coming to tell her that Master Bernard had crawled for the first time when he had been placed on his blanket on the floor of the nursery. When Daphne rose in great excitement to see this phenomenon, Nanny Weaver told Daphne that she would have to wait until the baby was awake again in the afternoon.

After luncheon, Daphne took some time for herself by having her hunter, Serene Masham, saddled. She could exercise him herself. The Ameschester Hunt was to meet in a few days, and she wanted to make sure that she was comfortable on horseback after all the time spent on other matters. However, she did not want to miss the chance to see her son's latest achievement, so she turned for home after an unusually short ride. When she arrived at Dipton Hall, she went immediately to the nursery without changing from her riding clothes. Bernard, much to her frustration, seemed to be much more interested in his feet than in becoming mobile when he was placed on the floor, though he did at least roll over for his mother. Her talk with Nanny Weaver about his amazing progress was cut short by the sound of a carriage in the driveway.

Looking out the nursery window, Daphne saw a coach pull up to the portico. She immediately recognized the man getting out of it. Giles was back!

In the past, Daphne had always rushed to Giles to embrace him warmly when he returned, a performance that had caused much secret amusement among the servants. This time, however, she was carrying Bernard. She descended the stairs sedately so that Giles had already handed his hat and gloves to Steves before seeing her.

"Lady Ashton," he intoned as he bowed formally, though there was a bright sparkle in his eye as he did so.

"Captain Giles," she replied while curtseying, completing the ceremony. "Welcome home."

That was as far as propriety could hold her. "Oh, Richard, it is so good to have you home! Why are you here? Has something happened to *Glaucus*? Did you get any of my letters? Oh, I am so keen to tell you everything that has happened! This is so wonderful!"

"Easy does it, Daphne. I'm here for a few days, and we can get all caught up together. I almost didn't recognize Bernard; he has grown so much!"

Giles had little experience with small children, and he seemed to be afraid of babies, even though he had spent a bit of time observing Bernard when last he had been home. He was visibly relieved when Nanny Weaver stepped forward to take Bernard from his mother's arms.

"I've been riding," said Daphne. "I need to change my clothes, and you probably want to as well, Richard."

Changing clothes was only one of the things that Daphne and Giles did while they were upstairs. Daphne learned the essence of what Giles had been doing, though dragging out of him the details of the battle that had led to the rescue of so many sailors had taken persistence on her part. She filled Giles in on the important things that had been taking place at Dipton. The mail packets with her letters on board had not found *Glaucus* for some time, so Giles also was not aware of the events at Dipton which had occurred after he had last departed. He was amazed that Daphne had succeeded in acquiring and disposing of all the smuggled goods. While he had been on *Glaucus,* he had sometimes reflected that he had no idea of how to deal with that problem. He had also lost all trust in Mr. Baxter based on what little he had seen of him and would not have liked to entrust the materials to him, but he knew of no alternative. Daphne's other enterprises also filled him with amazement. Even if he had been at Dipton, he doubted that he would already have had work started on the kennels so quickly, or even have decided what their design should be. Would he have found out that the timber of Hillcrest Grange made it a reason to purchase the property quite apart from the justifications that he and Daphne had used to persuade themselves that they must have it? He realized with great admiration that his wife was as capable of commanding in her sphere as he was in his.

Dinner was delayed by an hour that evening, for which the cook, Mrs. Darling was thankful. With only the three resident ladies expected for dinner, none of whom had large appetites; her planned meal had been a modest affair. That would not do when the master of the house returned from sea, even though Giles was not renowned as a trencherman. She kept Steves and the footmen busy with dish after dish, in such quantities that the next day a veritable feast was served in the servants' hall.

Conversation at dinner was dominated by one subject: Catherine's wedding to Captain Bolton. No sooner had they sat down than Giles mentioned to his niece that her fiancé would be arriving shortly and would have at least a couple of weeks to spend while his ship was being repaired. He knew that Captain Bolton would be more than happy to marry her on this occasion provided that she was ready for the event. Her fiancé would, of course, have to return to sea again as soon as his ship was repaired. That was just the nature of service in the Navy.

Catherine was overjoyed to hear the news. All the preparations for the event had been lined up. She knew when Lord David, who was her other uncle and whom she had asked to conduct her marriage ceremony, would be in Dipton. She even had made arrangements that his curate, Mr. Fisher, would be available should Lord David be required to be in London at the time. The other people who, Catherine thought, were critical to have at her wedding were Captain Bolton's parents, who lived in Norfolk, and her grandmother, Clara, Countess of Camshire. Giles was not surprised that the people whom Catherine wanted to have at her wedding did not include her grandfather, the Earl of Camshire, or any relations from the Crocker side of the family.

The principal delay in holding the wedding would come from the time needed to allow the Reverend Mr. Bolton and Mrs. Bolton to come from Norfolk. Catherine had yet to meet them, but she had already started a correspondence in which Mrs. Bolton promised to leave for Dipton as soon as news arrived about when the critical day would be. Realistically, five days had to be allowed for that journey in winter. Catherine had already persuaded Daphne to permit Geoffreys, a groom at Dipton who had formerly been a cavalryman, to ride to Norfolk as quickly as possible. The note was already written. All it needed was the addition of the date of the happy event. The party agreed that it would be possible to hold the wedding eight days later. Could Giles stay that long so that he could give Catherine away? If he couldn't remain at Dipton for such a long time, then Captain Bolton's parents would have to miss the ceremony which would be moved forward so that Giles could play his allotted role. He agreed that he could stretch his time at Dipton Hall as required, so the starting gun for the final preparations for the wedding was fired when the ladies withdrew at the end of dinner.

The next few days were hectic for Giles and Daphne. They crammed as much activity as possible into the short time before Giles had to leave again. The first morning they took their hunters, Serene Masham and Dark Paul on a tour of their properties. Dark Paul had a nasty tendency to try to throw his riders. Giles wanted to make sure that the horse would remember that Giles had established his mastery before the stallion attempted any of his tricks at the hunt the next day. Dark Paul wasn't above seeing if his rider had forgotten his deplorable tendencies. Giles and the horse had a breakneck gallop across the winter fields, jumping hedges as they appeared and scooting under low hanging branches before the horse fully appreciated that he would have to go where his rider dictated. Any attempts to unseat his rider had consequences for Dark Paul that were more unpleasant than they were for Giles. During this mad dash across the lands of Dipton Hall, Serene Masham carried Daphne in a no-fuss manner, letting her mistress find the best way of navigating the course and, by taking shortcuts, keeping up with the madly careening Dark Paul whom Giles forced to maintain a wild gallop even as the horse tired.

After Dark Paul had been forced to admit who was in charge, Daphne and Giles proceeded to examine the grounds for the kennels and the work done there and then continued on to Hillcrest Grange. Giles had not had time to explore the property thoroughly before he had had to go to sea and he had not received Daphne's letters detailing all that had happened. He was amazed to see how much had been accomplished, starting with the turning of the track joining Hillcrest Grange to Dipton into a road suitable for carriage travel and the emptying of the many storehouses that had been hidden in the woods.

Giles wasn't quite sure, even as Daphne's described them, just what changes were being undertaken to the house. He could hardly tell Daphne that, but she realized that she was not entirely clear about what was involved. Catherine's sketches would clarify things, she said. Giles, she discovered, was much more interested in the woods and the prospect of being able to sell some of the timber than in exactly what would be done to the house. From his experience in the navy, he knew how crucial was the quality of wood used in shipbuilding, but he had never thought about where it came from or how it was grown. He privately resolved to learn more about forestry, just as he had about agriculture. There must be books on the subject which he could study when next he went to sea.

Daphne and Giles finished their exploration by going to the canal landing that Daphne had discovered. Here Giles's interest was much greater than Daphne's had been. He realized that it should be improved if it was to be used more and it was undoubtedly the best place from which to transport the timbers that would be cut from the woods at Hillcrest Grange. Using the canal dock could also reduce some of the expenses involved in shipping corn from the area. That would be of benefit not only to the farmers but also to the coffers of Hillcrest Grange.

Giles insisted on plunging into the thicket that separated the landing from the main branch of the river to see whether a towpath could be developed to ease getting barges to this landing place. Daphne could not help laughing when he tripped over a surface root and fell into a mudhole. It was a sodden and grimy husband who remounted Dark Paul muttering words beneath his breath that would not be at all suitable in the drawing room.

They arrived back at Dipton Hall late in the afternoon with Giles still out of sorts from his mishap. A good scrubbing of his face and hands, followed by clean clothes restored his sunny mood, luckily since Daphne had learned that Bernard was awake in the nursery and a visit would be very suitable. She insisted that Giles join her and that he also get down on the floor to be at the same level as his son. Daphne had been reflecting on Giles's reaction to his son on the previous day and was resolved that she would try to wean him from his dislike of actually being a father instead of just being proud of having an heir. She knew both from Giles's mother and from Giles himself that his father had never shown any interest in or affection for his younger sons, quite unlike her own father who had been intimately involved in her life for as long as she could remember. She was determined that her husband should follow more nearly the pattern of her father rather than the one which her lady-visitors told her was the usual behavior of their husbands. On this occasion, she was rewarded by Giles, after several long minutes of looking very uncomfortable staring at his son, starting to make faces at him. This delighted Bernard, and his evident pleasure inspired his father to be even more daring so that in the end Bernard was gripping his father's index finger and trying to put it in his mouth. Daphne suppressed her urge to praise Giles for playing with his son, which would only embarrass him for engaging in such an unmanly activity, and she resolved not to mention it to others, at least not in Giles's presence. She had heard from her visitors that such behavior might be ridiculed by their husbands who might think it was unbecoming to a man.

The following day brought the meeting of the Ameschester Hunt. It was greeted with clear weather though cold. Giles and Daphne rode together and were among the few riders who were in at the kill. That evening, Daphne insisted that Giles go to the hunt dinner, even though both of them would have preferred to dine at home. Giles was now too important a landowner in the community that his absence would not have been noted, and many of the other men in the Hunt would feel insulted if he forwent the pleasure of their company. Appreciating that the local, famous hero welcomed their acquaintance and was part of the community of the men of the hunt would, Daphne realized, smooth the way for acceptance of his progressive ideas about many issues.

Much of the following day Giles spent visiting other men in the neighborhood. His younger brother, Lord David, the vicar of Dipton, was one, and Captain Bush, his former first lieutenant, was another. A third was his father-in-law, Mr. Moorhead. However, the one he spent the most time with was Mr. Griffiths, his stable master. There was little progress to report about the stud farm for it was a long-term project that had been fully planned and implemented before Giles had left Dipton to rejoin his ship. However, they could happily engage in discussion of racing and bloodlines and such matters. Mr. Griffiths remained adamant that Dipton Hall had no land suitable for a training race-course and therefore a racing stud would not make sense, quite apart from its being very expensive. But steeple-chase participation, at least in the older sense of being a cross-country race rather than one on a specially developed, artificial course might well be feasible. Of their present horses, Dark Paul might be a good prospect as a racer, though he would have to be ridden by someone who had already established who was in command. Giles was amused as Mr. Griffiths skirted around the fact that while Giles was the obvious person to control the hunter, he was also a very substantial man, which would slow the horse in a race. While Giles was not fat, he was tall and stocky, and his weight would be a handicap. Maybe they should breed Dark Paul with the objective of producing fast horses. The best mare among their present holdings to use would be Daphne's Serene Masham, but both of the men agreed that it was unlikely that she would consent to having her hunter be pregnant during the hunting season.

Giles returned to the house to discover that Daphne was with Bernard. Somewhat to his surprise, he realized that he would enjoy seeing his child again. Daphne was just as surprised when he entered the nursery and sank down onto the floor to be closer to him. His presence gave her hope that one of her keenest, though secret, desires might be fulfilled.

Daphne had known when she agreed to marry Giles that he would be away for long periods of time as a ship's captain. She had been sure that, just like other women she knew, the parting would not be unbearable once the initial excitement of marriage had settled down. Indeed, she knew that many of the ladies who visited her were envious of her not having her husband around all the time. But she was finding that she missed him more and more when he was away, even though she had been lucky in that his absences had been short compared to those of most seamen. Next time he might be away for months and months, even years and years, if he were sent to the West Indies or India. Could she endure that? She couldn't tell Giles her feelings on this subject; she knew that he regarded his service to the country as urgently needed in this time of peril from Napoleon. She also knew that, as a result of his growing reputation and wealth, he might be able to select his service so that he could be at Dipton more frequently. Dare she hint that to him?

Chapter XVI

Major Stoner returned to Dipton the next morning. His trip to Harksmouth had yielded some information, and he was bursting to tell Daphne about what he had discovered.

He had taken a room in an inn on the harbor in Harksmouth and settled into a place in the public bar with a view of the dock. He let it be known that he had recently returned from India with money which he was interested in investing in something that would give a better return than consols. It would not take long for the news that he had money to spend, he reckoned, and he might well be approached to fund smuggling ventures or otherwise get involved in the trade. While waiting, he was in an excellent position to observe what was occurring on the quay. The Major was a naturally convivial sort of person, so he had had little trouble striking up conversations with other idlers at the inn. He found out from them enough to be able to piece together the significance of what he was observing.

The Major had noticed several canal barges waiting a little way farther along the dock from the inn. No one was around them, and he wondered why they were idle. A one-legged old man, whom the major guessed spent much of his time in the inn, explained that the barges were awaiting cargo that would arrive on the quay soon. It would then be loaded onto them for transport up the river. When the Major showed surprise about this news, since it was evident from the grime on them that the barges were used to transport coal, the old idler put one finger to his nose. He said, in tones that indicated he was conveying a great secret, that the coal was loaded on top of the other cargo to protect it from danger, 'if you know what I mean.'

As the Major started to wonder how he could advance his cause more effectively than by sitting drinking the pub's best bitter and chatting with others who had no better use for their time, activity began on the dock. First, a ship came into view approaching the dock very slowly for the wind was light. His informant, whose name the Major had learned was Davie, told him that the vessel was a lugger, named the *Ruddy Fox,* which would quite possibly have visited France. This was more like what he had hoped to see!

"Did you say the *Ruddy Fox*, Major?" Giles asked. "She was among the ships I caught on my last voyage. So Harksmouth was where she was taking her cargo."

The Major resumed his tale after this interruption. The next development was the arrival of a man, dressed not for dock work but as an office holder, accompanied by two minions. He strode determinately up the quay towards the ship. Major Stoner had been intrigued by what might happen and, using the excuse that the sun on the lounge's windows was making the room stuffy, opened the casement so that he might hear better. His informant told the Major that the man approaching the ship was the chief revenue officer for the port. Davie added that something must be wrong for he was arriving too soon after the arrival of the ship.

As the tax official approached the lugger, a burly man with a white beard came on deck. He must have been the captain of the lugger since he was addressed as "Captain Creasey." A verbal dispute broke out between the two, the officer demanding to be let on board to examine the cargo and the captain claiming that he had come too soon and the official would have to get permission from the owner before he could board. After a few minutes of arguing about this, the captain summoned a lad and told him to get a Mr. Shockley. Major Stoner's drinking companion informed him that Mr. Shockley was a property owner whose buildings included a stable, a couple of warehouses and even the pub where they were drinking.

The lad returned with a well-dressed man who tried to take charge of the situation. To the Major's delight, he and the offical were soon shouting about an arrangement where the revenue officers were supposed to wait for a while after a vessel had docked before going on board to examine the cargo and impose any duties that were owed. The chief revenue officer did not contradict the property owner, but he said loudly that he was not being paid what was owed him under the agreement. He knew that more was being brought in than was being reported to him unofficially and he was not getting his fair share for looking the other way. Mr. Shockley retorted that those payments were not decided by himself and that the man should take it up with someone Mr. Shockley referred to as "the organizer." Apparently, that wasn't good enough for the revenue officer. If the problem were not sorted out immediately, he would board the vessel and if he found any contraband seize it until the full duty was paid.

The two men seemed to realize that it might not be wise to hold this discussion in public at the top of their voices. Also, they needed to get "the organizer" to come to settle the dispute. The lad was sent off to bring him, and the two combatants sat down at a table in the pub. They were quite close to Major Stoner. He was far too sly a fox to look at them, or show other interest in their conversation. Also, he boasted, he put his hand to his ear whenever his companion made a remark so that any observer would think him to be deaf. Whether or not as a result of his playacting, he was able to follow the conversation smuggler and the revenue officer perfectly.

The result of the Major's subterfuge was more information. He discovered that the local pattern was for the revenue officer to be warned when a shipment was due and told to keep away from the dock until any contraband had been moved. Movement, the Major suspected, involved shifting the material to the canal barges and covering them so that the contraband could not be seen. The revenue officer was then informed that the vessel contained some goods on which duty should be paid. The revenue officer made quite a production of calculating the sum involved, which Mr. Shockley paid and obtained a receipt. He failed to follow the prescribed script of their little play when he protested that he was not involved in determining how much the revenue officer received for his cooperation. He was just the person who transmitted the funds.

Major Stoner could not believe how much he was learning. He stayed in place even after the nearby conversation turned to other matters, getting himself another pint of bitter to justify remaining where he was and treating his companion to one as well. It took a while before anything further happened. Major Stoner suspected that "the organizer" must not be close at hand judging by the delay before he showed up. It was more than an hour later that he entered the lounge.

The newcomer was well dressed in clothes of fashionable cut. He appeared to be a prosperous gentleman, probably unused to being summoned to a waterfront inn. There was no doubt that he was annoyed at being called to deal with the problem, berating both Mr. Shockley and the revenue officer for requiring him to resolve their dispute. To Major Stoner's delight, he did not lower his voice. The major's companion informed him that the man, who must be 'the organizer,' was Sir Winthrop Shorthouse, a prominent landowner in the district, well known for having made numerous improvements to his estate which was close to Harksmouth.

Sir Winthrop was highly annoyed at being dragged into the dispute. He berated the revenue officer for not coming to him directly and for making a fuss on the dock. The official, however, stood his ground maintaining that he was owed more than was reckoned and that previously Sir Winthrop had refused to discuss the matter with him. He had watched what was unloaded in the past and knew that it was more than he was being credited with. This claim led to Sir Winthrop pointing out that the officer was already in so deep that he couldn't get out of his situation by stopping and any attempt to do so would result in his arrest.

Furthermore, the official's argument did not take account of the losses that happened to the cargos after being put on the barges. Why, only recently a whole barge load had been seized in Ameschester, and other goods hidden there had been taken. Sir Winthrop was trying to make more expensive arrangements at that town to continue supplying the area. In addition, customs officials elsewhere were demanding, and being paid, more. Sir Winthrop's letting the last fact slip opened the way to the revenue man arguing that it just proved that he should receive more too. Finally, Sir Winthrop agreed to pay the revenue agent an additional half-pence a gallon on spirits brought in. They could talk about other goods later, but, for now, they had to get the *Ruddy Fox* unloaded.

When the dispute ended, the three men left the inn and walked away in the opposite direction. Just before they disappeared from sight, Mr. Shockley blew a whistle. Suddenly there was activity. Navvies* appeared from various directions. Davie helpfully explained that they were laborers doing a variety of chores for Mr. Shockley. Their real job was to be available when the whistle blew to unload ships as quickly as possible. Other men appeared on the barges and threw off the canvas tarpaulins covering the cargo compartments. On the *Ruddy Fox*, the captain had the hatch boards removed. The workmen were soon lugging tubs that must have contained liquor from the ship to the barges, with each load's destination being read off by Mr. Shockley from a list he kept consulting.

It took only half an hour of frantic labor to complete the unloading. The navvies melted away. Mr. Shockley had disappeared sometime earlier. The scene returned to its picture of placid inactivity. Then, down the quay came the revenue officer accompanied by Mr. Shockley and another man who Davie said was the town constable. They were followed by a horse-drawn wagon. The group marched up to the *Ruddy Fox*, where they were welcomed aboard by the captain and disappeared into the hold. Soon they reappeared. Mr. Shockley gave a small purse to the revenue man in exchange for a piece of paper, and they shook hands before disembarking from the vessel. The crew of the *Ruddy Fox* hoisted one barrel out of the hold and placed it on the cart. Soon another one appeared. That apparently was the whole load. The wagon departed, and the sailors replaced the hatch boards. They then untied the ship, poled her away from the quay while raising the sails and off she sailed. The wharf returned to its original somnolence.

Davie told Major Stoner that the unloading had been much slower than usual, because of the altercation on the dock. What, the Major wondered, happened when the barges were away when a ship arrived. The answer, according to Davie, was that the goods were taken to the nearby church and stored there until they could be loaded onto the barges. Usually, a ship did not stay more than half an hour at the wharf, and the townsmen all pretended that they had no knowledge of the smuggling. Davie thought it was all a great joke.

Major Stoner stayed the rest of the day in the inn except for a few strolls he took around the town, but he learned nothing more and no one approached him to invest in smuggling or anything else. While returning to Dipton, he stopped at a couple of the larger towns on the canal, but all he discovered was that the ale tasted different in different locations.

Daphne and Major Stoner realized that they were at an impasse. Daphne had thought that all they would need to discover was how the canal barge got loaded and then fill it themselves with goods on which the duty had been paid. They had not expected to find such a well organized and extensive operation of which Ameschester's smuggling was only a small part. Giles pointed out that the customs officials were not likely to agree to only charge the material going to Ameschester while letting the rest be handled illegally. They would have to break up the whole smuggling operation at Hawksworth.

That was all well and good, argued Major Stoner, but with the very many tough laborers whom he had seen and who doubtless depended on the work, it would not be simple to destroy the smuggling operation without having a substantial force on hand. Violence was not out of the question as the smugglers' way of dealing with interference. The three of them could not call on nearly large enough forces to combat the smugglers effectively and, in any case, they had no authority to do so.

It was Daphne who came up with a solution to this impasse. She would write to Mr. Justice Amery to ask if he could somehow arrange assistance for them. She would do it immediately so that Giles might at least know what was in the wind before he had to take *Glaucus* to sea again. Before they had a chance to canvass any other actions, they were interrupted by the arrival of the Countess of Camshire.

Lady Camshire had become one of Daphne's favorite guests even though their acquaintance started off very badly. The Countess had not been able to imagine a proper lady who managed estates and could directly supervise the development of the gardens. Daphne regarded the peeress as a useless, ignorant, interfering creature. Lady Camshire had rapidly come to recognize that Daphne was, in fact, a very good match for her son Richard and that visiting Dipton Hall was much more enjoyable than staying on her husband's estate, Ashbury Abbey. Daphne found that Giles's mother had other sides to her character that were more agreeable. Nevertheless, the Countess still wanted everyone to make a fuss when she arrived. This time her hopes were only partially fulfilled. Right behind her carriage came Captain Bolton's, and, as the man of the hour, he stole some of the Countess's thunder. The situation was worsened by Daphne disappearing soon after the guests appeared to write the letter to Mr. Justice Amery and have it given to Griffiths, one of the grooms, to take to London as quickly as possible. Somehow, Daphne forgot to mention to Giles that she had suggested that handling the nautical aspects of converting the smuggling trade to a legitimate one would be greatly aided if her husband could participate.

Daphne had to put aside her concerns about dealing with the smugglers for a time after sending off her plea for help. The arrival of the groom meant that the whirl of activities centered on the coming nuptials became intense. Captain Bush, Mr. Moorhouse, and Lord David were summoned to join the others for luncheon. After that, everyone wanted to see Hillcrest Grange, even though Catherine protested that it was a shambles as the workmen had started on the changes. Everyone agreed to walk rather than take carriages, the Countess, in particular, announcing that she was not so decrepit that she couldn't walk all afternoon if called upon to do so.

Daphne managed to stay behind when the others left, pleading the need to organize dinner and some of the wedding arrangements. It turned out to be just as well that she did. Hardly had the party going to examine Hillcrest Grange left than a carriage with a coat of arms on the door came up the driveway. Daphne had told The Baron de Roy that he and Miss de Roy would be welcome to visit anytime, thinking it not much more than a polite and empty gesture. Now it turned out that the nobleman had taken her up on the suggestion. She could hardly send him off before the others returned or not let it be known that large celebrations were in store. She felt compelled to ask them to stay for dinner, which met the reply that it would be a great pleasure, but, of course, they had brought no suitable clothes. That was a problem easily fixed. Catherine was approximately Miss de Roy's size, and her father's clothes should fit the Baron adequately. So it was decided: two more added to the guest list, two more beds prepared, the cook and Steves warned.

Daphne was elated that the Baron and his daughter had arrived unexpectedly and were able to stay for dinner. The Countess had several times expressed surprise that Daphne's circle of acquaintances included no noblemen and thought that Ameschester was a very deprived area. At least, now, she had one baron to display. Dinner, which was held in the large dining room, was an animated gathering with people keyed up to celebrate the forthcoming nuptials and to put on their most charming faces for the people whom they were meeting for the first time. Needless to say, Daphne arranged for the Baron to take the Countess into dinner. She also selected Captain Bush for The Honorable Penelope de Roy. After the ladies withdrew, the men's conversation turned to the war with the three naval captains peppered with inquiries about the state of the conflict. The topic threatened to occupy a great deal of time even though all three protested that they were as ignorant as any of the others about the grand strategies for the conduct of a war in which not much seemed to be happening. Giles, realizing this, suggested they join the ladies after only a short time, a suggestion which was taken up enthusiastically since, by chance, the company included no heavy drinkers.

The next day saw the arrival of more guests. Two of Captain Bolton's lieutenants came unexpectedly together with all his midshipmen. Captain Bolton's parents arrived late in the day. Much to Daphne's surprise, the Countess took it upon herself to see that they felt at home. They were a rather dowdy pair for Mr. Bolton's parish was not a wealthy one, and they were a bit overwhelmed by Dipton Hall. The Countess was able to draw from them stories about village life in Norfolk. She contributed remarks about her experiences at Ashbury. Daphne had never before realized that the Countess's isolation at Ashbury Abbey, brought on by the Earl's neglect both of his wife and of the necessary expenses of his estate, had driven her to expand her interests and social contacts to the village where she lived. The last visitor was Mr. Justice Amery who came late in the day, having traveled overnight from London in response to Daphne's letter. He, of course, had to be accommodated, though Daphne firmly told him that nothing could be done about smuggling until the wedding was over.

Dinner the next evening was even livelier than on the previous night. This time, after the cover was withdrawn, the conversation turned to smuggling. Everyone knew that it occurred. Many had amusing stories about various aspects of the illicit business. Mr. Bolton's was generally agreed to be the best. His church was a splendid, Gothic building whose tower held a superlative ring of bells. Unbeknownst to him, his churchwarden sometimes used the tower to store smuggled goods awaiting distribution or shipment farther inland. One Sunday the warden had filled the tower too full of tubs of alcohol, so much so that the largest bell could hit the stored contraband contraband alcohol when it was rung enthusiastically. The bell ringers liked to conclude their summons to worship by making the last sequence of the ring extra loud. The result was that the bell thumped into a stack of tubs. It knocked the pile over and broke many of the containers open. Liquor started to trickle through the rough planking of the tower to drip onto the floor of the church. The processional had just begun when the calamity became evident to the congregation. Dozens forgot about Sunday worship as they tried to capture as much as they could, in any vessel that came to hand, of the liquid raining apparently from heaven. One man, known for his excessive drinking, ended up lying flat on his back with the liquid pouring down into his mouth even faster than he could swallow. He would have drowned if he had not been pulled aside by other men keen to taste what was clearly a gift from heaven. There was no peal of bells that evening to summon the faithful to evensong. There was not a single bell-ringer who was in any state to pull a rope.

The wedding the next day went off without a hitch, the only surprise occurring when a group of sailors from Captain Bolton's ship turned up to pull the married couple's carriage from the church. Luckily, the Dipton Arms had been expecting members of *Flicker*'s crew, and they were provided with suitable refreshments away from the more decorous wedding breakfast.

Daphne climbed the stairs of Dipton Hall after the newlyweds had departed for their marriage trip. She had been neglecting Bernard somewhat during the recent hectic days. Now she would be able to visit the nursery for as long as she wanted. She reflected on the differences between today's wedding and her own which had taken place less than a year and a half ago. This one had been more elaborate, but she thought her own had been better. How her life had changed in the last year and a half!

Giles joined her in the nursery. He had become fond of spending time on the floor with Bernard whose crawling skills were advancing rapidly, especially when his father gave him reason to want to move.

"I am sorry you will have to leave so soon," Daphne remarked.

"Not quite as soon as I expected," replied her husband. "Mr. Amery brought orders from the Admiralty that I should take another two weeks to help with his attempts to halt the smuggling at Harksmouth. He wants us all to meet tomorrow morning to plan what will be done. He has already enlisted

Captain Bolton's lieutenants and sailors, and he has even spoken to Captain Bush about joining us. I don't think it will take very long and so I should be back here for a couple of days before I have to return to *Glaucus*. I confess that every time I come here, it becomes harder to have to leave. The war keeps dragging on, and I am starting to wonder how crucial I am when many capable captains are on the beach."

"Oh, I would like you to be here! But could you be content not to be playing your part, especially as everyone knows that you are no ordinary captain? Couldn't you persuade Lord Gordonston to keep you in home waters so that you could be home more frequently while still doing your duty?"

"That's a good idea. The First Lord must owe me something by now."

Daphne decided not to pursue the matter. She wanted Giles at Dipton. She also wanted him to be happy. She was fully aware that the sea was in his blood, and she did not want him to give it up if doing so would make him unhappy. If he came ashore, it would have to be at his own instigation, not at her request.

Chapter XVII

It was a motley cavalcade that Mr. Justice Amery led from Dipton. He had commandeered the carriages belonging to Captain Bush and Dipton Hall, and he had arranged for a coach from the Fox and Hounds Inn at Ameschester. The gentlemen were joined in the carriages by the officers from *Flicker* as well as Giles's and Captain Bush's coxswains. In the coach and riding on it outside were the crew members from *Flicker* who had attended the wedding, most of them the worse for wear from the celebration of their captain's marriage.

Mr. Justice Amery had arranged for a company of dragoons to be on maneuvres bivouacking on the green at Harksmouth. His group arrived after dark at the town, and he left the sailors to camp with the soldiers while the others went to the King's Head Inn, which was a short way down the quay from the establishment where Major Stoner had gathered his information on his previous visit. Choosing the King's Head avoided any suspicion about why the Major was returning to Harksmouth.

The naval officers together with Major Stoner and Mr. Justice Amery had an extensive and lengthy breakfast in the parlor of the inn which provided a good view of the dock. Then after they had eaten, Giles, Captain Bush, Major Stoner, and Mr. Justice Amery went to put on their uniforms, or, in Mr. Amery's case, the robes and wigs of office, even though neither the judge's dress nor Major Stoner's uniform was technically appropriate for their roles. The judge had explained to Giles that the show of authority which the uniforms provided would be more important than their being the correct garb for what he intended. Similarly, Giles had a feeling that possibly Mr. Amery was sailing very close* to the wind in stating that, of course, the two naval captains were officers of the King's peace.

208

Giles's room was at the front of the inn so, when the men had changed into their uniforms, they gathered there to await developments. The morning seemed to drag on interminably until, finally, they observed the *Ruddy Fox* gliding up to the wharf. Still, they waited until the vessel had moored. A few minutes later, Mr. Shockley appeared. The four watchers went down the stairs, but the whole party delayed leaving the inn until Mr. Shockley blew his whistle to summon his laborers to start unloading the lugger. They then waited for another couple of minutes.

Giles stepped out of the inn in his full-dress Captain's uniform. He was accompanied by the others. He put a bosun's whistle to his lips and blew a blast. The call was for "All Hands on Deck," the same one which years ago had earned him a visit to the gunner's daughter* when he sounded it as a midshipman's prank. Straight from Harksmouth Green came *Flicker*'s seamen. They were supposed to be accompanied by mounted soldiers, but the planning had not allowed time for the soldiers to mount up and start moving. In any case, they would not have arrived with the seamen, who were taking a narrow alley unsuitable for horses so that they could reach the dock as quickly as possible.

The arrival of the sailors and their clear determination to interfere with the unloading was met with a shout of anger from the navvies. They dropped their loads to counter any attack by the seamen. Broken casks of liquor littered the wharf making footing treacherous. The seamen had armed themselves with various heavy sticks or other items to act as cudgels before leaving the green, while the dock-workers were not slow in improvising weapons.

Neither Giles nor Captain Bush was the sort of commander who would remain calm on their quarterdeck when their ships were boarding* another or being boarded. Bush waded into the fray immediately, having in the hook at the end of his wooden arm a formidable weapon. Giles aimed a kick at one of the tables the King's Head kept outdoors for patrons who liked to take their ale in the fresh air. The table broke apart, and he grabbed one of the legs to use as a club. Captain Bolton's officers, seeing what was afoot, also found weapons to join the melee. Although there were more laborers than sailors on the dock, the sailors had the advantage of being trained for boarding situations and this training was easily adapted to a street fight. It quickly became evident which side was winning, and the navvies broke and took to their heels to get away. Just as they approached the end of the dock, the dragoons finally appeared to seal off their escape.

The men who were manning the barges had come to join the fight, but now they tried to rejoin their vessels and cast off. Giles saw what was happening and blew his bosun's pipe to get the sailors to leave the dock-workers to the dragoons so that they could help him to prevent any of the barges from departing. Giles's men were in time: none of the barges succeeded in leaving the wharf. Some of their crews did succeed in escaping by jumping into the water and swimming away, but many more were rounded up. They joined the laborers in being marched off to Harksmouth Gaol.

Mr. Shockley had made the mistake of staying to watch the fight when the sailors appeared on the scene. He did not think to leave until it was too late. He tried to escape through the narrow alley which had been used earlier by the sailors, but one of *Flicker*'s midshipmen noticed him running away and followed, bringing him down with a tackle that would have been outstanding on a rugby pitch.

Giles together with one of *Flicker*'s midshipmen and a couple of her sailors went to the *Ruddy Fox*, which was in the process of casting off.

"Avast there, Captain Creasy," Giles bellowed. "If you try to escape, there is enough evidence to hang you whenever you reappear. If you co-operate, we can maintain our agreement to your profit."

Captain Creasy recognized Giles and seemed to realized that the tide was still rising too fast to allow him to get away from Harksmouth on the southerly breeze. He told his crew members to secure his ship to the dock again. Giles directed him to come ashore together with his crew and to leave the dock, assuring him that his lugger would be returned to him in the next day or two. The midshipman then took the *Ruddy Fox* away with a couple of members of *Flicker*'s crew to anchor a bit upstream.

The wharf returned to its usual sleepy appearance. Mr. Justice Amery took the somewhat battered Mr. Shockley into the inn. There, over a mug of bitter, he induced the man who had been directing the unloading of the contraband, with the threat of hanging for his offenses and the reward of only paying a small fine if he aided the judge unstintingly, to divulge all that he knew about the smuggling operation. Mr. Shockley even had a ledger in which he kept the names of ships that had recently arrived with illicit cargo, the amounts of smuggled goods involved and the barges into which they had been loaded. It also recorded the sums that Mr. Shockley had paid the captains of the ships for their cargos. Mr. Shockley did stress that he was just a middleman between the ships' captains and the man who was entirely in control of the smuggling in Harksmouth, Sir Winthrop Shorthouse. Ledgers detailing earlier smuggling activity had been given to Sir Winthrop and were presumably at his nearby estate, Eastrise Place.

Mr. Amery sent Mr. Shockley with an escort of dragoons to the Harksmouth Gaol, after emphasizing that only cooperation in breaking up the smuggling activity in Harksmouth could allow him to escape the gallows. Captain Bush was given the job of intercepting any further vessels coming to unload. He was to seize them and have *Flicker*'s officers and crew take them to anchor away from the dock.

Giles, Major Stoner, Carstairs, and Mr. Justice Amery then mounted horses supplied by the army. Together with the company of dragoons, they left to apprehend the spider at the center of the smuggling web.

Eastrise Place was a handsome, gray-stone building that appeared to have been built in the 1720's or 30's. It sat at the end of a straight, tree-lined drive that was in better condition than the road from which it came. The group from Harksmouth had just spotted the house when they saw a carriage come careering down the drive. Justice Amery realized as soon as he saw it that he had made a tactical error. Word must have gone ahead of them of the events in Harksmouth, and the carriage was most likely trying to escape before the authorities arrived. No doubt, the vehicle contained Sir Winthrop and, possibly, records of his endeavors. It would have been safer if the Judge had apprehended Sir Winthrop before intercepting the smuggling vessel, but he could hardly have arrested a titled gentleman without clear evidence of the offenses being committed.

Mr. Amery gave the view-halloo* just as if he had seen a fox started by dogs. He kicked his horse into a gallop to intercept the carriage. The rest of the cavalcade followed suit and raced toward the intersection of the drive from Easstrise Place with the road. The carriage reached the junction first, and the driver tried to turn the corner without pausing. In this, he succeeded, but only with the body of the conveyance rocking wildly. However, the road's condition was such that a moment later one of the wheels fell into a rut and the carriage tilted over on its side. The driver was hurled into a hedge and promptly took off at a run across the field on its other side. The vehicle lay on its side in the ditch. Luckily, as it was turning over, the shafts had cracked and broke so that the horses were not harmed.

"Go after that man," the captain in charge of the cavalrymen ordered a couple of his troopers. Their horses were not trained as hunters so they would have to take the long way around to the end of the field and possibly the next ones as the fugitive forced his way through the hedgerows that separated the fields. Giles was doubtful that they would be able to run down a man who knew the country. While the rest of the troop milled around the overturned carriage, Giles climbed up on it to look inside.

"There is someone in there," he announced. "Carstairs, come and give me a hand."

Giles and his coxswain pried open the door. There was indeed a man inside. He was unconscious and partly buried under some bags and other baggage that had not been stowed safely. Carstairs had to delicately lower himself into the carriage, taking care not to step on the man or to disturb the luggage further. When he had found steady footing, he started passing the items up to Giles who passed them to one of the mounted soldiers who in turn handed each piece of luggage to a man on the ground. Quite a pile of material had transferred before it was safe for Giles to join Carstairs in the coach while others assumed places on the side of the overturned carriage.

The injured man was dressed as a gentleman in expensive-looking garments. He appeared to be of mature age, but not old, and his red nose and chubby cheeks suggested a habit of over-indulgence in food and drink. There was blood matting his hair. It came, Giles supposed, from the knock on the head that had rendered the victim unconscious. In the cramped and awkward position in which Carstairs and Giles found themselves, it took some doing to lift the man without causing further injury and to hand him through the door to the men who had climbed onto the side of the carriage. It was accomplished with the victim showing no signs of recovering consciousness, and he was laid on the grass on the edge of the road after he had been lowered from the coach.

The captain in charge of the dragoons, whose name Giles had failed to catch when they were introduced, had sent a couple of troopers to see if they could obtain a wagon or other conveyance at Eastrise Place. One of them returned with a handcart saying that the other one was getting the grooms at the estate to harness some horses to a wagon on which they could transport the baggage. The well-dressed man, whom Mr. Justice Amery said must be Sir Winthrop Shorthouse, was loaded onto the handcart. Two dragoons were given the thankless task of pushing it up the hill to Eastrise Place, and the whole group set out for Sir Winthrop's mansion.

They were welcomed at the portico by a butler, who promptly called for servants to put Sir Winthrop to bed. He seemed to be very resentful when Mr. Amery stated that he was taking over the house and that his were the orders to be obeyed, but the servant realized that he had no choice. A doctor was sent for, even though Giles, with his long experience of knocks on the head – his own and others – felt that it was only a matter of time before Sir Winthrop awoke and medical intervention would serve no useful purpose. In Giles opinion, bleeding the victim, which undoubtedly a doctor would want to do, would only slow Sir Winthrop's recovering his wits. He did warn Mr. Amery that he would not be surprised if it were a while before Sir Winthrop could give any coherent answers to his many questions about the smuggling activities.

The wagon with all the baggage with which Sir Winthrop had been trying to escape pulled up in front of the house. Mr. Justice Amery ordered that it all be taken into the library where he placed a guard over it. That, thought Giles, was very wise. Among the items rescued from the coach was a small chest which had proved to be a struggle for two men to handle. Giles remembered it from his work with Carstairs in the carriage. It was one of the few items that had almost overwhelmed their joint effort to lift it through the door of the overturned carriage. Much to Giles's surprise, the lock on the chest had not been broken, for he was sure that it must be full of gold coins. In similar circumstances, he would not have trusted his crew not to smash the lock and help themselves to the contents.

Giles took his leave of Mr. Amery and Major Stoner who were settling down to examine the documents that had turned out to be part of the baggage. He wanted to get back to Dipton.

"Don't leave now, Captain Giles. There may be more things that I will need you to do, and there will be further news to carry to Lady Ashton. At least stay the night at the King's Head," the Judge begged.

Giles agreed, even though he very much wanted to spend as many of the extra days that this adventure had granted as possible with Daphne as he could. However, he didn't want to travel by night, especially as there was little promise of a moon, so it would be no hardship to wait until morning.

Morning came, but Giles was still not able to leave. Instead, he was faced with a crowd of ships' captains, those who had had their vessels peremptorily seized by Captain Bush on instructions from Mr. Justice Amery, and others who were anchored in the Harks River, awaiting cargo to take away. Giles would not have been surprised if they as well as the ones apprehended the previous day were involved in the smuggling trade, They just hadn't been caught doing it yet.

Giles first job was to sort the captains who had had their vessels taken from those who were just afraid of what might happen to them, but who had no immediate grievance. He told the second group that he would deal with them in an hour's time while he would deal with those whose ships had been seized immediately. Fortunately, while on the way to Eastrise Place the previous day, he had thought to talk to Mr. Justice Amery about what to do with the captains whose vessels they had taken. Except for the *Ruddy Fox*, which had been caught red-handed as it were, the other ships could claim that they had docked expecting to pay the necessary taxes on their cargos before proceeding. That talk made him realize how shaky was his position, though he was not about to tell the captains about how to evade the charges. Instead, he made it sound as if not charging them would be an unusual favor for which he would expect some things in return. First, in future, they would have to make sure that anything they brought in had the excises paid, even though Harksmouth had no customs hall. Second, when they visited ports in France, Spain or the low countries, they were to keep their eyes open to the state of naval preparations and of the number and type of naval vessels in harbor. They were then to relay this information to certain British naval ships, in particular to *Glaucus, Flicker*, and *Firefly* and to any other naval vessels about which they might hear later. If they encountered none of them, they were to inform the customs officials, when they docked, about what they had observed.

One of the captains wanted to know what they would be paid for the cargos they brought.

Giles didn't know how to answer this vital question.

"What are you being paid now?" he asked while trying to think up a satisfactory answer that would not commit himself to an outrageous price.

"It depends on what the goods are, of course," came the reply.

"Well, give me an idea. What do you get for a gallon of good French brandy?"

"Six shillings and eight pence, for good quality. Less if it needs to be treated with caramel before it can be sold."

Giles was surprised. Daphne and the Major had discussed what price they would need to get in order to sell the goods at a profit in Ameschester. They had used the same example for their calculations and thought that they could well make a profit at anything less than eighteen shillings a gallon before the tax was paid. He had had no idea of what sorts of figures would be involved. Nevertheless, he knew that Daphne would not be happy if he suggested the first price that came from the suppliers.

"It, of course, depends on the situation, but I can assure you that you will get what you are at present receiving, less fifteen percent because you would run no risk from the authorities here and would not have to sneak up to the dock to unload."

"Fifteen is too high," replied the captain. "Make it seven, and you might have a deal."

"Well, I can have you all thrown in gaol, I suppose. That's what will happen if we don't come to an agreement."

Giles wondered where in the world this figure had come from. He knew that bargaining took place routinely in business, but he couldn't remember when last he had participated in it. Well, in for a penny, in for a pound, as they say.

"Ten percent, and that is subject to the principals behind this endeavor agreeing."

"Still too high," came the response. "It won't be worth our while to come in here for less than what we are getting less eight and one-half percent."

"Make that nine, and we have an agreement," retorted Giles. The captains agreed.

"Now bring your vessels in one at a time, and we'll have them unloaded, as soon as I make arrangements to have the duty paid. You will get your money in bills of exchange on Coutts Bank on the Strand in London."

Giles realized that he was getting himself and Daphne into the business of supplying goods on which excise fees had been paid much more rapidly than they had decided. He just hoped that Major Stoner could arrange to dispose of the cargoes he indicated would be purchased.

Giles was more circumspect with the other group of captains when he met with them. All that he indicated was that

Harksmouth was no longer available as a port at which to land goods without paying duty. However, he was sure that there would be agents to facilitate the purchase of their cargos if they were brought in legally. He mentioned that, of course, the prices would be lower than they had been getting up till then, but there was no danger of getting into trouble with the law. To sell in Harksmouth, however, the captains would have to be ready to give information about naval conditions in the ports where they had loaded. They, of course, were not to tell anyone about that arrangement.

When the second group of captains had departed, Giles sat back priding himself on a good morning's work. Now, after refreshing himself, he could leave for Dipton and have several days at home with Daphne before he had to join *Glaucus*. He gazed out the window where he saw that Captain Bush was arranging for the transfer of the cargo from one of the ships that had been seized on the previous day. It seemed to be going smoothly, though he wasn't clear how Captain Bush had found the laborers. Then he realized the deficiency in his plan for dealing with the cargoes. The laborers would expect to be paid, of course, and so would the ship's masters. He had promised them bills of exchange on Coutts Bank, which they could undoubtedly have discounted at a bank in Harksmouth. However, if the bills were not written by himself, they might be considered dubious if the amounts specified were written in a different hand from his own. He would not be able to leave for Dipton before all the ships were unloaded unless he could straighten this matter out so that the payments could be made in his absence, based on bills on his London account, even in his absence. He would have to visit the bank to explain why there was a flood of such paper arriving at their door. Fortunately, his Captain's uniform, together with the fact that his likeness had appeared several times in the newspapers as a result of his triumphs, meant that he should have no trouble authenticating the paper. He would walk up to the bank now, and then return for lunch at the King's Head before leaving for Dipton.

Giles enjoyed strolling through the streets of Harksmouth to get to the bank. In his captain's uniform, he was recognized by several of the townsfolk who were keen to give him their gratitude for his feats against the French and to transmit to him their insights about how the war should be conducted. The officials in Sanders Bank, for that was the name of the establishment, including Mr. Sanders himself, the son of the founder, were more than pleased to assure him that his notes would be honored, without discount, at face value. He was almost sorry that he could not tarry longer in the town, but he was very eager to return to Dipton, even if his neighbors and the townspeople of Ameschester were more accustomed to his absence and so made a fuss over him when he was there.

Giles spent the few days remaining at Dipton in visiting his tenants with Daphne, seeing prominent people in the area and hob-nobbing with his friends. Daphne and he passed many happy hours with her playing the pianoforte while he sawed away at the violin. Marvelous pieces of music were coming from Austria, Germany, and Italy, some written for piano and violin, others adapted from works originally intended for different combinations. Daphne, the self-styled stay-at-home lady, was most intrigued by the new tacks that music was taking, while Giles was far from convinced that the innovations were an improvement. Giles tried to hide his worry about Daphne's now confirmed pregnancy while assuring her that another child was just what he wanted, especially as he was no longer terrified of interacting with his son. For the first time, Daphne became convinced that when he was at sea, her husband would miss not only herself and Dipton Hall but also his son, Bernard.

However, duty called. With Napoleon's army on the heights above Boulogne and with a huge number of somewhat ramshackle landing craft ready to convey that army to England,

Giles would never seriously consider letting someone else take his role while he remained at home. Carstairs and he left Dipton before any further news of what Major Stoner and Captain Bush were doing to supplant the smuggling that had for years been a fact of life in all the area served by the canal whose terminus was Harksmouth.

Chapter XVIII

Glaucus had resumed the search for French ships of the line in out of the way places along the French coast which had been interrupted by the clash with the brigs and the rescue of the sailors. The investigation was still the task to which Giles had been assigned, even when his consorts were not available.

It was tedious work. Giles had never been aware of how many creeks and sheltered bays there were in Normandy and Brittany. The charts that Mr. Brooks had were not informative or reliable about possible entrances to shallow bays where there might be a central pool which had enough water even at low tide to accommodate a significant ship. Most nights Giles found that he had to return to a place that might have looked promising from a distance during the day. He would then take one of the boats to sneak in after dark beyond the coastline to examine what might be hidden from a vessel that was far enough offshore to avoid the dangers of inaccurate charts and shifting sands. Often they did discover ships that they had not seen even from *Glaucus*'s mastheads. Unfortunately, so far, the discoveries had been fishing boats as well as some small coasting craft. None of the latter struck Giles as being worth taking as prizes, and he was loath to harm the sailors whose livelihood they were. He salved his conscience about letting French trade continue by reflecting that if he destroyed their ships, the mariners might well join the French navy, the quality of whose usual recruits, he believed, was abysmal.

Giles did encounter several English smugglers in these excursions. He would sneak up on them in the dark, and have his men on board their target before being seen by the crew, who usually spent their time at anchor carousing without posting any proper lookouts. Though scouting out these harbors could be done by his midshipmen and lieutenants, Giles often went on these exploratory trips himself because he had the authority to get smugglers to assist in providing information about what they had seen where his juniors inquiries might have been ignored. Giles was learning, however, that such vessels tended to avoid places where French warships might be sheltering out of sight. Recruiting smugglers and finding significant ships were quite separate activities. Meeting with the smugglers was also invaluable in that they often could tell Giles which of the many nooks and crannies in the coast could not possibly hold any naval vessel. As a result of that information, Giles was saved many fruitless investigations, though there were still more places to explore than he would have wanted.

As time passed, he became more proficient in recognizing from the sea which places might be worth examining, though he still had much time-consuming work. He might be involved in this search for fruitless months if he were to go all the way around the Bay of Biscay, a possibility now that Spain was allied with Bonaparte. The coast of Spain also had many inlets that could hide ships. Would he have to investigate them as well as the French ones?

Glaucus had almost reached Brest before her luck changed. There had been a nasty northwest gale a few days before, which *Glaucus* met without difficulty though she had moved somewhat offshore as the storm developed to give herself sea room. She resumed her investigation by approaching a headland which had a sandy beach to the north-east of it. The headland had two distinct points. The chart labeled it *Point Kermovan.* Beyond the next headland, the coast curved south-eastward towards Brest.

"Ships in the harbor," called the lookout at the masthead. "Two of them. A frigate and a full-rigged ship." Giles climbed to the crosstrees* to see for himself. Across the sandy beach, he could see a frigate and a large merchant ship. They were at anchor in the channel in front of a town.

222

Giles hoped that no one on shore had noticed *Glaucus* as yet. That situation could not be counted on to last long, and he would prefer that no one saw that a British frigate was coming directly towards the beach. A ship sailing by, at a safe distance offshore, would probably not be unusual and so it would be considered to be of no interest to those on the anchored vessels or to other people on shore. "Alter course to starboard, Mr. Brooks," he bellowed. "Steer south-west by south."

Giles had been practicing climbing the rigging since his break from the sea at Dipton. He decided to show off his skills by sliding down the backstay to return to the deck. That should help still speculation among the midshipmen and ship's boys that their captain was becoming a useless blob of fat. From his days in the midshipman's berth on previous ships, Giles knew that that was the lads' opinion of any even slightly rotund captain.

Giles gathered his officers in his cabin after *Glaucus* had settled on her new course.

"As you all know," he started the meeting, "there are a French frigate and a merchant ship in that stretch of water in front of the town. I suspect that they snuck in there to escape the storm since it is sheltered from the waves, though not from the wind. I intend to take them."

"How, sir?" asked Lieutenant Hendricks.

"We will have a cutting-out* expedition tonight. Mr. Brooks, do you know what the tide will be doing?"

"Not precisely, sir. The tide should be low at about three bells of the first dog watch and then will rise until roughly two bells of the middle watch."

"All right. Here is what we will do," Giles announced. "We will stand offshore today, though close enough to keep an eye on the harbor. After the sun sets, we will move in towards the mouth of the bay of *Le Conquet*. We will take all the boats to board and capture that frigate. I intend to do this just before the tide turns so that the frigate's bow will likely still to be pointed in the right direction. By the time we have taken her, it should be slack water or the tide will have just turned, and we will take her out on the ebb tide. If there is a breeze, we will sail her out of the harbor; if not, we will have to tow her using our boats. That's why we need the ebb tide. We may also be able to use her boats as well as our own if we have to. After we get through the harbor mouth, we will land her crew on the point, what is it called Mr. Brooks?"

"Point Kermovan, sir."

"Yes. The Frenchmen will have a long walk back to *Le Conquet* or even to a place where they might alert others on the opposite shore about our presence. We will keep her officers and maybe some of the petty officers as prisoners, but the rest of the frigate's crew would be a danger and a nuisance if we have to take them to England. It is more important to have as many of our people as possible with us on *Glaucus* than to have them guarding a ship-load of prisoners.

"After we have landed the captives, Mr. Miller can take the cutter to get the merchant ship. I am afraid, Mr. Miller, that you will have to row against the current.

"Normally, Mr. Hendricks would be in charge of the venture, but with that injured ankle, Lieutenant, I think you will have to stay here in command of *Glaucus* while I lead the foray."

Lieutenant Hendricks had twisted his ankle during the storm, and it had swollen drastically. Dr. Maclean had pronounced that no bone had been broken, but that the injury might take a long time to heal fully. The first lieutenant hobbled

224

about the deck during his watches, but the idea of his scrambling in and out of boats, or leading an attack if the French frigate happened to have alert lookouts, was laughable. He accepted his role in the enterprise good-naturedly, even though a cutting-out operation to capture a frigate would have helped his chances of soon being made commander and getting a ship of his own.

"Mr. Miller will take the cutter, and Mr. Marceau will take the jolly boat. I will be in my barge. I don't imagine that the French will have boarding nets* spread. If they do, we will need to adjust. If their nets are not in place, Mr. Miller will board at the waist. Otherwise, board at the bow. Have grapnels* ready so that you can climb aboard easily. Mr. Marceau will board on the opposite side from Mr. Miller. I will have the marines, under Mr. Macauley, with me in my barge.

"Mr. Hendricks, you will choose the boats' crews. It would be a good idea to have some of our people who have had experience in the merchant fleet among the cutter's crew. I am told that they do some things differently from our practice in the navy, and their familiarity might help to take the merchant ship out smoothly after we have captured her.

"Mr. Brooks, we will head offshore now, and hold our course until only our topmasts are visible from the shore, but so that we can still see the top of the masts of the French frigate at anchor. Then reduce sail, using only the mainsails so that we are less likely to be observed from the shore. A cutting-out venture always goes much more smoothly if the enemy is not expecting it. Of course, if the frigate sets sail, we will meet her after she emerges from the little inlet.

"Good. Now, carry on if there are no questions."

There was none. Though they would never have said so, all the officers felt that Giles had explained in far more detail than was required.

Glaucus proceeded south-west under all plain sail until the low land of the Finisterre Peninsula could no longer be seen from the deck. Even from the foremast top, the foreshore could not be seen. However, the lookout at the top of the main mast could still observe the spars of the French frigate standing out against the land behind it. Mr. Brooks then set the course to move slowly across the mouth of the harbor. He told the officer of the watch the courses to sail so that *Glaucus* would see if the French frigate made sail while they were waiting for nightfall.

Time crept by for all the men on *Glaucus*. The lookouts changed regularly, but none announced any activity in the French port nor were other ships spotted at sea. The wind was diminishing, but it did not die. It did back a bit, and the sea was losing the massive rollers that still told of the recent storm. Finally the sun set. Giles, who had been in his cabin, doing paperwork, came on deck. He glanced at the sails, the telltales*, and the sea. It was time to start the attack.

"Mr. Hendricks," he commanded. "Make sail. Take us back."

Glaucus's progress towards *Point Kermovan* seemed to go at snail's pace. Still, she arrived too soon at the harbor's mouth. Giles did not want to wait after taking the French frigate any longer than was required and he wanted to be sure that the tide helped to sail her from the harbor. Everyone had a nervous half-hour as they waited with backed mainsail for the time to come. Then the seamen, who had been told off for the duty, clambered into the boats, followed by the officers. Giles gave Carstairs the order to cast off, and they were on their way. *Glaucus* turned to get more sea room in which to wait for them to return.

The last of the flood tide carried the boats into the harbor before it ended. The three boats from *Glaucus* rowed slowly towards their target using muffled oars. Soon they could make out the French frigate. She was in the middle of the channel still bow-on to the harbor entrance. There seemed to be no lookout posted, at least no one whose head could be discerned in the ship's silhouette. That was all that they could see in the dark. No lights were showing on the frigate, but there were several in the town, and the sounds of revelry drifted over on water carried by the light land breeze.

Giles felt that what they could observe so far was encouraging, especially as he had been having doubts about the wisdom of this expedition as they neared the harbor. If her full crew were on board the French ship and were standing regular watches despite being at anchor, his attack was doomed to failure. Even with only a harbor watch mounted, the French ship could quickly get enough men on deck to overwhelm his limited force if she were given any warning. Only if he could somehow keep most of the French crew below decks until he had otherwise gained control of the frigate would he have success.

The Captain's barge slid up the larboard side to the waist of the ship. No alarm was raised, even though Giles could now see, in silhouette against the starry sky, a man who was leaning on the quarterdeck rail gazing at the town. They tied up and prepared to board. Giles led the way, matched by Carstairs and followed by sailors who spread out ready to stifle any objections the crew of the ship might raise. They were followed by the marines who moved smartly to block the passageways leading below. The men boarding from the starboard waist fanned out in the same way. The ship was now as good as taken, with any crewmembers who were on board trapped below decks. Finally, the man on the quarter-deck became aware that there was motion in the waist of the frigate.

"Qui va là?" he called. His head appeared at the rail looking down on the starboard side of the main deck. Mr. Stewart had already started up the starboard companionway to the quarterdeck and immediately stepped behind the Frenchman. The touch of the point of the midshipman's dirk on his throat was enough to silence the man.

Giles was amazed. With no resistance at all the frigate had fallen into his hands. The need for silence was now over. So was low water. Already Giles could sense that the frigate wanted to swing as the ebb tide started to pull on her to draw her towards the ocean He would have to get going if they were to use the gentle land breeze to help their departure and not have the problem of turning the ship in the narrow channel.

"Mr. Miller," Giles called, "Raise the anchor."

The bay was probably so shallow that it would be quicker to raise the anchor than it would be to find axes to cut the anchor cable.

"Mr. Macron, prepare to set the jibs and sheet home as soon as the anchor is weighed. Mr. Stewart, prepare to set the driver* as soon as we get steerage way. Carstairs, take the wheel," the orders continued. "Mr. Maclean, take your marines and find out whether we have trapped the officers in the cabin or the wardroom and take control of the lower deck and fo'c'sle to see how many of the crew were below decks when we took her. Since there are no boats, I presume that most of the crew are the people who are making that racket ashore."

Now there was a noisy bustle on deck. In minutes, the clank of the capstan started. Giles realized that he should have had some of *Glaucus*'s boys join them as nippers, but Mr. Miller commanded several of the sailors to take on this role as the anchor cable started to come on board. As Giles had suspected, not much anchor cable had been let out, so the capstan was also straightening out the ship so that the sails might catch the wind. In moments, the cry came to tell him that the anchor rode was up and down. "Raise the jibs" Giles ordered. The jibs and staysails* were hauled up and sheeted home even as the anchor came out of the water and was catted*. Carstairs held the wheel hard to starboard until he felt the rudder start to bite. "We have steerage way," he informed Giles.

"Set the driver and sheet home," was Giles next command. "Carstairs, can we clear the harbor mouth on this tack?"

"Yes, Captain. The wind has veered enough that the tide should carry us through."

"Mr. Miller, what have you discovered."

"There is almost nobody on board, sir. The only officer was the man who was looking over the rail. A midshipman, sir. The rest are all ashore, with most of the crew. That is why there were no boats, sir. I have the prisoners who were aboard under guard."

The captured frigate slid past the town helped along as much by the current as by the wind. Giles glanced the astern. He could make out several boats pulling hard after the frigate. In the dim moonlight, he had the impression that there were many men in them. The French officers and crews must have become aware of what was happening on their frigate. Maybe the clank of the windlass had caught their attention. He had been foolish not to cut the anchor line, even though not doing so rewarded him with a valuable anchor. Now it looked as if he had most of the frigate's company on his tail.

"Mr. Macauley, bring your marines to the quarterdeck. They are to fire into the boats which are pursuing us. Mr. Miller, prepare to repel boarders at the waist." Giles's orders spewed forth. The marines took up their positions at the taffrail, but their first volley, at too long a range, did little to discourage the attackers. It did force the French to make a wide circle in order to head for the bow and the waist of the frigate. The marines continued to fire, though with little success. The Brown Bess muskets were too inaccurate to do much damage even at only a few hundred feet.

There were six attacking boats in all, and they were all loaded with men. They appeared to have most of the French crew of the frigate that Giles had captured. They outnumbered his people by a significant factor. If they gained the frigate's deck in numbers, Giles was doubtful that they could be pushed back. Two boats on each side came up to the waist. The marines on the quarterdeck could do little damage since they had already fired at too long a range to be effective and now could not bring most of their muskets to bear. The defending force had to be divided. Giles ordered Mr. Miller to take the starboard side while he would handle the larboard. Mr. Marceau was to defend the foc's'le.

The marines on the quarterdeck again fired too soon, and their volley did little damage, though even wounding three or four of the attackers helped a little. Giles's men, armed with sabers, cut down the first wave of boarders where two of the boats had converged to try to board in the center of the larboard waist. Then the attacker's boats separated and were manhandled along the frigate's hull in opposite directions, leaving men hanging to the side of the frigate, waiting a chance to scramble on deck in an undefended place. There were too many of them for the defenders to cover all possible positions, and soon several attackers succeeded in forming a pocket where others could clamber over the bulwark and join the fight. Giles's force was being pushed back, even though the attackers were paying the stiffer price in casualties. He himself had already put two or three of them out of the fight.

The attackers on the starboard side had even more success in getting aboard the frigate. Soon they would have their full force on board. Meanwhile, the marines on the quarterdeck could find no safe targets. They were in some disarray since a wayward pistol-bullet had glanced off Lieutenant Macauley's skull, knocking him senseless. Their sergeant, not realizing this, took some time to recognize that he was now in command of the detail. When he did, he led a charge down the ladders to the waist where his men joined the others from *Glaucus*. The marines used bayonets and musket butts to even the fight.

The tide of battle turned. Now it was the attackers who were being pushed back. The positions in which they had left their boats meant that they could not scramble into them while fending off their enemies, and they surrendered. Battle was still raging on the foc's'le, but one of the attackers bellowed in an authoritative voice, "Rendez," which Giles knew meant "Yield." His supposition proved to be correct. The Frenchmen who had come aboard at the bow surrendered.

Giles turned his attention to the handling of the frigate. Carstairs had maintained his position at the helm. The captured ship was still responding very slowly to the rudder, but it was also being drawn through the harbor entrance by the tide. Nothing needed to be done in the next few minutes.

"Sargeant Evans," Giles called. "Gather all the prisoners together in the waist, both those we trapped below and those we have now defeated. Let them attend to their wounded.

"Mr. Miller, see to our own wounded and then report to me. Mr. Marceau, set the mainsail. I'll be below in the captain's cabin trying to discover just what we have captured."

The captain's cabin was sparsely equipped. It was easy for Giles to find the ship's papers. She was the frigate *Cecile* under Captain Robichamp. There were a muster roll, the captain's log, orders for the frigate, and the French signal book. That could turn out to be very useful. Her orders indicated that she had a rendezvous with someone off the Irish coast. It wasn't clear who she was meeting, but it could hardly be helpful for Britain. Indeed, information about such a meeting might be critical for those who were trying to prevent or suppress a revolt in Ireland. Giles would have to get these papers carried to England as soon as possible. Would he have to go himself? No, it would suffice to send in the prize, *Cecile*, immediately. He intended to do so anyway. Then he thought again. If the news was critical, sending it by *Cecile* risked having his prize retaken. One French frigate had successfully slipped through the blockade. It might not be the only one. A prize crew would not be able to fight a successful duel with another frigate. *Glaucus* would have to accompany her prizes to England.

Giles returned to the deck. Mr. Miller was waiting for him.

"Sir, four of our people are dead. Another five are seriously wounded, and a further dozen or so have minor wounds. They have all been bandaged up. We found the medical supplies in the orlop*, but the French doctor was not on board. The French fared worse. They have nineteen dead, and another six are not likely to live. That's not counting any who may have been killed trying to board. The total number of prisoners, including both those who were on the ship and those who boarded us is one hundred and eighty-eight."

"That seems a bit short for a frigate that had recently left harbor."

"I suspect that several other crew members were left ashore. Probably too drunk to be of any use in retaking the ship. What about taking the merchant ship?"

"I can't spare two boat crews unless I put the prisoners ashore. However, our captives can't possibly raise the alarm in time to interfere with our efforts if we put them ashore on the opposite side of the inlet from Le Conquet. I imagine that no one is expecting a second attack, especially as you will now have to pull against the ebb flow to get to the ships. "

"I would risk it, sir. If the merchant ship is ready for us, I can turn back without loss. We would only need one boat."

"No. Two would be better. Let's see. We now have eight boats. Ferry the prisoners ashore, with some marines to ensure that they do not try to take the boat. It will require several journeys, I would guess. After the last one, you and Mr. Marceau can try your luck with the merchant ship.

"Get ready to transport the prisoners ashore. Separate the French officers from the others. They won't be going ashore. I guess that I should talk to the French captain if he is among the captured, or whoever is their senior officer."

"Aye, aye sir. The captain is among the prisoners. I'll bring him to you."

Captain Robichamp turned out to be a short, dark-haired man, clean shaven but badly needing the attention of a razor. He had the hang-dog look of a man who could see no future for himself. Luckily he did speak English.

"Captain Giles," he said after the introductions were made. "You have destroyed me. I must beg you to take me to England. Anything is better than being returned to France after losing my ship in such a silly way. I – and my officers – are bound to be guillotined."

"Captain, I will happily take you and your officers to England, if you give me your paroles*. I cannot speak for the authorities there who may want to exchange you for English officers captured by your country, but I would hope not."

"Then I am happy to give my oath that I will not try to escape or attempt to make any hostile act towards you until I am exchanged. I am sure that my officers will also be happy to give their word. What will you do with my crew?"

"I am about to put them ashore on Point Kermovan. My frigate is just offshore. I will have you and your officers transferred to her when we meet my ship."

Giles turned away to give the orders to put the French crew ashore. They would be on the wrong side of the inlet to be able to go to Le Conquet to get help to disrupt the taking of the merchant ship. Giles now had many boats, but he still would need three separate transfers in only two boats to make sure that the prisoners would have no opportunity to overwhelm the crew including the marines and others whose only role was to suppress any attempt to take the craft.

After the third transfer had been made, Giles ordered Mr. Miller and Mr. Marceau to try to take the merchant ship, though he warned them not to proceed if they could not capture the vessel before the tide turned. The time available now made it doubtful if they could reach the merchant ship in time to take her out of the inlet with the current.

Giles again was faced with the need to wait for the outcome of actions without any way to speed them. He didn't even want to set more sail on *Cecile* so that he could meet up with *Glaucus* more quickly. He decided to read the documents he had discovered in the captain's cabin while waiting to learn the results of his lieutenants' attempt on the merchant ship.

The log told him little. Captain Robichamp had only recently been appointed to *Cecile*. He had a set of officers who had not served in her before. He surmised that the crew had been with her before, though the Captain's log and orders did not state so, nor did they give any information about her earlier history. The documents did contain some information about the merchant vessel, whose name was *Le Coq de Lorient*, and what the ships had been doing in the harbor. While it was not her principal purpose, *Cecile* was to protect the merchant ship until they reached the west coast of Ireland, where *Le Coq* would proceed around the Shetland Islands on her way to Stockholm with what was described as a valuable cargo and an important emissary. Or so Giles thought the papers said. His command of French, even written French, was still somewhat shaky. How much time had passed since he started on the documents? Shouldn't Mr. Miller be back by now?

Giles went on deck again. *Cecile* still had steerage way, but nothing more. However, her progress relative to features on the shore was greatly diminished. The current produced by the ebb tide had eased, indeed had almost stopped. Luckily, Mr. Brooks calculations had put the turn of the tide too early, but even so, it was almost upon them. It would already be very difficult to bring a ship out of the harbor in this light breeze. If the current turned, it might be impossible. It would be hard even to row the boats through the entrance if the current ran fast. The chart had not indicated what to expect. The moon was behind some clouds so lookouts on *Cecile* wouldn't be able to see *Le Coq* even if she were already at the harbor entrance.

Think as much as he liked, there was nothing that Giles could do in this situation. Time would tell, but if Mr. Miller had not returned in the next quarter of an hour, Giles would have to face the fact that his lieutenant might not be coming from the harbor on this tide. Should he turn *Cecile* around and go to the rescue? It might be possible. It would be hours before the French seamen he had put ashore would be able to get to Le Conquet, and they were unarmed. There might be other small boats in Le Conquet, but would they be able to mount an effective attack on *Cecile* or even be able to retake *Le Coq* if Miller had captured her?

Giles was about to give orders to turn *Cecile* about when the moon broke through a hole in the clouds. There, coming up to the harbor mouth was *Le Coq*. She had all sail set. Would she be able to make it through the narrows before the inflowing current countered her progress? The moon again disappeared behind the clouds, and it was impossible to judge her position. A nervous ten minutes passed for Giles until the moon again brightened the entrance. It looked as if *Le Coq* might be through the narrowest part of the passage, though there was no way of being sure, or guessing how strong the pull of the current on her might be. Slowly, slowly, slowly *Le Coq* came towards them. Even if she were past the narrowest part, where the flow would be fastest, the rising tide was also increasing the strength of the force drawing *Cecile* back to the narrows if the wind weakened at all. *Le Coq* might still not be free. She seemed to be balanced between the push of the wind and the pull of the tide, and the tidal current was probably increasing.

A gust of wind broke the impasse. The extra speed it gave the merchant ship allowed it to surge ahead so that when the breeze again weakened, *Le Coq* could still make progress away from Le Conquet. Soon she was close enough to *Celine* that Giles could order an increase of sail on the frigate and to signal to Mr. Miller to come to him.

The lieutenant's report was simple. It had taken longer to row to the target ship than they had expected, partly because the boat was loaded with more men than they thought were needed for the cutting-out operation. They were in the craft because of the need to guard the prisoners who had first had to be taken ashore. It made no sense to go back to *Celine* before going to try to capture the other ship. They would have lost too much time doing so.

When the boats finally got to her, *Le Coc de Lorient* was taken without difficulty since there was only an anchor watch on board. The master and the mates he gathered had gone ashore with most of the crew. The group from *Glaucus* immediately worked out how to set the sails, even though merchant rigging was somewhat different from naval standards due to the much smaller crews who were supposed to handle them. They encountered no difficulty in setting sails. Remembering what had caused the counter-attack on *Celine*, they cut the anchor rope. The problems they had to overcome arose from the lack of wind and from a back-eddy that countered the effect of the still falling tide. It had been nip and tuck to get through the narrows. Mr. Miller had been about to order the tired men back into the boats to see if they could pull through the current that was trapping them when the gust of wind carried them free.

"Did you find anyone on board who might be described as a 'special envoy,'" Giles asked.

"No," was the reply, "the harbor watch was composed of only two old sailors. I did bring the ship's papers, sir. I should tell you that there is a chest in the captain's cabin, which is so heavy that I believe that it must contain gold coins."

"Let me look at the papers you have brought." Giles repaired to the captain's cabin again to skim over the new documents. They confirmed that the ship was on a mission to Stockholm, disguised as a merchant ship. Its cargo was principally wine, cognac, and French lace and cloth. These were, of course, among the principal items smuggled into England, but this was not a smuggling venture. A little puzzling over the documents showed that the ship was in the hire of Napoleon's new-fangled Empire and was designed to keep the Swedes neutral and possibly to bribe them to aid the French side. There was a chest of gold to act as a subsidy and a cargo of luxuries to appeal to the powerful in Sweden. The ship was to go north around Great Britain, in the hope of avoiding being captured in the English channel or examined too closely in the area where the close blockade would make it likely that she would be boarded and kept, even though she might pretend to be a neutral vessel.

Once *Le Coq de Lorient* was west of Ireland, she would switch her identity to pretend to be an American ship, on her way to Sweden. She had a different name board, and her captain was fluent in the type of English spoken in the former colonies. If she were stopped later by British warships or privateers after separating from *Celine*, she would claim that she was a neutral ship sailing from one neutral port to another port, and rely on Britain's not wanting to anger neutral countries in the current delicate diplomatic situation.

Giles was learning critical information as he scanned what was to be gleaned from *Le Coq de Lorient*'s documents. He wondered again if he should take the discoveries back to England himself, to lessen the danger that it would not arrive. That would be a danger if he sent the documents and the money to England aboard his captured ships while *Glaucus* continued to perform her allotted tasks. The case for doing so was stronger now because he had more information which he wanted to keep from French hands and his ability to guard the ships and information would be non-existent unless *Glaucus* accompanied them. Revealing what Napoleon was contemplating concerning Sweden might help to frustrate the Emperor's intentions.

Chapter XIX

The light southerly wind died as *Cecile* and *Le Coq de Lorient* sailed beyond Point Kermorvan. It was soon replaced by a north-westerly, but one hardly any stronger. Dawn was at hand and with it came a call from the masthead that *Glaucus* was in sight. Giles was relieved to find her. Although he had every confidence in Mr. Hendricks, the unexpected could always happen at sea. Even so, he had to be cautious. He had arranged with Mr. Hendricks special, private signals so each could tell the other that there would be no unpleasant surprises when they met again. Giles had taken the precaution of having his own signals for this meeting since it was all too easy for the official "private" signals specified in the signal book to be discovered by the enemy if they took a British ship. *Glaucus* hoisted her version of the specified flags and Giles had *Cecile* respond with hers.

As *Cecile* got closer to *Glaucus*, Giles could see that his frigate was flying some other flags on one of the signal halyards. This suggested that there was a British ship further to windward. Giles wondered if the Inshore Squadron was in sight from *Glaucus*. If it were, he had no doubt that the admiral would have ordered *Glaucus* to close* with the fleet immediately. The admiral would not be pleased with the length of time it was taking *Glaucus* to obey the order.

Giles noticed that Mr. Hendricks seemed to have hoisted signals that said that the Captain was delayed. In this light air, however, it would be some time before Giles could reach *Glaucus*. Hendricks must be in a state of high anxiety. From his point of view, he was in charge of a frigate which was ordered to attend on an admiral while his captain was off on some adventure. Certainly, Giles expected to find him in the immediate neighborhood of Point Kermorvan while admirals expected their orders to be obeyed promptly.

There was nothing Giles could do about the situation. In the light breeze, it would take some time for him to reach *Glaucus*. The delay that Mr. Hendricks was taking in responding might be explained to the admiral when the lookout on *Celine* could see the ship that was farther out to sea, since then that ship could see Giles's captured frigate. But the wait for that to happen seemed interminable. Finally, the hail from the masthead came, "Ship to windward of *Glaucus*."

Further cries followed, though only excruciatingly slowly. Four line-of-battle ships were sailing in line ahead with the flag of an admiral of the Blue on the third ship. To windward of them were a frigate and two brigs of war.

It still took a long while before *Celine* could come up to *Glaucus* and Giles could be rowed to her. Mr. Hendricks said that *Glaucus* had spent a quiet night, but, as visibility came with the dawn, the lookout had spotted what he took to be the Inshore Squadron. A rear admiral's pennant flew from one of the warships, a seventy-four which had been identified as *Orestes*. It had taken some time for the squadron to spot *Glaucus*. When they did, the flagship issued the order to identify herself and then a series of commands, getting steadily more and more emphatic, that the captain report to the admiral. Lieutenant Hendricks had prevaricated, signaling that *Glaucus* had to finish her current task that had taken her captain on a mission in the harbor. He also claimed that he was having a great deal of difficulty reading the flagship's signals, which further delayed his obeying the admiral. Finally, the exchange of signals had reached the point where *Glaucus* was ordered to come immediately, the implication being that he should abandon his captain and whatever forces he had with him, no matter what Giles might be doing. The anger of the admiral had been shown in the very length of the last signal. Hendricks admitted that he had only turned *Glaucus* towards the squadron and started to make sail when it was verified that Giles was aboard the strange frigate emerging from the harbor at Le Conquet. Giles was impressed with the ingenuity of the signal midshipman. The signal book was not designed to convey the reasons for not obeying orders.

Giles clapped Mr. Hendricks on the back for *Glaucus*'s delay in obeying the admiral's orders. He would take responsibility when he reported to the admiral. Thank heavens he was sailing under Admiralty orders. That gave him some leeway in treating admirals' orders as requests rather than binding commands, though heaven help him if he ever came under this admiral's command.

"The flagship is HMS *Orestes,* Admiral Raymond Casterton, Captain Horace Chisler," Midshipman Stewart informed Giles. *Orestes* was a fairly new seventy-four, and Giles knew little about either Admiral Casterton or Captain Chisler. Of course, he had not seen many naval people recently, and therefore he did not have the latest gossip about the careers of other senior officers. He was surprised, however, that he could not remember hearing the name Captain Casterson even though the man would have had years of service in the rank of captain before he became an admiral.

Giles was welcomed aboard the flagship with no sign of warmth. Captain Chisler was not on deck to meet him, and the flag lieutenant was rather abrupt in telling him that Admiral Casterton would see him only when he had time. Giles was left to contemplate the seventy-four. This he did with curiosity. He noted that it was well maintained, as one would expect with a competent captain or first lieutenant, but somehow it lacked the sparkle that marked a crack ship. Lines were coiled, but without that last bit of neatness indicating pride in the task. The decks had obviously been holystoned* that morning, but not quite to the state where there were absolutely no marks or slight gouges on the planking, and so on.

Giles's attention was diverted by the flag lieutenant's coming, at last, to tell him that Admiral Casterton would see him. The Admiral was seated at a table in front of the stern windows of his cabin thus guaranteeing that his face would be in shadow. He was a small man, possibly forty-five or fifty years old, with a reddened, chubby face, a receding hairline, and a decided lack of chin. His authority was not enhanced by the high-toned, squeaky voice in which he addressed Giles.

"Captain," the admiral pretended to consult a slip of paper, "Giles. You have your orders for me to examine, I trust. You are joining my squadron, I presume. I am highly annoyed at the insolence you have shown me by not coming more promptly. Some nonsense about being on reconnaissance. What, checking out the bawdy houses ashore at Le Conquet, instead of doing your duty, were you?"

For a minute, Giles was puzzled by what the Admiral might mean, for he had pronounced the name of the town as "Luz-Conk-Quest."

"No, sir, I was following my orders from the Admiralty to explore possible hiding places for French warships of which we might not be aware."

"What nonsense! No one would ever keep proper seagoing vessels in that little cove. Never have, never will."

"Sir, be that as it may, I led a cutting-out operation that netted one French frigate and a French merchant ship."

"So your were off gathering prizes were you, instead of following orders? And capturing prizes that by right belong to me, I suppose." Admiral Casterson did not seem to be aware that this question contradicted his earlier reason for thinking that Giles's mission was a waste of time.

"No, sir. The orders given to me by the First Lord let me use my discretion to harass the French. Your fleet was nowhere in sight while I was accomplishing the task."

"What sort of orders were those! From the First Lord, you say! That accounts for the nonsense. That man is no sailor, is he? Sent you out hunting prizes, did he, just to feather his own nest one way or another, I'll be bound. Acted at the request of your father, no doubt."

"No, sir. My father and I are estranged, not that it has anything to do with this mission."

"So you say. What a waste! I am short of frigates. You would be better off under my command. Then I could set one of my other frigates to harassing enemy shipping. I have been told explicitly that I must have two between my little group and Brest. One very close in and the other to relay signals. Stuff and nonsense! The French are not coming out. And then *Incomparable* must be stationed between me and the main fleet and another frigate kept ready also to carry the news. Two of my precious frigates idle so that they can go looking for the main blockading fleet when they are blown into Torbay or somewhere else. Stupid orders, I can tell you, Captain Giles. Stupid! No prize money in it at all! That would be the proper way to harm the French. Use my squadron to harass the French and take their vessels. Impoverish them, sir, impoverish them!"

"Sir," Giles broke into this harangue, "in taking these ships, I learned some critical information about Napoleon's intentions. It should be transmitted to the Admiralty as soon as possible."

"So you think. That is just like you inexperienced men. There can be no serious doubts about Napoleon's intentions. He hopes to invade England. Everyone knows that. The only naval concern is to stop his fleet sweeping us aside to take control of the Channel. That isn't going to happen as long as we own the key to Brest! Your so-called information is irrelevant.

"More importantly, this morning, can you believe it, the lookouts found no trace of *Clytemnestra* – stupid name for a frigate -- and I've put my whole squadron on this easterly course to try to find her or to hear from *Hector*. Those are the two frigates that are supposed to keep me informed about what is happening in Brest."

Admiral Casterson's tirade was cut short by the Flag Lieutenant entering to say that *Hector* was in sight and signaling.

"What does she say?"

"She's against the sun, sir. Her signals cannot be read yet."

"Then there is not much point telling me, is there? I'd better go on deck so that there is no more of this tom-foolery. Captain Giles, I think we are finished. I am not happy, but there is nothing I can do about it. I do want you to stay to find out what *Hector* says. It may be something which would mean that I could insist that you give up your stupid activities."

On deck, there was no further news. *Hector* was coming to them close hauled to the north-north-westerly breeze, but it would be some time before she reached the fleet. Admiral Casterton did order a course change to starboard so that *Hector* could close the fleet more quickly. He was staring at the approaching vessel through his telescope as was Captain Chisler and the Fleet Lieutenant, all trying to decipher the flags that were streaming away from them.

"Whatever he is signaling, it is not enemy in sight," Captain Chisler remarked.

Several minutes passed before the signal midshipman announced, "It says *Clytemnestra* is missing."

"What does that mean?" wondered Admiral Casterton.

Though further signals were exchanged, the mystery was little clarified. Dawn must have found *Hector* with *Clytemnestra* not in sight to relay her messages. So the frigate most closely watching the Goulet had come in search of the relay frigate. When this became clear – the signal book did not make transmitting messages of any complexity easy – Admiral Casterton became agitated about the state of the French fleet in Brest. Would they be taking the opportunity provided by *Hector*'s absence to leave harbor on the ebb tide? A further exchange of signals established that the report which *Hector* had wanted to transmit was that there was no change observed in Brest, except for some exception that the men on *Orestes* still could not make out.

The mystery was not fully cleared up until *Hector* joined the fleet and her captain came aboard *Orestes*. After the usual ritual for a captain coming aboard had been completed, the captain of *Hector* was given a public grilling by Admiral Casterton. The full story was that he had wanted to transmit the information that two large merchantmen and one ship-of-the-line were no longer where they had been at dusk and might be presumed to have succeeded in sailing away during the night. There had been an overcast sky, and the ebb tide had occurred during the night, so Hector had not seen their exit from the Goulet.

The disappearance of *Clytemnestra* remained a mystery though Admiral Casterton was sure, based more on greed than any objective considerations, that she must have spotted the merchant vessels leaving and given chase. He seemed to be already claiming his one-eighth share of the hypothetical prize that *Clytemnestra* was capturing. She, of course, would not have tried to engage the ship-of-the-line, but of what significance was one stray battleship by herself?

The Admiral turned back to Giles, "You can leave your prize frigate with me, Captain Giles. I can supply the prize crew to take her in and also one for that merchant ship you captured. I am sure that the Admiralty will buy-in the frigate for a very pretty penny and the merchant ship will also provide much prize money. You will need all your crew for your search for unknown ships. I realize that now there is one more ship-of-the-line for you to find after *Hector* let her get away from Brest."

Giles was amused at the change of tone from the Admiral. It had apparently occurred to the commander that, if the admiral supplied the crew for the prizes, then a crafty lawyer should be able to get him his one-eighth share of the prize money that would otherwise be Giles's. The admiral had shown no interest in the missions of the two ships even when Giles had mentioned their importance. He had in fact brushed off Giles's remarks about his prizes. Their cash value seemed to be another matter altogether.

"That is very generous of you, sir," Giles replied. "However, the critical nature of the information I have requires that its transmission must be safeguarded by my prizes being escorted by a significant warship in case they meet another French frigate. As you mentioned, sir, you are short of frigates for your proper tasks, so I will have to perform the escort duty myself."

Admiral Casterton was unhappy with Giles's reply, but he could not think of a counter-argument. "You had better undertake your 'duty' immediately, Captain," he said in a bad-tempered voice. "I have wasted too much of my time on you already."

Giles was delighted to have the opportunity to return to *Glaucus* without more delay. He had been afraid that Admiral Casterton would saddle him with any number of reports to deliver to his superior in the Channel Fleet or to the Admiralty which the admiral had yet to write. Giles would not have been surprised if the senior officer had punished Giles by making him cool his heels while the messages were being prepared.

"Aye, aye, sir," he told the Admiral even as he turned from him to proceed to the entry port, causing consternation to Captain Chisler who had to hastily arrange the proper treatment for a post captain leaving his ship.

Giles wasted no time getting underway after returning to *Glaucus*. He had already assigned Mr. Miller to *Cecile* with Midshipman Stewart and enough of a crew to sail her, which meant that she could also partially man her broadside if required. He appointed Mr. Marceau to command *Le Coq*, with a master's mate to take the other watch. All three ships would be watch and watch* until they reached the Solent.

Giles invited Captain Robichamp to dine with him after the masts of the Inshore Squadron had disappeared in *Glaucus*'s wake. It was partly a matter of courtesy to a defeated opponent, but more it was curiosity about the French captain's request not be exchanged. He wondered if his guest's request indicated a lack of dedication to the French Emperor and he hoped that he could induce him to give some indications about the somewhat cryptic information he had found in *Cecile*'s papers. Before doing so, he wanted to review in more detail the captured documents.

Giles had almost finished glancing through the material when he came upon a sheaf of papers that he had thought belonged to *Cecile*'s master. Looking through them for the first time, he realized that they included the more detailed orders given to Captain Robichamp. Reading them, trying to decipher and translate the stylish French handwriting as he went along, Giles found that the mysterious rendezvous, news of which had him high-tailing it to Portsmouth, was with a French line-of-battle ship called *Honorable* and two troop-transport ships. *Cecile* would be under the orders of a Captain Grenier who would be landing a regiment of French troops to help Irish revolutionaries, led by a Douglas Reagan, to try to take Ireland from the English. The landing was to take place in Dangle Bay, and the orders must have been kept among the master's papers since it would be up to him to make landfall at the right point on the Irish coast. To that end, there was a sketch of the Bay with an 'X' marking the spot of the landing, together with more detailed charts of Dangle Bay and a poorly executed watercolor sketch which gave, Giles suspected, a view of the entrance to Dangle Bay from the ocean. The orders stated that *Cecile* was to stay well offshore until they had reached the latitude of Dangle Bay which was given as 52°5' N. Captain Robichamp was instructed to be careful not to be in sight of land farther south than 51°45' N.

Giles in all his voyaging had never seen the west coast of Ireland, and he knew very little about the island. He wondered if Mr. Brooks, the master, would be better informed. He indeed was though not having had first-hand experience of that shore. What he did know he had gathered from information provided by other mariners obtained during the frequent conversations masters had with each other about the hazards and landmarks of places all over the world. According to Mr. Brooks, Dangle Bay was a long inlet on the west coast of Ireland. He knew that there was some sort of harbor at the eastern end of the bay where a river emptied into the bay and had heard that, at least that part of the bay was deceptively shallow. The Bay was a dozen miles or so north of Bantry Bay where the French had tried to stir up a revolt in '98. From what little he knew, he thought that it might be a good place to land troops to form the heart of an Irish uprising.

Giles was even more convinced than he had been that he had to inform the Admiralty as quickly as possible about what he had learned. He wondered if the ships that *Hector* had reported missing were the ones who were headed to Dingle Bay. Well, he was on his way to inform the proper authorities, and going into Plymouth rather than Portsmouth would not speed up the delivery of the news. He would see whether his added knowledge of what was afloat could be used to pry further details from the feckless Captain Robichamp.

Giles's musings were interrupted by a hail from the masthead, "On deck, there. Ship ahoy bearing two points off the larboard bow! On a course to meet us." Giles gathered together the papers that were spread out on his table and went on deck. The fresh wind meant that the two ships were converging on each other rapidly. In minutes the lookout hailed that the unknown ship was *Flicker*.

Giles very much wanted to see Captain Bolton to find out how married life suited him and to learn about what was happening at Dipton in his absence. However, he was especially glad to see *Flicker* since the meeting opened another possibility for dealing with his important information. Rather than heave-to while they exchanged news, however, Giles ordered *Flicker* to take station on *Glaucus*'s quarter and for her captain to come on board so that they could converse, even as *Glaucus* continued to sail towards Portsmouth.

The two captains enjoyed several glasses of Madeira while exchanging news. Marriage was everything that Captain Bolton had hoped for, though he would now have to face repeated separations from Lady Marianne as he followed his calling. He had good news about the prizes that he and Giles had captured on the earlier part of their collaboration. The brigs would be bought into the navy, and each captain's share would be substantial.

When it came time for Giles to issue orders, Giles told Captain Bolton that he should take over accompanying the prizes to the Solent and there to deliver the news about the French plans for Ireland that he had discovered. *Glaucus* would head for Ireland once men from *Flicker* had relieved her crew members. Giles hoped that he might somehow interfere with Napoleon's plans to divert British attention and resources from the impending French invasion of England to quelling a rebellion among the Irish. He hastily wrote a letter to the Admiralty emphasizing what he had discovered and explaining what he was about to do. Next, he added closing lines with the latest news to his on-going letter to Daphne so that *Flicker* could carry it to England. His dinner with Capitan Robichamp would have to be canceled, but that was immaterial in the face of the urgent voyage in front of him. Of more regret was that his duty forced him to forego the visit to Dipton that he had been sure he could work into his trip to the Admiralty.

Chapter XX

Daphne found that she had little time to spend moping about as a result of her husband returning to his ship. Winter was releasing its grip and with it came the need to refine and implement plans for the coming spring and summer. She now had stewards for the three estates that were under her overall control. However, each of these men was newly appointed, and they knew that it would be wise to consult her about any plans they were formulating. Furthermore, many of the tenants needed reassurance that the stewards would not eliminate the methods that had worked well in the past and that, if they disagreed with the steward, Daphne was available to straighten things out. So far, what with teaching the stewards and reassuring the tenants, Daphne was not sure that hiring them had lessened her workload at all.

The Hunt Ball was fast approaching. Daphne and the staff of Dipton Hall had been through one Hunt Ball already. They had long since evaluated what had gone well and poorly and so had already decided what they should change for the next one. From Daphne's perspective, it should be an event that practically ran itself with the help of her servants. Unfortunately, Mr. Summers had many needless worries about the event that nevertheless required her attention since only Daphne could set his mind at ease. She found she was spending more time soothing his fears about the ball than she was making sure that it would be a success. In dealing with Mr. Summers, it became evident that Major Stoner must, in reality, be handling most of the arrangements for the meetings of the Hunt. With him away, Mr. Summers seemed to find that he had to consult Daphne on all sorts of small details having to do with the next meeting and the general operation of the Hunt. He seemed to think, because

Daphne and Giles had agreed to look after the hounds, that therefore Daphne should help with all aspects of the society. It was easier to deal with the problems herself than to guide Mr. Summers through each step of whatever was needed. Even when the members of the Hunt gathered in the cold morning of the next scheduled occasion to chase a fox, Mr. Summers was still dithering about small matters concerning the Hunt Ball. Daphne welcomed the view-halloo with relief.

The Hunt was not the only distraction for Daphne. She needed to catch up on visits to her particular friends as well as exchanging an unusually large number of visits with the ladies in the neighborhood. These were occasioned partly because she had done no visiting while Giles was home and partly because preparations for the Catherine Crocker's wedding had taken priority. The visits of the ladies also ate into the time that Daphne had for her most pleasant activities because the evident approbation of the residents of Dipton Hall shown by the Baron de Roy at his ball seemed to have increased the number of members of the fair sex who found it imperative for them to travel some distance to visit Lady Ashton. She was no longer plain Daphne Moorhouse who had married some naval captain. Now she was a viscountess, approved by the baron, wife of a war hero. She was clearly someone in whose circle others wanted to be included.

Catherine was now away on her wedding trip, but her place in the household activities was more than filled by Lady Clara. Bernard was her first grandchild and, though the Countess was usually a sensible woman, the slightest change in his behavior was taken as a clear sign of his exceptional talents or of an impending medical crisis, either of which had to be discussed at length with his mother. While Daphne's own attempts to soothe the Countess's worries were met with little success, her father had no difficulty in laying them to rest. In consequence,

Daphne was making sure that Mr. Moorhouse visited Dipton Hall more frequently than usual.

As time went on, Daphne was becoming anxious about the absence of Captain Bush and Major Stoner. She had received a couple of notes from the Major telling her that straightening out the smuggling situation in Harksmouth required much more time than he had anticipated. Mrs. Bush had heard similar news from Captain Bush, who had mentioned that Mr. Justice Amery was heavily involved in clearing out the smuggling activities that had been centered on Harksmouth. What could they be doing? The supplies that Daphne had obtained through the downfall of the smuggling ring in Ameschester were getting exhausted, especially in items relevant to there being another ball on the horizon. French lace and many other high-quality dress-making materials were again becoming in short supply in the neighborhood.

Major Stoner and Captain Bush showed up one evening at Dipton Hall just in time for dinner. Mr. Moorhouse again was among the people already scheduled to dine there, even though he was to have been the lone gentleman present. The conversation, both before dinner and also as they sat around the table afterward, was taken up with the adventures of the two arrivals and of Mr. Amery. While Giles had informed them of the situation up to the time when he had left the harbor town, everything after that had been a mystery. Everyone was interested in what had taken so long before the two men could return to Dipton.

The short answer to the question of what Captain Bush and Major Stoner had been doing was that they had been enjoying themselves. The full answer concerned how complicated and deeply rooted was smuggling everywhere and how difficult it was to suppress. The problems that they had encountered had started in Harksmouth. Mr. Justice Amery had discovered that it was not enough to eliminate the immediate corruption that had permitted the free trade to flourish so blatantly. Sir Lester Brownlee's tentacles had spread farther, and they had found that this was not limited to Harksmouth. The documents showed that two of the three men whom Mr. Amery had selected to be magistrates at Harksmouth to replace the ones complicit in the illegal trade were themselves already allied with Sir Lester. Canceling their appointments and finding others who were independent of the business ran into strong headwinds inspired by influence coming from various quarters, primarily, it turned out, from individuals whose direct links to the smugglers had not been revealed in the captured papers, but whose interests in the trade ran deep. When the problem of getting proper magistrates had been straightened out, and using the funds that Giles had provided, a regime of taxed goods that would provide the basis for legitimate trade had been established, at least in Harksmouth. While this was going on, the canal barges to transport the material inland were filling up waiting to carry what were now legal goods along the waterway, and the storehouses in Harksmouth had become full. The men who had stopped the smugglers would have to find ways to distribute their material in short order for their enterprise to be viable.

Dispensing the goods along the canal produced its own difficulties. The practice of the smugglers had been to have independent cells at eight main spots along the canal, including Harksmouth and Ameschester. Each site had a canal barge devoted to delivering to that one spot the contraband which was hidden by a legitimate cargo. The records were sketchy about who was conducting the business in each of the places except Harksmouth. For Ameschester, the documents revealed only the name of Mr. Wark, though there were people referred to by their jobs or by nicknames. Mr. Amery, with Major Stoner's assistance, had been able to assign names to the people mentioned and all the main ones were accounted for. They had already been apprehended or forced to flee the country. In the

254

other six places, the papers had referred to the nicknames given to the principals who were behind the illegal venture and not their names. The only exception was that, in some cases, the name of one contact, the local equivalent of Mr. Wark in Ameschester, was stated. These records let Mr. Justice Amery know how many men were involved, but not who they were. He could not even presume that the local magistrates' aid to smuggling consisted of much more than ignoring the illegal activities if no one called them to the officials' attention. As a result, he could not remove them all out of hand and find replacements, even if he had had candidates whom he was sure were not tainted already by more direct participation in the free-trade.

The smugglers used a system where they loaded different barges for the seven different places that they sent the smuggled goods. Mr. Justice Amery had decided to promise each of the bargemen immunity if they cooperated in breaking up the smuggling ring at each location. Captain Bush thought this was a very clever stratagem. He had felt that the evidence about their being knowingly engaged in transporting contraband was not as conclusive as might be wished. They might be able to get away scot-free claiming that they knew nothing about their cargos even though their complicity might be inferred from their knowledge of how the illegal goods were always hidden under innocent ones and from the rush with which the contraband material was loaded on and off the barges. Breaking up the local networks with the bargemen's assistance seemed more valuable than having them punished for their share in the activity. In addition, they might be useful when the smuggling was replaced by transporting goods on which the duties had been paid.

The smugglers had used different barges for each of the various locations as a matter of principle. Judge Amery felt that this had been a way of trying to isolate the different links in the chain so that if one were shut down by the authorities, as the

Ameschester one had been, the others might not be affected. What they had not made provision for was that the center of the network would be discovered and taken before all incriminating evidence was destroyed.

It had taken some planning before Mr. Amery could arrange a way to shut down the smuggling along the length of the canal. He had to get processes in place to hold any of the principal smugglers he caught without relying on the local magistrates. It would involve terminating the appointments of the justices of the peace and selecting replacements from among local gentlemen who turned out to be engaged in smuggling only as customers. He would use members of the army to apprehend and enforce the detention of suspected smugglers until the new civil regime was in place. Above all, Mr. Amery would have to move swiftly so that news of the shutting down of smuggling in one center would not warn those in other places to suspend operations until the crack-down on their activities faded away. Since crew members from *Flicker* had had to return to their ship when Captain Bolton's honeymoon had ended, the judge arranged for members of Captain Bush's crew to come from the Nore to replace them.

This delay had two effects. First, Mr. Amery was intercepting letters from some of the key men of the smuggling rings in the various locations asking about the delay in their shipments. The judge gloated over these missives since they revealed who were the ringleaders of the smuggling enterprise. He answered the letters with bland explanations about difficulties arising from sickness in Harksmouth, and the unusual difficulty smugglers were having in keeping clear of the revenue officials. All of them had delayed the shipments, he said in his answers which gave no hint of the real reason that the trade was interrupted.

Major Stoner broke into Captain Bush's account at that point to say, "That was all poppy-cock of course. We were being swamped with new arrivals of valuable cargos which would now enter the legitimate trade. No shortage of stuff to send up the canal, No shortage at all! Only problems were to make sure that we could find someplace to store what we bought and to find the money to pay the ship's captains for their cargoes. Captain Giles had provided what should have been plenty of money before he left, but now we were running out. Mr. Amery did not want to ask you, Lady Ashton, since your family had already spent so much. Anyway, he was afraid that we could not communicate with you quickly enough to solve the crisis."

"What did you do?" asked Mr. Moorhouse, who could not quite believe that his unexciting neighbors had been engaged in such activities. Daphne had been deliberately vague in talking with him about the extent to which she had become involved with the problem of smuggling. She felt that it would worry him to no useful purpose to learn that she might be putting herself into some peril at a time when Giles was away. Now her father was finding that she was virtually the ringleader of a group that included his friends Captain Bush and Mr. Justice Amery.

"Captain Bush came to the rescue. Like Captain Giles, he had an account at Coutts's Bank and stepped in with more bills of exchange which the local bank was happy to honor, having had no problems with Captain Giles's notes."

"That was very good of you, Captain Bush," Daphne broke in. "Of course, Captain Giles and I will reimburse you. I know you are not much of a financial risk-taker."

"I wasn't in the past, my lady," replied Captain Bush. "But that was mainly at the time when I only had just enough money to keep myself and my family in genteel circumstances. My fortunes improved after you showed me that being crippled did not mean that I had to forgo all activity and when Captain

Giles's summoned me to take command of a frigate. There was the prize money I got when we were rescuing the captured frigates and also from our fight with the French on that occasion. My command in the North Sea also produced a lot of prize money. Our taking the two frigates certainly will have helped some more in that direction. I am now far richer than I ever expected to be. I thought that maybe you would let me have a share in the counter-smuggling activities as an investor. I could certainly also help with some of the work involved, for it is likely to be much more complicated than I imagine you expected."

"Welcome aboard, Captain Bush. How will things be more complicated?"

"First, if you want to be able to control the sale of the goods that are usually smuggled into the places where we have interrupted the illegal trade, Mr. Amery thinks that you should try to include local gentry in the business. Second, it looks like we will need even more money. We can accompany both by selling shares to men of local influence. He suggests that you consult with Mr. Snodgrass to see if he knows how to set it up. Otherwise, there are solicitors in London whom he can recommend."

"Couldn't Mr. Amery handle the legal side for us?" Daphne asked.

"He says not. As a judge, he shouldn't even be advising about the terms to be incorporated in any documents."

"I see. Let's talk to Mr. Snodgrass about it."

Daphne summoned Mr. Snodgrass to come to Dipton Hall the next day, where she met with him and Captain Bush.

"You are very wise to consult me, Lady Ashton and Captain Bush," was the lawyer's reaction after they had laid out the situation for him. Quite apart from your need to expand your efforts – I will not quite call it a business, it is more an active investment, surely – it is always desirable for partners in a venture to have the terms of an understanding written down and agreed upon."

"Is that necessary?" Captain Bush asked. "I trust Captain Giles and Lady Ashton completely."

"That trust is fully reciprocated by us," added Daphne, a bit huffily.

"I am sure that is the case," Mr. Snodgrass said in soothing terms. "But you have to remember the hazards of living, especially as Captain Bush may be called again to serve in the Navy. Captain Giles is already at sea, and you, Lady Ashton, may yet face the challenges of childbirth. It makes things so much easier for those who have to sort out the affairs of the deceased if understandings about financial matters are made explicit.

"I suggest that you set up a private company. Initially, the shares should be divided in proportion to on the contribution which each of you has made. Further shares could be issued in exchange for money or services. For instance, Major Stoner may want to take some of the money you will be paying him in shares rather than in cash, or you may find that there are others who want to be involved financially in your activity. You, of course, would determine how much of a contribution is needed per share."

"It does seem to be getting complicated," Daphne complained.

"That is because even things that seem to be simple have a way of becoming very complicated if the untoward should happen. It is a good idea to take care before you start of the possibilities that might arise."

"Well, then, Mr. Snodgrass. Draw up the papers and bring them here for Captain Bush and me to examine."

When the lawyer had left the room, Daphne looked at Captain Bush and remarked, "I do wish that Captain Giles were here to consult about this."

"To tell you the truth, Lady Ashton, I think he would know even less than I do about these things and he would just rely on you."

"Maybe so, but I would be happier if he had a say in all of this. I just wish he were here, whether or not he could help with these problems."

Captain Bush was saved the need to respond to this remark by Steves who arrived to announce that the Honorable Penelope de Roy had come to visit Lady Ashton.

"Show her into the morning room, Steves. We will join her there right away."

"I'll take my leave, Lady Giles," Captain Bush said hurriedly as Steves left the room.

"You will do no such thing, Captain Bush. Miss de Roy will undoubtedly want to hear about your exploits in Harksmouth. And I want to show you off. Captain Giles is not here, of course, but I want to introduce my visitor to a genuine war hero. You must learn to take your place in society and not restrict yourself to only a few close friends."

Bush reluctantly agreed to accompany Daphne to the morning room to greet Miss de Roy. Daphne made him even more uncomfortable when she said to her guest, "Miss de Roy. I believe that I introduced you to Captain Bush at your ball. Captain Bush has just returned from helping Mr. Justice Amery suppress smuggling in Harksmouth."

That start to the conversation led Miss de Roy into questioning Captain Bush so that she could pry out of him some of the details of his adventures. She was not put off by one-word answers to her first queries, and soon she had him explaining in detail what was involved in taking a barge up a canal. The conversation went on for half an hour before Bush remembered that he was supposed to be reluctant about meeting the lady and found an excuse to leave. After he had left, Daphne said to her guest, "Miss de Roy, I had no idea you were so interested in how to handle a river barge."

Her guest laughed, "I never was before. But I have been told that the best strategy for conversing with men is to get them to explain what they have been doing. It puts them at ease and can be quite interesting. It is the quickest way to find out if they are blowhard bores or people worth drawing out. Excuse me. I suppose that blowhard is not a proper word for ladies to use. My father has not been much of a guide in such matters."

"I don't see why it would be inappropriate. Which category does Captain Bush fit into?"

"Oh, definitely the second one. Didn't you see how he downplayed his own role in everything?"

"Yes, that is rather a characteristic of Captain Bush. You seem to have found out a great deal about talking to gentlemen for the first time, especially for someone who came out such a short time ago."

Miss de Roy laughed. "Yes, I have had quite a few men show an interest in me. Even before the ball. My Aunt Doreen has said that for someone in my position it is desirable to get engaged to be married while one is new in society. Otherwise, the novelty wears off, and one may be overlooked."

"Someone in your position?"

"Yes. You may not know it, but my dowry is not going to be at all large, and, of course, I am only an 'Honorable,' not a 'Lady.' That means I am not much of a catch for someone who aspires to rise in society."

"And you have to get married?"

"Well, Aunt Doreen says so. My father is not rich, and his estate is all tied up in some silly escrow that means it will go to his cousin and I may be cut off without anything. I don't know what I would do then. But the idea of being tied down to some man who only wants me as a stepping stone to society does not appeal, even if they are rich. I confess, I would much rather have someone like Captain Bush, who is interesting and has led an exciting life. You have no idea how much more interesting his talk of river barges was than the boasting of the men my aunt has introduced me to."

"It sounds as if you might set your cap at him."

"I think that I might do that. I know that Captain Bush has his mother and sisters to look after, but that simply indicates what a good man he is. Many others would find excuses not to support them as generously. I suppose there might be the problem that he might think that he cannot support a wife, but I can hope not. But I am getting way ahead of myself. You saw how he rushed off after only spending a short time with us."

Daphne laughed, "Penelope – may I call you Penelope? – and you must call me Daphne -- I was amazed at how much time Captain Bush spent with us. I expected him to think up an excuse to leave us in the first five minutes. If you interest him, money will not be a consideration. When he arrived at Dipton, he hardly had enough to sustain him and his family in the style that he wanted. Since then he has earned a great amount of prize money."

The next half hour was spent by Miss de Roy grilling Daphne about Captain Bush, and by Daphne leading the conversation in ways which would let her know more about what her visitor valued. She concluded that Penelope would be a very suitable wife for her friend. However, she did realize that any pressure from her on Captain Bush to marry Miss de Roy would have to be subtle. Daphne would have to hold her tongue, but that didn't mean that she could not think of ways to put the two together, as long as it did not seem that she was pushing them together. "How to lead them to the altar," she wondered to herself. It would help if any of the three female residents of the Dower cottage were to marry, relieving Captain Bush's responsibilities in that direction somewhat. She was sure that, cautious man that he was when he wasn't engaged in a bloody fight, he would more readily think of marriage if his other responsibilities were diminished

Daphne shrugged the thought aside. She was being silly. She had too much on her plate as it was without adding scheming how to get others to share the same wonderful married state that she enjoyed. She was so lucky to have Giles, even if he was away at sea, that she would like everyone else to be as happy. However, these things had to take their natural course, and she shouldn't worry too much about speeding them along. She had enough other things to worry about as it was.

Chapter XXI

Mr. Justice Amery turned up the next day. He was staying with Mr. Moorhouse at Dipton Manor, but his purpose in returning was to see Daphne. She had just settled down in the morning room, with her guilty indulgence which was coffee, when Steves announced her guest. Why she felt guilty about enjoying the beverage wasn't clear to her. She could certainly afford it, and she took no pleasure in denying herself anything she desired. The coffee beans had not even been smuggled. Maybe it was because women weren't allowed into coffee shops and she felt that by having her coffee in the morning she was thumbing her nose at that most unfair custom.

Her pleasure at having coffee was enhanced by the fact that she had had to forego that luxury for some time due to lack of supplies. Coffee was, of course, among the items on which there was a high tariff. When Major Stoner was distributing the materials that Daphne had acquired by destroying the smuggling ring that supplied Dipton, he had set aside an adequate quantity of coffee to meet the needs of Dipton Hall. Unfortunately, after he had sold all the rest of the coffee, it turned out that sea-water had damaged the sacks destined for Lady Ashton's residence. The brew they produced was undrinkable. The Major and Captain Bush had arrived on the next barge which had unloaded at Daphne's landing which had been acquired when Giles purchased Hillcrest Grange. It spoke highly of Major Stoner's arrangements that some of the coffee included in the new shipment had already been delivered to Dipton Hall. Daphne was about to enjoy her first cup in a very long time. Of course, she was happy to share the coffee with Mr. Amery.

"I hear that your efforts to put down smuggling have met with great success, Mr. Amery," Daphne started the conversation.

"Yes, indeed, my lady. Captain Giles and Captain Bush were invaluable, as was Major Stoner. It was very good of you all to pitch in to help suppress the trade here."

"Well, we have been handsomely rewarded for it, even Captain Bush, who is now our partner in the new scheme."

"That is what I want to talk to you about, Lady Ashton."

"Yes?"

"I am sure that we have not rounded up everyone who was involved in smuggling in the other towns where we shut it down. Such people will have a vested interest in your failure to establish a legal trade."

"I hadn't thought of that, but I suppose that you are correct."

"I am afraid I am. We have not found all the tentacles of the trade in the other places in the way that we have been able to do in Ameschester, thanks to your assistance."

"Is there anything that we can do about this problem?"

"One thing that comes to mind is to involve some prominent men in each place in your new endeavor. If they stood to lose something by your business failing, they might be more prepared to help make sure that smuggling is not resumed."

"What do you have in mind?"

"I was wondering if there was some way you could let them share in the profits. In exchange for investing in the venture, of course. Some sort of joint-stock venture."

"Captain Bush and I are finalizing the terms of our partnership with our lawyer. They will make it possible for others to participate if they make the appropriate payment or assistance to the endeavor. Two things about it do give me concern."

"What are they?"

"First, many prominent people must have invested in the smuggling operation in the other places, just as they did in Ameschester. They will have lost their stake in the same way that the people here have. Would they want to invest again?"

"We'll have to see. I am always surprised how often men who have been duped with bogus canal projects come back looking for more. Your second worry is what?"

"Captain Giles is, of course, the major figure behind our venture into supplying duty-paid goods. As you know, he is the son of the Earl of Camshire. I am afraid that my father-in-law has a reputation for touting very dubious propositions. So much so that I am told he is no longer even asked to put his name even on shady endeavors, let alone genuine ones. Won't that reputation rub off, so we cannot get investors on practicable terms?"

"The estrangement of your husband from his father is very widely known. Captain Giles has a reputation for probity in his dealings and is, of course, a well-known hero. I don't think the Earl's reputation will be a problem. I think that the idea that men will be in league with the renowned Captain Giles, Viscount Ashton, will greatly enhance the desirability of joining the venture. To that end, however, it will make raising the money much easier if you make a little trip to meet with the men we have in mind. I know that you seem to be impervious to the wish to get reflected glory from associating with prominent people, but that is not true of most of the gentry. Just being in the same room with you would make them want to participate."

"I cannot believe it."

"Let me convince you."

"How?"

"By going to the nearest of the places, Netherham, and seeing some of the local gentry. It is only a morning's ride over there if we leave early, and we can be back before dark if you wish, or you could stay there."

"I don't think that would be quite proper, especially with Captain Giles away."

"You may be right."

"Well, let me think about it."

"Of course. But please don't wait too long. It will take a bit of time to arrange."

Daphne was of two minds about Mr. Amery's suggestion. She certainly did not want smuggling to become prevalent again in Ameschester, and it did make sense that stopping it all along the Harksmouth canal would diminish the chances of the nefarious activity reoccuring. Indeed, in terms of the Crown getting its due revenues to further the war, it little mattered where smuggling was reduced. However, even with Major Stoner taking over much of the management of the enterprise, the more elaborate it became, the more she would have to spend time on it. Daphne knew that she could not own something without being involved in making sure that it was being managed properly and she wanted to do other things with her time. Also, how would it affect Giles's and her standing in the community? Wasn't running a supply business becoming too involved in trade to be suitable for someone of her class? She wasn't sure. There seemed to be a great deal of arbitrariness in what was regarded as appropriate or inappropriate for the nobility. Unfortunately, she did not have anyone she could consult. Well, that wasn't true. The Countess of Camshire would certainly have an informed opinion on the subject. She would ask Lady Clara as soon as she had a chance to talk privately with her.

Daphne's opportunity to talk with the Countess came sooner than she had expected. After musing about what Mr. Amery had suggested for some time, she thought that a much better use of her time would be to visit Bernard in his nursery. That would also help her to focus on what was truly worthwhile in her life. When she entered the room, however, she found that the Countess was already there. Her mother-in-law was playing a game with Bernard which seemed to involve counting his fingers and a certain amount of tickling. The child was gurgling and giggling in delight. The Countess handed the child to Daphne while remarking wistfully, "I wish that I had done more of this sort of thing with my sons when they were at that age."

Daphne took up where the Countess left off, finding even more ways to keep Bernard interested in the marvels of his fingers. But all too soon, the child showed signs of being exhausted, despite being eager to continue the game. Nanny Weaver had been looking on very disapprovingly. Now she announced firmly that Master Bernard needed his nap. After the child had been taken away, Daphne had her chance to ask about the Countess's opinion on Mr. Amery's proposal. Daphne also wanted to know what Lady Camshire might think would be Giles's reaction if she undertook the visits.

Daphne had presumed that her mother-in-law would be against the idea. She was only asking in order to gauge how strong her objections would be and so judge much damage carrying out the scheme would do the reputations of Giles and herself. The Countess's reaction was not at all what she expected.

"I suppose, my dear, that you are worried about what other people will think, and especially how it will reflect on your husband's reputation, and what he will think of it."

"Yes, I guess I am. I do not fully understand how these opinions are formed."

"The rules governing general opinion are very complicated, and sometimes very silly. In this case, though, I think it is simple, and you should do whatever you want. Let me explain."

What the Countess said next was also not what Daphne might have expected.

"To take things in reverse order, Richard and what he will think. You know him far better than I do or than most wives know their husbands. But I do know that he has immense regard for your opinions, Daphne. If you think it is the right thing to do, so will he. You have to remember that he has received very little help from his father and he has made an enormous success of his profession. He did this entirely on his own merits and without toadying to the opinions of his superiors even though that is usually required for success. You must know that initially most of society, including myself, thought that marrying you was quite beneath him. He knew it too, but that didn't matter a jot to him. He is now in a position where other's opinions about any venture you undertake cannot affect him. Even if that weren't the case, I am sure that he would want you to do what you think is right.

"Next, how will it affect Richard's reputation? I wouldn't worry about it since he won't.

"Finally, how will others think of it. Richard won't care. Moreover, this endeavor is not at all like what the Earl, my husband, has been doing and which has brought him into such disrepute. He has been taking money to promote dubious ventures in which he has no real stake himself and making false claims about them. Even so, though he is not now thought of highly, it is the fools who are taken in by his claims who are at fault. And that is not what has driven him into hard times. No, his problems come from his gambling and from his throwing money away on the vilest of entertainments. There is no chance that Richard will do either of those."

Daphne was taken aback with how violently Lady Clara expressed her feelings about the Earl's activities; she had always presumed that the Countess had turned a blind eye to her husband's shortcomings about which Daphne had learned primarily from her brother-in-law, Lord David.

"That is very helpful, ' Daphne said. "It has clarified several things for me."

"I'm glad, my dear. Can I add a bit more advice, based more on what I have observed about how men behave rather than on any merits of your scheme."

"Please do."

"First, don't overpromise the returns that people can expect from your venture and make very clear what are any dangers to its success of which you are aware. Too many undertakings are sold on the basis of unreasonable expectations and so result in dissatisfaction with the results even though the returns are favorable. Second, try not to take money that the men cannot afford to lose. That one is harder, but I am told that you can sometimes guess that it is the case. Such people are very resentful if a venture does not succeed, even if it is not losing money for the investors."

"I'll keep that in mind. You seem to know a lot about business."

"Not really dear. I didn't form these opinions based on what men say, for they never talk to me about such matters. But their wives do, and they reflect the feelings of their husbands, especially the husbands who have not managed their affairs well."

Daphne saw Mr. Amery later in the day and told him that she was willing to try his scheme by visiting Netherham after the meeting of the Ameschester Hunt, which was only two days away. He said he would arrange the trip for a couple of days after that. He mentioned that, since the meeting was to be held on the side of Ameschester nearer to Netherham, some people from the other town might join the hunt and could help spread the word among their neighbors about what was happening.

The Ameschester Hunt met at the estate of Sir Warmouth Gravemend. Sir Warmouth had asked Daphne to stay the night before the meeting at his estate. The invitation surprised Daphne since she hardly knew Sir Warmouth, having encountered him at a few times hunts.

The reason for the invitation was explained by Daphne's brother-in-law, Lord David. His experiences as a Member of Parliament were making him increasingly both more worldly and more cynical. Sir Warmouth was a prominent member of the Ameschester Hunt. As such he had, of course, heard that Viscount and Lady Ashton were providing for the hounds. The news had come with thankfulness by many prominent men, including Sir Warmouth, that the problem had been solved with no drain on their pocketbooks. The status of the owners of Dipton Hall had also been elevated because, somehow, the naval captain and his wife had succeeded in increasing their income sufficiently that substantial expenditures could willingly be committed for the general good of the neighborhood. The reaction to Giles's contribution, Lord David noted, was remarkably different from that which had greeted Colonel Redferns' taking on the hounds. That contribution had been seen as an attempt at social climbing. Viscount and Lady Giles had already arrived. Lord David's acerbic remarks did not discourage Daphne from accepting the invitation happily.

Daphne was disappointed in her evening at Sir Warmouth Gravemend's estate. The men wanted to talk about hunting primarily and what they had read in the paper about the war, not realizing that Daphne, as a Captain's wife, might have some interesting insights into the situation. They had failed to follow up on any remarks on the subject which she made. It was clear that they were sure that no woman could make worthwhile contributions to their discussion. By contrast, the women were primarily concerned with fashion and the difficulties that arose from adapting to the recent changes in style. However, they were not dressed in remarkable ways which would indicate that they took the subject seriously. Daphne found their conversation tedious.

Daphne raised the subject of smuggling on two occasions. The first was at the full dinner table. The men stated that they were sure that there had never been smuggled goods in the area and that they would not buy them even if they were available. Only one of them knew that there were labels that proved that the appropriate duties had been paid on the goods. He had been at a loss to understand why this information was of interest to Daphne. He had never looked for them, leaving all such matters to his butler.

The position of the guests amused Daphne though she had the good manners not to reveal it. She knew that all of them, or at least their butlers, were good customers not only of the present endeavor but also of the previous illicit trade that delivered the goods to their doors. It would take very deliberate blindness not to know why their cellars had to be refilled by the light of the moon.

The second occasion for mentioning smuggling occurred in the drawing room after the ladies had withdrawn so that the men could drink in their absence. The ladies also claimed a horror at the thought of dealing in smuggled goods, even though Daphne was sure that their gowns were made of material that had come in smuggler's cargoes.

The next day dawned with what promised to be very fine weather. As the riders were milling around waiting for the hunt to begin, Daphne was pleased to see that Dipton was well represented. Lord David had ridden over with Mr. Moorhouse and Captain Bush. Daphne was relieved when Lord David suggested that she might like to ride with him until the fox was started and running well. She had had enough of Sir Warmouth's guests.

Daphne's interest in the social aspect of a hunt meeting was piqued when she saw that The Baron de Roy had come with his daughter. They were not regular attendees at meetings of the hunt. Indeed, Lord de Roy had told Daphne that he did not enjoy the sport. He did, however, seem to enjoy greeting acquaintances. Daphne was amused to note that, while her father was occupied in talking with his friends, Penelope had let her horse drift over to where Captain Bush sat waiting for the meet to start. Captain Bush was not one for idle chatter, but he did seem to be more animated than usual when making comments to his new companion.

The horn sounded. The whole group started off two-by-two, walking their horses slowly along a narrow lane. Daphne rode beside Lord David. A few horses ahead, Penelope was paired with Captain Bush. Daphne hoped that her new friend would not try to keep up with her partner when the hunt started to race after hounds because a fox had been discovered. Captain Bush, usually the most sedate of men, changed completely in the excitement of the hunt. He was known to ride recklessly in his eagerness to keep up with the hounds. Daphne, with her usual disregard for senseless conventions, was riding astride her horse, her hunting costume featuring a long skirt whose folds hid the fact that it was, in reality, a pair of trousers. By contrast, Penelope was riding side-saddle which made he much more liable for being involuntarily dismounted than did Daphne's style of riding. Penelope's trying to keep up with Captain Bush if he was dashing wildly after the hounds could be very dangerous. Would the naval officer remember this fact when the frenzy of following the hounds started or would he react in his usual boisterous manner?

The answer came soon. Captain Bush was mad keen to follow the hounds. He charged off towards the nearest hedge. Daphne guessed that he had presumed that Miss de Roy would set off at a more restrained pace if he had thought about it at all. Such was not the case. Penelope urged her mount into a full gallop as well. Disaster threatened. Daphne was particularly worried. Not only because the young lady was riding side-saddle, but also because her horse was not as smooth a hunter as Captain Bush's, while she was not as experienced as he was at dashing across the countryside.

What Daphne had feared happened at the first jump. Penelope's horse balked. She left her saddle and sailed over her horse's head straight into the hedge. It cushioned her fall, but she fell in a heap onto the ground. Daphne and Lord David spurred their horses to come to her aid. There was no sign of Captain Bush. Presumably, he had not heard Miss de Roy's cry and was still galloping after the hounds.

Lord David lept from his horse and ran towards Penelope. Daphne was close behind him. Their worst fears were not realized. Already the downed woman was shaking her head and starting to rise. She fell back with a cry as she tried to put weight on one of her legs. Daphne knelt beside her.

"Where does it hurt?"

"My ankle. Otherwise, I think I am all right, just shaken up a little."

"Please sit still while I have a look at your ankle."

Daphne as a girl had spent a good deal of time following Mr. Jackson, the apothecary-physician, around. He may have been annoyed at times by her presence, but he always had had the patience to explain to her what he was doing. As a result, she felt confident that she could evaluate how severe Penelope's injury was. Gesturing the other people to stand back, she knelt on the ground and eased off her patient's boot. She ran her hand up and down the injured ankle as Mr. Jackson had shown her. It was swelling most alarmingly, but Daphne was pretty sure that it was only a nasty sprain and that no bones had been broken. While putting some weight on the ankle would not be a good idea, that would not be as harmful as if there were a broken bone. Daphne had at first thought that they would have splint the leg, but now she was confident that it would be better to move her patient from the cold spot she was in.

Daphne had taken her carriage to travel to Sir Warmouth's estate accompanied by Betsy, with a groom riding her hunter, Serene Masham. She had given instructions that the coach could be used to follow the hunt to provide some entertainment for her servants. Luckily, the carriage was still where it had stopped in the lane at a place where they could watch the initial burst of activity, including the Honorable Penelope de Roy's spectacular fall.

"I think it would be best, Miss de Roy, if we take you in my carriage to your home where you can be more comfortable while a physician is summoned to evaluate your injury properly. I'll get my driver and groom to help carry you to the coach. The groom can then ride your horse to Bestercrest Hall."

Daphne was about to ask Lord David to go to the coach to get needed help when he made her request irrelevant by picking up the wounded woman and telling Penelope to put her arms around his neck. He then walked off in the direction of the coach carrying her as if her weight was a negligible burden. Daphne was left to gather up the reins of the three horses and follow him. She was astounded by his action. What had come over the Vicar of Dipton? While he was always a model of politeness, such impulsive action was not at all like him. Was it proper for him to pick up a lady and carry her off, even if she was injured and he was only taking her to a handy means of transport? It was hardly the action of a man more notable for carefully planning ways to sit on the Bench of Bishops than for acting as a gallant knight-errant.

Daphne's next surprise came after Penelope had been settled comfortably in her carriage and they were about to set off. Daphne would, of course, accompany the carriage to make sure that all went well. Without thinking about it, she had just presumed that Lord David would either ride off to see if, by luck, the hunt had turned back towards them so he could rejoin it or else he would return to Dipton. Instead, he insisted that he must also accompany the carriage to Bestercrest Hall. She was nothing adverse to being accompanied by him. However, it wasn't like him to take on such an unnecessary and unrewarding task.

The journey to Bestercrest Hall was uneventful. Her father returned almost as soon as Daphne had Penelope installed on a couch in the drawing room, with lots of blankets and cushions to ease her damaged leg, and tea and crumpets to mitigate her disappointment at missing the hunt. Though the

Baron invited both Daphne and Lord David to stay, they declined his offer promising to come soon to check on the state of his daughter.

Riding back to Dipton, Lord David extracted from his sister-in-law every bit of information about Miss de Roy that Daphne knew, asking particularly if she had any reason to think that the lady had suitors. He was clearly smitten with Penelope, Daphne thought, though she could not see any logical basis for it. Was he serious? She knew that he wanted to marry and that he had been calculating just what sort of match would best advance his hopes of becoming a bishop. Miss de Roy, though most acceptable in status since she was the daughter of a Baron, was without the ties to society that would advance his ambitions. Despite this shortcoming, it seemed that Miss de Roy might well have two very eligible suitors vying for her hand.

When they were about to part at the vicarage in Dipton, Daphne teased Lord David by saying, "David, it sounds to me as if you have a serious interest in Miss de Roy."

Her brother-in-law laughed. "She is an interesting lady, Daphne, but you will have to abandon your matchmaking in this case. I will need a wife better suited to being a bishop's helpmate, one who will be more advantageously placed to advance my progress."

Such a calculating approach to marriage was usual, Daphne knew. She had been lucky that Giles had not had similar concerns when they met. At that time, he had been a younger son of a nobleman with a career that might benefit from acquiring influential relatives by marriage. She had been fortunate that he had not considered marriage a way of finding such backing or, if he had, he had not let such considerations determine his choice. She had been lucky! It never occurred to her that, if Giles had been the sort of man who calculated the influence a wife might bring, she would never have been attracted to him in the first place.

Daphne's pregnancy manifested itself at that moment. The baby decided that it was the right moment to kick. It certainly was! She had begun to be apprehensive that this development had not yet occurred. It also reminded Daphne of her priorities. Now her most pressing job was to write Giles a letter with the fantastic news that the baby had kicked. Was it a boy or a girl? She knew that Giles would be happy with either, as would she.

Chapter XXII

Daphne had expected that she would have no worries about hosting the last meeting of the Ameschester Hunt and the Hunt Ball. After all, Dipton Hall had held both those events in the past. Steves was perfectly capable of supervising both events with aplomb. Indeed, he reveled in being in charge of the special occasions not only because it allowed him to show off his special and superior abilities, but also because of the kudos it gave him among all the other butlers in the neighborhood who had no such splendid events to supervise. Dipton Hall would put its best foot forward if he had anything to say about it. Luckily Mrs. Wilson, the housekeeper, and Mrs. Darling the cook took equally great pride in the event.

What Daphne had not realized was that word had spread throughout Society that the Ameschester Hunt Ball was the event of the year outside London. It wasn't just that the previous Ball had been a resounding success, though it had been. The fact was that almost everyone in Society had heard of Lady Ashton. Her husband was renowned for his repeated successes which were trumpeted in the press. Furthermore, Daphne's reputation as an able, unconventional and uncommonly effective woman in her own right was spreading through the parlors and the drawing rooms of all the best people in London. There was even just a hint of scandal in the tale of how she had hoodwinked some people of dubious stature that made her even more fascinating. Daphne's eccentricity in that she did not take part in the London Season further increased curiosity about her. To see the Viscountess Aston, one would have to attend the Ameschester Hunt Ball. As a consequence, many members of high society suddenly found a reason to check whether any friends or relatives, close or distant, lived near enough to Lord Ashton's estate to make going to the Ball a reasonable activity when visiting. If such a visit was possible, they then tried to secure an invitation to stay over the period in which the Ball would be held, even though normally they would avoid the hazards and dullness of the country in late winter and early spring like the plague.

Daphne had heard some rumors of this sudden interest in visiting country estates near Dipton, but she had thought nothing much about them. However, she did warn Steves that they might expect a few more guests than last year. Luckily, Steves had heard all about the sudden popularity of the Dipton area from his network of butlers. His realization of the need to prepare for an unusually large attendance at the Ball had been confirmed when Elsie told him, on one of his not infrequent forays to the Dipton Arms, that every room in the inn was booked for the time of the Hunt Ball. She had heard that unusually large bookings were occurring at all the inns nearby.

Daphne had already ordered a ball gown in the latest fashion like the ones that magazines reported were all the rage in Paris. She had access to the newest imported fabrics, the result of her bringing foreign material into the area. She, of course, got first pick of them. Her position at the center of the new enterprise to supply goods necessary to the gentry ensured that she would be very well dressed for the occasion. She had planned to have a stunning gown. It would show the many ladies in the area, who thought that she was just an inexperienced country mouse, what she was capable of when she showed an interest in the latest styles. Now, even if the most fashion-conscious of ladies from London attended the Ball, she was confident that she would not be outshone in her own ballroom by outsiders.

Despite her nonchalance in the weeks preceding the Hunt, Daphne started to worry about a range of items that could spoil the event as the day of the Ball approached. What if it rained heavily so that the roads were turned too muddy for a coach to pass easily? Worse still, what if a late heavy snowfall closed all the roads? What if the hounds failed to find a fox during the hunt as sometimes happened? Worst of all, what if some prominent rider were injured or even worse killed. Fatal accidents did happen when hunting. Would they have to cancel the Ball if one occurred? Why, oh why, had she persuaded Mr. Summers to hold the Ball on the day of the last hunt of the season? Her reason had been simple. The decision meant that there would be no all-male hunt-dinner from which she would be excluded on the occasion of Dipton Hall hosting the Hunt. Telling herself that there was nothing she could do about any of these possibilities did not prevent them from keeping her awake at night as the crucial date approached.

The day of the Hunt dawned clear and warm. Daphne, as usual, was up early. The only departure from her usual morning routine was to have Betsy spend extra time dressing her hair. Daphne had ordered a new riding costume for the occasion, in a finer cloth and a more stylish cut than the one she had been using for the last couple of years. It had, as was always the case with her riding clothes, a more full skirt than fashion dictated. The skirt was in fact trousers. Daphne would be riding astride, not side-saddle as would most of the other ladies.

When Daphne was ready, and before any of the other riders had arrived, a groom brought her horse, Serene Masham, to the portico and helped her to mount. Soon after, riders started coming, and Daphne became busy welcoming them. She found that, unexpectedly, she enjoyed the activity. Usually, she took care when going hunting to arrive only a little before the hunters set off. She didn't like milling around purposelessly waiting for the main event to begin. Now she had a role in the proceedings, so she had a good reason to talk to everyone. The rumors of a uniquely large turnout proved to be a reality. Daphne was kept busy not only greeting old friends but also being introduced to many who were unknown to her.

Daphne's most satisfying moment in the leadup to the start came as she turned away from greeting two ladies so that she could be introduced to some others. She overheard Lady Evans say to Lady Dallindly, "She really does look lovely. And that habit. Mark my words, there will be far more ladies riding astride on Rotten Row now." Daphne knew that Rotten Row was the place to see and be seen for Society in London.

Even though there were so many more participants than usual, the Hunt began on time. To Daphne's delight, a fox was started almost immediately. To add to the contribution that she and Giles were making to the hunt, the hounds found the fox in Hillcrest Grange's wood. It had been off-limits to the Hunt until it was added to the holdings of Dipton Hall. Off galloped most of the riders, although there were many, including most of the ladies, who hung back intending to follow the hunt at a less energetic pace. Daphne's duties as a hostess that morning were over. Away she went with the others, knowing that Serene Malsham was one of the best horses and could carry her to be first at the kill, seemingly with less effort than the other rider's steeds.

The fox was a wily one and led them a merry chase through the fields and woods, doubling back and finding lines that the dogs had trouble following. Several times the hounds lost the scent, but they caught it again and away they went with those riders who had kept up galloping in pursuit.

The conclusion of the hunt came late in the day. Daphne was in at the kill, Serene Masham tossing her head as if to say, "See, I knew we would be here."

Daphne rode home with Captain Bush and Lord David, who for once had neither been thrown nor lost the pack. There was little talk, but the silence was companionable. Daphne worried that people would be too exhausted from the Hunt to enjoy the Ball, but the others assured her that those who lacked stamina had undoubtedly abandoned the hunt long before the end. Otherwise, their conversation consisted of gossip about who had come and what was known about them. Daphne lapped it up. She had been introduced to a large number of important strangers that morning, and anything was welcome that might help her when she met them again that evening. Not surprisingly, Lord David had more information than Captain Bush. His duties as a Member of Parliament meant that he rubbed shoulders quite often with men from London Society and had been to several fashionable soirées.

Daphne very much enjoyed her role of introducing people to each other, especially men from London to some of the unmarried ladies from the Ameschester area. She was fully indulging her tendency to want to see a romantic and successful marriage among her acquaintances. The introduction she took most secret pride in was the introduction of Lord David to Lady Cecilia Westerly, second daughter of the Earl of Tamerstead. Lady Cecilia was beautiful. In chatting with her briefly as the hunt gathered, Daphne had noticed that she sounded more interesting than most of the young society ladies she had encountered. The Earl was said to have significant influence, and, in the brief introduction to Daphne before the hunt, he had hinted at an interest in church affairs. Lord David secured several lines on Lady Cecilia's dance card. Just the match, thought Daphne, for her relative who hoped to be a bishop.

Daphne's dance card filled up quickly with a variety of men asking for a place, both married ones and inveterate bachelors. Captain Bush was, of course, one of them and Daphne noticed when she saw his card as he wrote her name on it that several spots had already been designated for the Honorable Miss de Roy. When he was dancing with her, a waltz,

Daphne teased him gently about what she had noticed and that she had seen that the rest of his dance card had been empty. Captain Bush blushed a deeper red than even a lifetime at sea had given his face and changed the subject to their anti-smuggling venture. He mentioned that he had been talking with a Mr. Hesketh, a landowner with extensive holdings near Netherham. Captain Bush thought that he might be a man of influence in that area and that he was interested in maintaining an honest trade in foreign trade, provided that it was not much more expensive to purchase legal items than the smuggled goods that he had been acquiring. Mr. Hesketh had noticed the hiatus in deliveries of contraband in his area and had wondered at the cause. Yes, he also knew a few men who might be willing to back, in a small way, the effort to maintain a reliable and above-board supply.

When the time for supper arrived, Daphne realized that she had neglected to arrange one small detail. She was to lead the guests into the room where the refreshments were to be served, and she had neglected to arrange a partner. Luckily for her, the Baron de Roy spotted her difficulty and came over to help out. Daphne was amused to find that he was also scouting the marriage market for his daughter. Daphne endured a grilling about Captain Bush's character, wealth and reliability. She was sure that her answers would advance her friend's prospects just as she was sure that Penelope would be much more instrumental than she was in getting the Baron to see Captain Bush as an excellent choice for his daughter. One thing did become evident in the discussion. The Baron de Roy wished that Captain Bush had a title, a knighthood at the least if something grander could not be achieved.

Everyone declared the Ball to be a huge success. Those who attended were sure that they could boast to those who had not about what a shame it was that they had not been able to be there. The implicit debts that many had made to secure a visit to the area were felt to have been well worth taking on. Throughout the region, conversation in the breakfast rooms, morning rooms, and parlors of the gentry was restricted to the Ball and the merits and eccentricities of the hostess.

What Daphne had not anticipated was that many of the visiting women wanted to call on her after the Ball. A matter of common courtesy, they told their hostesses, many of whom had never exchanged visits with Lady Ashton before, but were maneuvred into believing that now was the time to initiate the practice. The local ladies were prone to agreeing to go to Dipton Hall as many of them had been curious for some time about Viscountess Ashton, and now it would not seem artificial for them to want to visit Dipton Hall.

Daphne, at best, tolerated the stilted encounters with ladies who had little in common with her. They were visiting to establish their status rather than for any other reason. Three days of having her morning room crammed with people she did not know and in whose activities and attitudes she had little interest were enough. She sent word to Mr. Justice Amery, who was staying at Dipton Manor with her father that she thought it would be an excellent idea to try out his suggestion for exploring interest in her venture along the canal. Indeed, it should be acted upon as soon as possible.

Three days later, Daphne settled down in her carriage with Mr. Justice Amery, Captain Bush, and Major Stoner. Betsey rode outside with the coach driver and a footman for the trip to Netherham. After the coachman had asked directions in the town, the coach drove on to their destination, Haversly Court. It was a rambling old house, that must have grown by stages as the needs and fortunes of the inhabitants increased. It was charming, though of no outstanding architectural merit. Instead, it blended smoothly into its surroundings in a way that hid the fact that the various additions, while not clashing with the existing house, also did not have the same architectural features. As the carriage drew up to the modest front door of the house, Daphne could hear the baying of hounds. Did Mr. Hesketh keep the hounds for the local hunt? Perhaps she could learn from him more about the problems that having the hounds might present.

Mr. Hesketh was a ruddy-faced large man with an accent that, though refined, hinted strongly of his county. Daphne quickly took to him since he was a no-nonsense type of country gentleman with a good knowledge of his fields and what was being grown on them. He showed surprise when he learned that Daphne knew as much about agriculture as he did. The presence of others meant that they could not indulge in their conversational preferences immediately, though he did invite Daphne to see some of his recent changes after luncheon.

Mrs. Hesketh was a match for her husband, a buxom friendly woman with no pretensions to fashion or elegance, though her gown was of high-quality material and cut in a contemporary manner. After a few general words, the men in the party drifted into their own conversation while Daphne and Mrs. Hesketh were left, implicitly to talk of women's matters. Daphne was more amused than angered by this development. It was just what she expected.

Mrs. Hesketh startled Daphne with her opening question, "When is the baby due, Lady Ashton?"

"I didn't think it showed yet," she protested.

"It doesn't unless one knows what to look for. You are glowing as only a pregnant woman can, though I am afraid many go the other way and look drawn out and wasted."

"My best guess is August."

"Is this your first child?"

286

"No. I have a son, Bernard. He is just starting to walk."

"Oh, that is such a wonderful age! I remember how special it is."

"Do you have children, Mrs. Hesketh?"

"Yes, we had five, but only two have survived. One girl and one boy. Harold is twenty-eight, not yet married. He didn't like working for his father, so now he has taken a position as a steward at another estate near here. That is not going very well either. The man for whom he is working isn't willing to spend any money on maintaining and improving his property and, if his tenants try, he takes any gain from them by raising the rents. My daughter, Angelina, is eighteen, so you may have seen her at your Ball."

"I probably did, but I have to confess that there were so many people there whom I didn't know that I cannot remember most of them. Very wicked of me, I know."

"Nonsense, I don't know how you managed so very well. Mr. Dalrumble and I thought it was, by all means, the best ball we have ever attended, and I know that doesn't happen without the hostess putting in a lot of effort. Angelina also loved your event. It was her first ball, and she had a wonderful time. She danced most of the dances."

"I am glad that she enjoyed it. I do hope that some of the men she met will be seriously interested in her."

"Let's hope so. Angelina has many of the accomplishments that are supposed to make young ladies attractive to possible mates."

"Does your son take after his father in his interest in modern farming ways?"

"Yes, he does. They can argue for hours about it. He only left us because he thought that his father would never let him try out his ideas when they disagreed."

"I may need a steward who is familiar with modern farming ways. The position is in Ashton, so it is not in this neighborhood. If your son might be interested, ask him to contact me."

Luncheon was an uneventful time, though entirely pleasant. When Mr. Hesketh took Daphne for a tour of his property, his astonishment at her knowledge only increased, while she was full of admiration at how his land was being managed. The soil at Netherton was a bit different from that at Dipton, and they were mutually interested in how each dealt with the problems presented by their area, and in some cases got some ideas that they might try on their own properties. He did mention that his son was equally knowledgeable about how to handle the challenges of getting good yields over the long haul from different fields.

Daphne had agreed with Mr. Amery and Captain Bush that probably the most effective way to find out the interest of the leaders of Netherton society in their venture was to have them discuss it after dinner with the people whose aid they were soliciting. Mr. Hesketh, however, did raise the subject when he and Daphne were sitting on their horses by the side of the river, which was part of the canal system in Netherham. They were admiring the estate across the river which was sited in such a way as to have a swath of lawns with clumps of shrubs sloping down to the river bank.

"I wonder who will take that property over now," Mr. Hesketh mused.

"Is it for sale?" Daphne asked idly.

"Yes. Oh, I suppose that you wouldn't know about it. That is Bryne Hill, Sir Lucas Wharton's estate. He was one of the central figures financing the smugglers along the canal. I didn't know anything about it until Mr. Justice Amery started rounding up all the ringleaders. Sir Lucas's place suddenly became empty. He had left announcing that he had an exciting venture to pursue in Maryland. We were all puzzled by it until the smuggling operation was smashed. Then it emerged that he was deeply involved in the illegal activity.

"I must say that I am glad that you and Captain Bush are trying to find a way so that we don't have to rely on smugglers. Until now, of course, we had no choice if we wanted any number of goods. It wasn't just a matter of cost, though that was a big part of it, of course. Things simply were not available here, unless you were prepared to place orders, sight unseen, from a very long way off."

"I hope you will support us in trying to make sure that the excise has been paid so that we can all have uninterrupted supplies."

"Yes, I will. I confess that I had no idea how the canal was being used for smuggling, even though it should have been obvious. I think we all presumed that the stuff came in over the roads at night and that it was healthier for us all to ignore it. I should have known because I am one of the people who have seen some of the advantages to be gained from the improvements to the river bank and the course of the river.

"You can see that the towpath runs along the bank of the river on my land. This part of the riverbank used to be a muddy, sloping area, good for nothing and a problem if one wanted to keep a boat to go fishing or what have you. The river rose and fell a good deal over the year. Now, one can count on good banks and the same level of water from one lock to the next. I had a pleasure barge built so that we could enjoy the river on summer afternoons and evenings. Come, I'll show you."

They turned their horses and followed the towpath around a copse of beech trees. Ahead, there was a barge moored to the side of the canal. It had benches for rowers at the bow, followed by seats that had a canopy over them. At the very stern, there was a place for the helmsman. The craft was beautifully finished with gleaming varnish and brasswork.

"There it is!" Mr. Hesketh said with pride. "Got the idea from pictures of the boats used on the Thames in London. It's amazing what you can learn from magazines, isn't it, Lady Ashton?"

"I suppose that it is. What do you use the boat for?"

"Oh, only trips up and down the river. Sometimes we go through the locks and go to Hammersby, the next town along. Mainly it is very nice to use on a summer evening. You have no idea how relaxing it is to be rowed along this stretch. Often, Angelina plays her violin so that we have music. Of course, this is all very new. Building the barge was only finished last September, and it went back in the water only two days ago. I expect that I will use it a good deal this summer. I want to take it up to Ameschester for one thing."

"Then, when you do, you must visit Dipton Hall."

"I might take you up on that, my lady."

"I hope you do."

Haversley Court had a huge dining hall, that easily seated the large company who had been invited to meet Lady Ashton and Captain Bush. When Daphne commented on it, Mr. Hesketh told her that it was the oldest part of the house, dating from medieval times when the house had been part of a walled residence. The walls were long gone, but the hall had remained.

It was rarely used, but it was the most remarkable feature of the house.

After dinner, when Mrs. Hesketh was leading the ladies to the drawing room, which was some distance from the hall, she took Daphne aside. "Lady Ashton. Mr. Hesketh informed me about the purpose of your visit. I told him that we should invest in your venture because it makes sense in that it supports a better way to secure the availability of some of the things we use. I will let you in on a little secret we have. Mr. Hesketh is excellent at managing what is grown, but he has no real sense of business. He has learned to take my advice on all such matters, though he would never confess that fact to his friends. There are several other ladies here who direct their husbands' financial decisions. They will be the people deciding on your proposal in their households. I'll point them out to you, and you can try to persuade them. I'll also start a general conversation about the subject when we are settled if that is agreeable to you."

Mrs. Hesketh was as good as her word. In the general conversation that served as an introduction to Daphne, she led her guest through an account of her interest in countering smuggling along the canal. Daphne also explained why she thought it would be desirable to have local involvement in the project, though she neglected to mention the reason that it would prevent the men reverting to smuggling if it seemed to them a good idea. The ladies listened with an attention which might have surprised their husbands who, if they had thought of it at all, would presume that the ladies were talking fashions, children, and the marriage prospects of their children.

Later, when the ladies broke up into smaller groups to gossip, several approached Daphne to learn more about how their husbands could be part of the venture she was forming. It was evident from their questions that they were better informed about the state of their husbands' coffers than their husbands might suspect and that to a large extent they did control the purse strings.

The following morning saw the visitors from Dipton board their carriage amid expressions of mutual pleasure at their visit to Netherham and with suggestions that they visit each other in the future. Excepting Mr. Hesketh, none of the local leaders had committed to joining the venture to replace smuggled goods with legal ones. However, Daphne was confident that at least three others would. The party from Dipton was satisfied with their effort and decided that Mr. Justice Amery should arrange for visits farther along the canal soon.

Chapter XXIII

Giles turned *Glaucus* onto a course to clear the south-east corner of Ireland. Conditions were perfect with a fresh breeze from the North-cast. Mr. Brooks advocated having all sails set to the top gallants for maximum speed. The frigate tore through the water. The sky was clear, the air cool but not frigid. It was a day to make any true seaman's heart sing!

Giles stayed on deck, ignoring the piles of paper demanding the captain's attention as a result of taking the prizes and transferring their care to Captain Bolton, not to mention all the routine reports that he was supposed to read and initial. He only went below to change for the dinner he was hosting for all his officers to celebrate the haul that they had taken at *Le Conquet*. The prize money would be highly significant for all their fortunes, even though they had to forgo some head money as a result of Giles's decision to set the crew of *Cecile* ashore.

It was late the next afternoon when Mr. Brooks reported that Fastnet rock was abeam with Cape Clear behind it. Giles ordered the correction of course so that they could beat up the coast. *Glaucu*s stood out to sea on a long tack away from the Irish Coast. He hoped that any watchers on shore who spotted them would assume that *Glaucus* was bound for Newfoundland by the northern route, rather than that she was tacking up the Irish coast.

Night had fallen before Mr. Brooks reported that they should now be able to make Dangle Bay if they came about. Later the Master suggested that it would be wise if they hove to and waited for the moon to rise before going closer to shore. When it was high enough to provide adequate illumination, it revealed the silhouette of the coast that the Master was expecting. Giles ordered that they close the coast to determine better where they might be. Soon Mr. Brooks announced that he could make out all the critical features that indicated that they were off Dangle Bay. Giles had enough faith in his Master that he ordered that they enter the bay, though under reduced canvas. They were well into the outer part of the bay before Mr. Brook's felt that discretion might now be the better part of valor. He recommended that Glaucus anchor and await dawn before proceeding any farther into the bay.

Giles was unwilling to wait for dawn to discover whether the French were already farther up the bay or whether, instead, he should prepare for their arrival. It was just possible that *Glaucus* had arrived ahead of the seventy-four. To be caught in the bay by the much more powerful vessel would be fatal. Maybe he should not have been so eager to find out what was happening and stayed offshore till morning. Now that he was here, however, he should find out if the French were in the bay. If they were not, he would still have time to get more sea room before dawn.

Giles ordered the jolly boat lowered. With Carstairs at the helm, the boat's crew rowed into the bay. Once they had passed the narrows, the channel widened enough so that Giles could see what ships might be lying in the inner bay out of sight of the entrance. The bright moonlight allowed him to make out three large vessels. One was, based on the silhouette of her rigging, a line-of-battle ship, a seventy-four most likely. The other two were substantial merchant vessels, suitable for use as troop carriers. He was not on a wild goose chase. He had found the French force mentioned in *Celine*'s papers! Now, what was he going to do about it?

The stern cabin of the warship was ablaze with light. Giles ordered that the oars of the jollyboat be muffled with rags. Then the crew rowed towards the anchored vessels. The moon was well to the north of the line between the jolly boat and the ships so that Giles's approach would not be in the path of the moonlight leading to the seventy-four. Even if they were spotted, the French were unlikely to think anything remarkable about a small boat rowing in the bay. The enemy would likely presume that they were observing some fishermen pursuing their trade.

The jolly boat headed slowly towards the line-of-battle-ship, her crew handling their oars carefully so that no splash occurred. There was no indication from the ship to indicate that they had been spotted. Possibly, the watchmen had been lulled into intention, or maybe no watch had been set. After all, it was unthinkable that any ship that could threaten the seventy-four would traverse the narrows in the dark with the tide against her. Whatever the reason, no one seemed to notice Giles's approach to the enemy vessel.

The jolly boat slid successfully under the stern of the French warship. A board well above Giles's head named her as *Clytemnestra*, the ship he had read about in *Celine*'s orders. Some windows of the stern cabin were open, and Giles could hear loud voices. As his ears became attuned to the racket in the cabin, he could start to distinguish individual words and phrases, some in English and some in French. He realized that he must be listening to a meeting between the French and the rebel Irishmen. He suspected that the gathering had started with everyone consuming considerable amounts of spirits which had led to so much noise being made. Possibly the Irish had greeted their allies with some of the celebrated Irish whiskey. Certainly, it did not sound as if it was a sober group in the French captain's cabin. From the snippets he overheard, Giles gathered that they were discussing the landing of the French troops and horses the next morning. There might still be time to do something to disrupt the French intentions. He would return to *Glaucus* now with the information that he had collected.

Even as the jolly boat pulled away from the French ship, Giles was formulating plans in his head. There was, of course, no way that a cutting-out expedition against the French seventy-four could succeed. He thought of the chaos that cutting *Clytemnestra*'s anchor cable would cause, but he realized that trying to sever it with an ax or a saw would be spotted long before it succeeded. Could he blow the rope apart, he wondered? It was very doubtful that that would work, especially as any slow match would likely be seen and quite possibly countered. Anyway, the currents in the bay seemed to be minimal. The ship would anchor again, and he would have lost any advantage that surprise might give him.

That line of thinking did suggest what might be done. If Giles could sneak a boat loaded with gunpowder under the stern of the ship in the way that the jolly boat had succeeded in positioning itself to glean information about the French, he could blow the stern off her. That should sink her. Once the warship was out of the way, he should be able to capture the other ships and prevent a successful landing.

It seemed to take forever before the jolly boat reached *Glaucus* even though they were now rowing with the current. Once aboard, Giles issued a string of carefully thought-out orders. He had retained the boats which he had acquired at *Le Conquet*, so he had two large craft which he could sacrifice. He wouldn't even have to explain to the Admiralty how he had happened to lose two valuable pieces of equipment.

Giles ordered that the two boats be filled with kegs of gunpowder. Lieutenant Hendricks's ankle had not yet healed enough for him to be able to lead the expedition, and Giles wanted the other two lieutenants to be in charge of the tricky business of setting the fuses. He would command his barge and take off the crews of the explosion craft when they had lit the slow fuse. In no time at all, the boats were loaded, and the expedition was ready to proceed. Giles ordered Mr. Hendricks to take *Glaucus* to Portsmouth if he did not return and the foray was a failure. Then he descended into his barge. The adventure was underway.

The small flotilla of boats rowed smoothly past the narrows and turned toward the anchored warship. Her stern still pointed towards them, and a slight sea-mist helped to mask their approach to their target. Silence was more important than speed. The gathering in the stern cabin of the battleship was still in progress, the voices now louder and more boisterous than before. When Giles got close, he realized that the words were now slurred. If the French were to disembark in the morning, many officers would do so with aching heads.

The two boats loaded with gunpowder reached the stern of the seventy-four and made no perceptible noise as they touched it. Silently, the craft were tied on each side of the rudder. Giles's barge slid up beside the first boat to take off everyone except Lieutenant Miller. Then the second crew boarded the Captain's barge though leaving Lieutenant Marceau behind. The lieutenants uncovered their flint boxes and struck small flames. When the tinder was burning nicely, each lieutenant plunged the end of the already placed slow match into the flames. They then scrambled into Giles's barge. He ordered his men to pull with all their strength with Carstairs steering a straight course for the narrows. Giles anxiously stared behind him, silently counting off the seconds before the smoldering slow-match would reach the explosives. Excitement must have speeded up his count for the crucial moments passed with no explosion. He was about to order a reversal of course so that he could explore the failure of the slow match when a flame shot into the air from the stern of the *Clytemnestra*. It briefly illuminated the whole bay. Moments later the sound wave from the explosion enveloped the British crew, and then a monstrous wave threatened to swamp their barge.

"Turn around," Giles ordered Carstairs. "We have to try to rescue survivors."

Giles had thought that the explosion would have ripped a hole in the stern that would have made the French ship rapidly sink by the stern as water poured into her. No such effect was evident. The force of the explosion must have gone straight up. Even with only moonlight illuminating the scene, it was clear that the stern cabins were no more. Even if she did not sink, without a rudder and with her stern open, it would be a long time before the *Clytemnestra* could sail again.

Then Giles realized that there might only be minutes before the seventy-four was gone. Flames were jumping up from the stern of the ship and setting the rigging alight. Fire was also spreading along the deck steadily. It was unlikely that the crew of the French seventy-four could put the fires out, at least not before they reached the magazine. The resulting explosion would make the one Giles had set off look like a Guy Fawkes day firecracker.

"Belay* that order. Pull for your lives for the harbor entrance," Giles ordered. The sailors pulling on the oars also realized the danger and put all their strength into rowing the boat as far from the burning inferno as they could. Their effort must have helped, but they were still too close when *Clytemnestra* blew up with a spectacular flash of light, followed by a mighty boom. Now all French ship was burning. The crew of Giles's boat could see another enormous wave rushing towards them. They could not possibly out-row it. It spoke highly of their discipline that on order from Carstairs they pulled their oars into the boat, hooking the ends under the opposite gunwales, and holding on for dear life. Even with these precautions, the barge was almost swamped when the wave reached them, while three sailors were injured, and two oars were lost. One of the injuries was a broken arm, which Giles splinted before doing anything else. Their next task was to bail the boat. Then they recovered the oars that had been swept overboard but were still nearby. Giles looked back in time to see the seventy-four, still burning brightly, sink. Of course, this doused the flames. It took a few minutes for their ability to see in the moonlight to return.

Giles realized, when his night vision returned, that the situation on the remaining enemy vessels was chaotic. Rigging and spars were dangling higgledy-piggledy on both ships. He would not be surprised if they failed to launch any boats to rescue survivors from the warship, or even from themselves, who were alive in the water.

The rule of the sea was imperative in Giles's mind. He ordered his barge to reverse course and go to seek survivors. The next hour was spent searching. They did indeed find many men clinging to flotsam and even more corpses which had not yet sunk. Before he abandoned the search, the barge was dangerously overloaded. Giles did not dare take the men he had rescued to the merchant ships which might be crammed with soldiers all too keen to capture the perpetrators of the disaster, and he had no idea what sort of a welcome he might receive if he went ashore. As a result, he ordered the barge to return to *Glaucus*. He gave orders that all his crew and the men he had rescued be given a tot of rum, and ordered his rowers to take to their hammocks without regard to which watch they were in.

Giles ordered the purser to find dry clothes for the survivors that he had picked up. He swept aside the man's worry about who would pay for them by saying to put them down on his bill. The purser was right. The petty-fogging clerks at the Admiralty would see no justification in providing dry clothing to captured enemies and would expect the accounts to reflect that the items had been paid for.

Giles got only a couple of hours rest before he was awoken at first light. He and Mr. Brooks consulted for some time over the chart of the bay before taking *Glaucus* farther towards where the French ships were. The channel to the inner bay was treacherously shallow, and slack water was upon them. However, Giles wanted to proceed. At least, if they grounded, the rising tide would likely float them off. Giles sent two boats ahead to measure the depths before the leadsman in the *Glaucus*'s bow could report any sudden shallowing. The British frigate crept forward with only enough canvas spread to maintain steerage way.

Nothing untoward happened. *Glaucus* passed the narrows and spotted the two merchant ships, still at anchor. The French sailors appeared to have done little in the dark to clear up the damage which had occurred when their naval escort had blown up. Their boats had been swamped, and they were still bailing them furiously. On the ships' decks, soldiers in French infantry uniforms were milling about while on one of the transports there also appeared to be a large group of cavalrymen. The invasion force had yet to be landed.

On shore, just back from the beach, was a camp with groups of men looking anxiously towards *Glaucus*. They must be part of the rebel Irish force that the French had come to support. Their numbers were not impressive, but Giles presumed that there were others elsewhere, ready to join a rebellion when it was evident that they had active French backing. Well, Giles reflected, it was up to him to make sure that that did not happen. He could not take control of the merchant ships by boarding* as he would normally do when capturing a merchant ship as a prize. These two vessels had far too many armed soldiers on board who might try to prevent any such capture from happening. Instead, he would have to force them to surrender, and that before they had could land any significant numbers of soldiers. Luckily, it should be a simple matter to overwhelm them.

Giles ordered *Glaucus* to anchor and a spring* be put on the anchor cable so that he could turn his ship as he wanted. He pointed *Glaucus*'s bow directly at one of the French ships, which fortuitously made his broadside aim at the Irish camp. *Glaucus* had cleared for action already. Indeed, it had been part of the dawn routine. He had, of course, ordered that the readiness for action not be undone on this occasion.

"Mr. Hendricks," he announced, "I think we should force the French ships to surrender, and we might as well see if we can get that Irish rabel to disperse. Have the broadside fire at the Irish encampment while you use the bow chasers to see if the transports want us to reduce them to matchwood. Fire when you are ready."

"Aye, aye, sir," responded the first lieutenant, glad, for once, that his ankle injury did not relegate him to a spectator's position as Giles undertook another blow against the French. The two bow chasers roared out first, followed immediately by the broadside. Giles could not make out exactly what damage had been done on shore, but the Irish did not wait for a second broadside. They took to their heels to put as much distance as possible between them and the English bombardment before they suffered more casualties. They had not been disciplined troops to begin with, and Giles would not be surprised if the Irish force melted away even before a proper British army could be brought to confront them.

The damage to the leading troop ship was more evident. One ball had slammed into the side of the vessel, well above the water line where it had staved in one plank. The other ball had caught the railing and sent deadly splinters into the packed groups of soldiers standing on deck. Chaos now reigned on the ship as men sought shelter wherever they could find it. Giles could see one small group consisting of several army personnel and a couple of sailors haranguing each other. The soldiers' uniforms told Giles, who had had some experience with French troops and their uniforms, that they were non commissioned officers while the dress of the sailors suggested that they were officers of the merchant ship. Giles suddenly realized that, in blowing off the stern of the seventy-four, he might have sent most of the officers of the invading force to kingdom-come.

Another pair of cannon balls from *Glaucus* settled the argument. As the smoke cleared, Giles could see one of the sailors madly hauling on a flag halyard to bring down the French colors. The ship had surrendered. The other transport followed suit after he ordered that the spring line be used to make the bow chasers point toward it.

Giles realized that capturing two large merchant ships packed with foreign troops on a coastline that might be considered hostile was a dubious success. He couldn't land the troops ashore because that would complete for them the mission on which the French were engaged. If he sent his marines aboard the French vessel, was there a danger that the French soldiers might try to overwhelm them and hold them as hostages? There must be garrisons in Ireland where he could unload the French troops, but neither he nor Mr. Brooks knew where they were. Well, he would have to take it one step at a time and hope for the best.

Giles's next orders were directed to Lieutenants Miller, Marceau, and Macauley. They were to take two boats packed with marines to verify the surrender of the first ship and to find out exactly how many people she was carrying. He told Mr. Marceau to mention that his Captain was a blood-thirsty commander who would be quite happy to open fire on the captured ships if there were any attempt to take his party hostage. With Lieutenant Macauley and Mr. Miller maintaining order, Mr. Marceau was then to return to *Glaucus* to report on what they discovered about the ship and her cargo.

Even as the boarding party was being readied, Giles ordered Midshipman Stewart to take the jolly boat to cut the lines of the boats that were trailing behind the same ship. The tidal currents should take the boats well away from the captured vessel so that the French could abandon any plan to overwhelm the men he sent to receive their surrender. If they had the boats, they could ferry men ashore unseen because their ship would be creating a route to the shore that could not be observed from *Glaucus*. That is what Giles would try to do if he were in the Frenchmen's situation.

The plan wasn't foolproof, Giles realized. It would be a nervous half-hour or so until he could determine the French response. He sent a second lookout to the masthead who was to concentrate only on the two French ships while the other one would have the broader duty to look for any vessels approaching the narrows.

Mr. Stewart accomplished his mission without aid from *Glaucus*'s other boats. Without further orders, the midshipman went to the second ship and dealt with its boats in the same way. Now the only way for the French to get ashore would be to swim, Giles doubted that they would take that option in any numbers.

Mr. Marceau returned after a period that seemed endless to Giles. The party from *Glaucus* had met with no resistance. The only officers aboard were a couple of Captain's mates and three soldiers whose rank, Mr. Marceau thought, was the equivalent of subaltern*. Giles's suspicion had been correct, all the other officers, including the ship's captain, had been on board *Clytemnestra*. When it blew up, they had all been killed. The holds of the captured ship were filled with supplies, field guns, and gunpowder. It would take a considerable effort to empty them using untrained soldiers. They would not be suitable places to lock up the soldiers who were on board. The French troops did seem to be cowed by the threat from *Glaucus*.

One of the reasons for the full holds on the first ship, Mr. Macreau had discovered, was that the corresponding spaces of the other ship had been converted into stables for the hundred or more horses of the cavalry contingent. That ship held over 300 soldiers, Mr. Macreau had discovered, while the first ship was carrying well over four hundred. Both transports were severely overcrowded. Indeed, it had not been possible for all the soldiers to sleep at the same time below deck. The French had been gambling on good weather for the short crossing from Brest to the corner of Ireland.

Giles realized that his problems would be eased if the stables on the second ship were emptied and he used the hold as a prison. At least then, he could keep most of the French soldiers locked up. However, irrational as it was, he didn't want to kill all the horses, and he knew that he would have an angry crew if he slaughtered the animals.

There was little Giles could do to get rid of his captives since he had no idea where to unload them in Ireland. It would be quickest and easiest to return to England with them rather than to try to find a suitable place in Ireland. He would do what he could to minimize the danger of their overwhelming their captors and seizing one or even both of the captured vessels.

He gathered Mr. Marceau, Mr. Dunsmuir, Mr. Stewart, and the two most senior master's mates together before issuing more orders.

"What we are going to do is sail these two captured ships back to England, Plymouth, in fact. The weather looks favorable. Hopefully, we will get there before it changes. You will take eighteen experienced seamen for each of the two vessels. You should be able to handle the ships with all plain sail. We won't be in a rush.

"Now, I want one of the ships on the starboard side of *Glaucus* and the other on the larboard within easy cannon range. I shall have *Glaucus* cleared for action and her guns run out ready to fire on both sides. I want the Frenchmen to know that I am prepared to blow them out of the water immediately if they try to interfere with the operations of their ships. I expect you to reinforce the view that I am a ruthless captain who will not hesitate to lose some of my crew for the greater good."

Midshipman Stewart tried to stifle a guffaw at this claim, knowing how false it was, and that set off the others.

"Play acting, Mr. Stewart, play acting! It is at the heart of how a good commander gives his threats. Remember that when Mr. Marceau is painting me as a ruthless pursuer of glory. If you laugh then, it will drastically weaken the effect of his words.

"At night, I want lanterns lit along the sides of the ships facing *Glaucus*. We will be showing lights too. Mr. Marceau, make it clear to the captured Frenchmen that, if their lanterns are doused, I will not hesitate to blow them to pieces. The same will be true if the course of their ship veers away from mine."

"Mr. Stewart, you will lead the way out of the inner bay. *Glaucus* will follow and then Mr. Dunsmuir's ship. Mr. Marceau, I want you to return to *Glaucus* as soon as you have established our control of the second transport. Your coming back to *Glaucus* will strengthen their impression that I will fire on them if they try to take over their ships. I am afraid that it is usually presumed that junior officers are expendable in armies, and those ships have mainly soldiers on board.

"We will get underway just as soon as possible. I want to be out of here. Once away, we will head for Plymouth."

Giles dismissed his officers, but he continued to think about his plans. They should work. It would have been easy if those French ships were not loaded with soldiers, but he believed that he could manage. Luckily he had not had to contend with more vessels, either naval or troop transports. Such a situation would have had a very different outcome.

Chapter XXIV

Giles had become steadily more anxious about becoming trapped in Dangle Bay. He had presumed that *Clytemnestra*'s only supporting ship was to have been *Celine*. However, he had based that belief on the fact that *Celine*'s orders had only indicated that *Clytemnestra* held the senior captain. If other warships were involved in the foray to Ireland, they had not been mentioned in the captured papers. However, any such vessels might also have been scattered by the storm. If they existed, they might even now be approaching Dangle Bay. The more he thought about it, the more unlikely it seemed to him that the French would have sent only two troop carriers. There could easily have been more transport ships and therefore more escorts to protect them.

Giles did not want to have the tables turned on him through any slackness on his part in dealing with the possible situation. Already, he had lost too much time by being very careful in dealing with the transports, though there was not much he could have done to speed things up. The tide had yet to turn. He would not be able to take his ships through the narrows until that had happened. Still, he did not want to jeopardize his present control of the tricky situation by being careless.

His subordinates were losing no time in following out his orders for dealing with the transports. Nevertheless, it would be some time before the captured vessels would be ready to proceed. Giles sent the jolly boat under Carstairs to the narrows to signal if any ships were sighted approaching Dangle Bay. If they did spot an enemy, it might be possible to get *Glaucus* through the narrows so that she could engage her in the outer bay.

He did not have long to wait to find that his fears were materializing. He was idly watching the jolly boat as it approached the narrows when it spun about and picked up its pace as it rowed back toward *Glaucus*. Carstairs was holding up the solid red flag that was used to signal "enemy in sight." French ships were in the outer bay.

Giles had no time to try to traverse the narrows to engage whatever enemy had been sighted in the outer part of the inlet. Could he position *Glaucus* so that he could rake* any ship that attempted to enter the inner bay with his opponent having no chance to retaliate? He was about to give the orders when Carstairs arrived on deck. There was a naval vessel approaching, but behind it were two others. His coxswain thought that they were merchant ships, but he had had little time to study them in order to assess what guns they carried. He had felt that he should report to Giles as soon as possible when he caught sight of the enemy.

It was tempting to try to block the entrance, but its most likely result was a stalemate. The French ship could also anchor. She would prevent Giles from leaving, just as *Glaucus* would keep his opponent from entering. Furthermore, it would take time to raise his anchor and set sail, and he certainly did not wish to be caught adrift. From her present position, *Glaucus*'s guns could easily reach a vessel emerging from the narrows.

Giles gave orders so that his broadside was aimed at the exit to the outer bay. *Glaucus* was still cleared for action due to the need to maintain the threat to the transports. Now he could only cover his existing captures with his stern guns, and those cannon still had to be moved into position. Only two would be enough to do the job. The others could still be used in the broadside.

Only two more items remained to be done before *Glaucus* was as prepared as she could be to engage the enemy.

First, he ordered all the gun ports to be closed, though the guns were to be loaded and ready be run out and fired the minute that he gave the order. So that there would be no unnecessary waste of time, he stationed one of the powder monkeys at each porthole with orders to raise their lids even as the cannon were being run out. Until the moment for action came, everyone manning the guns was to hunker down so that they could not be seen from a ship in the narrows. Second, he ordered Mr. Fisher to lower the union jack and instead raise the French tricolor. The midshipman was to stand by ready to exchange the French for *Glaucus*'s true colors at exactly the time that the gunports opened. Flying false colors was an accepted *ruse de guerre* provided that the true flag was shown before engaging the enemy.

Giles knew that one of his weaknesses as a commander was to not wait for subordinates' reports when he could check a situation for himself. He knew that he had that weakness. Nevertheless, he wanted to see for himself what might be coming through the passage. He climbed to the top of the mainmast to observe what might be emerging from the outer bay. While he could see only a little farther into the narrows along the surface of the water than he could from the deck, being at the masthead gave him a view over the trees that hid most of the narrows from *Glaucus*'s deck. He would be able to see the masts of the enemy before any part of the French ship would be visible from *Glaucus*'s deck.

Giles had hardly settled himself at the masthead before he saw a ship's topmast creep into sight. For a couple of moments, he was puzzled. It did not look like a warship's top-hamper. A glance at where the two transports were still anchored confirmed his guess. What he could see of the newcomer looked like the ships he had already captured. Giles had brought gloves with him anticipating that he might have to return to the deck quickly by sliding down the backstay. He made use of that way to return to the deck so that he could make sure that firing on the transport would not spring the trap that he had set for the naval vessel. Even as he slid down the rigging, he was confused. Carstairs had said that he had seen a warship. Of course, his coxswain had turned tail the moment he had spotted the enemy. In his haste, could Carstairs have mistaken this ship as a greater threat than it truly was? Or was there still a warship in the outer bay, one which had accompanied the transport and which the naval commander had decided to send first into what he might presume was an inlet which was either empty or else controlled by the French.

Giles reached the deck to find that Mr. Marceau had returned to report on the progress being made to ready the captured transports to leave.

"Mr. Marceau, go over to the ship that is coming out of the narrows and tell her to anchor near the other transports. State that you have been sent to guide him through some waters that are more tricky than his chart may indicate. With luck, the ruse may get the newcomer to anchor under *Glaucus*'s guns without immediately realizing the true nature of the situation."

Giles climbed to the masthead again. Mr. Marceau appeared to have persuaded the merchant ship to follow his orders. How lucky he was to have an officer who spoke perfect French with a French accent. He realized that it was also fortunate that he was wearing ordinary working clothes, not his Captain's uniform. Anyone spotting a captain up the mast of his ship would smell a rat.

Giles turned his attention once more to the narrows. Another ship was coming through. Its rigging looked much the same as on the previous vessel. God, he was having enough difficulty devising ways to control two ships loaded with hostile soldiers. Was he now faced with dealing with four? Of course, this worry was probably moot. There was still the warship to

310

come. He would have to defeat it before he need be concerned with how to control the transports. He was glad to see that Mr. Marceau was taking the initiative in giving the second ship the same directions as had been specified for the first one.

Turning back to look over the trees hiding the narrows, Giles spotted the fore top-gallant mast of a warship. It was followed by two other top-gallant masts. Giles could see a seaman who must have been stationed as a lookout on the first mast. The man was looking at him. He pantomimed calling down to the quarter-deck with the news and then started to descend, not by the backstay this time, but, instead, by the ratlines. By the time that he reached the top of *Glaucus*'s mainmast, the French masts had disappeared behind the trees, and he slid down the rest of the way.

On deck, there was little to do before springing his trap. The French ship slowly emerged from the narrows. She was large, bigger than *Glaucus*, a two-decker, but smaller than a line-of-battle ship. She was one of the old-fashioned fourth-rates, probably with fifty guns. That size of ship had gone out of fashion. It was now considered to be too small to stand in the line of battle, while she was slower than a modern frigate. Old fashioned or not, she was more powerful than *Glaucus,* and she had Giles's ship trapped. She had cleared for action, and her gun ports were open.

The logical thing for Giles to do was to surrender at once. However, his experience had shown him that the inevitable did not always happen in a fight and it was possible that some fortuitous event would interfere to turn the balance of battle his way. He had positioned *Glaucus* so that he could fire the first couple of broadsides on the enemy while his rival would not yet be able to turn so that it could hit *Glaucus*. There was no need to surrender at this point. He warned his crew not to show any signs of excitement until he gave the word. Instead, he told several men to lean on Glaucus's rail and appear to be looking with curiosity at the ship now emerging from the narrows. They thought this play-acting to be a great lark, and it helped to relieve the tension that waiting quietly for action induced.

The French ship was moving quite quickly under all plain sail, aided by the tide which was still flooding. She was certainly going faster than Giles would have done if he were in command. She also seemed to be more to starboard in the channel than Giles thought was wise. On she came until she was in perfect position from Giles's point of view.

Glaucus's ports opened. Her guns ran out.

"Mr. Stewart, raise our flag… Larboard battery, open fire. Mr. Hendricks begin adjusting the spring lines so that our full broadside continues to bear."

The guns roared out. The smoke shrouded Giles's view of the target. When it cleared, he saw that most of the balls had struck home, but they had not inflicted any significant damage, such as hitting a mast centrally enough to bring it down or destroying the enemy ship's large steering wheel.

The enemy kept sailing, even as *Glaucus*'s second broadside crashed out. Before the gunsmoke cleared, the French ship fired. Only a few of her balls hit *Glaucus*. One of them clipped the quarter-deck rail and sent a cloud of splinters at the men who were on the deck. Several of the wood fragments struck a couple of sailors, killing one instantly. Another one speared Giles, glancing off his rib cage and ripping a hole in his arm. Surprisingly, even though the force of the blow almost knocked him down, Giles felt little pain immediately.

A sudden, brief gust of wind whistled through the anchorage. It cleared away the gunsmoke from *Glaucus*'s broadside to reveal that the wind had caught the enemy ship and pushed it far over to starboard. One of *Glaucus*'s balls from the last broadside had severed the stay on which enemy's driver was raised. The loss of that sail, together with the unexpected gust of wind, had swiveled the French ship to starboard. It had also forced her to roll far over to that side. As the blast of wind passed, she straightened up and continued swaying, now to larboard. Just when she had rolled as far as she could go, the French ship ran aground. Her bow was pushed up out of the water as she slid up a mud bank. When she stopped, she was still listing to larboard. Her broadside now was aimed at the water. The list was so great that even at maximum elevation her guns could not hit *Glaucus*.

Giles stared incredulously at his opponent. The French ship was at his mercy. Even as he took in the changed situation, *Glaucus*'s broadside roared out again.

"Cease fire," Giles bellowed.

The smoke from the broadside cleared. More damage to his opponent was evident, but the most significant development was that her flag was being hauled down. She was surrendering.

"Mr. Hendricks, do you think your ankle can allow you to climb into and out of my barge so that you can take her surrender?" Giles asked.

"Yes, sir, I am sure that it can."

"Then have the honor, if you please."

"Aye, aye, sir." The first lieutenant seemed to be overjoyed at the request. Too long had he been relegated to the less exciting aspects of *Glaucus*'s adventures. At the back of his mind must be a suspicion that the report stating that he had accepted a French fourth-rate's surrender could not help but advance his career. Giles hoped that it would. He would have to praise Mr. Hendricks explicitly in his report. Now that he had some influence, maybe he should mention to the First Lord of the Admiralty that it was high time that Hendricks was both promoted and also given a command of his own.

"Mr. Dunsmuir," Giles called. "Have the two new transport ships also surrendered?"

"No, sir. Sir, there is a group of army officers on the decks of each of them. They are waving their arms about in a most agitated way. In one case, someone who looks like a merchant captain seems to be the center of attention."

"We had better deal with them before they can form any plans. The stern chasers should be bearing on them. Fire a shot to land between the two ships. If that doesn't make them haul down their colors, start firing into them. Use one gun for one ship and one for the other. Keep that up until they give up.

Surveying his ship, he saw that one of his opponent's cannonballs had carved a large chunk out of the mizzen mast. That must be the source of his wound. He should get it attended to by Dr. Maclean. The mast would have to be strengthened before it would be safe to use it. Mr. Evans, the carpenter, was already dealing with it. There was nothing much that Giles needed to do immediately. His side and his arm were now hurting abominably. He felt weak and light-headed as he sank to the deck with his back resting on the helm. Dr. Maclean found him there a few minutes later.

"Two dead, three injured – not seriously – and you, Captain. Yours is not a serious wound, though it probably hurts like hell. The danger is from infection due to foreign bodies carried into the wound. I will have to clean it and try to remove any bits of cloth or wood that have been carried into it. Cleaning it up and stitching it is going to hurt, I warn you. A stiff dose of laudanum is called for, I think."

"No, I have to have my wits about me."

314

"Have it your way, Captain, but you may well faint from the pain. I'll have my loblolly* boys hold you down. If you change your mind about the laudanum, tell me at once. Now, since the sliver is still in place, I am going to have to cut your clothes away. Luckily, you don't seem to be wearing your best coat and shirt."

It did hurt as the surgeon extracted the splinter and probed for bits of wood and of cloth that might have been carried into the wound. Giles concentrated on thinking of something else, something pleasant. He focussed on Dipton, his wife, his child, the second child who was on the way, his plans for the place, the problems that he had had to leave to Daphne to solve. Finally, the surgeon was satisfied with the slash across Giles's ribs. He doused it with rum. Giles had a hard time suppressing the scream that the treatment provoked. Dr. Maclean rubbed some gooey stuff onto the wound before bandaging it.

"What is that ointment, Dr. Maclean?" Giles asked through gritted teeth

"A salve I got from your Mr. Jackson," the surgeon replied. "He thinks it tends to reduce the likelihood of infection. Made from some sort of mold. It does seem to work a bit, though nothing can guarantee that infection won't occur. Now sit still while I work on your arm."

Another ten minutes of pain passed slowly for Giles. At one point he must have passed out, for he became aware, rather groggily, that the surgeon was bandaging his arm without his doing anything like pouring run into the would or using Mr. Jackson's salve, but he could smell both the rum and the salve.

"There, that is finished," Dr. Maclean told Giles. "I've done the best I can. As long as infection does not develop, you should be right as rain before long. I'll just fashion a sling for your arm. The bandage will need to be changed before long. Let me know if your wounds start to throb or the pain increases markedly. I suggest you rest here for a while."

Giles decided to sit in his position on deck until he recovered his strength a bit. Right now the main thing to do was to give orders that would direct the next steps of the business of making sure of his captures and getting them ready for the journey to England. He could wait until more was known before becoming active.

The first substantive news arrived when Mr. Marceau returned. He had accompanied Mr. Hendricks to the French naval ship. Her name was *Achille*, the lieutenant reported. There had been no problem going aboard her and taking the French captain's surrender. All the officers had given their parole. Mr. Hendricks would soon be sending them to *Glaucus*. The French sailors had been imprisoned in the hold with Mr. Macauley's marines guarding them.

Giles told Mr. Marceau to go to the newly arrived merchant ships to see if his language skills were needed there. He then turned to Carstairs who had also come back from the French fifty-gun ship and was waiting for his captain's attention. He was carrying a large, waterproof bag.

"Well, Carstairs, what do you have there?"

"*Achille*'s – that is the name of the French ship, sir – *Achille*'s logs and other papers, probably her orders."

"How in the world did you get them? Didn't they throw them overboard before surrendering?"

"Yes, sir, they did. I noticed that an officer threw something off the taffrail before they hauled down their colors. I looked there after Lieutenant Hendricks accepted their surrender. I could make out something on the bottom – the water is very clear and, of course, shallow. We succeeded in raising the bag. Here it is."

"Has Mr. Macreau seen the papers?"

"No, sir; he had already left when they were recovered."

"Open the bag and give me the contents."

The bag contained a variety of papers. Scanning them, Giles found the orders under which *Achille* had been sailing. She had been anchored at Lorient, along with two merchant ships which were at a quay all prepared to load half a battalion of infantry soldiers and a company of cavalry. They were preparing to sail when a messenger from Brest announced that *Clytemnestra* had already sailed. The new orders said that *Achille* and the ones carrying the troops were to sail to Ireland immediately and unload the troops at Dangle Bay where they would rendezvous with Irish rebel forces. Because of the danger that either contingent might be intercepted by the English navy, the groups from Lorient and Brest were to proceed directly to Dangle Bay without meeting at sea first. The commander of *Clytemnestra* was to be in overall command.

Giles hoped that his weak command of French had not led him astray. The crucial aspect of the captured orders was that he could expect no more French ships to enter Dangle Bay. He would make sure that Lieutenant Marceau confirmed his understanding of what the documents said. Even without the threat of more French warships appearing in Dangle Bay, the situation was fraught with difficulties. He had to get six ships safely to England, five of which were captured vessels full of French troops or sailors. If he waited in Dangle Bay for help, there was a very real danger that the French would find some way to get ashore from the transports before he could stop them. Since landing the troops in Ireland was the essence of the French endeavor, preventing them from doing so was his major priority. The best way would be to get to sea as quickly as possible. *Glaucus* was ready, the damaged mast having been reinforced to make it strong enough to use. What about the other ships?

Giles stood up. It took him a minute to reorient himself after a wave of confusion washed over him as a result of standing up too soon after being injured. When he had steadied himself, he saw that Mr. Hendricks had laid out a kedge anchor and was even now hauling *Achille* off the bank on which she had grounded. Good The tide had remained high long enough to refloat her. He would not have to wait until the next high tide to get her afloat.

Turning to see farther into the bay, Giles spotted that a boat was leaving the second pair of French captive merchant ships. He would not have long to wait before he had the information he needed to determine when and how to get underway.

Mr. Macreau was the first of the officers sent to the French prizes to return. He reported that this pair of merchant ships carried the same number of French troops as the previous ones. In total there was a battalion of infantry and half a squadron of cavalry, with their horses. The main difference was that these ships had on board their naval and army officers as well as the lower ranks. The officers had given their paroles, though Mr. Marceau was somewhat doubtful about whether all of them fully understood to what they were committing. He had come back to *Glaucus* to get boats and crews to take the officers to the frigate. The soldiers had been confined to the holds of the ships.

Mr. Hendricks arrived a few minutes after Mr. Marceau departed. He came with the officers of *Achille* having left Mr. Macauley to make sure that the crew was secured in the hold. Surprisingly, the ship had suffered no major damage from running aground. She was ready to proceed once she was in the hands of a prize crew.

Giles summoned his officers to meet with him. Before they assembled, he had completed his plans. He wasn't happy with what he had decided to do, but he could think of nothing better. He couldn't count on the admiral in charge of the Channel Fleet responding quickly, if at all, to the news that Captain Bolton would be bringing with *Celine*. Rather than immediately dispatching a squadron to counter the French initiative, he would expect the admiral to await news from *Glaucus* about what he had discovered. He could expect no help from that quarter.

Giles was confident that he could return to England with *Achille*. He was more worried about the troop transports. At least, if he lost those ships, he would only lose a few of his people. Without their officers, and with a threat of being sunk if they tried to escape, he might well have a reasonable hope of getting them to England. Of course, he was unlikely to be able to keep them within range of his guns if a storm blew up. But otherwise, he should be able to keep them together for the five or six days that might be necessary. With luck, he might meet some British ships on the way. The quickest way to get rid of his unwanted captives would be to go to Brest so that he could hand his problems over to Admiral Casterton. But Brest was not on the way to England, and he might have to waste time searching for the Inshore Squadron. Truth be told, he had little confidence that Admiral Casterton would not try to steal as much of *Glaucus*'s glory for himself as he could or find some way to take a large chunk of the prize money that rightfully belonged only to the crew of *Glaucus*.

"Gentlemen," Giles addressed his officers. "As you know, we have made an unprecedented capture of French forces. I do not know what the political situation in Ireland may be, but the French army came to meet and support a rebel uprising, I am sure. Even without their weapons, those soldiers may provide an invaluable force of trained men to take on whatever British troops are in Ireland. So I do not think that I can put the soldiers ashore, hoping that our people will round them up. We will take them to England, just as we planned to do when we only had two other ships to worry about. We are going to be spread very thin, but I think we can do it. "

"The main thing that I plan to do is to provide *Achille* with enough of *Glaucus*'s crew so that she will be able to fight one side and sail the ship adequately. Mr. Hendricks, you will command *Achille*. You should pick some of our more experienced men for your crew since they will have to handle without any practice rigging and armament that is unfamiliar. Work out watch and station bills for *Achille* and *Glaucus* which will allow *Achille* to fire one broadside into one of the transports if necessary. That's why it will have to be a larger crew than we would usually use for a prize. Unfortunately, we will be at sea for several days – and, more importantly, nights – before we reach home waters. Plan accordingly.

"The merchant ships are a different challenge. Before we sail, I will have all their weapons thrown overboard. I think it unlikely that any of our soldiers would be happy being armed with French muskets or sabers. We will carry out that activity this afternoon using Mr. Macauley's marines and a large number of our people to suppress any resistance. The ships full of French soldiers will sail using their own crew and their own mates, with only one of our midshipmen or master's mates to supervise. At night, we will require them to show lights and keep close to us.

"Our guns must be loaded and run out, though with tampions to protect the charges. If necessary, we will blow any ship that tries to slip away out of the water. Our people on board them, in that case, should take cover and hope for the best. A warning gun will be fired across the bow of any who veer away from us. If that doesn't produce the appropriate response immediately, we shall fire on them. Mr. Marceau, emphasize what will happen if the French try to escape when you go with Mr. Macauley and the marines to throw the weapons overboard."

Giles filled in several blanks in the plan in response to questions and then his officers set about their tasks. Giles wasn't sure how Mr. Marceau did it, but he succeeded in getting the French sailors to dispose of the weapons with enthusiasm. Giles reflected that he would have to try to make good on any outlandish promises his subordinate had made.

By late afternoon, they were ready to set sail. *Glaucus* led the way past the narrows followed by the four merchant ships. *Achille* brought up the rear. Once in the outer bay, they formed up as Giles had planned. The troop ships were close enough on each side to the two warships that they would be easy targets if a cannon were to be fired at them.

Giles went below and took to his bed. He left orders to be woken if anything untoward happened. He somehow forgot to mention that he should be roused when a change of course was required

Dusk was upon them when they had got far enough out to sea that the little convoy could turn to the south without any of the captive ships getting out of range. The wind was perfect for a nice run south-south-east. At two bells of the middle watch, Mr. Brooks calculated that they were abreast of Fastnet Rock. Giles had considered trying to maintain the same course until dawn to avoid the need for his little group to alter course in the night, but he had been afraid that doing so might place him so far south that he would be forced to beat eastward to reach home waters if the wind veered. He had given detailed orders as to how the turn was to be accomplished while keeping the captive ships in range of the guns. He had presumed that he would have to be woken to supervise the change of course, but his officers saw no need to do so in the absence of specific orders.

The turn went off without a hitch. The lookout at the masthead reported that he had spotted Fastnet Rock at some distance to larboard. Now, if the wind would only hold for the next while, they should be able to reach the Channel without making further changes to their course. The slowest of the merchant ships could sail no faster than four knots. They would have at least another night to spend at sea before they were in home waters.

The wind held constant. Giles's convoy kept together all day and through the next night. Late in the afternoon watch of the following day, Mr. Brooks announced that, by his reckoning, Land's End should soon be in sight. Before it could appear, however, the lookout shouted that he saw a sail, two points off the starboard bow. The strange ship was on a reciprocal course. Minutes later, he cried that the ship was *Flicker*, Captain Bolton's frigate. The next call announced that *Flicker* had altered course to close with the convoy.

It seemed, as always, to take forever for the two ships to come together even though they were on reciprocal courses. Giles was happy to doze in his hanging bed while the distance between the ships shortened. Mr. Hendricks was disturbed by this development. It was so unlike his captain. He pestered Dr. Maclean as to whether Giles's wound was more severe than he had previously believed. Luckily for Giles, the surgeon maintained that Giles would benefit far more from rest than

322

from being poked again by a surgeon who had already done all that he could to see that the wound healed properly.

Lands End was in sight from the deck of *Glaucus* before Captain Bolton came aboard. He had taken *Celine* into Portsmouth as directed. Urgent messages had been dispatched to the Admiralty, with no official willing to take any action until word was received from London. He had spent several of long, and frustrating days trying to persuade various admirals that *Glaucus* might well need immediate support, but no one was prepared to take responsibility for assembling even a small force to sail for Ireland until news from the Admiralty had been received. Finally, Captain Bolton had given up. Announcing that his orders had been to rejoin *Glaucus,* he sailed, intending to go to Dangle Bay to discover what was going on. He was most relieved to see that *Glaucus* and, particularly, Giles were safe, though he noticed that Giles was injured.

The arrival of *Flicker* was a godsend for Giles. He had another frigate so it would be easy to run down any of his merchant ships that tried to wander away from the convoy. Now he could be confident that his gamble in taking them all from Dangle Bay would pay off. *Flicker* could even provide space for some of the French officers who were overcrowding *Glaucus*'s wardroom and gunroom distressingly. More importantly, now he could give in to the tiredness that was almost overwhelming him since he had not been able to sleep even on his watch-off in the previous two days. His wounds also were hurting and were making it even more difficult to stay alert.

His final decision before going below was that the group of ships would go to Portsmouth rather than to Plymouth. The wind had backed a point or two. To sail his convoy to Plymouth would require some beating into the wind. With his slow captives ships, which he suspected could not lie at all close to the wind*, it would take at least as long to get to Plymouth as to Portsmouth.

Even in his exhausted state, Giles had made sure that everything that might require his assistance was attended to before he went below. He then took to his bed. This installment of his mission was as good as completed. Five merchant ships, one forth-rate, and one frigate taken, and one third-rate blown up, not to mention most of a battalion of infantry and a troop of cavalry, with their horses, captured. A good cruise, even if he had not found anyplace where the French were hiding ships of the line. Not very heavy casualties, though *Glaucus* had an injured mizzen mast and he had a damaged arm and ribs. At least, the latter two would give him an opportunity to visit Dipton. How he longed to see Daphne! What had happened to the ventures to replace smuggling? How was Berns? How was Daphne's pregnancy going? Giles dropped into a deep and much-needed sleep, still mulling over the vital parts of life that he was missing. Would this fool war never end?

Chapter XXV

Daphne returned to Dipton to find that any number of things required her attention. The Ball had put some of her other duties behind time, and it was, in truth, the busiest time of her year. It was the first spring in their positions for each of the men who were managing her properties. None of them had previous experience in her employ. One at least, her nephew-in-law, Thomas Dimster, did not appear to have a good knowledge of what decisions spring brought that he had to make, or how to discuss the coming year with her tenants. Furthermore, the building of the kennels and the changes to Hillcrest Grange required an array of decisions to be made before the best season for building was upon them. Daphne's opinion was sought about these problems as well. She could, of course, leave all these matters to others, but that had never been Daphne's way. She was having difficulty realizing that it might be better for her if she took less of a hand in a large variety of matters. Despite these demands on her time, Daphne kept her promise to herself to spend more time with Bernard. This did not entirely suit Nanny Weaver, who was of the opinion that the children of ladies needed very little attention from their parents, at most a half-hour in the parlor before dinner.

All of these calls on her time meant that Daphne was not able to plan more visits along the canal with the aim of making smuggling less attractive to the prominent men of the area. Lady Marianne and Major Stoner were to get married. Having both her daughters married meant that there was no obstacle placed in front of Lady Marianne's nuptials occurring anytime, but she wanted Giles to give her away, not so much because of any affection for her half-brother, but to demonstrate to everyone that she was no longer the black sheep of the family. She also wanted an extensive marriage trip to follow the ceremony. Major Stoner felt that it would be sometime before the anti-smuggling venture was running so smoothly that he could leave it for any length of time. Daphne's help was sought. She avoided giving an opinion, saying that they should wait until they knew more about Captain Giles's activities. Daphne always referred to it as their anti-smuggling venture rather than their import business. The one sounded like noble patriotism while the other was clearly a branch of trade. As long as Lady Marianne was living at Dipton Hall, Daphne kept getting involved in planning the wedding. She heartily wished that they would follow the naval custom of getting married as soon as it could be arranged, even if it meant a very brief period for the couple to get to know each other before the husband had to sail away.

A more unusual request came from Lord David, her brother-in-law who was the Vicar of Dipton and a Member of Parliament for Dipton. She knew that his principal objective was to become a bishop as quickly as possible, and she wasn't sure that he did not regard that position as a stepping stone to become the Archbishop of Canterbury. Some of his speeches in Parliament had been noted in the press. They made what would be regarded as sound points about church matters without being in any way revolutionary, or even reforming. Just the thing to get a man recognized as a sound bet for elevation. It also did not hurt his chances that his brother was a naval hero who was gaining in importance as well as in wealth.

The next ecclesiastical step in Lord David's progress would be to become the rural dean for the Ameschester region. It was a sinecure, the important functions that had once been attached to the position having largely fallen into neglect. However, it would make him the leader of the clergy in his area, and give him some say in church matters in the diocese. The position was vacant. Lord David was not the most obvious candidate to be appointed by the Bishop, the Right Reverend

Chesterton. Lord David would have to change the Bishop's mind.

Bishop Chesterton was known to be very sensitive to all issues having to do with status and influence. He was coming to Dipton allegedly to participate in a special church service, but really, Lord David thought, to evaluate him in his role as the vicar of Dipton. Lord David's position would undoubtedly be enhanced by showing off the material success of his older brother and providing a not very subtle reminder that Viscount Ashton would soon become Earl of Camshire with all the influence that would entail. Of course, Giles was not in residence, but Daphne could easily host the Bishop and his wife.

Daphne became aware of this situation when Lord David called upon her to explain what was at issue in the appointment of the rural dean and how she could help. She was amenable to providing what assistance she could, though she did point out to him that she would have to include Lady Marianne in the company, as well as Catherine Bolton, both of whom were living at Dipton Hall. That left her one man short.

"You know, David," Daphne commented after agreeing to host the Bishop, "I suspect that the Bishop would find your candidature even more appealing if you were married. And your advancement in the Church more generally would be made easier if you had a wife."

"I believe that you are right, but there isn't much I can do about it before the visit, is there?"

"You seemed to be very keen on Lady Cecelia Westerly at the Hunt Ball."

"I did manage to call on her twice while I was in London."

"And?"

"Lord and Lady Tamerstead were welcoming and even invited me for dinner."

"Is Lady Cecelia engaged? Does she have a suitor?"

"I don't think so. Lady Westerly somehow got passed over in the year in which she came out. I don't know why, except that she is a lady of very definite opinions. Furthermore, she doesn't suffer fools gladly. She's worse than you, that way, Daphne."

"She may be just what you need. Much better than some mindless ninny who will have little to converse about with you, and will gladly gossip behind your back. If you like, I can ask Lord and Lady Tamerstead and Lady Westerly to visit over the period when Bishop Chesterton is here. If you want, you can propose to her, and that is the sort of thing that will get Mrs. Chesterton on your side. Women love engagements and weddings. From what they tell me, much more than they like marriage itself, which is silly, I think. Maybe I am just very fortunate."

"Richard is the lucky one in getting you, I think. Daphne, you are right, though. I think that Lady Westerly would be an excellent wife for me, both as a companion and also as a help in achieving my proper place in society."

"Then I shall invite Lord Tamerstead with his wife and daughter for the weekend when Bishop Chesterton will be here."

Daphne was satisfied with this development. Maybe her schemes to make sure that the guardians of her son were married were coming to fruition. Now there was just the question of Captain Bush. That would, of course, be helped if his mother and sisters were to get married. She wondered how things were developing between the Bush household and the vicarage of Hillcrest.

Daphne realized that she was getting too busy again. The baby in her womb took that moment to remind her of his presence, even as she started to mount the stairs to go to the nursery and play with her son. She must learn to say 'no' to Mr. Amery when next he showed up.

Daphne had only three days for her various activities before Mr. Amery reappeared at Dipton. Again, he was ostensibly visiting his friend, Daphne's father, but she suspected that his real purpose was to see her and to persuade her to take part in another of his schemes. Her suspicions were confirmed next day when Mr. Amery came to call. After only a minimum amount of polite chatter, he got down to business.

"Lady Ashton, Captain Bush and I have been exploring the possibilities of recruiting sympathetic landowners at the other centers along the canal. He has been very successful, by and large, though he is not as effective as you in recruiting people. Our support in other towns has not been as strong as in Netherham. Captain Bush suspects that the difference has to do with the appeal you make to the ladies. We noticed at Netherham that when you convinced the wives, their husbands always agreed with them. The ladies who said that they never had an opinion on business matters had husbands who, if they did not join our endeavor initially, did not do so on reflection either. Captain Bush and I are convinced that you would be more successful than we have been in convincing members of the gentry to support us. I am hoping that I can persuade you to visit some of the places remaining. With the two of us and Major Stoner as well, of course."

"How many places are there?"

"There are eight towns between here and Harksmouth. Captain Bush and I have done two of them, and Netherham is a third, so there are still five to go."

"Oh, that is too many for me. I do have other responsibilities, Mr. Amery."

"I'm disappointed, Lady Ashton. I am mainly worried about two of the towns: Crowspir and Angleton. They appear to have a stronger tradition of smuggling than the others. Angleton still had rivalry between the people who brought contraband by land and those who used the canal before we destroyed the canal trade. That town has a good road to the coast, where the smugglers can bring in the stuff and transport it inland. They use, I understand, quite a large crew and there had been clashes with the previous group who were using the canal. We have been undercutting the overland group. They are not at all happy about it. I need to get the landowners generally onside and make sure that the magistrates and the constables know that they have the support of the influential people. Giving the gentry a financial stake in your operation will make them less likely to be willing to help the other group.

"Captain Bush did succeed in appealing to the patriotism as well as the greed of two of the prominent people, but otherwise we have no commitments there and some indication that at best they are waiting to see which group prevails. One of our supporters in Angleton is Sir Geoffery Thompson, who was in the dragoons before his brother died and he inherited the estate and title. Very patriotic chap even though he has never seen battle. Captain Bush appealed to his sense of duty, and Sir Geoffrey would be willing to host a visit where we – you especially – could try to recruit a significant group of supporters."

"Speaking of Captain Bush," said Daphne. "He needs a reward for his success as a sailor and for his help to the crown in this endeavor. I think that he should have more than a medal recognizing his service. A title, so that his contributions will be acknowledged whenever he is addressed, is what I think he deserves."

"I agree with you. In fact, the last time I was in London, I raised the subject. There is a difficulty on the Admiralty side."

"Oh?"

"Yes. While Captain Bush has been a highly successful frigate-captain, the major actions he has been in have all been with your husband."

"Why should that matter?"

"Captain Giles has been the more prominent captain and the one given the most credit for the successes – not necessarily fairly – in the press."

"That's not a reason to deny Captain Bush."

"The problem is that Captain Giles is already a Knight of the Bath. He also has most of the standard forms of recognition. Many think that a such a young captain should not have received such an honor and they deeply resent it. It's not just that he was so young and that it wasn't really a strategic victory which he won, or so they say. It is also that there can only be a fixed number of Knights of the Bath, and giving your husband one of the places was seen to mean that some deserving admiral or senior captain – or so they thought themselves to be – couldn't become one. To make matters worse now, he is already a viscount, which is a very unusual title for someone in the navy to be awarded. Usually, even very distinguished officers have to settle for a knighthood or becoming an Earl. Even though your husband's is only a courtesy title, his having it is resented. Furthermore, he will soon be an Earl. So there is a great reluctance to give him another noble title. It is regarded by the government as not worth creating the bad feelings and resentment that would be caused among admirals or other post-captains, who have distinguished themselves in fleet actions – not that there are many of them nor that their claims to a title are compelling except in their own eyes – and were not ennobled. The difficulty is not helped by Captain Giles's father, the Earl of Camshire. He is very strongly disliked and even held in contempt in many quarters by men of influence who would not like to see his son rewarded however much he deserves to be."

"So are you saying that there is nothing that can be done for Captain Bush?"

"Not quite. I think that I have the government looking favorably on making him a baronet. It would be for services rendered to the crown, which covers both his naval successes and his help in stopping a certain amount of smuggling. There are those, however, who think that his contributions in either area are not yet enough to warrant knighting him."

Daphne realized immediately that Mr. Amery was indicating that a knighthood for Captain Bush required that she visit the towns that he regarded as critical. Well, she did want Captain Bush to be knighted, so she would help Mr. Amery by visiting the two problem towns.

"I am very busy, as you must know, Mr. Amery. However, I might be able to get away after the visit of Bishop Chesterton in two weeks time. Do you have gentlemen who will act as hosts in Angleton and Crowspir?"

"In Crowspir, I have succeeded in persuading Sir Thomas Lambert to invite you. Lady Lambert is primarily interested in meeting you, I believe, rather than smuggling. Tales of your activities are becoming spread widely, Lady Ashton, and all to your credit, I must say. Other ladies also seem to be highly interested in you and your doings. The gathering in Cowspir would be much the same sort of gathering as we had in

Netherton, though, of course, you have not yet met Sir Thomas and Lady Lambert.

"Angleton is a different story. Mr. George Hastings is the leading landowner there. He has a large estate, but it has a limited, old residence. It's not suitable for a large gathering. He has suggested that he might have a small dinner for a few of the leading men and their wives, and a more extensive meeting in the church the next afternoon."

"Are you thinking of having the two visits on the same trip."

"Yes, if that is agreeable to you."

Daphne was not happy about having to agree to do this task for Mr. Amery, but it was clear that she should undertake the trip for Captain Bush's sake in addition to aiding the company she and Giles and established to counter smuggling. However, she wanted to maneuver Mr. Amery into another obligation that he would find difficult to get out of. She had better try to secure it before agreeing to what he wanted.

"Mr. Amery," she said after mulling his proposition over for a short while, "I cannot go on these visits for a few weeks because of my duties here. One is to host Bishop Chesterton for a visit which may influence him to advance my brother-in-law's career – Lord David Giles."

"Of course, I know him and can speak highly of him."

"Thank you, but that is not what I am concerned with primarily. Among the guests is likely to be Earl de Roy and his daughter, the Honorable Penelope de Roy. Captain Bush wants to marry her, but Lord de Roy would prefer that his daughter marry a man who has some sort of a title. I am sure that you will find a chance to mention your endeavors on behalf of Captain Bush when you join us for the occasion."

"I would be most happy to attend, Lady Giles. I know the Bishop, of course, and have followed Lord David's career with admiration. I do not know Lord de Roy and will look forward to meeting him. Of course, I cannot promise anything, but I will tell him what I have heard about Captain Bush. I will also mention that I believe that before much longer the knighthood will be a reality instead of an expectation."

Daphne was kept busy as the date of the Bishop's visit approached. This pregnancy was bothering her a little more than had the first one, and she found that her energy level decreased as the number of tasks to undertake increased. She was glad that she had insisted on the need to get through the Bishop's visit before going to the two towns for Mr. Amery. Preparing for the occasion involved more of her attention than she had expected. This was partly because the Countess of Camshire got wind of the Bishop's visit to Dipton and its connection to the future of her son, Lord David. Luckily Lady Clara had not also got wind of Daphne's scheme to get Lord David engaged. With the Countess coming, Daphne, of course, had to find another man to squire her to dinner, a task which fell to Mr. Moorhouse. All seemed in order until Lord David returned from London.

He had somewhat mixed news about his courting Lady Cecilia Westerley. He had told her that he would ask her father for her hand in marriage, and, after some dithering, she said that she would accept, provided that her father agreed. Difficulties arose at that stage. While the Earl of Tamerstead did not flatly refuse the request, he did express worries about Lord David's ability to support his daughter appropriately. The financial circumstances of the Earl of Camshire were all too well known, so Lord Tamerstead knew that Lord David could expect no legacy on Lord Camshire's death. Lord David had a comfortable living as vicar of Dipton, but it would hardly suffice to provide all the luxuries and the style of life which his daughter would expect as the wife of a Member of Parliament. While Lord

David's brother had more livings in his gift, they were at present filled by other men and could not be awarded to his brother. In addition, Lord David had to tell Lord Tamerstead that his brother did not approve of clergymen holding several livings. In that case, the Earl asked, were there any perks that he could with certainty count on as an MP to supplement his income? Lord David had had to answer that he did not take that sort of payment and, if he did and his brother found out, that would be the end of his parliamentary career.

Lord David had emphasized to Lord Tamerstead that his prospects for advancement in the Church were bright and he was sure that before long his emoluments would be more than large enough to satisfy Lady Cecilia's wishes. That had evoked a doubtful snort from the Earl, apparently induced not by the likelihood of Lord David progressing, but by the idea that his daughter's wishes could ever be satisfied.

Daphne was not sure what Giles's opinion of Lord David's needs might be and what was appropriate for him to give his brother. After all, he had already supplied a good living, though better ones would fall into his hands eventually. Would he approve of an annuity for his younger brother? She thought he would, and was confident that she could persuade him even if his initial reaction were negative.

"How much are we talking about?" Daphne demanded in her straightforward way.

"£3,000 a year, give or take."

"How much would the rural deanery bring in?"

"With various emoluments, it is worth £4,500 at least."

"Then I'll tell you what I will suggest that Captain Giles do. He should give you an annual supplement of £4,000 to last until you are made rural dean or get an equivalent increase in

your income from some other position. I do hope that Lady
Westerley is the right woman for you."

"I'm sure she is. Definitely. Excellent background, good
dowry, and an influential father. Just what I need. She is also
charming and intelligent as I am sure that you will find out
soon."

"I am glad to hear it."

Daphne, if she were telling the truth, would admit that
she was disappointed in Lord David's evaluation of his bride, or
at least in the order of priorities his reply had indicated.
However, she would continue to do everything she could to
accommodate his desire to advance his position in the world.

"You know, David," she said. "It would undoubtedly be
better if he heard about your brother's decision about a
temporary annuity directly rather than as a claim that you make.
Richard, of course, is away, but I think I could stand in for him
in this case. It might do some good if he were to see Dipton for
himself. It gives an indication of your brother's wealth and
standing. If you like, I will invite Lord and LadyTamerstead and
Lady Westerly to visit Dipton Hall on the occasion of the
Bishop's visit. I can mention the annuity when I am singing your
other praises. That might advance your suit."

Lord David accepted the suggestion eagerly. His future
was evolving much more favorably than he could have imagined
just a few days ago, and he was aware that the progress was
largely his sister-in-law's doing.

Daphne had a few days to herself while awaiting the
Bishop's visit. Both the Earl of Temerstead and the Earl de Roy
had accepted her invitations, and all the preparations needed for
the event had been scheduled. Her next task, undertaken just for
herself after spending so much of the morning with Berns that he
was completely worn out, was to visit Elsie at the Dipton Arms.

Business was good, Daphne's friend reported, though fewer men were whiling away long winter days in the snug and were only looking in for a pint to be consumed hastily between other activities. Her child was the same age as Berns and was making equal progress. Indeed, Daphne was called on to admire the amazing feat of standing up without falling over again in two seconds. Daphne had mixed feelings about seeing Elsie when she herself was pregnant. Her former maid was pregnant too, and she was having a much harder time of it than Daphne. Daphne had to hide her thankfulness that she was hardly bothered by pregnancy while her friend was suffering.

The weekend of the Bishop's visit was blessed with good weather, which Daphne found to be a relief as she could suggest that her visitors explore the best features of the neighborhood, while she got on with more serious tasks that somehow arrived with spring good weather. Both the principal visitors had proved to be a bit of a trial.

Bishop Chesterton was a sullen-looking man, with a notable pallor with the exception of his nose which matched his clerical bib, a bright lavender color. He seemed to be concerned with only two things: that the diocese received its financial dues under any circumstance and that everyone knew that his wife was the daughter of a marquis. Lady Clara was heard to mutter under her breath that she was more likely the offspring of the king who had awarded the title to the understanding husband who had encouraged the King to seduce his wife. The woman, herself, was a rather mouse-like creature from whom Daphne had been able to extract no interesting comment on anything. The Bishop had the worst type of parsonical way of talking, dropping his voice mournfully at the end of every sentence, a habit that Mr. Moorhouse claimed was adopted by clergyman since it put God to sleep during the prayers and the congregation during the sermon.

The Earl of Tamerstead could talk of nothing except the high price of everything, how important was his work in the House of Lords, and how unfair were the entail laws and the income tax. His estate would go to a second cousin whom he despised. He firmly believed that it was beyond question that it should go to the husband of his daughter, whoever that might be and, of course, only whenever Lord Tamerstead had no further use for the title. Such a circumstance would undoubtedly enhance her marriage prospects, but it was entirely out of the question. At least, the Earl claimed, he could provide an adequate dowry for his daughter and a generous widow's portion to his wife. The latter, he confided to the Bishop in a voice that all could hear, would go to the Church when she died and not return to his heir for whom he had little liking.

Daphne had no difficulty in explaining how promising a man was Lord David. He was backstopped financially as well as being a member of an influential family. If Lord Tamerstead inferred that this indicated that Giles would use his influence to ensure that his brother's career advanced whatever the merits of the case, so be it. It was noticeably the case that Daphne had said no such thing explicitly.

Lord Tamerstead gave his consent to Lord David's marrying his daughter. Her mother, who had a lot of valuable connections on her side of the family, was enthusiastically in favor of Daphne's brother-in-law. Whether Daphne's talk of Giles's plans and the contribution he would undoubtedly make when he became the Earl of Camshire had helped Lore David's suit was unknown, but both Daphne and Lord David suspected that, in a world where influence was everything, being in the orbit of the new star of society and politics carried great weight.

Mr. Amery had done his bit as well, assuring Lord Tamerstead of the degree with which Giles was respected by the government as well as by members of the opposition not only

338

for his military achievements but also for his recent diplomatic success in Russia. The value of a family connection with Lord Ashton was likely to become invaluable.

Mr. Amery had been even more successful in influencing the Earl de Roy. He had suggested strongly that Captain Bush was a most effective force in civil affairs, roles the naval officer would never boast about, but which, Mr. Amery was sure, would soon lead to a knighthood and might well lead to further rewards. A coming man, was Captain Bush, according to Mr. Amery, definitely a coming man. Daphne had overheard the critical parts of this conversation and was amused by how successful the Judge had been in telling nothing but the truth while implying much more.

When the last of the guests had departed, Daphne heaved a sigh of relief. She had found it much more nerve-wracking than she had expected to try to guide the different sets of interests in play on the weekend. Everything she had hoped for had been realized. Two of Bern's guardians were engaged to be married and to women whom she thought were right for them. Her only worry was about what Giles would think of this meddling in other people's affairs. Her recent activities might not be at all what he had expected of her when he married his wife. But she trusted him to allow her to have her head, though she would dearly love to have his advice about all that she was doing. Indeed, what she truly wanted was to have him home. What in the world was he up to? The last she had heard from him, he was off to Ireland in pursuit of the French. What was that all about? It seemed to be ages since he had written that letter, though, in reality, it had only been a short time. She had no reason to think that she would have any more news for many days.

Was Giles even safe? Her father had pointed out to her news articles saying that Admiral Villeneuve had somehow fooled Admiral Nelson and escaped from Toulon. There was much speculation about where the French fleet might have gone and what its admiral was planning. With that force loose in the Atlantic, would Giles have the bad luck to encounter it? What if Ireland were the target of the French fleet? Well, there was nothing she could do about it. She might as well do what Mr. Amery wanted as quickly as possible so that she would be home again if Giles should happen to return to England.

Chapter XXVI

The captured French fourth-rate, *Achille*, led Giles's small flotilla into the Solent with *Flicker* and *Glaucus* bringing up the rear like sheepdogs herding a flock of sheep. Near the entrance, they were challenged by a frigate on picket duty. That resulted in a flurry of signals being relayed from the senior admiral anchored at Spithead, inquiring for more and more detail about the captured ships and their escorts and giving conflicting orders about what to do with the captives. The sequence ended with a command for Giles to go to the flagship immediately. The admiral in question was not the commander of the Channel Fleet, who presumably was with the bulk of his fleet somewhere off Ushant, but one who was subordinate to that officer.

Giles was tired and fed-up with admirals who had taken a report on a possible invasion of Ireland and dithered about what to do about it, rather than acting upon it. One of them now dithered even about ensuring the orderly landing of the enemy troops which his flotilla carried. Nevertheless, although he was sailing under Admiralty orders that meant he was not, in fact, subordinate to the admiral, the man had power enough to make it highly unwise to ignore him if Giles wanted to end his duties in guarding the captured ships and men as quickly as possible. However, Giles did take advantage of his status as an independent commander to signal to the port admiral in Portsmouth to get ready to receive a battalion of infantry, a troop of cavalry with their horses, and the crew of an enemy fourth-rate. He also reported that the French officers he had on board had given their paroles and would have to be found accommodations. He felt for the poor flag lieutenant to whom would fall the task of immediately dealing with the influx of enemy prisoners. The prison hulks that held many of the captured French combatants had already been full the last time he had been in Portsmouth.

Word had spread throughout the flagship about Giles's convoy. In reading off the signals, the midshipman of the watch had told not only the admiral but also everyone on the seventy-four's quarterdeck about what Giles was bringing into port. All the other ships at anchor must have read the signals too, so word of his feats would be the subject of conversation throughout the fleet, even though no one as yet knew that he had also succeeded in blowing up a French seventy-four. Murmured words of commendation greeted him as he came through the entry port of the flagship and saluted the quarterdeck and Giles noted the glint of telescopes on other ships directed in his direction. The flag captain also gave him the warmest of congratulations before taking him to the admiral. That warmth evaporated when he was ushered into the admiral's cabin.

Admiral Carnarvon was a short, thin, gray-haired man, surprisingly pale for a seaman. Giles knew little about him. The admiral had spent most of his career in ships-of-the-line. Like many such men, he had never been in a battle. Even in the smaller ships in which he had served after getting his step* to the rank of master and commander, he had been tied to the apron strings of admirals of fleets, with his vessel serving as a messenger-carrier rather than as a fighting ship. Age and influence had carried him to his present position aboard a line-of-battle ship, not success in warfare.

"So you are the famous Captain Giles," Admiral Carnarvon opened the meeting with a sneer. "The captain who felt that he was above the need to report to higher authorities when he was lucky enough to capture some enemy orders. Couldn't be bothered to bring them here and await orders, could you? Instead, you went tearing off on a wild goose chase without orders."

"Sir, I am sailing under Admiralty orders, and I felt that what I had discovered should be brought to the attention of the Admiralty as soon as possible. Only when I met Captain Bolton did I feel confident that I could try to discover what the enemy was doing while *Flicker* delivered the documents and news to you."

"Stuff and nonsense! You were simply going off after more prizes, I am sure, especially when you have a chance to do an admiral out of his proper share of any prizes. I see that you have caught some instead of waiting for orders from us on how to counter the French endeavor."

"No, sir. I sailed to Dangle Bay to discover what the French were doing. I knew that Captain Bolton would be able to deliver the news and the evidence I found for their going to Ireland just as well as I could. Captain Bolton tells me he did just that and then you did nothing."

"Captain Bolton! Captain Bolton! Another man who couldn't wait for proper orders. How am I supposed to fulfill my duty when no one gives me the ships and support I need? I should have you both court-martialled!"

"I am not aware that you have that authority, sir. All I know is that you, as well as the Admiralty, have yet to act on the news which I captured about the French plans."

"Stuff and nonsense. We are in the process of forming a plan that will counter this move against Ireland. But we have to be sure not to weaken the defenses of the Channel. Napoleon may come any day. Now, what is this about capturing French soldiers that my fool of a midshipman claims you signaled us?"

"Yes, sir. As I stated in my report to the Admiralty, of which I have given a copy to you, I proceeded to Dangle Bay where the French force was directed to go. When I arrived there, I entered the inner part of the inlet to see if the French had already arrived. They had, but I was fortunate enough to blow up the seventy-four that was there together with two transports."

"Blew up a seventy-four? I have never heard such nonsense in my life. Frigates don't blow ships-of-the-line out of the water! That is a preposterous claim! What would the world be coming to if that could happen? You must have been dreaming or drunk. I see that your arm is in a sling. Probably rum or laudanum has given you hallucinations. Anyway, that puny ship you brought in just now is not a seventy-four. And you didn't blow her out of the water, obviously."

"No sir, that is another French ship that came later. She is *Achille*, fifty."

"Well, go on with this fairy tale."

"Aye, aye, sir. But it is no fairy tale. When I reached Dangle Bay, I discovered that there was a French seventy-four, *Clytemnestra*, at anchor near the head of the bay with two merchant ships. Night had fallen by then, so I took some boats loaded with gunpowder which I placed below her stern and blew it off. She sank immediately. I found out later that on board she had had not only her own officers but also the army officers of the expeditionary force sent to Ireland.

"Next day, I secured the two merchant ships, which turned out to be troop carriers, before they could land their men or their guns or their horses."

"So what happened next?" Admiral Carnarvon asked, his hostility to Giles being forgotten at least temporarily.

"Because of the tide, we could not leave the inner part of the bay immediately. While we were waiting for the tide to turn, another French warship with two other troop carriers came into the outer bay."

"Is that the ship you have brought in just now?"

"Yes, sir," Giles replied and went on to explain his capture of the French arrivals, how he had obtained *Achille*'s orders and how he had convoyed his five captures to England without losing any of them.

By the time Giles had finished, he had won over Admiral Carnarvon to admitting that Giles had had a remarkable success, no matter how wrong-headed his behavior in going off to Ireland on his own without explicit orders might have been. Rather pompously, the admiral said he would be mulling over the report before forwarding his recommendations to the Admiralty. Giles had no idea what the superior officer had in mind. Admiral Carnarvon also said that he would take under advisement how best to land the soldiers that Giles had captured.

Giles was fuming as he returned to *Glaucus*. He wanted to get rid of the prisoners and the prizes immediately, get *Glaucus* repaired and get back to sea after a visit to Dipton. He did not want to spend time idly at anchor at Spithead waiting for senior officers to decide what to do. Giles's mood improved after he had been piped aboard *Glaucus*. Midshipman Stewart informed him that the port admiral must have read all the signals that *Glaucus* had exchanged with Admiral Carnarvon as well as the ones directed explicitly to himself. He had signaled that arrangements were being made to land the French troops at eight bells of the afternoon watch. An officer would be coming to *Glaucus* to give the details and to help guide the prize ships to the appropriate quay. The port admiral also ordered Giles to visit him immediately.

Giles was annoyed at first that another admiral should be ordering him about. When he reflected further, he remembered that the signal book had no way of distinguishing between an order, a request, or an invitation. Thinking about the communication some more, he became both surprised and very pleased to find such efficiency from the port admiral. He immediately ordered his barge to be readied so that he could comply with the admiral's order or request.

The port admiral, Admiral Jerrycot, wanted details on the number of people, of guns and of horses that Giles's ships were carrying so that the prisoners could be dealt with expeditiously, with the soldiers separated from the sailors, and the appropriate treatment awarded to the officers and the cavalry mounts. The admiral was astounded to hear about how many soldiers had been captured, having presumed that the description given by the signal midshipman of there being a battalion of infantry and a troop of cavalry with the corresponding artillery was due to the shortcomings of the signaling system instead of being a fair description of the magnitude of the capture. On being told that the figures were not exaggerated, Admiral Jerrycot, without fuss, called for his flag lieutenant and altered the details of what was needed to deal with the prisoners when they were taken ashore.

When the interview with Admiral Jerrycot was almost through, his flag lieutenant entered the room to give the admiral a message which had just arrived by the telegraph connection to London. The admiral had mentioned earlier that, when he had received the signals from *Glaucus*, he had immediately sent a summary to the Admiralty in London.

"Amazing how fast the messages go. Most of the delay in getting a response comes from the clerks and others dithering about what to reply, not the time of transmission. Usually, we get an acknowledgment that a message has been received a

346

quarter of an hour after we send it. That, of course, presumes that you are at the telegraph station. It often takes longer for the message to get from here to the station than for it to get from the station to London. I still can't get over how fast is the system even though it has been working for several years now.

"The Admiralty's order is for you to appear there as soon as possible, Captain Giles. That means the overnight coach, I am afraid, even though you no doubt deserve several nights in your own bed. You can, of course, supervise the disembarking of all your prisoners. My flag lieutenant knows where to moor your prizes. I understand that you have all the French officers aboard *Glaucus*?"

"Yes, sir, both army and navy."

"I don't imagine that they will be needed for the disembarkation of the soldiers and the cavalry horses. Their non-commissioned officers are with them on the transports with the troops?"

"Yes, sir."

"Very good. I am handing the soldiers over to the Army. The prison hulks are all disgustingly full. I told the local colonel that it is his job to take them and find them somewhere to stay. Good experience for him! If Boney comes and doesn't wipe them out immediately, they will have to deal with a lot of prisoners. My flag lieutenant will tell you where to moor your prizes and where to dispose of your captured French seamen and officers.

"You mentioned, Captain Giles, that *Glaucus* was damaged in your fight with the French fifty."

"Yes, sir. I need a new mizzen mast."

"I can try to get the dockyard to give you priority, but I would not be hopeful."

"I was thinking of taking her to Stewart's Boatyard at Butler's Hard."

"That would be better, I think. Now, a glass of Madeira before you go?"

Giles was delighted. Admiral Jerrycot showed a measure of efficiency that he wished other senior officers displayed. He would enjoy spending some time with him. The Admiral was quite ready to admit that his promotion had come about solely on the basis of length of service as a captain. The powers-that-be had wanted someone farther down the captain's list to be an admiral, so those above him had been promoted willy-nilly. It was good luck for Jerrycot, for he had been without a ship for some time, living on half pay. He had served since '92 in ships-of-the-line. He had never been in a fleet action, and he had had no chance to get prize money. He had lost his command when it was given to some countess's protégé.

Admiral Jerrycot was not bitter about the system, though he did mention that his wife had found things a bit constrained living on a captain's half-pay. He would have welcomed the extra income from being a yellow* admiral, but by some luck, for he had no powerful sponsor, he had been made Port Admiral in Portsmouth. He knew most of Giles's history already, though he ate up every word about Giles latest adventure. All too soon, Giles had to return to *Glaucus* while the Admiral resumed the thankless tasks of being the port admiral in the busiest of ports.

Disposing of the prisoners and of the prizes proceeded without a hitch. Giles boarded the overnight coach to London and slept through the whole trip. A substantial breakfast and a quick wash at the coaching inn had him ready for the short walk to the Admiralty. There he was whisked into the presence of the First Lord of the Admiralty. He was soon joined by other senior members of the government or their deputies. They paid close attention to Giles's story which confirmed and illuminated the

348

terse signals that they had received from Portsmouth. However, he could not answer most of their subsequent questions since they concerned either what Napoleon's longer-term intentions for Ireland might be or else what the rebel forces were that he had seen at Dangle Bay.

The First Lord soon cut off further discussion, suggesting that the men consult with their departments about the import of Giles's news and the implications of his capturing a significant force. He then proposed that Giles and he have luncheon in a chop-house in the Strand. There the First Lord gave Giles more information on the possible significance of his discovery.

The importance was not only in frustrating the immediate intentions of the French. It was also finding out that that the French were again thinking of causing trouble in Ireland, no doubt to draw England's all-too-scanty forces away from the likely landing places in the south-east of England. The First Lord was sure that candles would burn late into the night in the Admiralty and Whitehall as officials and their minions debated the situation. Did Giles's discoveries reveal that the French had intended only to divert English attention from the main threat, or did it portend that the French were going to mount a serious attempt to promote a successful Irish uprising? For opening the Channel for invasion, controlling Ireland and having a base for friendly naval support would be invaluable in forwarding Napoleon's invasion plans that at present were stalled by the English control of the Channel and the bottling-up of the main French fleet in Brest.

"We don't know what Boney may be doing," remarked Lord Gordonston. "The French tried an invasion of Ireland in '96, and then there was an uprising in '98. Certainly, the scheme you broke up would have caused us to divert attention and soldiers to Ireland from defending the southern and eastern counties where Bonaparte may land. It's a difficult time. We are reinforcing the defenses continually, but nobody knows whether they are enough to stop the French. It is very worrying with that giant army at Boulogne and a French Fleet at large somewhere in the Atlantic."

"Surely the Channel Fleet and the North Sea Fleet can prevent the French from getting control of the Channel."

"We hope so, but I sometimes have my doubts. My fears would be increased if the French had command of a good harbor in Ireland."

The two men reflected on this unhappy line of thought until Lord Gordonston changed the subject. "Captain Giles, I suppose that you must now want a ship-of-the-line."

"No, my lord, I think I can contribute more in a frigate. Being given a ship-of-the-line would be an honor, of course, but those ships are only truly useful in the line of battle against another fleet. There is nothing much for the captain to do the rest of the time, especially if his first lieutenant is competent. Furthermore, I would run the danger of having an admiral on board, and I would not make a good flag captain. There are many deserving post-captains on the beach who are more suitable than I am for those duties."

"I would tend to agree with you. Speaking of first lieutenants, I will promote your first lieutenant – Mr. Hendricks isn't he – in recognition of your successes while he has been with you.'

"He certainly deserves it, sir. But I don't want you to promote him just to have him sit idly waiting for a command."

"No. I think that training with you will prove invaluable to us in one of the sixth rates. He won't be idle, not as long as we are at war."

"Good. While we are on the subject of recognition, Captain Bush deserves to be recognized for his battle with two French frigates last year."

"Yes, we have been considering the subject. Especially as Mr. Justice Amery has been pressing his case to have his endeavors against smuggling recognized."

"Captain Bush has contributed greatly to that cause, I know."

"The only trouble is that all his successes have come with you. And you already have had significant recognition. There is quite a bit of opposition to giving you any further reward of a major sort, partly because of envy, I am afraid, and partly because of their dislike and distrust of your father. You will be an earl in no time at all, so it is felt inappropriate to give you another earldom, though I disagree. Even being made a viscount in your own right would raise any number of hackles among admirals and other captains who think they are more deserving than you and they do but do have powerful patrons. You are already a Knight of the Bath."

"I don't see why any of the facts that you mention should prevent Bush from being recognized. I don't even think your reasons are valid in my case, though further recognition for me is not of any concern. As you say, I have the KB and am a courtesy viscount, and anything more in that line would produce duties that I would not be comfortable ignoring, such as attending in the House of Lords. Captain Bush should have a knighthood at least."

"That is what I have been thinking. Making him a baronet is appropriate. The document granting the elevated status should mention his service to the crown on domestic matters as well as his naval triumphs. That should do the trick in justifying the award. I hope that I can pull it off.

"Now, I can't promise not to give you a seventy-four, whether you want it or not, and then make you a commodore on some special mission, but for now I expect you to spend some time at Dipton while you and *Glaucus* recover. I should warn you that news of your latest victories will be all over London by now. No. I haven't said anything nor has anyone else at the Admiralty, but the newspapers keep dispatch riders at Portsmouth to report the latest developments in the war, and they will have brought the story to London. You were lucky to get to the Admiralty without being mobbed, but don't be surprised if you are treated as a hero when we leave here."

As Giles made his way back to the coaching-inn*, he heard his name shouted by news sellers many times. However, no one recognized him. Post captains on foot were not unusual in the area, and the pen and ink sketch used to represent him in some news reports looked nothing like him. What was clear was that his successes at Dangle bay were being treated as a much more significant victory than he himself considered it.

The post-coach to Ameschester was about to leave. Carstairs had already secured places for them on it. Some of the people inside the coach with Giles wanted his opinion on the news about Ireland, but he stifled their curiosity by replying only with grunts as he pretended to fall asleep even before the coach started. At Ameschester, Giles wasted no time arranging transportation to Dipton, and he succeeded in getting away before the news of his feats in Irish waters was circulated. In Ameschester, of course, he was not just another anonymous post-captain, and he could expect to have a fuss made over him if his name was attached to news.

Disappointment awaited him at Dipton Hall. Steves reported that Lady Ashton was not at home. She had gone on an expedition with Captain Bush, Major Stoner, and Mr. Justice Amery to the towns of Angleton and Crowspir. Steves expected her to return in a few days' time. He mentioned that they had departed on a barge vessel of some sort, propelled with oars, he understood. It had taken Lady Ashton from the dock at Hillcrest Grange.

Giles was upset that his wife was not at Dipton Hall to greet him, irrationally, he knew, because there was no way that she could have known that he was back in England and he had been encouraging her activities in supplanting the smuggling trade. He was also out of sorts because his son's schedule did not allow him to see Bernard right away. Nanny Weaver stood firm on the point. She was accustomed to thwarting the desires of parents whose wishes she considered to not be in the best interests of her charges.

Giles was sure that a ride would do him good. He could see some of his estates and get some badly needed exercise at the same time. He could not ride cross country now that the fields were planted, but there was no lack of roads and lanes that could give him and his horse a workout. He might stop by Mr. Jackson's to get news of the district and have him look at his wound to make sure that it was healing as well it should. Yes. A ride and a visit to the apothecary, a pint at the Dipton Inn and then a visit with his son in the nursery would fill in the time before dinner. Still, he did wish that Daphne had been home to greet him. She was the only person to whom he felt that he could boast about his successes and tell about his doubts. Being with her was what he most looked forward to whenever he returned to Dipton.

As he mounted his horse, Giles thought about how far removed were his concerns from the grand dilemmas he had been discussing with Lord Gordonston. He also realized that he was much happier thinking about which horse he should mate with which mare in his stud farm rather than considering Napoleon's wily ways. He would have to see his stable master sometime soon and spend some time with him. He would do it tomorrow if Daphne had not returned by then.

354

Chapter XXVII

The trip to Crowspir and Angleton took place a few days after the weekend that had focused on impressing Bishop Chesterton with the merits of Lord David. The excursion promised to be more enjoyable than Daphne had expected initially. Rather than travel by coach, Mr. Hesketh, who had welcomed the anti-smuggling consortium to Netherham, provided his special oared boat to journey along the canal. Traveling by boat in comfort and with refreshments laid on would be a new experience for Daphne.

Mr. Hesketh had brought the boat up to Dipton the day before. He had stayed with Mr. Moorhouse at Dipton Manor as had Mr. Amery and Major Stoner, but they had all been to dinner, together with Captain Bush, at Dipton Hall on the night before they were to set off. It had given them a chance to plan their strategies.

Before dawn, the travelers assembled again for breakfast, a hearty meal much to the satisfaction of Steves, the butler, and Mrs. Darling, the cook, who found little challenge in the modest breakfasts that Daphne and the other ladies living at Dipton Hall usually wanted. With well-filled stomachs and with the high spirits that might partly have been the result of the beer that the men had consumed to wash down their breakfast, the party set off as the sun rose for the landing at Hillcrest Grange.

The boat proved to be even more luxurious than Daphne had remembered from seeing it at Netherham. There were cushions aplenty on the seats and blankets to wrap one in against the morning chill. There was a canopy over the seating area to protect from sun or rain if a shower should interrupt the spring day. They set off to the sounds of the birds' dawn chorus, the rowers quickly establishing a rhythm which took them swiftly along the canal. It was developing into a glorious, spring day, with a myriad of different greens from the newly unfolding leaves and flowers along the more marshy banks of the waterway to the reawakening meadows and trees. As the day warmed, the blankets could be put away, and the passengers could enjoy the promise that the day gave of the warmth of summer still to come.

Daphne sat back and enjoyed the boat ride. It was an experience very different from bumping along a road in a carriage, no matter how good the carriage's springing might be or how even the surface. It was also different from the cramped boats in which she had been rowed while visiting Giles's ships or being taken up and down the Thames in London. Of course, there the scenery had been much more compelling, but she preferred the bucolic scenes they passed. Entertainment here was provided by grey herons standing while waiting patiently for a fish to come near and by voles moving along leaving a long 'V' behind them. What would Giles think of their having a boat like this one?

Their progress was only interrupted once when they arrived at a lock, and they had to wait for a barge coming toward them to be poled through. The boat paused briefly at Netherham where a new set of rowers replaced the ones who had brought them from Hillcrest Gange and luncheon supplies were brought aboard. Then they were off again, gliding down the still waters of the canal until they reached their destination at Crowspir.

Their host at Crowspir, Sir Thomas Lambert, was a jovial country squire with a wife who struck Daphne as being the shrewd member of the family. Sir Thomas was a pleasant man with no pronounced enthusiasms and a life of indolence which he had pursued happily for many years. The title must have come from a forebear since Daphne could see nothing remarkable in the present holder of the baronetcy. Lady Lambert was a matronly woman who had more opinions about society and political events than her husband. Her conversation indicated that she must spend a good deal of time reading newspapers and novels.

Sir Thomas and Lady Lambert had assembled a group of locally prominent people who might be able to help take a stand against smuggling. As at Netherby, Daphne's task was to indicate before dinner what a good idea she had had in supporting the continuance of the distribution of luxury goods on which the excises had been paid. Then, after dinner, while Mr. Amery and Captain Bush told the men about the advantages of taking a small stake in their endeavor, she was to persuade their wives that it was a sound proposition.

Daphne was confident that she had won Lady Lambert to her cause and suspected that she would then carry a good deal of weight in forming the opinions of the other ladies. As Daphne gained more experience with the affairs of married gentry, she was becoming convinced that the picture of a submissive wife who had no opinions or interest in the areas in which her husband was supposed to be supreme was not accurate in many instances. She was confident that getting the women's support would significantly increase the goodwill of their husbands which would then be demonstrated in their taking shares in the legal-distribution endeavor.

The group left the next day to go to Angleton, again by Mr. Hesketh's canal boat. Mr. Amery had not been too happy about the arrangements which he had been able to make in Appleton. However, he thought it was worth making their presentation there. The problem which Mr. Amery faced was that the leading figures in the area were not interested in aiding him or in providing accommodation. One such person was Baron Leslie Fisher, an irascible old gentleman, suffering from gout which he treated by consuming ever larger quantities of port. Lord Fisher had indicated no enthusiasm at all for their cause or their business. Indeed he had expressed distinct hostility. He boasted quite openly that he obtained his favorite drink from smugglers with whom he had dealt satisfactorily for years.

The second and more important leader in Appleton was Viscount Appleton. He was prominent in London Society and regularly participated in the House of Lords. He had shown no interest in aiding Mr. Amery in the mundane task of preventing smuggling and had made it quite clear that he would be away whenever Mr. Amery chose to visit Appleton. Mr. Amery reported him as saying, "Look, Amery, old boy. There has always been smuggling in Angleton, and there always will be. Ashton's interest will be only a passing one, and I d expect the old ways will come back just as they were. No sense disturbing a good thing, is there?"

The upshot of these problems with the local nobles was that no one would host the group from Dipton in the way in which they had been received in Netherton and Crowspir. Mr. Amery had had to settle for using the large room of an inn to host a reception for those he hoped to interest in the canal-shipment scheme. He was not happy about the situation, as he had heard rumors that the one-time canal smugglers had joined forces with their former overland rivals in bringing in the contraband by road and cart-track. The two groups were united in having no love for Daphne's venture which was taking food from the mouths of their children, or so they claimed. To avert any trouble that might arise, he intended to have the town constables present at the meeting and had arranged for a company of dragoons to be at hand in case they were needed.

When Mr. Amery expressed his doubts about the safety of Daphne's attending the meeting, she shrugged him off with the comment that if it was safe enough for the three men of her party and Mr. Hesketh, she was sure that it was safe enough for her. Surely the constables could suppress any ugliness until the dragoons arrived. Her stand met with no concurrence from the men. Nevertheless, Daphne would attend to lend support even though it was thought by everyone else that it would be inappropriate for her to say anything publically about the importance of having goods available on which the excises had been paid.

The Appleton Inn was a warm, welcoming, half-timbered building that looked as if it had been added to repeatedly over the years as it had prospered. It served a hearty dinner to the guests from Dipton together with a handful of leading people from the area. The food was accompanied by a superlative, vintage wine. Mr. Amery pointed out with pride the excise stamp on one of the bottles from which an old cork had been drawn. That stamp would not have been on the bottle only a few months ago, he declared. Indeed, such good wine would not have been available at all.

Daphne enjoyed the informal discussion of how she and her companions were intending to maintain the service in luxuries and more mundane goods that the government had decided to tax very heavily. People were interested not just in that subject but also in the exploits of Captain Giles. They were also curious about whether the rumors were accurate that Lady Ashton managed the estates of her celebrated husband when he was absent. She found that she was eager to encourage women to take a more significant role in their own lives than most were used to. Furthermore, she realized from odd remarks that many women were operating in precisely that way, whether or not their husbands recognized what they were doing. As far as Daphne was concerned, the trip to Appleton was going very well, and surely Mr. Amery's worries were unfounded.

The next morning brought news which had arrived on the coach from Portsmouth late the previous night. According to the reports spreading throughout the small town, the celebrated Captain Richard Giles had won a stunning victory over the French, destroying a French fleet and capturing thousands of French soldiers who were about to seize Ireland. The first that Daphne knew about it was when Betsy reported the news breathlessly as she woke her mistress with her breakfast. Daphne rather pooh-poohed the idea of such a success, but Betsy held her ground maintaining that that was what she had heard. The lady's maid had been basking in the reflected renown that she obtained by being in service to such a distinguished master as Captain Giles. That Giles's victory was the news from Portsmouth was confirmed when Daphne met up with the others in the parlor after breakfast. Could Giles have possibly won such a success, she asked her collaborators.

"Not the way it is being reported," replied Captain Bush, the acknowledged expert on matters nautical. "Captain Giles could not single-handedly have taken on a whole French fleet and defeated it without suffering fatal damage to *Glaucus*. There is, indeed, no officer who could have done anything of the sort."

Could Giles have done damage to a French expedition to Ireland and even captured some troops? It was certainly possible. Having served with Captain Giles, Captain Bush asserted that his former captain could succeed in doing the highly unlikely, but not the truly impossible.

"If he hasn't accomplished something important in frustrating Bonapart's intentions towards Ireland," added Mr. Amery, "there would not be this sort of news circulating. The report may be grossly exaggerated, but something of significance must have happened."

"I'd say it must have been a jolly good show whatever it was!" declared Major Stoner. "Jolly good! And it should help us in getting people interested. Association with the hero of the hour always pleases people. You can be very proud of your husband, Lady Ashton, very proud!"

More gentlemen than expected entered the room where the meeting was to be held. Mr. Amery thought that the surprising influx of men must be the result of the sudden prominence of Daphne's husband and the knowledge that his wife was at the Appleton Inn. There was also a substantial crowd outside. If Mr. Amery had any qualms about proceeding in the face of the unexpectedly large gathering, he gave no indication of them to the others. Instead, he opened the meeting at the scheduled time. Daphne, of course, was not at the front of the room as Captain Bush and Major Stoner were. Instead, she was off to one side but still in a prominent position. Everyone could see her, but she was not among those who would make a presentation and answer questions.

Mr. Amery opened the meeting by referring to the role Giles had played in putting down smuggling along the canal. Now, thanks to the naval hero, the people of Appleton could enjoy cheaper and better supplies of many goods while they supported the navy and the army by the taxes they paid on their purchases. What could be better?

At that point, Mr. Justice Amery was interrupted, something to which he clearly was not accustomed.

"What about all the carriers and others who have been put out of work?" a large and poorly dressed man interrupted. "The night trade has provided good work and lots of money to the people here. Why should we let outsiders benefit when the job is rightfully ours?"

Other voices joined in, and soon the meeting was out of hand.

361

"We ought to tar and feather this toff for taking work out of the hands of honest men," shouted another man with threatening gestures. A large group at the back of the hall started to make their way forward to carry out, it seemed, the threat. Daphne could not believe what was happening. Surely no one still carried out tarring and feathering. It must be just a figure of speech.

Mr. Amery called on the local constables to seize the man who was interrupting his speech, only to discover that the officers seemed to be intent on aiding the protestors, rather than on stopping the interruption. There could be no doubt that the meeting was over.

Daphne arose from her chair preparing to leave with the others before things got even more out of hand. The men advancing upon the group at the front of the hall seemed intent on violence. If their purpose was in any doubt, it disappeared when one lout, who appeared to be the worse for drink, staggered against Daphne while violently yelling, "Out of my way, you doxy." He knocked her over. In falling, she hit her head on the wooden arm of a chair which promptly disintegrated under her weight.

Major Stoner and Captain Bush both found it intolerable that any lady should be treated in this way by being abused both verbally and physically. With a roar from the Major, they threw themselves at the miscreant throwing him violently to the ground. That marked the start of a free-for-all battle between those who supported the legal canal trade and those who wanted it stopped so that conventional smuggling could continue.

Daphne was dazed by the knock on her head, but she had never been the sort to cower in a corner when things got difficult. Without thinking, she picked up the arm of the chair which had broken loose as the chair collapsed and used it to hit a man who was about to attack Captain Bush from the rear. He turned and completed Daphne's work by striking the man in the face with the hook that replaced his missing hand.

Seeing that they were about to be overwhelmed, Captain Bush and Major Stoner joined forces to protect Daphne. Their intention probably was to stand facing outwards with Daphne safely between their backs to protect her from the mob. In practice, Daphne was having none of that. They formed a little circle with Daphne using her convenient chair-arm to hold off some of the attackers while the major and the captain protected the group from men attacking from the other directions. Captain Bush was using the flat of his sword, which he had been wearing as part of his uniform which he had donned to impress the meeting. Somehow Major Stoner had wrenched a club from one of the people supporting smuggling. Their joint defense of each other held up very well until, finally, the dragoons arrived. The fighting ended as the aggressors took to their heels in the face of trained soldiers who were quite prepared to use their cavalry swords to quell the disturbance.

Those who did not get away before the soldiers had restored order, found themselves herded into a group to be marched off to the Appleton Goal. Among the miscreants captured were the three town constables. Mr. Amery had received a cut on his cheek in the melee, but he was otherwise unharmed. Even before he could take charge of making the miscreants pay for their crimes and adding to the magistrates who would be dismissed so that others could be appointed to mete out punishment to the rioters, Daphne insisted that Mr. Amery's wound be bandaged. She suddenly realized that what she had always supposed was an apocryphal exaggeration by storytellers was a practical necessity. The only clean cloth to serve as a bandage was her shift, and she had to tear a strip from it before she could dress Mr. Amery's wound.

363

"Surely, Lady Ashton, you do not intend to bandage me while your own face is covered with blood," protested the Judge. The side of Daphne's head still hurt where she was hit when she was pushed aside by the leader of the fight. She touched it with her hand which came away sticky with blood. Luckily at that point, Betsy appeared and was pressed into service to take her mistress somewhere more private to attend to her wound.

Daphne was embarrassed at the turn of events that had led her to participating in a bloody fray. Ladies were not supposed to be knocked out of their chairs, of course. If they were, they were not supposed then to respond violently. Daphne knew that she would have been expected to cower in a corner while the fight went on, not to take up a handy cudgel so that she could use it to thump ruffians who attacked her. Her head hurt, and she had started to worry about what Giles would say when he heard of this scuffle. She must remember to downplay how extensive had been the battle when she wrote to him. Nevertheless, she was both proud and pleased with her part in it. Her dress was ruined, unfortunately, not only from her wound but also from the man whose nose she had smashed with her chair-arm when he got too close. That had been worth wrecking her dress, she confessed to herself. The ruffian certainly deserved it!

Her companions were horrified that they had brought Daphne into such a violent situation, but neither Captain Bush nor Major Stoner was particularly surprised about how she had defended herself. Captain Bush had long observed how independent Daphne was and how prepared she was to do whatever was necessary to accomplish her ends or to help a friend. He could hardly condemn her lack of judgment in this case for he knew how he would lose all sense of caution when he became engaged in a melee. Major Stoner knew Daphne as a strong-willed and independent woman whose approach to difficulty was to meet it head-on. Mr. Amery, realizing that

Daphne seemed to be managing on her own, turned his attention to dealing with how to quell the near-riot and have the miscreants, including the town constables and one of the magistrates, carted off to Appleton Gaol.

Only Mr. Hesketh was shocked by Daphne's situation. He felt highly responsible for bringing her into danger where she had been injured and had to defend herself. His team of rowers had been near the inn where the ruckus had broken out, and he immediately organized them into a cordon to shepherd the visitors from Dipton, with the exception of Mr. Amery who was otherwise engaged, to where his rowing-barge was moored. They left immediately, the rowers taking the boat quickly away from Appleton. Daphne noticed that the pretty, tranquil picture the town showed from the water gave no hint of the turmoil that had recently upset the presentation of the benefits of having trade operating in the same tranquil, legal way.

They by-passed Crowspir on the way to Netherham. Their picnic on the boat was not as jolly a time as it had been on their way down the canal. Their original plan had been to spend another night in Appleton and then go all the way back to Dipton on the following day. However, they had left Appleton later in the day than they had planned initially. Mr. Hesketh invited them to stay the night at his estate before proceeding to Dipton the following morning.

Mrs. Hesketh was the soul of hospitality when they arrived. She fussed over Daphne's wound anxiously even as she was expressing displeasure to the men of the party for putting Lady Ashton at hazard. She insisted that Daphne's wound be cleaned again, and a new bandage of the proper material replace the make-shift one used in the aftermath of the ruckus at Appleton.

The warm reception that Daphne and her friends received from the Heskeths did much to clear away the doubts about what she was doing that arose from the treatment of her endeavors in Appleton. Good, honest people like the Heskeths were ready to go out of their way to support her and her cause. The least she could do was to continue to encourage the honest trade that her discoveries at Dipton had made possible. However, until the baby was born, it might be wise for her to refrain from the more prominent ways of supporting her cause.

Mr. Hesketh's canal boat was scheduled to arrive at the Hillcrest landing in the late afternoon, and the coach from Dipton was supposed to meet it there. Steves, being the fuss-budget that he was, had fortunately sent the coach far in advance of their expected arrival, despite Giles having been sure that if Daphne said she would arrive late in the day, then that was when she would come.

Giles had again gone riding in the morning and was returning to Dipton for a late luncheon when he turned into his driveway. There in front of him, he saw the carriage going towards the entrance to Dipton Hall. What could be the matter? He spurred his horse, Dark Paul, to go as quickly as possible to solve the mystery, and arrived only a minute or two after the coach. Daphne had just been aided out of the carriage when she heard the sound of hoofs and turned to see her husband riding like a demon on the large hunter that was bearing down on them. Giles pulled Dark Paul to a halt close to the carriage and leapt to the ground. He had noticed the prominent bandage on Daphne's head. In his urgency to find out what was wrong and to comfort her, he lost all sense of caution. The result was that he twisted his ankle in coming to earth, fell over and could only stand up again with great pain. Daphne rushed towards him and almost knocked him over once more. They clung to each other to express their affection and also to steady their precarious balance.

When they had become untangled, Mr. Jackson was summoned. The apothecary-physician had been called primarily at Giles's insistence that Daphne's wound needed to be examined and properly dressed. After looking at her and reporting no serious damage, he spent more time working on her husband. Giles had broken a small bone in his foot as well as spraining his ankle. Mr. Jackson treated both before examining Dr. Maclean's efforts to heal the wound on Giles's ribs and arm. The news about those wounds was good. They were healing without infection. The ankle and foot had to be bound tightly so that the bone could knit and the sprain recover.

"You'll need to keep that bandage on for several weeks to make sure your foot heals properly," Mr. Jackson told Giles. "No boots, I am afraid, just shoes. It shouldn't cramp your style when next you decide to blow up an enormous ship."

The news about Giles's latest trip had evidently reached Dipton. It accounted for the exceptionally warm welcome that he had received from Steves on his return home, though the butler was far too well trained to comment on the successes or failures of his master.

The injuries hardly affected Giles. Hours and hours were spent with Daphne, checking on parts of the estate and admiring at frequent intervals the amazing feats of their son as he explored the limited confines of the nursery. Nanny Weaver was not pleased. She believed that, in the nursery, parents should be seen rarely. Pregnancy suited Daphne and she looked more radiant than ever in Giles's eyes. The only shadow on their lives was that soon Giles would have to leave again.

Mr. Justice Amery came to Dipton several days after Daphne had returned. He was uncharacteristically nervous about the welcome he might receive, especially from Giles, after putting Daphne in harm's way. To his surprise, Giles did not blame him for the encounter at Appleton. Giles knew Daphne well enough to realize that, having set her mind to establishing an anti-smuggling network, she would be enthusiastic about going to different towns to further the cause. If he had been home, he would not have tried to prevent her from going, though undoubtedly he would have accompanied her. He could hardly expect Mr. Amery to have stopped her going. Giles and Daphne had, however, agreed that she would curtail her activities until the baby was born.

Mr. Amery confessed that he had badly underestimated the strength of the smuggling faction in Appleton. The local magistrates who had been appointed after he purged the former ones did not have ties to the canal smugglers. Instead, they were adherents of the overland smuggling clique. The same was true of the new town constables. Another group of gentlemen was now slated for trial on various charges and many of them would now, no doubt, be taking up residence for at least seven years in New South Wales. Mr. Amery was hopeful that this time he had removed or neutralized the principal sources of funding and guidance for smuggling in Appleton.

The great shadow on Daphne and Giles's reunion was that stalemated war had still not been resolved. The need of the navy for all ships that could be mustered remained pressing. Captain Bush received news that he had been given a frigate currently at Spithead, one that was manned and ready for battle. His orders did not specify why the position had become available. He would be under the command of Giles engaged on a mission whose nature remained unclear. Mysteriously, he was also ordered to attend a levée with the King in St. James's Palace before taking up his command. He was invited to an audience later that day.

Giles and Lady Ashton were also invited to the audience as well as to an evening affair at Carleton House, the Prince of Wales's residence. Giles was also summoned to London to find

368

out what his new assignment might be. Undoubtedly, he would have to leave Dipton. Daphne would probably have to manage alone in the later days of her pregnancy. Though she had known that separations in time of war would be inevitable, it was becoming harder and harder for both of them to accept this kind of life. Giles sensed that something must happen soon to change the complexion of the never-ending war. His greatest hope was that the change would be such that he could abandon the sea with honor.

Author's Note

This is a work of fiction set in a historical context. None of the events detailed happened, and none of the main characters existed. It is, if you like, an alternative history. Many positions, such as the First Lord of the Admiralty, are real, but they are occupied by fictional characters. Of course, many prominent people mentioned did exist such as Admiral Nelson or Napoleon Bonaparte.

The places central to the story are mainly fictional as well, though Portsmouth, Spithead, and the Nore among others are all real. Another exception is *Le Conquet* in France. By contrast, Dangle Bay is fictitious though it closely resembles Dingle Bay in Ireland. The latter site was not used for the story because it has one or two critical physical differences from what was envisioned in the plot.

There was no explicit French attempt to help an Irish uprising in 1805, though it might have been anticipated. France had intervened in 1796 and encouraged revolt in 1798, and aiding another Irish rebellion would undoubtedly have diverted soldiers from defending England against the threatened invasion. There was also no canal joining the south coast to the Thames valley or other inland parts of England, though at least one had been seriously proposed, and it might well have been profitable if it had been built.

Smuggling was endemic in England during the 18th and early 19th centuries, as it had been for hundreds of years before that. A staggering number of goods had quite exorbitant taxes imposed on them, and it seems that wherever surreptitious transportation was feasible, substantial amounts of smuggling occurred, despite government efforts to stop it. Records and firm evidence is sketchy, not surprisingly since it was a criminal activity not likely to leave detailed records. It is known that in one way or another much contraband material reached parts of Britain that were far inland despite the higher cost involved in not openly transporting the material and the need to hide it at various way-stations. It is then not implausible that canals would be used for transporting smuggled goods nor that the difference in transportation costs of using them openly rather than secretly might well cover the tariffs that legally supplied goods would have to pay, ridiculous though they were in many cases. The use of violence by smuggling interests to protect their business from the revenue officers is well documented. The involvement of prominent people in local societies is also documented. However, I know of no instances where a member of the gentry set up an enterprise to defeat smuggling by efficiently transporting duty-paid goods whose presence and conveyance did not need to be hidden or disguised.

I always appreciate getting letters from readers, especially ones which are helpful for improving the books. I would like to thank Mr. Bill Boswell for suggesting that Giles should be officially recognized for his accomplishments even though I have not acted on his suggestions as yet. Giles and

Daphne still have a lot of unresolved issues, and I expect to find out more about them in the future.

The best way to reach me is by email at jgcragg@telus.net.

Glossary

Beak   Slang for "magistrate."

Belay (v.)   Tie down. Regularly used by mariners to also mean stop.

Board(ing)   Refers to attacking another ship by coming side to side so that men from one ship can attack the other one in an attempt to capture it.

Boarding-nets   Loose nets hung from the spars of a ship to prevent enemies climbing aboard from boats.

Brig (1) A two-masted ship square-rigged.

(2) Slang for the prison on board a ship.

Camperdown   The Battle of Camperdown in 1797 between the Dutch Fleet (then under the control of France) and the British North Seas Fleet resulted in a complete victory for the British. After that, the Dutch Navy played no significant role in the Revolutionary and Napoleonic Wars.

Cat (out of the bag)   Traditionally, when the cat (q.v.) had been made by the bosun, it was stowed in a baize bag until needed. Hence the expression, which has evolved into a somewhat different meaning over time.

Close (verb) Closing with another ship (or fleet) was to sail towards it by the quickest path.

Close hauledSailing as much to windward as possible

Close to the wind   A ship is sailing close to the wind when it is going upwind as much as it can without stalling. Slang meaning is that the action is almost illegal.

Coaching-inn   An inn that served as a stop or terminus for coaches carrying passengers about the country. Usually the most lively and noisy inn in the area.

Cloth (drawn)   Refers to the stage of a meal when the final dish had been consumed, the tablecloth had been removed, and the men in attendance gathered together to imbibe liquor stronger than wine, usually accompanied by nuts and fruit. When ladies were present, they withdrew to the drawing room just before the cloth was drawn. It was often a time of more pointed conversation than occurred during the meal.

Consol   A bond issued by the British Government with no stated redemption date, paying the holder a specified amount per annum.

Crosstrees   Two horizontal spars at the upper ends of a topmast to which are attached the shrouds of the topgallant mast.

Cutting-out Entering an enemy harbor in boats to capture a ship and sail her out to sea where the warship would be waiting.

Driver   A gaff-rigged sail on the mizzen mast. It was a fore and aft sail with the leading edge attached to the mast rather than a square sail whose center would be at the mast.

Entail   A provision that the inheritance of real property would go to specified members of a family (or another specified group) usually to the closest male relatives. An entail typically prevented the present owner from leaving the property to someone else, and it was usually put on a property to prevent the immediate heir from dissipating the inheritance but would pass it intact (more or less) to the next generation.

Entered (in books) Young men of influence were often entered in ship's books at a young age even though they were not yet on the ship so that they could become lieutenants at the minimum age without having spent the required time at sea.

Examination (lieutenants) To be appointed as a lieutenant midshipmen (and master's mates) had to pass an oral examination by a board of post captains who also checked their records. Candidates had to be at least nineteen years of age.

Fighting top A Platform on the mast where the main part met the top mast from which marines could fire their muskets on to the deck of an opposing ship.

Grape (shot) Musket balls, or sometimes small scrap metal, used to fill bags which were then inserted into cannon as if they were cannon balls.

Grapnel   A metal hook or set of hooks attached to a line that could be thrown and hook on to the edge of another ship or a wall or other object.

Gunner's daughter   Midship were made to lean over one of the ship's guns when they were whipped.

Heave to   Stopping the forward motion of a ship by turning one sail to work in opposition of the others.

Holystoned On naval ships, the decks were scrubbed each morning using sandstone blocks. Since the crew had to perform the task on their knees, they were called holy stones and holystone became the verb to indicate the activity.

Larboard   The left-hand side of the ship looking forward. Opposite of starboard. Now usually called "port."

Living   The term 'living' was used to describe the position of the parish ministers. It was usually in the gift of a local landowner, who if his properties were extensive might have the right to appoint men to several different parishes.

Loblolly boy A medical assistant in the Navy

Lubber's hole   A hole in the top (q.v.) of a mast so that access can b e gained from below, either to get to the top of to be able to reach the next set of shrouds to clime farther up the masts. Experienced topmen avoided its use when climbing the mast, preferring to climb up the ropes on the outside of the top.

Nore (The) Anchorage in the Thames estuary off the mouth of the Medway River. A major anchorage for the Royal Navy in the Age of Sail.

Orlop (deck) The lowest deck of the ship, below the waterline.

Parole   It was common for officers who had been captured to give their word (parole) that they would not try to escape or aid their side in a war until they had been exchanged for officers of the other side.

Portion (marriage)   Another term for a dowry

Quarterdeck The outside deck of a ship at the stern.

Rafted   Ships or boats are rafted together when they are tied to each other.

Rake (a ship)   Fire a broadside into the bow or stern of an opponent who would not be able to return the fire.

Rate Naval ships were rated according to the number of guns they carried. They were

First rate -- 100 guns and over

Second rate – 80-98

Third rate – 60-78

Fourth rate – 50-60

Fifth rate (frigates) – 28-48

To make matters confusing, not all guns were counted in the rate. Carronades and bow-chasers being the main exceptions.

Shrouds   A rope ladder formed by short lengths of rope tied tightly between the stays of a mast.

Sheet   A line controlling how much a sail is pulled in.

St. James('s) District of London about St. James's squares. Developed in the seventeenth century as a residential area for the nobility and rich gentry, by the early nineteenth century it also housed many exclusive gentlemen's clubs and other establishments devoted to the entertainment of high society.

Staysail   A fore-and-aft rigged sail fastened to a line (stay) running forward from a mast. When attached to the foremast, it is frequently called a jib.

Step Promotion from lieutenant to commander.

Spring (line) A line attached to the anchor cable leading to the aft of the ship that can be used to turn it while at anchor

Strike   Lower the flag of a ship to indicate surrender.

Subaltern   The lowest commissioned rank in the army.

Tack   (a) Change the direction in which a ship is sailing and the side of the ship from which the wind is blowing by turning towards the direction from which the wind is blowing.

(b) (as in larboard of starboard tack) The side of the ship from which the wind is blowing when the ship is going to windward.

Taffrail   Railing at the stern of the quarter deck.

Telltale   A ribbon, usually sown to the rigging used to indicate wind direction.

Toulon   The main French naval base in the Mediterranean. It was under loose blockade both in 1805 and also earlier when it slipped out of the harbor and evaded the Britsih Fleet under Nelson to go to Egypt. Nelson's ability to contain it was no greater in 1805.

Tub Liquor was not usually smuggled in regular barrels but in smaller containers, made like a barrel, which could be carried by one man.

View-Halloo The cry made when the huntsman first spots that a fox has been found and is being chased by the hounds.

Wardroom   The area in a ship used by the commissioned officers of a ship when off-duty.

Watch   (1) Time: A ships day was divided up into fur hour watches with one further divided into two. The watches were

First watch: 8 p.m.- 12 midnight

Middle watch: 12 midnight - 4 a.m.

Morning watch: 4 a.m. – 8 a.m.

Forenoon watch: 8 a.m. – 12 noon

Afternoon watch   12 noon – 4 p.m.

First dog watch 4 p.m. – 6 p.m.

Second Dog watch   6 p.m. – 8 p.m.

In each watch, time was marked off in half-hour segments so the one bell of the First watch would be 8:30 p.m., two bells would be 9:00 p.m., and so on.

(2) Division of the crew. The crew was divided (usually) into two watches, the starboard watch and the larboard watch, which alternated when they worked (in normal circumstances) and when they were at leisure or asleep.

(3) the time when officers were on duty. Referred to as "being on watch" or "watch."

(4) Police force on land.

Watch and watch   Refers to a situation where a ship's crews are divided into two watches of four hours each, or when officers have to change with each other every four hours.

Printed in Great Britain
by Amazon

37874135R00217